Michelle Sma... ...
she was a baby... ...
voracious read... ...g...s, s...e ...a...d ...r ...v... of
romance established when she stumbled across her
first Mills & Boon book at the age of twelve. She's
been reading them—and writing them—ever since.
Michelle lives in Northamptonshire, England, with
her husband and two young Smarties.

Chantelle Shaw lives on the Kent coast and thinks up
her stories while walking on the beach. She has been
married for over thirty years and has six children. Her
love affair with reading and writing Mills & Boon
stories began as a teenager, and her first book was
published in 2006. She likes strong-willed, slightly
unusual characters. Chantelle also loves gardening,
walking and wine!

THE GREEK'S PREGNANT CINDERELLA

MICHELLE SMART

WED FOR THE SPANIARD'S REDEMPTION

CHANTELLE SHAW

MILLS & BOON

First Published in Great Britain 2019
by Mills & Boon, an imprint of HarperCollins*Publishers*
1 London Bridge Street, London, SE1 9GF

The Greek's Pregnant Cinderella © 2019 by Michelle Smart

Wed for the Spaniard's Redemption © 2019 by Chantelle Shaw

ISBN: 978-0-263-27349-6

Printed and bound in Spain
by CPI, Barcelona

THE GREEK'S PREGNANT CINDERELLA

MICHELLE SMART

CHAPTER ONE

TABITHA BRIGSTOCK WHEELED her trolley to the laundry room and heaved the sack of dirty linen and towels from the suites she'd spent the morning cleaning into the white dirty washing tub, then left the laundry to wheel the trolley further up the corridor to the storage room, where she locked it away with the other trolleys. Her hands were red and sore but there was no time to go to her room to rub the hand lotion on them that sometimes stopped them cracking too badly. The staff quarters were right at the other end of the hotel, a good fifteen-minute walk away.

Instead she climbed the stairs and headed to the far end of the first floor. She knocked on the door out of habit then used her master key to unlock it.

'Hi, Mrs Coulter,' she said cheerfully as she walked into the opulent suite. 'How are you feeling? Sorry I couldn't pop in earlier but they needed me to help out on the second floor.'

At eighty-three, Mrs Coulter was the oldest guest at Vienna's Basinas Palace Hotel and had been in residence for three months. The poor woman had been floored by a virus that had left her bed-bound for two weeks. Tabitha had been very concerned and had taken to dropping in on her regularly to make sure she was okay. Thankfully, Mrs Coulter had been much improved the last couple of days, and today she was up and dressed and eating her lunch at the table by the window that overlooked the palace's vast grounds.

Mrs Coulter smiled, the twinkle in her eye that had been missing all week very much back. 'I'm feeling much better, thank you. And thank you for getting Melanie to check on me earlier.'

'Not a problem. I've got the vitamins you asked for.' She pulled the small plastic pot out of her handbag and put it on the table.

Gnarled arthritic hands covered hers. 'You are an angel. Will you sit and have a cup of tea with me?'

As Tabitha still had twenty minutes of her lunch break left, she took the offered seat and poured them both a cup from the bone-china pot.

It felt wonderful to sit after six straight hours of physical exertion. The hotel was in a state of great excitement. The Greek owner, Giannis Basinas, was hosting a masquerade ball there that evening for the world's elite.

Tabitha had caught a glimpse of him earlier. She'd just finished cleaning a room and was wheeling her trolley down the corridor when he'd strolled past. Her heart had soared to see him but, as normal, he didn't spare her so much as a glance.

In the five months since she'd started working there, she had seen the billionaire widower, who was rumoured to be descended from Greek royalty, only a handful of times. The Basinas Palace Hotel was but a small part of his vast empire. When he did bother to show his face in Vienna, the excitement and fear amongst the staff was palpable. The hotel had once been a royal palace and was now regarded as Europe's most prestigious hotel with a price tag to match. Working there was a coup in itself but, should standards be deemed to have dropped, the risk of being fired was all too real.

Tabitha could not afford to lose her job and had no idea what it was about Giannis that meant every rare glimpse of him played on her mind so much or made her stomach come alive with butterflies. As a live-in member of staff, to be fired would be to be made homeless. The salary here was much better than her old job in a small English hotel, and the tips were often amazing, but even with all the overtime she grabbed she still hadn't saved anywhere near enough for a deposit on her own home.

That was all she wanted. A place of her own. A home where she could be safe. A home that no one could ever take away from her.

'I was hoping you would come see me this lunchtime,' Mrs Coulter said.

Tabitha raised an eyebrow. 'Are you ready for a game of cards?' The two women had taken to playing rummy most days when Tabitha's day shift was over.

'My head's still too fuzzy for that, my dear. No, I wanted to discuss tonight's ball.'

'The masquerade ball?'

'Is there another one I should know about?'

Tabitha laughed. 'I hope not. I'm grateful for the extra shifts it's giving me but I'd need a holiday to recoup if we had another one too soon.' And she could not afford a holiday.

The twinkle reappeared in Mrs Coulter's eye. 'I have a ticket for it.'

'No way!' Tickets for the ball were forty-thousand euros. To have the privilege of forking out that astronomical amount of money, you had to be invited. To be invited, you had to be rich and part of the global elite. It was an open secret that all the single women who'd been invited were under the age of thirty, the rumour—not denied—being that Giannis Basinas was using the ball as a means of finding himself a new wife. Mrs Coulter was rich and recently widowed but she was not part of the global elite and she absolutely was not under the age of thirty. 'How did you get that?'

Mrs Coulter winked and tapped her nose. 'A lady has her secrets, dear.'

Tabitha felt a surge of excitement for her. To go to the ball… She'd seen all the preparations for it, heard all the whispered talk, and it was obvious it was going to be the ball of century. 'Do you want me to do your hair and nails for it? My shift finishes at four, so I'll have time…'

'No, dear. The ticket is for you.'

'Sorry?'

'I bought the ticket for *you*.'

Tabitha was momentarily struck dumb. She stared at the wizened old woman with the white wispy hair and twinkling eyes and wondered when she'd gained such an evil sense of humour. It had to be a joke. Who would spend forty-thousand euros on a ticket to a ball for a chambermaid?

The gnarled hand covered hers again. 'Tabitha,' she said earnestly. 'You have been a godsend to me. You have looked after me since I first arrived in Vienna and often in your own personal time. You've cared for me this week when my own selfish children could hardly be bothered to call to see if I was okay. You work your fingers to the bone for little money and you never complain. You're a ray of sunshine in a dark world and I wanted to show my love and appreciation for all that you do.'

Tabitha swallowed. A ray of sunshine? Her?

The only people who had ever said such nice things to her had been her father and paternal grandmother. Her lovely grandmother had died when she'd been seven but her memories of her were strong. Mrs Coulter had the same mischievous twinkle her grandmother had had and the same easy affection. Tabitha supposed that was what had drawn her to the elderly lady to begin with and partly why she felt such deep affection for her.

'The ticket is in my name. Tonight, you will be Amelia Coulter, and you will dance with handsome men and drink champagne and spend an evening being who you were born to be.'

Tabitha blinked, partly to push back the tears threatening to spill down her face and partly in shock.

Being who you were born to be...?

She had spent the past four years trying her hardest to forget her birth right. The memories were too painful. All she could do was tackle each day as it came and look to the future.

Her heart thumped. Did Mrs Coulter know...?

The twinkling eyes were steady on hers. If Mrs Coulter knew Tabitha's true identity, she was keeping her cards close to her chest.

But Tabitha had never hidden her true self. Her name was the only thing her stepmother had been unable to take from her. She'd taken everything else, though. Her home, her education, her money, her future...

'Take a look in my wardrobe. Go on, dear.'

On legs that felt strangely drugged, Tabitha stepped through to the bedroom.

'Right-hand door,' Mrs Coulter called.

'What am I looking for?'

'You'll see.'

And she did see.

When she opened the right-hand door of the wardrobe, all that hung on the rail was a floor-length ball gown that could have leapt off the pages of a fairy tale.

She stretched out a hand and ran her fingers over the delicate material, her eyes soaking up the pastel-pale pinks and greens overlaid with embellished gold-threaded patterns and encrusted with jewels and the palest of pink roses. An eighteenth-century princess would have been thrilled to wear something so beautiful.

On the shelf above it lay a pair of white-gold high-heeled shoes, a white eye-mask with gold detailing and gold braiding around its edges and a plume of wispy pale pink feathers shaped into a flower on the left cheek.

Hands now shaking, she took hold of a shoe and examined it in awe.

It was her size.

Dazed, she went back to the living area of the suite. 'How…?'

Mrs Coulter smiled. 'A lady has her ways.'

'I can't. I wish…' She took a deep breath and hugged the shoe to her chest. 'I wish I could go but I can't. If I get caught, I'll be fired. We've all been warned.' And warned unambiguously. Any member of staff caught trying to enter the ball would have their contract of employment terminated.

But Mrs Coulter was not to be deterred. 'We will make you unrecognisable. No one will know it's you—no one will be expecting you to be there. In my experience, people see what they want and expect to see. They will not see a chambermaid. Come back here at five. I've arranged for a beautician to join us. She will turn you into a princess. And then tomorrow you can join me for lunch and tell me all about it.' She gave a tinkle of laughter. 'I admit, I'm not being entirely altruistic. I'm too old and my knees too shot to go to the ball myself but I can live it vicariously through you.'

Hot tears prickled the back of Tabitha's eyes. No one had ever done such a thing for her before.

'Do not be afraid, my dear. Tonight you will be a princess and you will go to the ball, and I will not hear another word of argument about it.'

Giannis Basinas left the apartment he used as a base when in Vienna and strolled up the rose-hedged path that led to his hotel. He could have earmarked one of the suites for his own use but he preferred to give himself at least an illusion of privacy. Privacy was a concept frequently ignored by his large, exuberant family.

It was partly down to his family that he was making this walk now dressed in an all-black, leather swallowtail suit and hosting this masquerade ball. His sisters had been dropping hints since he'd turned thirty-five that he needed to find a new wife. He'd come to the reluctant conclusion that they were right.

When his oldest friend Alessio Palvetti had pulled in a favour owed from their school days and asked him to host a masquerade ball, using a specific event team to manage it, Giannis had figured the ball could work in his favour. He could repay his debt *and* let his sisters believe he was serious about finding a wife. Everyone would be happy.

He didn't hold much hope that his ideal woman would emerge tonight but this was as good an opportunity to find her as any. He'd even let Niki, his youngest sister and the biggest socialite in his family, select fifty of the four hundred guests to invite. These fifty guests were unmarried women, their wealth determined by their ability to pay the forty-thousand-euro price tag he'd set the tickets at.

If Giannis was going to marry again, he had three criteria. Firstly, and most importantly, his potential wife had to be independently rich. He would not make the same mistake as he'd made in his first marriage. Secondly, she must be of childbearing age, a criterion that was self-explanatory. Thirdly, and least importantly, she must be pleasant to look at. She didn't have to be a model, or even be particularly beautiful, but if he was going to spend the rest of his life with one woman he would prefer it to be with someone he found attractive.

Slipping through a rear door into the hotel he'd bought less than two years ago, he made his way to the ballroom.

Giannis's business interests were varied but mostly concentrated in shipping and property across the globe.

This former palace he'd spent millions on renovating into a world-class hotel was his first venture into the tourism industry outside his Greek home. As a status symbol, there was none better.

About to open a side door into the ballroom, he spotted a female guest on the cantilevered stairs. Her fingers trailed the railing as she made her descent. Her other hand clutched the gold invitation all ball guests were required to show on their arrival.

There was something hesitant about her graceful walk that made him look twice.

He looked at her. Then looked again.

Although much of her face was hidden behind a white-gold eye-mask with a plume of dusky-pink feathers on the left cheek, there was something about her that set his pulses racing.

He couldn't tear his eyes away.

Her beautiful dress, all delicate pale greens, dusky pinks, golds and jewels that sparkled when the light caught them, was strapless and form-fitting to the waist then puffed out to fall in layers to her hidden feet.

She looked like a princess.

She could *be* a princess.

He imagined the dazzling circle the skirt of the dress would make on the dance floor…

Leaving the door he'd been about to enter, he approached her as she reached the bottom of the stairs.

She was shorter than he'd thought and, up close, even more ravishing. Honey-blonde hair had been coiled into an elegant knot at the base of a graceful neck adorned with a gold choker necklace covered in jewels, and roses that matched her dress and the drop earrings hanging from the lobes of her pretty ears.

She was the most exquisite creature he had ever set eyes on.

'You look lost,' he said in English.

A pair of cornflower-blue eyes met his from behind the mask.

Full, heart-shaped lips curved into a hesitant smile.

'Do you need directions to the room the guests are meeting in? Or are you waiting for someone?' She wore a glimmering diamond on her right hand but there was no ring on her left.

She shook her head in obvious shyness.

'You don't need directions or you're not waiting for someone?' Or did she not understand him? It was a rare event to meet someone in his world who did not speak English.

When she finally spoke, her cut-glass English accent contained a huskiness to it. 'I'm not waiting for anyone.'

Better and better.

He held an arm out to her. 'Then allow me to escort you, Miss…'

'Tabitha.' Colour stained what he could see of her cheeks. 'My name is Tabitha.'

'A pleasure to meet you, Tabitha. I'm Giannis Basinas and it would be my pleasure if you would allow me to escort you to the ball.'

Tabitha could have screamed at her stupidity.

Why had she given him her real name?

She hadn't even reached the ballroom yet and already she'd blown her cover. And with Giannis Basinas of all people!

She was supposed to be Amelia Coulter, the name on the invitation in her hand.

She should have turned Mrs Coulter's incredibly generous offer down but she'd been caught up in the moment, her head turned by the beautiful dress, her heart aching for one night, just one night, of freedom from the unrelenting drudgery of a life spent scrubbing bathrooms and cleaning rooms.

This was the sort of ball at which, if her father had lived, she could have been a real guest. She would have been here by right, not deception.

If Giannis suspected for a moment that she was a lowly hotel employee she would be fired on the spot.

But there was no hint of recognition.

But then, he'd never looked at her before. And why would he? He employed hundreds of people at this hotel alone. Chambermaids came bottom of the pecking order, a faceless army who flitted unobtrusively through the corridors and cleaned the rich guests' rooms.

The thought calmed her a little but it was with a heart that raced that she slipped her hand through his offered arm, then found it racing even harder.

Tall, with dark brown hair cut short at the sides and long at the top, Giannis had a nose that was too long and his chin was a little too pointed for him to be considered traditionally handsome. But there was something about him, whether it was the high cheekbones, the clear blue eyes or the full bottom lip, that drew attention.

It had drawn her attention from her first glance.

His was a face that had lived and had the lines etched in his forehead and around the eyes to prove it.

He might not be traditionally handsome but in the black leather swallowtail suit and black leather eye-mask he wore as his masquerade costume, which gave him an almost piratical air, he was devastating.

'Which part of England are you from?' he asked as they strolled down a wide corridor.

'Oxfordshire,' she answered cautiously.

'A beautiful county.'

It was, she thought wistfully. She'd avoided the entire county since she'd been thrown out of her home. It hurt too much to think of everything she'd lost and everything she missed.

However, she smiled, nodded her agreement and prayed for a change to the conversation.

What would be even better would be an increase to the pace Giannis had set. They were walking so slowly a tortoise could have overtaken them.

Her mind raced as to how she could slip away from him before she had to hand over the invitation written in the name of a woman who was not Tabitha.

If she had left Mrs Coulter's room a minute earlier or later she wouldn't have bumped into the one person she'd really needed to avoid.

'I went to university in Oxford,' he said. 'Boarding school at Quilton House in Wiltshire. Do you know it?'

That explained his flawless English.

'I know of it.' Quilton House was one of the oldest schools in the world and certainly the most expensive. Only the filthy rich could afford to send their children there. A few of her school friends' brothers had attended it.

'What school did you go to?' he asked.

'Beddingdales.'

He laughed, a deep, rumbly sound that played melodically in her ears. 'My first girlfriend went to Beddingdales. I would ask if you knew her, but I suspect you're a lot younger than me.'

'Probably.'

He laughed even louder. 'You don't waste words, do you?'

'I'm sorry, I didn't mean...'

He stopped walking and fixed clear blue eyes on hers. 'Don't apologise. Honesty is a rare, refreshing trait in this world we live in.'

They reached the door that led into the area where the guests were to wait before the ball was declared open. In a moment she would have to hand over the invitation for her name to be confirmed on the guest list.

Her heart pounded.

She needed to slip away.

Before she could think of an excuse to flee, Giannis took hold of the hand tucked into his arm and brought it to his lips. His eyes sparkled as he razed the lightest of kisses against the knuckles. 'I have a couple of things I need to check on before the ball starts. I will find you.'

Then he bowed his head and turned on his heel, leaving nothing but the scent of his spicy cologne in his wake.

Tabitha slowly released the breath she'd been holding and closed her eyes.

Her heart still pounded, although whether that was an effect of the kiss on her hand or the close call she'd just had she couldn't determine.

'Are you coming in, miss?'

The uniformed guard had opened the door for her.

She swallowed.

It wasn't too late. She didn't have to do this.

But then she caught sight of a waiter holding a tray of champagne and the longing in her heart overshadowed the fear.

She could stay for one glass of champagne, she reasoned. That couldn't do any harm. One glass of champagne and then, when the ball was declared open, slip away and return to her room and the safe anonymity of her servile life.

But she would have one glass of champagne first.

She stepped into a small holding room. Another uniformed guard stood on the other side of the door, a large tablet in his hand. Her heart almost stopped.

She recognised him. She'd spoken to him numerous times in the staff room.

There was not a flicker of recognition in his returning stare.

He greeted her with a polite smile. 'May I see your invitation please, miss?'

Hoping he didn't notice the tremor in her hand, she passed it to him.

He peered at it closely then turned his attention to his tablet until he found her name on the list. He pressed his finger to it then smiled again at her and nodded at the double doors at the other side of the room. 'Guests are assembling through that door. Enjoy your evening, Miss Coulter.'

Air rushed out of her lungs.

Mrs Coulter had been right. The dress and the mask acted as the perfect disguise.

'Thank you,' she murmured.

Straightening her back, Tabitha held her head high. Yet another doorman opened the double doors for her to step through.

The noise she was greeted with from the reception room made her blink. The guests already congregated were in high spirits. Laughter and the buzz of excited chatter filled the air, melding with the music coming from the corner, where a pianist was playing a familiar tune.

She soaked up all of this in the time it took to step over the threshold.

A waitress holding a tray of champagne approached her.

Tabitha took a flute with a smile and restrained herself from tipping the contents down her throat in one swallow.

Whatever the circumstances of her life now, she'd been raised to be a lady. Ladies did not tip drinks down their necks.

She brought the flute to her mouth and took a small sip.

The explosion of bubbles in her mouth was enough to make her want to cry.

Only twice in her life had she tasted champagne. The first time had been at her father's wedding when she'd been ten. The second had been when she'd been fourteen. Her stepmother had thrown an eighteenth birthday party for Fiona, the oldest of Tabitha's stepsisters. The party had been an elaborate affair with no expense spared.

The celebrations for Tabitha's own eighteenth birthday had been markedly different. Her stepmother had celebrated by throwing Tabitha out of the family home.

The big wide world she'd looked forward to embracing had shrunk overnight.

Any alcohol she'd consumed since then had been whatever was cheapest. No Freshers' Week at university for her. While her school friends had scattered to various higher education institutions around the country—the majority intent on having a fantastic three years getting drunk and attending the odd lecture when they could fit it in their busy social schedules—Tabitha had already been gaining callouses on her hands from working as a cleaner in the small family-owned hotel. The pay had been terrible but the job had come with accommodation.

The call for silence broke through her sad reminiscences.

The master of ceremonies greeted the four hundred guests and then, with a flourish, declared the masquerade ball open.

CHAPTER TWO

CAUGHT IN THE tide of bodies, Tabitha entered the enormous ballroom.

Her hand flew to her throat as she took in the lavish transformation the already opulent room had undergone.

From the grand high ceiling hung balloons of gold, silver and white, the walls lined with heavy drapes following the colour theme. In the far corner sat the champagne fountain the staff had been talking about for days.

Everything glittered. Everything shone, especially the colourful, fabulously dressed guests.

It was like entering a magical wonderland and Tabitha's heart ached at the beauty of it.

She finished her champagne, placed the empty flute on the tray of a passing waiter and took her place amongst the ladies forming a long line to the left of the springy wooden dance floor.

The gentlemen lined up on the right and then the orchestra struck the first note of the first tune. Four ballet dancers appeared and performed a short but exquisite dance for them. No sooner had they danced out of the ballroom to rapturous applause than two-dozen professional ballroom dancers, notable for the ladies' all-white gowns and the gentlemen's traditional black tail suits, took to the floor and performed the first waltz.

It had been a long time since Tabitha's ballroom dancing lessons at school. It was the one lesson every pupil had looked forward to and she'd been no exception. She'd never imagined then that she would have to wait so long to put the moves she'd learned into practice.

These dancers were incredible and the whispers around her indicated there were world champions amongst them.

Yet she found her gaze darting over the line of gentlemen on the other side of the room.

She shouldn't be looking for him, she scolded herself. Hoping that his words about finding her were true was nothing but a fool's wish, and a dangerous one at that. If Giannis discovered she was an employee, she would lose everything.

And, even if he had meant it, there were one-hundred and ninety-nine other women here, most of them far more attractive than she was.

He'd probably forgotten her already.

The professional dancers finished their waltz and then came the words Tabitha had once longed to hear in a setting just like this, and not from a school mistress: *'Alles Walzer!'*

Everyone dance!

The gentlemen set off towards the ladies.

Excitement surged inside her.

For so many years she had dreamed of this moment, yet for so many she'd stopped believing it could happen.

She didn't even care that the gentleman making a bee-line towards her was old enough to be her father and short enough to fit in her handbag.

When he was only a couple of feet from her, his path was suddenly blocked by another, much taller and broader figure who seemed to appear from nowhere.

Her heart stopped then, after a breathless pause, kick-started back to life with fury.

Giannis stood before her, his head tilted, a gleam in his eyes as bright as the chandeliers hanging amidst the balloons above them.

'Darf ich bitten?'

The traditional way of asking a lady to dance at a Viennese Ball.

The very words Tabitha had once dreamed of hearing.

She stared into the clear blue eyes, the strangest of feelings forming in her veins.

Her knees sank into a curtsey without any input from her brain.

Strong nostrils flared. He put a hand to his stomach and inclined his head in a bow.

Then he took hold of her right hand with his left and slipped his other hand around her waist to rest just above the small of her back.

Sensation shot through the fingers being held in his, seeping straight into her bloodstream.

Muscle memory took control of Tabitha's left hand and she placed it on his right bicep, splaying the thumb away from her fingers to cup it.

The orchestra struck the first note and then she was being spun across the great ballroom in his arms.

In Giannis Basinas's arms.

Her first ever dance with a man.

This man.

This man who controlled their moves effortlessly and steered them around the other couples without his clear blue eyes ever leaving hers.

She couldn't tear her gaze from the face that had captured her attention from that very first glance either.

And nor could she stop herself breathing in his spicy scent.

But, even with the feeling that she had entered the most magical of dreams strong inside her, there was a voice in her head whispering that this one dance was all she could have with him.

Never mind the danger that being with him put her in, he would want to dance with other women. If the rumours were true and this ball was a ruse for him to find a new wife then he would want to spread himself out and talk and dance with as many women as he could.

It felt as if no time had passed at all when the dance finished. The couples around them parted like the Red Sea.

Tabitha let out a breath that contained both relief and disappointment and moved her hand from his arm. But there was no relinquishing her hand by his. His grip on it tightened.

He brought his mouth to her ear. 'You don't think I'm letting you go, do you?'

Brand new sensation skittered down her skin at the warmth of his breath on her ear and cheek.

She tried to think of an excuse to pull away but her brain refused to co-operate.

Her body refused to co-operate too. Her hand reached back up to cup his bicep.

Around them, new couples formed.

The orchestra played the first note of the next dance and then she was being spun around the floor again.

All the reasons she needed to escape seeped away as the music made its way through her body and down into her dancing feet. Masked faces floated around her, dresses twirled, beautifully played music...

And the heavenly arms of Giannis Basinas.

When that dance finished and the master of ceremonies took to the floor to announce that it was time to dance the polonaise, she met Giannis's eyes. There was a question in them.

She nodded. She remembered this dance.

He smiled and, holding her left hand, led her to the forming line of couples.

In and out they wove, separating then coming back together, curtseying, separating... She curtsied and danced with other men but her attention was always on Giannis.

She simply could not tear her gaze from him.

Not until they'd danced another waltz, and then a fox-trot, did he steer her away from the dance floor to one of the round tables on the raised dais running the lengths of the ballroom walls with a murmured, 'Time for a drink.'

Unwilling to leave her side for a moment, Giannis signalled for champagne to be brought to them.

He had a feeling this ravishing creature would disappear if he turned his back on her.

She hadn't exchanged one word with him during their time on the dance floor.

Their champagne was brought to them. He held his flute to hers then drank from it. 'Are you hungry?'

She shook her head.

'You don't speak much, do you?' he observed. In his experience, women always had to fill any silence with chatter, however inane. His sisters were the worst for it. Their mother always said Niki had been born with a never-ending battery in her tongue. He'd caught a glimpse of Niki in the arms of a bemused man trying to cut above her incessant chatter to waltz her around the dance floor.

Slim shoulders raised in a tiny shrug. 'I do if I have something to say.'

He laughed. 'And do you have anything to say, Tabitha?'

She shook her head again.

'I thought Beddingdales taught its girls how to make small talk in social situations.'

There was the faintest spark of amusement in the corn-flower eyes. 'I failed that class.'

He laughed. 'But obviously not the ballroom-dancing lessons.'

'I liked those.'

'Do you go to many balls?'

Another shake of the head.

'I'm going to have to stop asking you closed questions, aren't I?'

Now there was the slightest of curves in the full heart-shaped lips to accompany her shaking head.

He laughed. 'Tell me about yourself.'

The faint amusement he'd detected vanished. She looked away from him, her lips pulling in together. 'What do you want to know?'

Everything.

'Let us start with how old you are.'

'Twenty-two.'

That surprised him. The features he could see beneath the mask covering her face indicated youth but the way she carried herself suggested someone older.

'Have you graduated from university yet or did you take a gap year?'

'I didn't go to university.'

That surprised him too. University was a rite of passage in his circle whether the person was academic or not. 'What do you do?'

He waited for the stock answer of 'charity work'.

There was a momentary hesitation and her face flushed with colour. 'I'm in hospitality.'

He could have laughed. After charity work, hospitality was a great favourite for the idle rich wanting to make a point of their usefulness.

No wonder she blushed at the admission.

It surprised him, though. Tabitha struck him as being from a different mould to the usual socialites who filled his world.

What a waste of a good brain and a life, being content to spend days shopping and holidaying. It was a mind-set he'd never understood. Giannis had been fortunate to be raised within one of Europe's wealthiest families and, like his sisters, had inherited thirty million euros on his twenty-first birthday, but it was not in the Basinas nature to be idle. Undoubtedly wealth was something to be enjoyed but it was also a tool to create more wealth, not just for him but for others.

Giannis's inheritance had been used to build a diverse portfolio of businesses which collectively employed over five thousand people. He had exacting standards, and demanded the best from every person he employed, no matter their position, but he rewarded them well for it both in pay and perks. The staff here in his palace hotel, for example, were considered the best paid hotel staff in the whole of Europe.

He did not understand how people could sleep if their wealth was generated by the unrewarded sweat of others.

He did not understand how people could actively seek to be freeloaders.

His wife had been a freeloader. She'd been many things. A liar. A gold-digger. A cheat. Even now, five years after the fact, five years since she and her unborn child had died, the anger and bitterness still lived, muted but still there.

He'd buried his wife and her child, and while the other mourners had mourned he'd had to bite his tongue to stop himself from ripping into their grief.

He would never allow himself to lose his anger entirely. If he forgot what it felt like he would lay himself open to making the same mistake again and Giannis never made the same mistake twice.

He'd been blinded by his wife's beautiful façade to the lies beneath it.

What lay beneath this woman's façade?

His fingers itched to pull the mask off Tabitha's face and see if it was as beautiful as he suspected.

Her own fingers lifted her champagne flute to her lips.

A tiny drop of gold liquid spilled out of the corner of her mouth. A pink tongue darted out to capture it.

Veins heating at the less than chaste images that tiny action produced, Giannis drank some more of his champagne and swallowed it slowly.

Theos, he could not remember when he'd last been so physically aware of a woman.

He could not remember ever being so captivated by one.

Whatever lay beneath her façade, he could enjoy their time together and enjoy the heady feelings that erupted through him to hold her in his arms.

He rose to his feet and held out a hand to her. 'Ready for another dance?'

Cornflower-blue eyes met his. A shy smile formed on her lips.

When her fingers wrapped around his he felt a shock of electricity dart through his skin.

Time slipped away from her.

Tabitha knew she was a fool for saying yes to another dance. She was a fool for not having made her excuses and left.

She could make all the excuses she wanted but the simple truth was she wanted to stay. She wanted this feeling to last as long as it could because she would never feel it again.

She would never have this night again.

Once the ball was over she would never dance with Giannis again.

Come the morning she would revert back to being a chambermaid and this night would be nothing but a memory.

She was in the midst of the most wonderful of dreams and she didn't want to wake up.

They danced. They drank more champagne. They danced again.

The hands that held as they danced clasped tightly, their forearms pressing together.

The hand that had rested just above the small of her back moved up so it palmed her bare skin. She had never imagined the thrills that could race through her veins at a mere touch of flesh upon flesh.

Their eyes stayed locked. The guests surrounding them were nothing but blocks of colour in the periphery of her vision.

When the next group dance started there were no words to communicate their unspoken agreement to leave the dance floor.

More champagne was consumed.

Time slipped even faster. She tried her hardest to hold on to it but the great clock on the wall ticked on.

As midnight approached the dances slowed in tempo but Tabitha felt giddy. The champagne she'd drunk, the setting, the arms holding her so closely, the undiminished attention from the clear blue eyes holding hers…

She felt as if she were coming to life. Never before had she been so aware of the blood pumping through her body, of the beats of her heart, of the sensitivity of her skin.

And never before had she been so aware of another. Giannis. The olive skin, the strong throat, the strong jaw, the rise and fall of his chest…the sensuous mouth.

She no longer cared that he had the power to make her homeless with nothing but a single word. Maybe it was the champagne doing her thinking for her but these were feelings she had never known before. Tomorrow was tomorrow. Right now it didn't exist.

'The fireworks start soon,' he murmured into her ear. 'Watch them with me.'

She shivered at the sensation of his breath against her skin. Her fingers reflexively tightened on his. They were pressed so tightly together her breasts were crushed through the fabric of her dress and his suit against his chest.

She smiled her answer.

His lips curved.

The orchestra was reaching the end of its piece.

Giannis put his nose to her ear and breathed in the soft, floral scent.

He ached to take this ravishing creature somewhere private and feel those heart-shaped lips against his own.

When he had imagined this night he had seen himself dancing with a parade of women, making bored small talk in the vain hope one might capture his attention.

He'd never imagined he would find someone before the dancing had even started and be greedy to keep her in his arms. Ballroom dancing was a chore he'd endured at his boarding school but there was nothing chore-like about dancing with this enigmatic woman with whom small talk had proven itself unnecessary. He could dance with her all night. He *would* dance with her all night.

But the dancing was about to finish for a short period while the orchestra took a break and the firework display took place.

He knew the best spot to watch it with her.

Drifting his hand further up her back, marvelling at the soft texture of her skin, he found the spot where her spine formed at the base of her neck and circled a finger around it. Then he pressed his cheek against hers, a last contact of their bodies before he pulled away and guided her out of the ballroom.

Hands clasped tightly together, they walked past the champagne fountain. He picked a glass up and handed it to her then took one for himself.

The corridor they stepped into was deserted but the rooms they passed were full of revellers wanting a break from the dancing for food or to rest their feet.

Outside in the gardens, the scent of roses in bloom filled the warm air.

Giannis loved the palace hotel gardens at night. Beautiful though it was by day, the night brought a new dimension to it, imagery from childhood books coming to life amongst the carved statues, water fountains and, further back, in the thick hedges that formed the famed maze.

The spot he took Tabitha to was in a white gazebo in a secluded part of the garden. She stared at the vast structure perfectly suited to such lavish grounds and imagined aristocracy from centuries ago treading this same path.

Flutes of champagne in hand, they stood at the balustrade, arms pressed together, and watched the guests spill out onto the vast lawn, but they were blurs in Tabitha's eyes, her senses too attuned to the man beside her for anything else to sink in with any substance.

'How long are you in Vienna for?' he asked casually, a question to make her stomach turn.

Before she could think of an answer, the moonlight caught one of the figures on the lawn, mask removed. Tabitha's blood turned cold in an instant as recognition flashed at her.

It was her stepsister, Fiona.

She hadn't had any communication with her in well over four years, not since Tabitha had been forced to leave the family home.

So many emotions rushed through her to see Fiona there, dressed in a beautiful gown that no doubt had been paid for by money intended to be Tabitha's inheritance, but the primary emotion that shot through her like an echo was fear.

Fiona had made her life a living hell.

Tabitha's fingers tightened around the now empty champagne flute, but she must have exerted too much subconscious pressure for the glass shattered in her hand.

She jumped back as shards of glass fell to the ground, too shocked at seeing her stepsister—how had she not noticed her before?—to realise her hand was bleeding until she caught Giannis's concerned stare.

He snatched at her hand and peered closely at it. 'Are you okay?'

She inhaled deeply through the shock and stinging pain and managed to nod.

'We should get a doctor to look at this. I'll make a call and see if we have one here.' Still holding her hand, he used his free hand to tug off the black cravat around his neck.

'I don't need a doctor.' A drop of blood rolled off the palm of her hand. She took another deep breath. 'It's superficial. Just a cut.'

She would have argued against a doctor even if she'd severed half her hand. The last thing she wanted was to draw attention to herself. The mask and the dress gave her anonymity amongst her colleagues but if anyone who knew her were to look too closely the game would be over. Now she knew Fiona was here—and maybe Saffron too—she dared not risk it. It wasn't just that her identity would be blown. The thought of seeing either of them without any preparation was an ordeal she was in no way ready to put herself through.

She remembered the day she'd first met them and how excited she'd been at the thought of having two big sisters, along with a new mother, and her heart clenched at the trusting innocence of her ten-year-old self.

The cravat freed, Giannis gave it a sharp flick then wrapped it gently around her bleeding hand. 'That's a lot of blood for a superficial cut.'

'That's the body doing what it's designed to do. I'll find a bathroom and clean it out.'

He kept his hand on the cravat wrapped around her cut. 'My apartment is right behind us. We can clean it there and assess for damage.'

She was quite sure the flow of blood seeping from her wound increased at the casual way he said 'we'.

When her gaze drifted back up to meet his eyes there was a lurch in both her heart and stomach.

If the choice was to dart across the garden and risk facing her stepsister, or to go to the apartment of this man who, despite his being a virtual stranger, she felt a strange sense of safety being with…

CHAPTER THREE

TABITHA DIDN'T THINK of the foolhardiness of going to Giannis's one-storey apartment until he closed the front door behind them and even then it was more of a dim chiding in the back of her head. And it wasn't about the foolishness of being alone with a man she hardly knew while fireworks exploded in the sky around them.

It was the foolishness of her own feelings.

Her every action that night had been foolhardy from the moment she had accepted Mrs Coulter's wonderful generosity.

She held Giannis's cravat tightly against her stinging wounded hand and tried to take in her surroundings.

Tabitha knew he'd converted the old staff quarters into a base for himself for the few days a month he was there— she currently lived in the new staff quarters—but none of the staff had been invited in before.

But as she followed Giannis down a wide hallway the huge living room they passed barely registered, her attention completely taken with the man before her.

He pushed open a door to the right and stepped over the threshold.

She did the same and came to an immediate stop.

This was Giannis's bedroom.

He stopped walking and turned to face her. His features taut, his voice serious, he said, 'The light in my bathroom is the best to see with but if you don't feel comfortable coming in here we can clean the cut in the kitchen.'

How many foolish actions could a woman make in one evening?

She walked into the bedroom.

Her legs feeling as if they were walking on a cloud, she followed him past the largest bed she had ever seen in her life, vaguely noting the impersonal nature of the space and its lack of pictures or photos, her heart hammering, breaths shortening.

Tabitha had never been in a man's bedroom before.

Trying desperately to affect nonchalance, but knowing she was failing, she followed him through another door into a bathroom that was as luxurious as the bedroom was sparse.

Heart in her throat, she went straight to the double sink. From the corner of her eye she saw Giannis open a tall cupboard door and pull out what looked like a black leather washbag.

Carefully unwinding the cravat from her hand, she placed it in the right-hand sink then turned the left sink's tap on.

The bleeding had definitely lessened in flow.

'Your cravat is ruined,' she said in what she wanted to be a conversational tone but which sounded shaky even to her own ears. The cravat might be black but it was made of silk.

'It doesn't matter.' He placed the washbag beside the sink just as she put her hand under the running tap.

She clenched her teeth as the cold water hit.

'It hurts?' he asked.

'Only a bit,' she lied, feeling foolish to admit that a cut so minor smarted so much. There was soap in a dispenser above the sink and she squirted some onto the cut and rubbed it in, then held it back under the tap to let it clean out properly, all the while intensely aware that Giannis stood close enough that she could feel the heat emanating from him.

They had danced together for hours, their bodies almost flush, but her awareness of him had not been as heightened as it was now.

Every cell in her body had come to life and strained towards him.

'May I have a towel, please?' she asked when done.

'Let me,' he murmured, taking her injured hand back into his own.

Tabitha held her breath, suddenly aware of her heart hammering so hard its beats were thudding in her throat.

He'd removed his mask. The features she found so captivating were right there before her, the closest they had ever been, unadorned.

Head bowed in concentration, a lock of his dark brown hair fell over his eye. He dislodged it with a quick flick of his head. 'You can move your hand without problem?'

She cleared her throat and whispered, 'Yes.'

His movements unhurried, he wrapped a small grey hand-towel around her hand and gently pressed it to her palm.

Palm dry, he removed the towel. Fresh droplets of blood seeped from the cut, although noticeably less heavy than before. 'I should have a bandage for that.' He placed the towel back on the palm, took Tabitha's other hand and pressed it on it. 'Keep the pressure on.'

He unzipped what she'd assumed to be a washbag but was in fact stuffed with bandages and other first-aid equipment.

'Are you a secret doctor?' she asked, again striving for lightness of tone and failing dismally. His spicy scent was filling her senses again and she struggled to even open her vocal cords.

Clear blue eyes briefly met hers, creasing at the corners, before he pulled out a large padded plaster in a protective packet. 'A habit from my university days. My mother insisted I take a medical kit with me.'

Using his teeth, he ripped the packaging, the tendons on his olive throat straining.

The blood running through her heated a little more and she had to fight the fog in her brain to think of something to say. 'Was your mother over-protective?'

He gave a grunt-like laugh. 'She was sensible. I was rather wild and reckless in my younger years. Hold your hand flat but curve your fingers a little for me.'

She complied then held her breath again as he carefully fixed the plaster to her hand, smoothing it down at the sides.

'There,' he said, lifting her hand to his mouth and placing a kiss to the plaster. 'All done.'

Her belly flipped over so hard the effect rippled through the rest of her. 'Thank you.' But her vocal cords had now knotted themselves so tightly the words hardly formed.

He was so close. The cells in her body were no longer merely straining towards him; they were trying to fly out of her skin to him, abetted by the violent beats of her heart.

Giannis studied the delicate palm spread out on his hand and traced his fingers over her elegant ones, surprised to find the tips hardened and calloused.

About to ask how this could be, he met her cornflower-blue gaze and his throat closed up.

He'd tended to Tabitha's wounded hand with the best of intentions, promising himself they would clean it up and bandage it then go back outside to watch the fireworks together.

He hadn't considered that his attraction to her would burn even brighter when they were alone in the confines of his apartment or that he would be so aware of her every movement and every breath.

He hadn't considered that he would tend to her hand and have to stop himself from running his tongue over it.

Since Anastasia's death he had hardly lived like a monk.

He'd been with a considerable number of women, both before his marriage and after he was widowed.

Not one of them had made his loins ache and his chest tighten with one shy smile.

Not one of them had captivated him like Tabitha had, and he still hadn't seen her face...

Suddenly he found himself needing to see it, to see the whole face of this woman who had enchanted him so much that he couldn't determine if it was her or the champagne he'd drunk inducing it.

He released his hold on her hand and brought his fingers to her face.

Not a breath of sound could be heard between them as he slowly lifted the mask up and over the honey-blonde hair.

Heart pounding, he stared at a flawless face far more beautiful than he had suspected.

Truly, ethereally beautiful.

He rubbed the back of his fingers down high, rounded cheekbones in wonder, that wonder growing at the sudden pulse he saw in the cornflower eyes.

She gave a sharp inhalation before her own hand reached for his face and tentatively touched his jaw.

A bolt of electricity charged through him, strong enough to knock a weaker man off his feet.

The light delicacy of her floral perfume whirled into his senses.

Everything about this woman was delicate and faultless. Were it not for the warmth of her soft skin and the slight trembles he saw vibrating through her, he could have believed she was made from porcelain.

He traced his fingers across her oval jawline then dragged them down the elegant neck, lingering at the pulse throbbing at the spot before he reached her collarbone and took the one step needed to do what he had spent the entire evening hungering to do.

He brought his face down and captured her heart-shaped lips in his.

Another bolt of electricity rocketed through him, far stronger than the first, crashing hot through his veins and skin with a buzz that must have seeped through him, for Tabitha jolted too.

Pulling back slightly so their lips were barely touching, he opened his eyes and found hers fixed on him, a dazed expression shining at him. The fingers resting on his jaw had frozen.

The walls around him began to spin, heat flowing through him so fast and so thick he wondered if he *had* drunk more than he'd thought.

He found he didn't care.

Champagne, desire or a combination of both, at that moment he wanted this woman more than he had ever wanted anyone or anything.

Sliding an arm around her waist, he pulled her to him and moulded his mouth to hers, exploring the plump softness of her lips, then parting them to dart his tongue inside and explore the hot champagne-scented depths.

Tabitha succumbed to her very first kiss feeling like she'd fallen into a dream.

The whole night had been a dream.

But this…

It was mesmerising.

She met the strokes of his tongue tentatively at first but the heat bubbling inside her being fed by his heavenly kisses grew at a ferocious pace and smothered any inhibitions she should have had.

Grabbing at the soft leather of his swallowtail jacket to keep her suddenly boneless legs upright, she arched into the hard contours of his body and moved the hand clutched at his cheek to hook tightly around his neck.

She felt intoxicated, could feel the blood pumping in the

veins of her mouth and moving relentlessly through the rest of her, heating wherever his firm hands swept over her.

She only realised he'd unpinned her hair when it spilled down over them.

He broke the kiss to turn his face into her hair and breathed it in deeply before bringing both hands to her face and smoothing the hair back.

His eyes had darkened, his hunger for her so stark that her stomach contracted.

Never had she imagined that this man would look at her with such desire in his eyes.

Before this night she hadn't imagined Giannis would *ever* look at her.

When his mouth found hers again, the kiss harder and hungrier, fresh heat assailed her, threading through the very fabric of her being, and she tightened her hold around him, suddenly aching for him to rip the beautiful but constricting dress from her burning, sensitised skin.

As if his mind was aligned with her own, Giannis lifted her effortlessly into his arms, the motion making her belly swoop.

The world's biggest rollercoaster could not have had a greater effect. Or felt a fraction as heady.

The feelings rippling through her were like nothing she had even suspected could exist. Her world—her *universe*—had shrunk so it contained only Giannis.

He carried her to the bedroom and set her down gently on her feet beside the bed.

During that short walk he'd turned the bedroom light off so they were illuminated only by the light pouring in from his bathroom and the fireworks lighting the sky outside.

His throat moved as his hooded eyes stared at her so hard, she felt stripped naked beneath it.

'*Eisai omorfi,*' he breathed as he tugged her to him again.

She didn't have a clue what he'd said but pleasure soaked through her at the way he'd spoken the words.

Their arms wrapped around each other and she sank into another invasion of his hungry tongue assaulting her in the most heavenly way.

Reckless, intoxicating madness had caught Giannis in its grip. He *knew* this was madness: making love to a woman he knew only by first name. Tabitha could have stepped out of one of the fairy-tale books his sisters had read as children, an enchantress casting her spell over him.

If this was a spell, he did not want to find the cure to it. Not yet. He wanted to stay under her enchantment and let it take him wherever it desired.

He dragged his mouth down the column of her throat to where the pulse at the base of her neck now raged while her fingers snaked into his hair and dug into his scalp.

Too many clothes, he thought dimly, his fingers working furiously at the back of her dress, trying to find the hidden buttons. His thumb ran over the bump of a small clasp. He popped it open and immediately found the hidden zip.

In one fluid motion he pulled it down to the base of her spine.

He ran his hands flat over the length of her back and sucked in a breath when he found no bra.

He brought his mouth back to claim her in another hot, hard kiss and shrugged his jacket off, then stepped back, giving himself just enough room to undo the top three buttons of his shirt, then tugged it up and over his face. He threw it to the floor.

Breathing deeply, he gazed again at the captivating face in front of him before closing the small distance he'd just created to place his hands on her shoulders.

His fingers drifted over the soft skin to the band of her dress, which was defying gravity and staying up.

All it needed was one small tug at the waist to help it on its way.

It fell with a whoosh to her feet.

His throat closed as he drank in the body now naked bar a pair of skimpy white knickers.

Thee mou.

Upturned breasts, plumper than the dress had allowed his mind to imagine, a slim waist and rounded hips…

She was all woman.

She was exquisite.

Unthinkingly, he cupped one of the breasts and ran a thumb over the erect tip.

She swayed. Her lips parted and a small gasp escaped from her.

He gripped her tightly at the hips and lowered himself down to capture the breast his hand cupped with his mouth.

Blood pooled hot and hard in his groin, making his rock-hard arousal throb tightly against the constriction of his leather trousers.

She tasted…incredible.

She swayed again, legs visibly trembling, the fingers on his head digging in harder.

Rising, he shuffled her back until the back of her legs touched the bed.

Chest rising and falling rapidly, hands still reaching for him, she sat.

His arousal had become too painful to endure a moment longer and, not tearing his eyes from hers, he quickly undid his trousers and pushed them down his hips.

Tabitha gazed at the first erection she had ever seen in the flesh and her pelvis contracted all over again.

Her mouth full of moisture, heart thumping painfully, her gaze drifted over the rest of him.

Giannis was beautiful.

His tall frame was broader and far more muscular than

she'd imagined—and she *had* imagined it, in many unbidden moments when the only thing she'd needed to use her brain for was changing bed sheets. Only a small line of hair covered his chest, starting from just above his abdomen, but thickened and darkened considerably at the area where his huge length jutted out proudly.

She felt too intoxicated with all the heat swirling like a furnace inside her to be scared.

Never in her life had she craved something as much as she craved Giannis in this moment. There was something about him that sang to her on a fundamental level she had no chance of understanding so she did the only thing she could do and embraced it.

When he'd divested himself of the rest of his clothing and joined her on the bed, pushing her down so she was flat on her back, she opened her arms to him.

His lips found hers in another crushing kiss and then he was exploring her, using his hands and mouth to cover her body, setting fire to her skin, melting her bones.

He lavished attention on breasts she had never suspected could be so sensitive and yet so receptive. He kissed her belly button, he kissed her sides…and then he tugged her knickers down and kissed her right in the core of her womanhood.

At the first touch of his tongue on her swollen nub she jerked wildly, sensation shooting through her.

Dear God…

One hand grasped his head, the other reaching up to grab a pillow.

Pleasure pooled thick and heavy deep within her and she instinctively lifted her bottom; instinctive, as the action came not from her brain.

Her brain had ceased to function on anything but a primitive level.

Her *body* had ceased to function on anything but a primitive level.

The only coherent thought in her head was Giannis's name playing like a distant echo.

Only when he'd snaked his way back up her body, sheathed himself deftly and his mouth hovered over hers for another kiss, his hips lodged between her parted legs, his arousal hard at the top of her thigh, did she get the coherence to gasp, 'Please be gentle.'

The lips that had been about to claim hers reared back, a question forming in the crease of his brow.

Suddenly afraid that the truth would put an abrupt end to this most magical of moments, she hooked an arm around his neck and pulled him down to mould her mouth to his.

He kissed her back hungrily and shifted his hips so his erection was right where it needed to be.

And then he slid inside her damp heat. Slowly, deliberately slowly, stretching her, giving her the time to adjust and accommodate...

Her eyes flew open as a sharp pain seared through her, fleeting then dissolving...

And then *she* dissolved.

Her bones softened, her hips arched, she scraped her fingers into his head and parted her lips as he drove into her, the pleasure so intense that all she could do was cling to him and let him move inside her with long strokes, every thrust increasing the sensation, every groan from his lips against her ear feeding it.

He filled her completely. Perfectly.

A large hand skimmed roughly down her side and reached under her bottom, lifting her so their groins ground together, heightening the pleasure to a level that turned her into a mass of nerve endings.

Faster and harder he thrust into her, and faster and harder her hips bucked back, and all the while the sensation that had started life deep inside her spread until, without any warning, pleasure ripped through her, so intense that colour brighter and more explosive than any firework filled her.

It must have been enough to tip Giannis over the edge too for the fingers still holding her bottom clamped tightly on her flesh and his huge body tensed then shuddered.

Long moments later, he collapsed on top of her, breathing heavily in her ear.

It took a long while for Tabitha's world to right itself and for her heart to regain something that resembled a normal rhythm.

A delicious lethargy came over her. Her eyes closed and the world drifted away.

The sound of a door closing woke Tabitha with a start.

She sat bolt upright, horrified to find dusky light pouring through the bedroom window.

She looked at her watch and saw the time was six a.m.

No, no, *no*.

She was due to start work in an hour.

She strained her ears and heard the sound of a coffee machine working.

Giannis must be in the kitchen.

How long did she have to escape?

She cursed herself and tried her hardest to breathe but panic had set in.

Clutching her fuzzy head, she darted her gaze around the room, looking for her dress.

It was draped on the arm chair in the corner. Giannis must have put it there.

She swallowed back a surge of nausea and cursed herself again.

Stupid, idiotic, fool!

Bad enough she'd got so carried away with the romance of the evening and the undeniable yet fatal attraction that had sparked to life between her and Giannis to sleep with him in the first place, but to stay the whole night?

What complete and utter stupidity.

Her cheeks burned as she recalled them making love a second time…

She staggered off the bed and instinctively covered her nakedness.

She had never slept naked in her life!

Snatching the dress, she found his own masquerade costume beneath it, his black shirt at the top.

She debated for a nanosecond before pulling the shirt he hadn't fully unbuttoned over her head and hurriedly pulled her knickers on, all the while thinking of the best way to escape, wishing she had paid more attention to the layout of the apartment when she'd had the chance.

But of course, she hadn't paid attention. She'd been too drunk on the strange alchemy of Giannis and champagne to pay attention to *anything*.

Quickly she scanned her surroundings from the window. The grounds were empty of life but they wouldn't be for long. Any minute an army of workers would be out there to clear up any mess revellers had made during the event.

She opened the window, threw her dress and shoes out of it, then squeezed herself out behind them.

Bare feet on the cold ground, she scooped her belongings into her arms and fled.

Giannis whistled as he poured the freshly brewed coffee into glass cups, placed them on a tray with milk and sugar and continued whistling as he made his way back to his bedroom where he'd left his enchantress sleeping.

He could not remember the last time he'd awoken in such a good mood. Years.

Could Tabitha be the one his sisters had been nagging him to find? He knew next to nothing about her but if she could afford a ticket to his ball, and that dress which must have cost more than the ticket, she obviously had wealth. She'd been educated at one of the UK's finest boarding schools. And they had a chemistry that was off the scale.

He'd never known a night like it.

Whether Tabitha was the future Mrs Basinas or not, right then his intention was to bring her coffee and climb back into bed with her. He hoped she hadn't made any plans. He'd already messaged his PA to inform her he wouldn't be returning to Santorini that day and to rearrange his appointments.

Still whistling, he carried the tray to his bedroom and opened the door…

The bed was empty.

'Tabitha?' he called. She must be in the bathroom…

The bathroom door was open.

He placed the tray on his dresser and, as he did so, he noticed something else that had gone. Her ball gown.

Two minutes later, every room in the apartment searched, he returned to his bedroom perplexed and angry.

She had run out on him.

From the corner of his eye, something sparkly caught his eye.

He strode to the bed where the sparkly item was and found, on the pillow on which her exquisite head had rested, one of her earrings.

CHAPTER FOUR

'THE FILE IS INCOMPLETE.' Giannis tapped his long fingers on the thick file which allegedly contained the details and photograph of every guest who'd attended the masquerade ball two weeks ago, when he'd learned there had been no guest by the name of Tabitha on the list. He'd spent the morning studying the dossiers so thoroughly he was quite sure he could bump into any of the guests in this file and relate their name, age and occupation without introduction.

But the one face he'd wanted to find was missing.

His PA sighed. 'That is the entire list of attendees. It has been triple checked.'

'Then someone must have gate-crashed the ball.'

At this, Giannis's head of security spoke up. 'Every guest was checked off on the system.'

'Then the system must have been faulty or someone forged an invitation.' He hadn't explained why he thought this. Giannis hadn't explained himself to anyone for years. Unless you counted his sisters, who pried into his life with a thoroughness that would make a Russian spy envious.

'Every invitation was inspected and the names ticked off electronically. The only way it could have been done was for someone to steal an invitation but there were no reported thefts. Everyone who should have been there was there and accounted for. There was only one no-show: an elderly Swiss gentleman who was hospitalised after a fall that day.'

Giannis drummed his fingers with more force against the file, thinking hard.

Tabitha had vanished without a trace. Were it not for the earring left on his pillow and his missing shirt—had she taken it?—he could have believed he'd been under a real enchantment and imagined the whole encounter.

He'd had unplanned one-night stands before but never had he had a woman run out on him as Tabitha had done.

That was if she was even called Tabitha.

Somehow, a woman had foiled the ball's tight security. She had made a fool of his security system and made a fool of him.

It brought a rancid taste to his tongue to imagine how she must be laughing at him.

He would have let the whole thing go, put it down to experience and forgotten all about her...were it not for the strong suspicion that she'd been a virgin.

Pushing his chair back, Giannis got to his feet. 'I'm going to take a swim. Josie, call my flight crew. Tell them we'll be returning to Santorini in two hours.'

Leaving his PA to make the arrangements, he left his office and strolled through the lobby of his hotel.

What a waste of a valuable day. He could have read the thick dossier of guests from the comfort of his home, should have distrusted his gut which had nagged him that being here at his Viennese palace hotel would bring him closer to Tabitha.

Now he intended to do what he should have done the moment he'd found her gone—forget about her.

Striding down the long, wide corridor that led to the hotel's luxury leisure facilities, he saw in the distance a couple of chambermaids talking, their heads bowed over something.

When he was three doors from them, the chambermaids separated, one entering the room to the left, the other the room to the right. By the time he passed they were wheeling their trolleys loaded with fresh bedding and cleaning products in behind them.

There was something about the blonde one…

Unbidden, his feet ground to a halt and he turned around, only to catch a glimpse of a swishing blonde ponytail before the suite's door closed behind her.

His heart suddenly pounding, Giannis stared at the shut door for a long moment before he blinked some sense into himself and carried on his way.

He had to accept that the woman he'd shared the most miraculous night of his life with was some form of confidence trickster and the chances of him ever finding her were slim.

It was time to forget about her.

Tabitha, her back resting against the door of the suite she'd just entered, held her trembling hand to her beating chest, hardly daring to breathe.

Had he seen her?

Worse, had he recognised her?

Legs shaking, she slid down the door until her bottom reached the floor and dragged long gulps of air into her lungs.

When she'd been told by a panicking colleague that the big boss had unexpectedly turned up she'd been grateful to have her trolley to hold on to. It had stopped her visibly swaying. She'd felt the blood pooling from her head down to her feet.

The two weeks since the ball had been awful, her feelings alternating between guilt at running away from Giannis and terror that he would discover who she really was. A lowly worker. Not the rich woman he'd assumed and which she'd let him believe. Every time there was a knock on her bedroom door in the staff quarters fear would grip her that her identity had been discovered. Visions of being unceremoniously escorted from the palace hotel plagued her.

Guilt consumed her too. Recalling how she'd been swept away by the romance of the ball, by the attraction that had blazed between them, by the consumption of all that champagne, didn't change a thing.

The champagne had lowered her inhibitions but it hadn't acted for her.

She should have left the ball and returned to her quarters the moment Giannis had showed an interest in her.

But if she had then she would never have shared such a wonderful night with him.

She hugged her knees, wishing she could run after him, explain herself and apologise but there was no way she could do that and keep her job. He would be rightly disgusted with her.

She was disgusted with herself, a disgust that had grown ever since she'd used the staff computer to seek pictures of him. All she'd wanted was to see his face again but all she'd done was unleash a whirl of new emotions within herself. The first pictures that came up in the search were of Giannis and his dead wife. There had been many pictures of the happy couple together.

Tabitha had stayed glued to that computer for so long, her eyes had become gritty.

Anastasia Basinas had been the sexiest, most beautiful woman Tabitha had ever seen, a stunner with thick, glossy raven hair and a knowing gleam in her cat-like eyes. There had been a particular picture of the two of them together on their lavishly celebrated wedding day. Giannis had looked at his new bride with what could only be described as devotion.

They had clearly been madly in love.

Anastasia's death, which she read had occurred in a car crash five years ago, must have devastated him.

The mild nausea that had been swirling in her belly since she'd taken her break intensified and she forced herself back to her feet and propelled herself to the bathroom, where she heaved the contents of her lunch up.

'You're looking very peaky, dear. Are you not feeling well? You're not still worrying about the earring are you? I did tell you not to.'

Tabitha managed a smile and shook her head. She *did* still feel guilty about the lost earring but that wasn't the reason she looked peaky.

Mrs Coulter gave a stern stare. 'Then eat something. You're going to waste away.'

To stop the elderly woman worrying, Tabitha took a small bite from a cheese and cucumber sandwich.

'That's better. What time do you finish today?'

'Midnight. I've got four hours off from three.'

'You should use that time to rest. You look exhausted.'

Tabitha swallowed the small morsel and prayed her stomach would keep it down until she'd left Mrs Coulter's suite.

It had been the same thing now for two whole weeks. Every day at around the same time, she became nauseous. What she'd initially thought was shock at Giannis's unexpected appearance at the hotel had become a daily occurrence. As had the strange exhaustion that cloaked her, which Mrs Coulter had picked up on.

And then had come the realisation that her period was five days late.

She'd taken the test three days ago. Then she'd taken another.

For three days she'd felt as if she were living in purgatory. She was sure Mrs Coulter would give her a sympathetic ear but she'd resisted confiding in her.

The first person she needed to tell was Giannis. And

that was who she was going to see as soon as her shift was finished.

He'd flown into Vienna that morning and, as far as Tabitha was aware, was staying for one night only.

It was too late to worry about her job. Too late to worry that she could hit rock bottom again.

She'd already hit it.

The knock on Giannis's office door interrupted his perusal of the palace hotel accounts. When he was satisfied that everything was in order, he would read through the guest book for feedback from the people who really mattered. The paying guests.

'Come in,' he called.

Josie, his PA who travelled everywhere with him, entered the office, a crease on her usually unflappable brow. 'I have a young lady here to see you. I've told her you're not to be disturbed but she won't take no for an answer.'

'I'm too busy,' he dismissed. Once he'd finished his monthly appraisal of the books and guest satisfaction he had his monthly meeting with the hotel senior management team to chair, followed by a dinner date with his sister, who'd turned up at his villa that morning announcing she was coming to Vienna with him.

'She says to tell you her name is Tabitha.'

His heart inflated like a hot air balloon, punching the air from his lungs, and he had to grind his feet to the carpeted floor beneath him to stop himself jumping out of his chair.

She was here?

Tamping down the eruption that had exploded inside him, Giannis nodded curtly. 'Give me two minutes then let her in.'

Josie, betraying no surprise, nodded and slipped back out of the office.

Once the door was closed, Giannis rested back in his chair and sucked a lungful of air back in.

His throat had run dry.

He poured himself a glass of water and drank it in three swallows.

Once he'd regained a little of his equilibrium, he bent his head over the accounts spread out on his desk, dragging more air into his lungs, trying to establish regular breathing.

By the time the next knock on his door echoed, he was prepared.

'Come in.'

The door opened.

A petite figure appeared, dressed all in black, blonde hair tied back.

His heart slammed against his ribs.

She pushed the door shut behind her.

Cornflower-blue eyes met his.

His heart slammed again.

Not a word was exchanged between them.

Blood whooshed in his head as Giannis stared at the face that had haunted him this past month.

His efforts to forget her had been spectacularly unsuccessful.

This was the woman he had shared the most incredible night of his life with, the woman who had then run away and stayed away...until now.

She was much paler than he remembered. More fragile looking. But, even in ordinary clothing, every bit as beautiful.

Slowly he let his eyes drift over her and as he did so he noticed other details.

Like that the ordinary clothing she wore was the black trousers and black polo shirt with his hotel's motif embroidered on the left side of the chest that all his hotel's cleaning staff wore.

He flattened his hands on the desk and leaned forward, hardly able to believe what his eyes were telling him. 'You work for me?'

Hands wringing together, she pulled her lips in and nodded.

Incredulous, he swept his eyes again over the anonymous uniform designed to make the predominantly female staff who cleaned his hotel's rooms and suites feel safe. 'How long?'

She closed her eyes. 'I'm sorry.'

'How long?' he repeated icily. The shock and elation that had suckered him at the first mention of her name was steadily morphing into anger.

He had spent weeks searching for this woman. He'd thrown numerous resources at the futile attempt to locate her and then, when he'd made the choice to abandon his search, had still found her lodged in his thoughts. She'd become an earworm he could not rid himself of.

The throat he had run his tongue down moved. 'Six months.'

Six months?

She'd been in his employ and under his nose all along? His anger ratcheted up a notch.

'How the hell did you get a ticket for the ball?' he asked in the same icy tone. 'Did you steal it?'

'I was given it.'

'Someone gave you a forty-thousand euro ticket?' he mocked. 'What extra services did you have to do to receive that?'

Colour slashed the rounded cheekbones. 'Nothing like you're thinking.'

'And how do you know what I'm thinking, Tabitha…is that your real name? Or something else you lied about?'

'It's my real name,' she whispered then, hands still

wringing together, paced to the small sofa in the corner of his office.

'I did not invite you to sit down,' he snapped.

Slim shoulders rose in a shrug and she sat regardless and hunched forward, forearms resting on her thighs. 'I'm sorry for lying. I was given the ticket and the dress.'

'By who?'

'It doesn't matter.' Tabitha was struggling to breathe. She'd entered Giannis's office full of resolve and determination but then she'd found herself engulfed by his spicy scent and everything inside her had cramped and tightened, all except for her heart, which thundered hard beneath her ribs.

She had dreaded this moment. She had longed for it too. Longed to see him again.

How could you miss someone when you'd shared only one night with them? One night out of over the eight thousand she had spent on this earth but it had altered her place on this earth.

The most wonderful night of her life. With the most unimaginable consequences.

She could feel the antipathy radiating from him. She couldn't blame him for it. She deserved it. Her behaviour, especially when she had run out on him without a word of goodbye, had been unforgiveable.

If she could live that night again she would do everything differently but wishing for the past to rewrite itself didn't change the facts of today.

She'd expected to be met with anger but she couldn't deny the faint hope that had lived inside her that he would be happy to see her.

The clear blue eyes that had stared into hers with such hunger were icy cold as he leaned forward. 'I want to know who gave a chambermaid of my hotel a ticket for my ball when the guest list was by strict invitation only.'

She clamped her lips together. The darkness emanating from him made her think she would be better off protecting Mrs Coulter from this. Her wonderful friend didn't deserve to have Giannis's ire turned on her.

Tabitha had shared one magical night with this man but she didn't know him. From his reputation, she knew he had a ruthless streak. She would not risk turning that ruthlessness onto an elderly woman who'd wanted only for Tabitha to have one night of fun.

His eyes narrowed at her silence. 'Then you leave me no choice. Hotel staff were warned the ball was for paying guests only and that any attempt to infiltrate it would lead to the termination of their employment. On that basis, you're fired.'

'I'm pregnant.'

The words blurted from her tongue before she could stop them. They'd been hovering there since she'd walked into the office, waiting for the right time to be uttered.

But there had been no right time. What right time could there be for two virtual strangers to learn they were going to have a baby?

Never had she seen the colour drain from someone's face so quickly.

Clear blue eyes ringing with shock stared at her. 'What?'

'I'm pregnant.'

'Pregnant?'

She nodded and finally expelled the breath she'd been holding.

'Who's the father?'

Those three words landed like individual slaps to her face but she didn't drop her gaze. 'You are.'

He stared at her for the longest time and then, to her utter astonishment, Giannis threw his head back and laughed. The maniacal quality to it made her want to cover her ears.

'Please, don't,' she beseeched.

Still laughing, he pushed his chair back and got to his feet. Striding to the door, he opened it. 'Your time is up. I will let Giselle know your contract is to be terminated with immediate effect. Either you leave voluntarily or I call security and have you escorted out.'

'Giannis, please.'

The humour vanished. 'If any of what you say is true then a DNA test will prove it once the so-called baby is born. Until that time, your benefactor can deal with it. Now, get out before I throw you out.'

'You don't believe me, do you?' she whispered, hugging her arms across her chest to stave off the chill that had enveloped her.

'*Believe* you?' Without any warning, he slammed the door he'd been holding open for her shut, making her jump with the force of it. When he looked at her there was nothing but contempt to be found in his stare. 'You let me believe you were a real guest and a woman of wealth.' Anger thickened his accent. 'You shared my bed then ran out on me and now you expect me to believe you're pregnant even though we used contraception?'

'We didn't the second time.'

The memory of reaching for her in his sleep suddenly flashed in Giannis's mind and his blood chilled.

He hadn't used a condom to begin with. He'd groped in the dark for one when he'd already been deep inside her.

The memory alone was enough to heat the sudden chill and thicken his loins.

It didn't matter that she was a liar of extraordinary talent, better even than Anastasia, who could have won a gold medal for deceit. His awareness for Tabitha had not abated in the slightest.

He remembered when he'd discovered that Anastasia had been playing him for a fool. Every lick of desire for her had been extinguished in that instant.

Tabitha was every bit as bad as his wife had been but the ache to haul her into his arms and taste those delectable lips anew thrummed inside him.

Never in a thousand years would he have believed her to be anything but a woman of breeding and wealth. She must have practised that cut-glass accent. The nerve it must have taken to tell the barefaced lie that she'd attended Beddingdales, one of the most exclusive all-girls boarding schools in Europe... She hadn't skipped a beat. It had been a prepared lie, just as everything else had been.

'Who is the puppet master behind your honey trap?' he demanded to know.

Her face paled again, cornflower eyes widening, pretty brow creasing. 'What...? There was no honey trap. You approached me first.'

'Do you expect me to believe it was coincidence you were walking down the stairs at the exact moment I entered the hotel from my apartment? It would have been easy to watch me walk from my apartment from a window on the first or second floor and time your appearance to match mine.'

A flash of anger sparked from her eyes. 'That's absurd.'

'Is it? Someone bought you, a chambermaid, a ticket and outfit to wear for the ball. What was the reason behind it if not to seduce me and entrap me?'

'I didn't seduce you!' she cried. 'Don't rewrite what happened between us just because you don't like the idea that you slept with the hired help. What happened between us just...happened.'

'I could understand if someone had paid for your ticket to accompany them but you attended the ball alone. Why was that? Why did your benefactor not attend with you?'

'They couldn't.'

'Why not?'

'Because...' Her shoulders hunched as she obviously

thought of the most convenient lie to tell. 'They just couldn't. But, I promise you, there was no ulterior motive. They just wanted to do something nice for me.'

'A very expensive way of doing something nice,' he mocked. 'Who was it? A rich family member?' That would be the only answer he would find vaguely acceptable, although that would then beg the question of who would allow a member of their family to work in a job that involved cleaning other people's messes if they had the kind of wealth at their disposal to purchase a forty-thousand euro ticket for a masquerade ball.

She took a deep breath and shook her head.

'Who is your benefactor?'

'It isn't important.'

'I disagree. No one would spend that amount of money on someone without expecting something in return. I want to know who your benefactor is and what you had to do in lieu of payment for attending a ball which you were expressly forbidden from attending.'

'I don't know what circles you mix in but you should look at expanding it.' There was a tremor in her voice. 'There are good people in the world and my benefactor is one of them. There was no ulterior motive. I know I let you believe I was a wealthy woman, and I'm sorry for that, but I didn't have a choice—if I'd confessed who I was you would have fired me on the spot.'

'You can try and talk your way out of it but the facts are indisputable. You posed as a paying guest. You spent the evening in my arms on the dance floor and in my bed. Strange behaviour for a woman who now claims she couldn't tell me her true identity for fear of losing her job. If you were so concerned with keeping it, you wouldn't have attempted this charade in the first place. You certainly wouldn't have gone to bed with me.'

Even though her gaze was now on his carpeted floor, he could see the stain of colour on her cheeks.

It was the same colour that had flushed on her cheeks when she'd come with him buried deep inside her.

Theos, every cell in his body ached to feel that sensation again, of being so deep inside her they could have been fused together.

This woman could confess to being a mass murderer and he would still want her.

But she wasn't confessing to anything and made no attempt to defend herself.

'Your denials are pitiful,' he said coldly, hating her but hating himself more for still wanting her. 'You set out to entrap me and, if your claim that you're pregnant proves to be true, then you have hit the jackpot.'

She lifted her head to look him square in the eye. 'How?' she challenged. 'Tell me, please, how an unplanned pregnancy can be described as hitting the jackpot?'

'If you really are pregnant and the child proves to be mine, you have a meal ticket for life.'

'*If?*' She jumped to her feet. 'I *am* pregnant and you *are* the father. Go and buy me a pregnancy test if you don't believe me! There hasn't been anyone else. And I don't want a meal ticket. All I want is some financial support...'

Fury thumped violently through him. He strode over to her and stared at the angry, beautiful face, his heart pumping harder as that delicate scent swirled into his senses.

One night he had spent with this deceitful woman and her scent had imprinted itself on him.

He had never despised anyone as much as he despised her at that moment.

'I knew there would be a financial aspect in all this. There always is with women like you.'

'Women like me?' Her outrage vibrated from her very pores then her face contorted, her hands flew forward and she shoved his chest. 'Are you implying that I'm a whore because I slept with you?' she shouted. 'What does that make you? A gigolo?'

He grabbed her wrists before she could push him again. 'I did not call you a whore!'

'You implied it!'

'I did not. That must be your conscience.'

'I was a *virgin*.'

CHAPTER FIVE

TABITHA WAS SO fired up with anger and shame, her awareness of him fizzing over her skin and buzzing through her veins, that if he hadn't had such a tight hold of her wrists she would have slapped him.

Suddenly she found herself against the office wall, his hands either side of her face.

His features were taut as he stared at her, his long nose inches from hers, clear blue eyes pulsing with fury but also with something she recognised from their night together...

Her heart thrashed so wildly he must have been able to feel the beats against his chest which brushed against her breasts.

A thrill laced her treacherous spine when he pressed his cheek to hers.

'You put me under an enchantment.'

She shivered at the whispered words, although the actual words barely registered, not when his breath was hot against her ear, hot enough to seep through her skin and melt her bones.

Then, just as suddenly as he'd trapped her, he stepped away. *'Sygnomi,'* he muttered.

Legs like noodles, Tabitha kept her back propped against the wall for support and watched, dazed, as he turned his back and ran his fingers through his hair.

She had never known silence could be so charged.

He kept his back to her. 'Were you really a virgin?'

'Yes.' She'd gone to an all-girls boarding school, had looked forward to starting university and finally being able to mix with men, only to find herself homeless before she'd finished her boarding school education and having to work her fingers to the bone to make ends meet, leaving no time for *any* kind of life.

His broad shoulders rose and she heard him inhale deeply. 'And you really are pregnant?'

'Yes.'

He muttered something in his native tongue she didn't understand but which, judging by the tone, she guessed was a curse. She didn't want to know if it was aimed at herself or the situation.

Resisting the strong urge to step over and place a hand on his shoulder, she took a deep breath and tightened her ponytail with shaking hands.

The effect of his touch still blazed through her body. Her lips still tingled from the anticipated kiss that had never come. If she strained her ears she'd be able to hear the electricity still crackling through the tense silence between them.

As hard as it was, she had to ignore the tumult of feelings just sharing his air evoked in her. Tabitha might have been a virgin until their night together but she wasn't naïve. She knew sexual awareness did not automatically equate to emotional feelings. Many people were capable of having physical affairs without emotional intimacy.

She'd just never thought she would be one of them.

The times when she'd allowed herself to think of a future where she could drag herself out of the drudgery of her life and find happiness, she'd always imagined it with a faceless man and a handful of children. She'd imagined happiness. Laughter. Love.

All the things that had been denied her since her father had died and her stepmother's true nature had come out.

All the things that had got her out of bed at the crack of dawn every day, working so hard her hands were red and sore, the tips of her fingers calloused and cracked. Dreams of a future.

Those dreams were the only thing that had stopped her spiralling into a pit of despair.

At first it had been a matter of survival but what use was surviving if there was nothing else? She'd had to believe there was something else out there for her.

And now she had to believe there was something else out there for the tiny life growing in her belly. This man with whom she shared this most inexplicable of attractions had created a life with her. He had the means and the power to give their child a life without poverty.

Giannis turned back to face her, breathing heavily.

For a long moment all they did was stare at each other.

Tabitha straightened her shoulders. 'What happens now? Do you want me to go and buy another pregnancy test? Only, I need to get back to work soon.'

His eyes narrowed dangerously and his brow furrowed.

'You can't sack me,' she said with a bluntness that belied the knots in her belly. 'I don't expect any help from you until the baby's born but I still need to support myself. I need to eat, a place to sleep… At some point I'll need to buy maternity clothes. I can't do that without an income. I have little savings. If you sack me, I'll be homeless.' She tightened her ponytail again to mask her agitation. 'All I want is for you to let me keep my job until I can legally take maternity leave. Hopefully I'll have found somewhere to live by—'

'No.' Giannis gritted his teeth and swallowed the bile rising up his throat. His guts were churning acid. All these things were happening within him but stronger than the rest was the sick compulsion to touch her, to keep touching her, to make her his again. Every part of him ached to drag her back into his arms, the few moments spent with his back to her, trying to take back control of the desire raging through him, fruitless. 'You are not returning to your duties here. You're coming to Santorini with me.'

She stared at him, the soft, full lips open but no words coming out.

'I cannot leave you here knowing you might be carrying my child.'

Could it be true? Was there a child of his loins forming within the softness of the stomach he had kissed every inch of?

'I thought you didn't believe me,' she whispered, cornflower eyes not leaving his face.

'A visit to an obstetrician will prove if you're pregnant and give a good indication of conception.'

He knew that first-hand. It was how he'd discovered it was not possible he'd fathered Anastasia's child.

But there was a big difference, he had to acknowledge. His suspicions that Tabitha had been a virgin had been confirmed. He'd read stories about women selling their virginity to the highest bidder. Was this a different version of the same thing? A woman giving her virginity to a rich man with the express desire to get pregnant?

Her virginity was the only thing he would allow himself to believe. He'd been cuckolded and humiliated once. His pride had been wounded far more than his heart and he would never put himself in that position again. It was the reason he'd decided that his next wife would be chosen using cold, hard logic.

It made his guts twist to remember how the morning after he'd thought that Tabitha might be the woman for him. She'd fitted all his requirements and the desire between them had been off the charts.

But she hadn't. She was nothing but a liar. She didn't have the independent wealth he required his next wife to have as a form of surety that she wasn't a gold-digger.

The only truth had been the desire between them and

that desire had proved itself to be dangerous. It had driven him to become carried away and forget to use a condom until it had been almost too late.

Had it been too late? Tabitha was twenty-two. Helena, the second-oldest of his sisters, had fallen pregnant within a month of her marriage at the age of twenty-one. Giannis remembered his mother's delighted comment that it was because she was in the prime fertile years of her life.

He could not allow this attraction to cloud his thinking any more than it already had. He'd been led by 'feelings' before and had vowed, as he'd watched his wife and her child be lowered into the cold ground, that he would not be made a fool of again.

He looked hard at the woman who had already fooled him once with her deception. He could never trust her and he could not trust the feeling in his guts that she spoke the truth.

Giannis hadn't taken anything on trust in five years. He liked proof. Cold, hard facts.

'You will come to Santorini with me and meet with my sister's obstetrician,' he said, voicing his thoughts as he decided them.

'Aren't there obstetricians in Vienna?'

'This is one of the best obstetricians in Europe. If you are carrying my child he will be the one to monitor you throughout the pregnancy and deliver it.'

'Hold your horses.' Her hand shot out, palm up, dark, angry colour slashing her cheeks. 'Ten minutes ago you thought I was lying to you.'

'If you told me it was raining I would put my head out of the window to check. I'm still to be convinced about the pregnancy, but you would have to be the most audacious of fools to try and pretend something so easily disproved.'

'And you would have to be the most audacious of arrogant twonks to think I would let you decide anything on my behalf!'

'It's my money that will be paying for it. You, by your own admission, don't even have a home of your own to raise a child.' Ignoring her splutters of outrage, he continued, 'If things are as you say, a visit to the obstetrician will confirm it. Once it has been confirmed we can move things forward. I will put you up for the duration of the pregnancy and pay for all your expenses. If, however, the obstetrician proves that you're lying…' He smiled. 'You can find your own way home.'

The dark colour on her cheeks had drained away. She took a step back and wrapped her arms around her stomach. 'I didn't have to tell you. I could have kept the baby a secret. You could have seen me every day in this hotel and you would never have recognised me because you would never have deigned to look at a lowly worker like me. I told you because…'

'You needed my money,' he supplied sardonically.

'And because I thought you had a right to know. You might be a gazillionaire but that does not give you the right to use your money as a weapon.'

'I can use my money however I see fit. But I'm not using it as weapon, I am merely giving you my terms. If you are convinced I am the father of your child, then you can have no objection to accompanying me to Santorini. If you want the best for the child you claim is mine then I fail to see how you can object to spending the pregnancy living in luxury with the best medical attention on hand if it is needed.'

Oh, she could object, all right, Tabitha thought, panic clawing at her throat as she recognised that he was serious. He wanted to take her to Santorini. Once he had her on his home turf she would be trapped. She had enough in her bank account to fly back to Vienna but she had no doubt there would be no job to return to and that no references would be provided.

She could fly back to England but where would she go?

Back to the small hotel whose owners had taken pity on her when her stepmother had first thrown her out? Back to the tiny room too small for even the least discerning guest where there was no space for a cot? And that was if that tiny room wasn't being used by someone else.

She rolled her shoulders and tried to clear the panic away to think clearly.

Giannis's offer was more generous than she could have hoped. He was giving her a way to get through the pregnancy without having to worry about finances or worry about the physical aspects of her job harming the baby the further into the pregnancy she got. What woman wouldn't want to be under the care of a top obstetrician in her first pregnancy?

So what if he didn't believe her? She couldn't expect him to take her word on trust, not after the lies by omission she'd told at the ball.

What was there to be so afraid of?

They would fly to Santorini and the obstetrician would confirm that everything she'd said was true. She had nothing to lose by going with him and everything to gain for her baby.

So why was she so afraid?

'Well?' he asked, folding his arms across his chest and staring at her with an imperious expression that made her heart ache for the generous lover who had swept her off her feet. 'What are you going to do?'

'I'm coming with you.'

He looked at his watch. 'Then I suggest you pack your belongings. We leave in two hours.'

Giannis wrapped up the meeting with his senior management team much quicker than he usually did.

He'd hardly paid attention to a word that had been exchanged.

His gut was telling him loud and clear that he was going to be a father. This was the same gut that had told him loud and clear that he was not the father of Anastasia's baby.

Striding back to his office, he went straight to his computer and clicked on the hotel's staff files. Every current member of staff was listed on it alphabetically by surname.

He didn't know Tabitha's surname.

He found her quickly, though. Tabitha Brigstock. A quick scan of the other names showed this to be the only Tabitha, which was not surprising. Tabitha was not a common name. He clicked on her name and brought up her file, which contained a copy of her résumé, a copy of her contract, copies of her appraisals and a file of all the shifts she'd undertaken over the past ninety days.

He clicked on the résumé first. His brow creased as he scanned the sparse information. It contained her full name, Tabitha Louisa Brigstock, her date of birth—her twenty-third birthday was approaching—and her employment history. There were no educational qualifications listed. She'd spent four years working as a cleaner and evening waitress at a hotel in Northamptonshire which he'd never heard of. The owner of the hotel was named as a referee. The other referee was a name he recognised—his current Head of Housekeeping, Rachel.

He brought Rachel's file up and found that she'd started working here when he'd first turned it into a hotel. Her previous employment had been at Tabitha's old hotel. Tabitha's employment in Vienna had coincided with Rachel's promotion. He deduced that Rachel had been the one to encourage Tabitha's move from England to Vienna.

He then clicked on Tabitha's contract which had been signed six months ago. She was contracted to work thirty-five hours a week as a chambermaid at a subsidised rate to account for her living in the staff quarters.

On the file listing all the shifts she'd undertaken, his

eyes widened to see she worked an average of seventy-hour weeks, often covering evening housekeeping shifts and occasionally filling in at the hotel bar and restaurant. She obviously grabbed any overtime she could get.

He thought back to when he'd touched her fingers and had been surprised to find them hard and worn.

Her fingers should have been a warning sign that she wasn't who she claimed to be, he thought ruefully, smothering the ache coursing through him to imagine the long, back-breaking days Tabitha spent working herself into exhaustion. He had never encountered a woman in his social circle whose hands weren't looked after with the same zeal as her face.

On a whim, he typed her name into a search engine. No immediate matching results came up.

A knock on his office door took his attention away from any further Internet search.

He cleared his throat, his heart suddenly setting off at a canter. 'Come in.'

The door opened and, as expected, Tabitha appeared.

Her honey-blonde hair loose and impossibly long, much longer than he remembered, she'd changed out of her work uniform into a pair of slim-fitting jeans and a T-shirt that must once have been black but was so worn it had faded to a dark grey.

For some reason his heart wrenched to see it.

It was like looking at a beautiful butterfly with its old, faded cocoon still attached to it.

She carried an oversized sports bag, its strap hooked over her shoulder. Like her T-shirt, the bag was obviously well worn.

'You're still here, then,' she said lightly, pushing the door shut with her bottom. Only the tremor in her voice showed her nonchalance was nothing but a façade. 'I thought you might have run off.'

'Running off is your department.'

She winced and dropped her gaze to the floor. It was a long few moments before she lifted her head to look at him. 'I never apologised for that, did I? I'm sorry. I panicked. I was going to be late for work and I didn't know what I could say to explain myself without giving myself away.'

A boulder had lodged itself in Giannis's throat. He couldn't speak for it.

She didn't seem to expect a response, putting her bag on the sofa on which she'd sat earlier when she'd told him she was pregnant.

She unzipped it and pulled a black item out.

He didn't notice her hands were shaking until she carried the item to him and placed it on his desk.

It was his shirt from the ball.

'I need to apologise for taking this. It was a spur-of-the-moment thing. I never meant to keep it.'

Curiosity got the better of him. 'Why did you take it?'

'It was easier to put on and escape in than my ball gown.'

'Did you escape through the bedroom window?'

She gave a sheepish nod. 'I'm sorry. And I'm sorry for not giving it back. I couldn't think how to without giving myself away.'

He leaned forward to take the shirt. Then he got to his feet and, without any ceremony, dropped it in the waste bin. 'Are you packed?'

Her eyes darted from the bin back to him. 'Yes.'

'Where's the rest of your stuff?'

She patted the bag. 'It's all in here.'

'Everything?'

She nodded. 'I've given my work uniforms back.'

A whole life enclosed in one oversized sports bag?

For some reason, his heart made that wrenching feeling again, although why that should be he didn't know, not when Tabitha didn't seem to think there was anything strange in having all her worldly possessions contained in one bag.

Not his concern, he told himself sternly. *She* was not his concern.

The only thing that should concern him was the child she purported to carry.

He would know in the morning if the child was his.

CHAPTER SIX

TABITHA LOWERED HERSELF into the biggest bath she'd ever bathed in and closed her eyes as the warmth of the foamy water enveloped her.

It was hard to believe that only eight hours ago she'd knocked on Giannis's office door, sick with apprehension.

Everything that had passed since then had gone at warp speed. Their confrontation. His ultimatum. Packing her belongings. The silent journey in the back of the chauffeured car to the airport. The flight from Vienna to Santorini in Giannis's private plane, Giannis studiously working on his laptop, Tabitha dozing but not sleeping—she'd been too overwrought to sleep. The chauffeured drive from the private airfield they'd landed in to his home… One continuous blur with no time to get her bearings and no privacy to think.

She had privacy now, though.

Giannis had left her at the entrance of his breathtakingly beautiful home saying his housekeeper, Zoe, would show her to her designated room and provide her with anything she needed. She hadn't seen or heard from him since.

She'd walked through the vast, cavernous rooms of his clifftop home with its thick, white walls feeling like she'd slipped through the looking glass.

One minute she'd been in the beautiful city of Vienna, speaking a language she'd learned at school and in which she'd become able to converse fluently, the next on what could be the most beautiful island in the whole of Europe. The sun had begun its descent when they'd arrived, the sky a glorious deep orange shining enough light to showcase the pristine white homes they'd driven past, the architecture like nowhere she'd been before.

The looking-glass feeling had continued when she'd tried to speak to Zoe, who'd taken her straight to her room. The housekeeper didn't speak a word of English. Greek was not a language on the Beddingdales curriculum so Tabitha had been stuck. Her stomach had kept rumbling but she'd been too shy and feeling too out of place to find the kitchen and communicate her hunger.

The room she'd been given was lovely, though, dual aspect windows giving her a fabulous view of the Aegean Sea now glinting under the stars of the moonless night sky. Her *en suite* bathroom had been stocked with all the toiletries a woman could need, a soft white robe hanging on its door.

She was tying the sash of the robe around her waist after she'd got out of the bath and dried herself when she heard a knock on the bedroom door.

Hurrying through the bedroom to open it, her heart leapt into her throat to find Giannis standing there.

From the dampness of his hair and the fresh, spicy scents seeping off him, he'd showered or bathed recently too. He'd also changed out of his business suit, his muscular body wrapped in a pair of casual tan chinos and a short-sleeved khaki shirt unbuttoned at the throat.

His eyes flickered over her robed form, a pulse in them that hardened to stone when he met her gaze.

'Are you going to bed?' he asked stiffly.

Suddenly feeling as naked as she was beneath the robe, she pulled the sash tighter, painfully aware of the heat engulfing her face. 'No, I've just had a bath.'

There was the slightest flare of his nostrils before his jaw tightened. 'Are you hungry?'

Her stomach rumbled loudly in answer.

It was the most mortifying sound she'd ever heard and her cheeks flamed brighter for it.

'Dinner will be brought to you in five minutes.'

'I have to eat in my room?' What was she? A prisoner?

'I've spoken to the obstetrician,' he said, ignoring her question. 'He's flying to the island first thing to meet us at his clinic here. We'll leave at eight. Do you need a wake-up call?'

'I'll set the alarm clock on my phone.'

He nodded. 'I'll see you in the morning. Goodnight.'

And as suddenly as he'd appeared, he left, heading off down the wide corridor and disappearing from sight.

Giannis got into the back of his car, his head swimming.

He could still hear the baby's fledgling heartbeat ringing in his ears.

Neither he nor Tabitha had exchanged a single word since the obstetrician had confirmed the pregnancy. And confirmed the conception date to a narrow period which coincided exactly with the date of the ball.

As much as he would like to think Tabitha was the sort of woman who could lose her virginity to a man one day and sleep with another the next, he just could not see it.

His gut had been right. He was going to be a father.

Resting his head back against the soft leather upholstery, he closed his eyes.

'Are you okay?'

Tabitha's softly spoken words soaked through him.

He jerked a nod.

He'd hoped for a different outcome. He'd hoped the visit would result in him driving Tabitha back to the airport and never having to see her again.

But he could not deny that the confirmation had delivered a bolt of pure joy inside him. There had been a moment when he'd had to fist his hands to stop himself from leaning over to kiss her.

Every moment with her was a fight against himself not to touch her.

The spell she'd woven over him a month ago still lived in his blood. He'd felt it on the flight from Vienna when he'd worked diligently on his laptop but found his attention wrapped solely in the woman reclining on the seat opposite him, sleeping. He'd felt it on the drive to his home, felt it sharpen at the shine in her eyes when she'd seen his home, then felt it burst through his veins when she'd opened her bedroom door, wearing nothing but a robe and a cloud of her divine scent.

The evening meal he'd planned to share with her...

A snap judgement had decided for him that it would be better if she ate alone.

Merely sharing the same air as her did things to him that could not be explained by any degree of logic.

His desire for Tabitha was like a sickness and he had to treat it as such. To touch her and make love to her again would only drag him further into her duplicitous web.

And now that delectable temptation would be under his nose for the next eight months. If he didn't take drastic action she would be a permanent part of his life, this woman in whose web he'd foolishly allowed himself to be caught.

'Name your price,' he said heavily.

'My price for what?'

'For me to have sole custody of our child. Name it. Cash. Property. Whatever you want.'

She was silent for the longest time.

His heart thudded as he awaited her response.

When she finally answered there was an iciness to her tone he had never heard from her before. 'That is the most offensive thing I have ever heard.'

'Why? You are not in a position to raise a child. You have

nothing. I can give our child everything it desires and the best education money can buy.'

'Are you saying that being poor disqualifies me from being a good parent?'

'You cannot tell me that you want a child,' he said roughly, ignoring her question. Of course he didn't believe that. He remembered the old Basinas family gardener who'd had three children he'd doted on. They'd lived hand to mouth in a tiny home but they'd been the happiest kids he'd known, secure and loved. He'd loved playing with them when he'd been a child and still kept in touch with them as an adult.

He also knew plenty of rich people who were lousy parents and whose children were spoilt brats.

None of this was the issue. The issue was Tabitha, this duplicitous temptress, who even now had every cell in his body singing for her. 'You're young, single, you have no home, no money…'

'That last issue can easily be resolved by child support from you, which I will be legally entitled to. I'm young but I'm not a child—'

'What can you inspire a child to be?' he interrupted, knowing even as the words came out that they were cruel, but unable to stop them, the determination to talk Tabitha out of his life far stronger than decency and compassion. 'I've seen your résumé—what qualifications do you have? I assume you have none, seeing as you did not list them. Or do I have that wrong?'

'What do qualifications have to do with raising a child?' she hissed indignantly. 'Children need one thing only— love. To say only the best educated and those with a disposable income are the only people capable of raising a child well is unspeakably snobbish and cruel.'

'Anyone can love a child,' he conceded. 'But, if it came

to a choice between love and a roof over their head, every child would choose the roof.'

'Twaddle. I lost my mum when I was a little girl. If you'd asked me then if I would prefer to live in a big, swanky house or have my mother I would have chosen my mother every time. I would have happily lived in a cardboard box if it had meant having her with me.

'And,' she continued before her words about her mother could really penetrate and before he could get a word in, 'I take umbrage with your assertion that anyone can love a child. There are people on this earth—rich people, poor people—who shouldn't be allowed within a thousand miles of one. I will not give you custody of our child, not now or ever, and if you ever make such a suggestion again you will never see me or our child again.'

If they hadn't been in the back of a moving car, Tabitha would have stormed off.

She resisted the urge to kick the seat opposite her and resisted the even stronger temptation to kick Giannis.

Instead, she twisted so her back was to him and looked out of the window at the passing scenery, breathing hard to regulate the tumultuous emotions rippling through her.

Her heart ached to think of the generous lover under whose spell she had fallen for one magical night. He had been warm.

This man was cold.

This man hated her.

He hated her so much that he'd made her dine in her room alone rather than share his evening dinner or breakfast with her. He hated her so much that rather than allow the sound of their baby's heartbeat to bond them together as parents, if not allies, he had stabbed her heart with his cruel offer to pay for her to abandon the life growing inside her.

What would he have done if she'd said yes—locked her

away while the baby incubated inside her as if she were livestock?

Nausea cramped in her stomach and she put a protective hand to it.

Give up her child? She would rather die.

They had made this life together but the truth was Giannis didn't think she was good enough to be a mother to his child. She'd been good enough to sleep with when he'd assumed she was wealthy but now he knew the truth of her circumstances he wanted nothing to do with her. He didn't want to touch her, didn't want to look at her.

She didn't want him to touch her, she told herself defiantly. If he was so shallow that he judged a person's worth on their income and job title then he could go stick his head up his backside.

She heard him shift in his seat and caught a whiff of his cologne.

Her heart ballooned as fresh awareness raced through her, moving too fast for her to take any kind of control over it and squash it back in a box where it belonged.

Pressing her forehead to the window, she stared miserably at the pristine white homes they were driving past.

She didn't want his touch. She didn't.

This sick awareness of him was not her choice and how she could still feel it was beyond reason. Even now, sitting here, despising him and despising his cold cruelty, her senses were alert to his closeness. She'd lain on the obstetrician's medical bed and rolled her T-shirt up over her belly, had the sonographer place the cold gel onto her skin and, until the moment the tiny blob that was her growing child had appeared on the screen, had been consumed with Giannis's presence. When the first sound of a heartbeat had rung out in the small consulting room, their eyes had met for the only time since leaving his home that morning, and for one beautiful moment she'd experienced a connection with him that had filled her with so many emotions she'd wanted to throw her arms around him, press her head to his chest and hear his heartbeat too.

All her hopes that they could find an agreement to be amicable co-parents had evaporated.

A prickle on the back of her neck told her Giannis was looking at her.

A moment later his deep voice cut through the silence. 'If you ever threaten to take my child away from me again, I will sue you for full custody. And I will win.'

His cold words almost knocked the air from her lungs.

Inhaling deeply, she clenched her hands into fists. 'Don't treat me and my child like a commodity and I won't have to make that threat. Oh, and I wasn't threatening you—I was promising. Take me to court. See how a judge reacts to you throwing your money around to buy a baby.'

She heard his own sharp intake of breath.

When he next spoke, it sounded as if it were coming from between tightly gritted teeth. 'I was merely trying to think of the best way to proceed—the best way for all our interests.'

'All *your* interests, you mean. If I was as shallow and money-grabbing as you keep implying, I would have accepted your offer and you wouldn't have to face a future explaining to all and sundry that the mother of your child is a chambermaid. You could say the child was conceived by a surrogate.'

His phone suddenly vibrated in his pocket. He pulled it out and saw it was Niki.

He sighed and switched it off without answering. His youngest sister was furious with him for abandoning her in Vienna, although there was some debate as to whether 'abandoning' was the correct term, considering he'd put her in the best suite of the hotel and sent his plane back to collect her that morning. He was not ready to tell her or any of his family about Tabitha. Not when he was still trying to get to grips with the situation.

It was a situation he knew his family would be delighted about. He also knew what they would expect him to do about it. They would expect him to marry her.

His driver turned onto the long driveway that took them to Giannis's home. Staring out of the window at the home he loved and had expected to be filled with children long before now, an overwhelming weariness flooded through him, and he bowed his head and rubbed the back of his neck.

'I've appointments in Athens to get to. I'll be back later this evening. We can discuss the situation more then.'

He reached out to touch the honey-blonde hair splaying down her back and over her seat and pulled his hand back with only inches to spare.

He needed some legal advice because the only future he could see now involved marrying this woman who evoked the stickiest desire he'd ever known and a maelstrom of emotions in him. If marriage was the route they needed to take then he needed to get a grip on it all. And fast.

With the sun already blazing high in the azure sky, Tabitha rolled her jeans up her calves as far she could and put a black vest on. It was the closest thing to beach wear she could create from her limited wardrobe.

Then she walked down the long pebbled steps that led from Giannis's clifftop house to his private beach. She'd just reached the bottom of them when Giannis's house-keeper came tearing after her with a bottle of sunscreen and a large bottle of water.

Touched at the thoughtful gesture, and wishing she could thank the kind woman in her language, she kissed her cheek as a means of conveying her gratitude.

Alone with nothing but the clear Aegean Sea, she sank onto the dark volcanic sand and, for the first time in over four years, spent a day doing nothing. No cleaning. No washing. No scrubbing. No ironing. She just sat on the beach with the sun toasting her skin and got lost in her thoughts.

Slowly her fury at Giannis's offer to effectively buy their baby from her lessened but threads of agitation grew in its place. He wanted to talk more about the 'situation' later.

What would happen to her now? What would happen to her baby? She wished desperately that her father were still alive. Just a warm embrace from him would be enough. He'd been such a good man, always wanting the best for his only child. It would have devastated him to see what had become of her. It would have devastated him to learn the wife he'd chosen with such care for his daughter's sake had been a wolf in sheep's clothing. He'd known Tabitha's relationship with her stepsisters hadn't been the loving one he'd envisaged but he'd never dreamed the rot went all the way to the top. If he had, he would never have put his second wife down as a trustee to his estate. He would have better protected Tabitha.

Would Giannis only want the best for their child? He'd implied as much but what did his interpretation of 'best' even mean? Did it only mean material things? Or did it include love and affection?

His assertion that she had nothing to offer a child had stung but not as much as his cruel question as to how she could inspire their child.

Giannis looked at her and saw an insignificant nobody.

She wished it didn't make her heart ache so much to know that that was who she'd become.

But now she needed to become someone. She needed to be the mother her child deserved.

Giannis took a deep breath before knocking on Tabitha's door.

A long day had been broken up with a quick chat with

his lawyer, who'd confirmed marriage was the most sensible route to take if he wanted any rights over his child. The law in Greece gave unmarried mothers sole custody. He would only have rights to his child if Tabitha consented. He could take her to court. With the legal minds he would employ, he could be reasonably certain of winning, but there were no guarantees in life. Marriage cut out any risks. He would be his child's legal parent in the eyes of the law and seamlessly solve any future problem regarding custody and maintenance.

Marriage protected him. The sooner he tied Tabitha down the better, before she learned for herself that she held three out of the four aces in the pack. Which meant he needed to go on a charm offensive.

The door opened slowly.

When their eyes met he had a moment where all thoughts flew from his brain.

She looked dishevelled in rolled-up jeans and a black vest top, her pretty feet bare, long honey-blonde hair tumbling messily over her shoulders.

She tucked a lock of it behind her ear, colour rising on her rounded cheekbones.

Damn it, even resembling a grubby urchin she was beautiful.

There was a smudge on her left cheek. He rammed his hand into his pocket to stop himself from reaching out to wipe it clean.

His beautiful liar was the greatest temptation he had ever known. That made her more dangerous than she could understand.

But she was here, in his home, under his roof. If he wanted his rights to the child growing beneath the stomach that looked only a little rounder since their night together to be guaranteed, he needed to marry her. To marry her, he needed her consent.

He cleared his throat. 'Dinner will be served for us on the terrace in twenty minutes.'

There was not the slightest softening on the beautiful stony face before him. 'You want to eat with me?'

No. He never wanted to be near her again, never have that astounding beauty in his sight, never have her scent dive into his senses, never hear that fake cut-glass but utterly melodious, husky voice, never have his own fingers itch to reach out and touch the soft skin he so vividly remembered the texture and taste of…

Loins thickening uncomfortably, he gave a sharp nod and stepped back. 'I'll meet you out there.'

Then he turned and headed straight to his own room at the other end of his home to the room he'd put her in, far out of the reach of temptation.

Standing under the shower, he knew he had to get a grip. If she did consent to marry him then the temptation that was Tabitha would no longer be a temptation. She would be his wife. She would share his bed. Share his life.

Frustrated and furious with himself for his weakness around her, he punched the wall.

Damn it to hell, how had he got so carried away that he'd failed to put the condom on before thrusting inside her?

But that was the wrong question to ask because all it did was make his already aching loins remember the exquisite pleasure of being bare inside her.

CHAPTER SEVEN

WHEN GIANNIS ARRIVED at the terrace he found the table set as he'd instructed but no Tabitha.

Pouring himself a large glass of white wine, he took a seat and waited.

She appeared ten minutes later in the same rolled-up jeans and black vest she'd answered her bedroom door in, her hair brushed, her face clean but her cheeks flushed. 'Sorry. I got lost.'

Awareness stabbed through him so hard that all he could do was raise a brow.

Her nerves came out in her voice. 'I thought you meant the terrace at the back with the swimming pool. I didn't know there was one overlooking the beach too. It's very well hidden.'

'It's secluded,' he agreed. 'Please, sit. Would you like a drink?'

'Just water, please.' Tabitha took the seat she assumed had been set for her—judging by the cutlery setting, they were having a three-course meal—and looked out at the magnificent view so as to avoid meeting his eye again until her heart had slowed to a more manageable beat.

Trying desperately to distract herself, she inhaled the fragrant floral air mingled with the scent of the sea that glimmered before her. This terrace had to be right below her bedroom.

The more she explored Giannis's home, the more there was to discover, including that the vast majority of it was carved into the cliff itself.

He poured water for her from a jug and indicated the pitta bread and dips already laid on the table.

Being alone with him had killed her appetite quicker than the gory pictures her stepsisters had liked to show her to scare her when she was a child but this was a much different appetite suppressant. This suppressant was because large butterflies had suddenly formed in her stomach, their wings fluttering hard all the way up to her throat.

Although she knew she wouldn't be able to manage more than a small amount, Tabitha dipped some of the bread into the pink *taramasalata* and took a tiny bite.

Giannis was the one to break the silence. 'Forgive me for not asking this sooner, but how are you finding the pregnancy?'

She swallowed her bite-sized morsel and forced herself to look at him. 'Exciting and frightening.'

'That is understandable. What about physically? Have you noticed any changes?'

'I suffer with afternoon morning sickness.' She managed a small smile to see the furrow in his brow. 'Every afternoon, without fail, I get nauseous. I've learned to only eat plain food for lunch then it's less severe but, either way, it doesn't last long—an hour or so. I also get tired easily but that's it. So far, so good.'

She crossed her legs to stop the jitters.

Why were they pretending? Why was *she* pretending? Pretending that sharing a meal with Giannis was normal, that she wasn't suspicious at this change in attitude towards her? She wanted to be thankful for it but she couldn't. When he'd dropped her back at his home earlier he'd hardly been able to look her in the eye. Now he was pouring her drinks on the terrace of his home, sharing a meal in a setting that could only be considered as romantic.

'Maybe the sea air here will help with the sickness,' he observed.

'Maybe. I was nauseous earlier but I wasn't sick.'

'That's encouraging.' He dipped a large chunk of pitta into the humus and popped it whole into his mouth.

Unable to take this stilted, fake politeness a moment longer, she wiped her fingers on the cotton napkin and raised her chin. 'Why are you being nice to me?'

He didn't pretend not to know what she was talking about. He took hold of his glass but, instead of drinking from it, he swirled the wine within it. 'I have been harsh with you. For that I apologise. The news about your pregnancy came as a shock but now we have to move forward...'

Before Giannis could finish and tell her he thought they should marry, there came the sound of clacking footsteps followed by his sister Niki bursting through the French doors.

'What are you doing here?' he asked in Greek, rising from his chair.

'To tell you off. You left me in Vienna without a word of explanation and have been avoiding all my calls since.' She cast a beady stare at Tabitha. 'Is *she* the reason for...?'

But then Niki cut herself off and stared even harder at her with widening eyes. 'Tabitha?'

Giannis watched as recognition flickered in the cornflower eyes. 'Niki?'

'You two know each other?' His mind raced. His sister had not spent a great deal of time at his palace hotel but she was a gregarious soul who made friends easily. It would be just like her to befriend a chambermaid.

An enormous smile spread over Niki's face and, in English, she said, 'It *is* you! What are you doing here? How do you know my brother?'

The shock on Tabitha's face told its own story. 'Giannis is your *brother*?'

Niki beamed and nodded, then pulled out a chair to sit, uninvited.

'How do you two know each other?' Giannis asked again, his curiosity outweighing his frustration at this rude interruption.

Grabbing Tabitha's unused wine glass, Niki poured herself a glass. 'Tabitha was at Beddingdales with Simone, Melina's cousin. We used to meet up at weekends if we had the same leave.'

Melina was Niki's best friend. Melina had been the reason Niki had refused to go to Beddingdales herself, begging their parents to send her to the same English boarding school that Melina was being sent to. As Niki could wrap her parents around her little finger, they'd agreed.

But none of this was what Giannis was thinking of.

He stared at Tabitha, met her expressionless gaze and felt the ground shift beneath him.

Then Niki burst into a peel of laughter. 'I've just realised— you're the woman who took Giannis's attention for the whole of the masquerade ball! I was sure you were familiar but with your mask on I couldn't place where I knew you from!'

He whipped his head round to look at his sister.

She'd mentioned his 'mystery woman' a couple of times in the days after the ball but not once had she said the woman in question was familiar to her. After he had shut her up about the subject, she had stopped mentioning it.

If he had known Tabitha had rung a bell with Niki he would have made her think hard about who she could be.

He looked again at the woman carrying his child.

How the hell did a girl from one of the world's most exclusive and expensive all-girls boarding schools grow into a woman so impoverished she'd become a live-in chambermaid?

The next hour passed with Tabitha in a daze.

Niki was Giannis's sister? She'd never known her well

but had always remembered her, mostly because she was one of the most fun people she'd ever met. A few years older than Tabitha, she'd exuded a glamour Tabitha would have killed to achieve for herself. Whenever she'd come with Melina to visit Simone in the town near their school, Tabitha had been thrilled to be included in the group.

Whether she was oblivious to the tension in the air or whether she just chose to ignore it, only Niki knew, but she stayed, happily helping herself to Tabitha's leftovers, of which there were many, from all the delicious courses they were served. There were many instances of, 'Do you remember?' to which Tabitha would nod and smile but chatterbox Niki didn't require input from either of them. From the way her merry eyes darted between them, she obviously thought they'd got together at the ball and had been seeing each other in secret since.

When she finally took one of the enormous hints Giannis kept dropping and said her goodbyes—and Giannis insisted on seeing her out, most likely to ensure she actually left—Tabitha got to her feet and stood at the thick white wall that acted as a barrier between the terrace and sheer drop beneath them.

She breathed in deeply, inhaling the wonderful night scents, trying hard to compose herself.

Something was about to happen. She could feel it in her bones: an anticipation.

But whether it was an anticipation of dread she couldn't tell. Whatever it was, she needed to keep herself together. She needed to be strong.

His footsteps were heavy when he joined her back on the terrace.

He poured himself another glass of wine from the second bottle to be opened after Niki had demolished most of the first one and drank half of it before putting the glass on the table and coming over to stand beside her.

The night sky and the romantic lights illuminating the terrace cast his handsome face in shadows that gave him a gothic, piratical look. It made her heart ache, reminding her strongly of how he had looked the night of the ball when she had fallen under his spell.

The heady awareness that lived in her blood for him flickered to life with all the ease of a switch. Without the barrier of the table between them he was close enough to touch.

For a long time he stared at her with a hard curiosity. 'Who are you?'

She forced herself to maintain eye contact. 'Are you asking because you saw me as a dirt-poor chambermaid and assumed that's all I ever was?'

His eyes narrowed. 'I never thought that.'

'Didn't you?' she challenged. 'I saw the shock in your eyes when Niki said how she knew me. You assumed I lied about Beddingdales, didn't you? You were so confident it was a lie, you never bothered to ask. You didn't think a privately educated woman could possibly get her hands dirty working in domestic service. It was easier to assume I was a liar than give me the benefit of the doubt.'

'If I thought you a liar, it's because you lied about your identity to get into the ball. You lied about who you were,' he ground out.

'The only lie was the name on the invitation I entered the ball with. I told you my real name. I told you I worked in hospitality, which was stretching the truth, I admit, but it was the closest I could get without telling a lie. Everything else was the truth. I was an imposter that night but I'm not a liar, Giannis, whatever you may think of me.'

His lips thinned, a pulse throbbing on his jawline. 'You made assumptions too. You ran out on me without giving me a chance. You didn't even attempt to tell me the truth.

You assumed that I would be furious that you worked for me and sack you.'

'With good reason.' Tabitha held her ground and tried to hold on to her train of thought which was threatening to slip away. His spicy scent had slowly mingled with the fragrant bougainvillea and was seeping through her airwaves with every inhalation. If she stretched out her hand, she would reach his chest. Her hand was begging her to do just that. 'And you proved it when you tried to sack me the moment you realised I worked for you.'

'I'd spent...' He cut himself off and ran his fingers roughly through his hair. 'I was angry. You say you didn't tell me one lie, but you let me believe you were someone you were not. Or *are* you the person you pretended to be?'

'I was that person once, but that was a long time ago, and I would say you were more than angry when I came to you and you realised I was nothing but a chambermaid. You were disgusted and don't you dare deny it—it was written all over your face.'

'I was disgusted with myself for falling for a woman who wasn't who she claimed to be. I've been there before. My wife... You know I was married?' It was a question framed as a statement.

The picture she'd seen of Giannis and his stunning wife on their wedding day flashed immediately into her mind, the way they had stared into each other's eyes... It felt like a hand had grabbed hold of her heart and twisted it.

Since she'd arrived in Santorini, Tabitha had tried hard not to think of the woman who had shared his life here before tragedy had struck, because every time she did she had the sick feeling of stepping on another woman's toes and something else, something much deeper and stomach-twisting, which she dared not think about in any depth.

But hearing him acknowledge his wife for the first time...

'Yes.' The clenching in her heart softened to imagine the hell he must have gone through losing the love of his life as he'd done. 'I'm sorry for what happened to her.'

Giannis shrugged and raised his chin.

By the time of Anastasia's death he'd grown to hate her but not as much as he'd despised himself for believing her lies.

That he felt guilt and a responsibility for her death were things he could not fathom. He hadn't been driving that car. She had.

She'd been driving it to her lover.

'I'd learned she was a gold-digger who was cheating on me.'

He watched Tabitha stiffen before he cast his eyes away from her to the dark sea before them.

Too many emotions curled through him when he looked at her. The spell she'd bewitched him with the night they'd conceived their child breathed powerfully in his blood stream, his desire for her threatening again to cloud his thoughts. How easy it would be to cup her beautiful face in his hands, plunder that enticing mouth and lose himself in the pleasure they had created together all over again.

Always he'd been the master of his desire, even during his short, ill-fated marriage.

With Tabitha he felt a breath away from losing control without even touching her.

A yacht sailed past them in the distance. He focused his attention on it, using it much like the anchor the yacht would use when it reached harbour, wherever that would be.

'Anastasia tried to pass her lover's child off as mine,' he said in as emotionless a tone as he could manage. He heard a sharp intake of breath but ignored it. 'She fell pregnant three months after we married. I should have been delighted but my gut told me something did not feel right. She had the scan done without me, only telling me about it after the fact, so I visited the obstetrician privately. I asked if the date of conception could be determined from the scan and learned that it could to a good degree of accuracy.

'The child Anastasia claimed was mine had been conceived during the ten days I was in Brazil. It was not possible I was the father. I set a private investigative team onto her and learned our entire marriage was a sham. All she wanted was my money and the lifestyle. She never wanted me.'

He could not bring himself to tell Tabitha about his confrontation with Anastasia's lover and his admission that she'd planned to leave him after the birth. Giannis would have been the legal father and liable to pay maintenance. Anastasia would also have been entitled to a good chunk of his money in her own right.

He'd just shared more with Tabitha than he had with anyone else. Not even his family knew Anastasia's child had not been his. A man had his pride.

Anastasia's actions had humiliated him. The bruises to his pride still lived in him.

But Tabitha's child was his and, whatever virulent, dangerous emotions his child's mother evoked in him, all that mattered was securing his child to his side.

'It's no secret that one of the reasons for me hosting the masquerade ball was to find a new wife,' he said into the stunned silence. 'The time was right. I'm thirty-five and I want to be a father before I'm too old to play football with my children. I wanted my next wife to be a woman who was independently wealthy. I do not want love in my next marriage—I've done love and it tastes bitter—but I wanted security in my wife's motives for marrying me. You are carrying my child. It would be wrong of me not to give our child the same opportunities it would have had with the mother of my choice. As you won't countenance me having custody of our child, the next best thing is for us to marry.'

'I beg your pardon?' Tabitha must have misheard him, too dazed at his unexpected revelation about his marriage to have been listening properly.

She didn't want to feel sorry for him but she did. What a blow it must have been to a man as proud as Giannis to learn he'd been cuckolded, and what a blow to his heart too. He must have been devastated.

No wonder he'd doubted Tabitha about the pregnancy. If she'd been in his shoes she might have demanded proof too.

'I want us to marry,' he repeated.

She twisted her face to look at him but all she found was his profile gazing into the distance, his jaw clenched, hands gripping the wall tightly.

Marriage?

That feeling of having slipped through the looking glass hit her strongly again, the pebbled ground beneath her feet starting to spin. 'Marriage? You and me?'

'If you marry me, our baby will not want for anything.'

'That applies even if we don't marry,' she managed to croak. 'You would still have to pay child support.'

Of all the things she had expected him to suggest about a way forward for them as parents, not once had it crossed her mind he would suggest this.

'It is better for a child to have two parents together.' Suddenly he turned his face to her. His eyes bored into hers with an intensity she could feel right in her core. 'Marry me and our child will have a mother and father living under the same roof. Two parents available at all times. No being shunted from one home to another. No insecurities about which home is their home, no wondering which parent they are spending the weekend or school holidays with. And you would have greater security too—the law would give you that.'

'Why offer this now? Only this morning you wanted to buy our child from me and cut me from its life.' But, before he could respond, the answer came to her and all the sympathy she'd felt for him vanished. 'Coincidence, is it, that you suggest marriage within hours of learning I was privately educated? Does it make me more acceptable to your standing in your world?'

His features darkened, becoming taut. 'You insult me.'

'You insult *me*.' All the emotions she'd been trying to supress for so long, all her fears and insecurities, merged with the anger she hadn't felt creeping up on her at his cruel words, colliding to crash through her in a wave. 'You tell me you want us to marry in the same breath as telling me I'm not the woman of choice to be mother of your child. You say I don't disgust you, that my job isn't an issue...'

'It has *never* been an issue.'

'But half the time you won't even look at me!'

She'd hardly finished uttering the last word when two huge hands lunged at her and gripped her shoulders, pulling her to him. His piratical features only inches from hers, he snarled, 'Look at you? You have turned my world on its head! I am trying to navigate my way through everything, trying to do what's right and best for my child, but just sharing the same air as you distracts my thoughts. Yes, *matia mou*, I have an issue with looking at you but it's not because I'm the snob you think I am. I look at you and all I want is to throw you over my shoulder, carry you to the nearest bed and rip the clothes from your body with my teeth.'

Heart thumping, Tabitha stared into the clear blue eyes that were filled with the same anger and desire that coiled in her and felt something low inside her melt.

And then Giannis's mouth caught hers with a savage possessiveness that sent everything else inside her melting too.

Sticky warmth flooded her. The ache she'd carried inside her since the night they'd conceived their child bloomed as her senses filled with his spicy scent and dark, wine-laced taste. Wrapping her arms around him, she sank into the hungry urgency of his mouth.

One touch from Giannis was like the spark of a match on kindling: immediate and utterly combustible. And yet there was so much more than the flames licking her skin. There was a sense of rightness. Where she turned his world upside down, he righted hers. Being held in his arms…it felt as if this was where she was meant to be.

Their tongues wound together in a heady, sensuous exploration while his fingers threaded down through her long hair until he reached the base of her spine, evoking sensation that made her stomach contract and blood move relentlessly through her veins. Splaying his hand, he moulded her closer to him so the hard contours of his body were flush against hers.

She hardly noticed when his hands gripped her waist and lifted her from the ground to carry her effortlessly to the far wall covered in a tumbling display of flowers, not until her feet were placed back on the ground and she had to tighten her hold around him to stop her watery legs giving way beneath her.

His hard mouth wrenched from her lips to graze over her cheek and burrow into her neck, his hands pushing up her vest and bra, fingers brushing over her ribcage to her breasts to capture and knead the tender tips before capturing her breasts whole. A rich wave of sensation darted heavily through her sensitive flesh.

Capable fingers dragged down her belly to the button of her jeans and wrenched them open. His mouth crashed back onto hers at the same moment his fingers dipped beneath the band of her knickers and her gasp was smothered by the weight of his heady kisses.

Her body had become a playground of tingling nerves and her hips arched towards him of their own volition. When his fingers edged down through the soft curls of her pubis to the slick heat at the core of her womanhood, she writhed, helpless against the exquisite pleasure engulfing her.

The pleasure grew in intensity, a yearning growing with it, stronger, needier, reaching, searching, all of it centred on Giannis and his magical manipulations, until she reached the tipping point and she pressed her cheek to his throat and held him tightly as an explosion of rippling pleasure roared through her.

She was still awash with the waves of bliss flooding through her loins when he disentangled himself and stepped back, visibly fighting for air.

Pressing herself against the cold wall for support, she stared at him, dazed, fighting for her own breath.

His throat moved then he rubbed his head angrily.

'You see what you do to me?' he said roughly. 'How can I hate you when you make me feel like this? What you do to me...'

What she did to *him*?

Had he not just seen—*felt*—what he'd done to her?

Hands shaking, she straightened her clothes and fumbled the buttons of her jeans back up.

She couldn't speak, could only watch mutely as he strode heavily to the table and downed what was left of his wine.

He rolled his shoulders and breathed deeply before looking back at her. 'I am serious about us marrying, *matia mou*, and I want you to think seriously about it too. Sleep on it. I don't wish to fight you but be under no illusions—I will not accept anything less than being a permanent part of my child's life. All custody battle will do is give the press a meal to feed on and line our lawyers' pockets.'

And then he left the terrace without looking back.

CHAPTER EIGHT

By the time Tabitha woke the next morning after a tumultuous night of very little sleep, she found Giannis had gone. Zoe, the housekeeper, handed her a note from him with a smile. All the note said was he had gone to work and would see her at dinner.

His absence was an unexpected mercy.

She wasn't ready to face him. Not after what had happened on his terrace.

But she couldn't deny that the sinking of her stomach at his absence felt very much like disappointment.

Back in her bedroom, she rooted through her limited wardrobe for something clean to wear that she wouldn't swelter in. In Vienna she rarely left the hotel, and normally just stuck to wearing her work uniform, so had had little need for a summer wardrobe. Or a winter wardrobe. Without that uniform, she was stuck, especially in the Santorini summer heat.

She kneaded her forehead, nauseous that she needed to spend some of her savings on something as frivolous as clothes. She had few savings as it was. If things got ugly with Giannis she would need every cent she had…

Who was she trying to kid? If things got ugly with Giannis she had no hope of fighting him. Compared to those of a normal person her savings were pitiful. Compared to a billionaire's they were laughable. He probably carried more in spare change than she had in her bank account.

After dressing in another pair of rolled-up jeans and the thinnest top she had, she left Giannis's house and headed off in the direction she remembered driving through, which led to busy streets. Unfortunately she underestimated the distance and it was a good hour before she found civilisation. By then perspiration soaked her skin and clothes and she'd drunk all the water from the bottle she'd taken.

Thirsty, she stopped at a small café packed with holiday makers—at least she'd found a tourist hotspot, and if there were holiday makers that meant shops—and ordered a large glass of lemonade and a slice of pizza.

Finding a table tucked away in the corner, she waited for her order and sank back into her thoughts.

That was all she'd done since she'd left Giannis's home. Walked and thought. Walked and thought.

Those thoughts continued to consume her as she ate her small lunch and then hunted for the shops selling cheap clothes, continued as she rifled through rows of generic beach dresses and as she tried on dress after dress, eventually settling on the cheapest two she liked the most and which might survive more than a couple of washes.

Her thoughts continued when she eventually, reluctantly, began the walk back to Giannis's home.

To raise her child in that magnificent home on this beautiful island was the stuff of dreams. Fantasies. Her child would want for nothing.

But her child would want for nothing even if she refused. Legally, Giannis would have to pay child support.

If she married him, her child would have two parents under the same roof. That was the best way to raise a child. Everyone said so.

Except Tabitha's happiest childhood memories were of when it had been just her and her father. She had only vague memories of her mother. She remembered the feeling of love and security she'd had with her and she'd always missed her, always felt a part of herself was missing, but she'd died before solid memories could form.

Her father had remarried when Tabitha had been ten. He'd introduced Emmaline as her new mother. He'd married her because he'd been lonely and because he'd believed, his own mother having since died, that his pre-pubescent daughter needed a mother. The two older stepsisters his marriage had given Tabitha were supposed to have been an additional bonus for a lonely child.

If Tabitha didn't marry Giannis that would leave him free to marry someone else who would become stepmother to her child.

A pain shot through her heart every time this particular thought entered her head and it was a pain that terrified her.

Because it wasn't just the fear of a stepmother resenting her child, as Emmaline had resented her, or fear that that resentment could become as poisonous as Emmaline's had become towards Tabitha. It wasn't the thought of Giannis with another woman that hurt. It was the thought of Giannis gazing at another woman with the same intense devotion with which he had gazed at Anastasia.

Her thoughts darkened with each step, and her legs were aching as she ascended a particularly steep narrow road. A car appeared at the crest of the hill she was walking up and her heart began to thump before her brain had even fully registered it.

It was the sports car she'd seen parked at the back of Giannis's house.

Pressing her hand to her chest, she tried to breathe through a throat that had closed.

This was the real reason she found herself shying away from doing the right thing by her child. Her attraction to its father was too strong, too overwhelming and more rooted than all the other emotions she felt towards him. She was the kindling to his flame. She had debased herself on his terrace, coming undone in his arms like a wildling, and for all his accusations about her doing things to him he hadn't been the one to lose control. She had.

She thought of the night when they had conceived their child as a magical dream. There had been a connection between them she could never explain in words but she had felt it so acutely. It had breathed through every part of her. Falling into his bed had felt like the most natural thing in the world and she had closed her ears to all the dangers because she had been caught in a spell so wonderful she hadn't wanted it to end.

That inexplicable connection was still there but it had transformed into something darker, their fledgling relationship containing something explosive and elemental that she was too inexperienced to understand.

She wished desperately that she had told him the truth instead of running out on him. He was right that she'd never given him a chance. She had made assumptions.

But if she had stayed and taken her chances with the truth then she strongly suspected the outcome would have been everything that had stopped her revealing it. He would have felt duped whether she had told him then or not.

They would never have had a chance.

The car stopped beside her. The driver's window slid down with a soft burr.

Their eyes met.

Her heart bloomed.

'Get in.'

'Sorry?'

'It's not safe for me to park here.'

Blinking furiously, she hurried round to the passenger side and climbed in. The interior smelled of leather and Giannis's spicy cologne.

He put the car in gear and they roared off.

'Where have you been?' Giannis asked tightly. The fresh air pouring in from the open window pushed away the faint trace of Tabitha's scent his greedy nostrils had detected when she'd sat beside him but that did nothing to stop his pulses reacting to her close proximity.

To distract himself some more, he pressed the button that opened the roof.

He'd called home after his second meeting to be told by his housekeeper that Tabitha had been gone for four hours. An hour later she still hadn't returned and, unable to shake the angst that gnawed away inside him, he'd cut his day short and taken the small plane he used to commute between Santorini and Athens back home. Finding that she still hadn't returned, he'd jumped in the car and set about finding her, cursing himself for not taking her phone number.

'Shopping,' she answered.

He glanced at the thin plastic bag she clutched on her lap and loosened his clenched jaw. 'You didn't tell Zoe where you were going. She was worried about you.'

'I couldn't. She doesn't speak English and I don't speak Greek.'

He looked again at the bag on her lap and swallowed back his rising temper. 'You've been gone for seven hours.'

'Am I on a curfew?'

The roof now fully open, her long hair caught in the breeze. Although he knew intellectually that he couldn't smell its fragrance, his senses reacted as if they did and he tightened his grip on the steering wheel. 'You should have told someone.'

'Told who? *None* of your staff speak English and, in any case, since when do I need to account for my movements?'

'Next time, leave a note.' He couldn't stop himself from adding, 'You haven't got much to show for seven hours' worth of shopping.'

And that cheap, thin plastic bag should not make his heart ache. All the women in his family went shopping and returned with their goods packed in pretty boxes and carried in smart designer bags.

'That's because I haven't got much money,' she retorted icily. 'Would you like a blow-by-blow account of my movements?'

'You are carrying my child.'

'And? Do you think it gives you autonomy over me?'

He sighed as he slowed for a bend and changed to a lower gear. 'I listen to you speak and I wonder how I thought you uneducated. You're quick. Literate—'

'And you're changing the subject.'

'I don't want another argument.'

His home gleamed bright on the clifftop in the near distance but, instead of taking the right turn that would have led to his driveway, he continued on the road they were already on.

Having to concentrate on the road before him meant they could talk without his thoughts being entirely consumed by ripping her clothes off.

Theos, he still couldn't get what had happened on the terrace last night from his mind. He'd had no fulfilment for himself but it hadn't mattered. Tabitha's uninhibited, wanton responses to his touch had been as heady and fulfilling as anything he had ever experienced.

'Okay, but before we stop arguing I would like to point out that not going to university does not make someone ignorant or uneducated.'

'I've seen your résumé, remember? You had no educational qualifications. That makes you uneducated by anyone's standards but I listen to you and I can't square the circle. You went to one of the best schools in the world. Why no qualifications? Why have you only worked in hotels?'

This was what he wanted to talk about. The mystery of who Tabitha really was.

'My stepmother kicked me out on my eighteenth birthday and stopped paying the school fees.'

She said it so matter-of-factly that it took a moment for the implications of what she'd said to penetrate.

Giannis swore under his breath.

He'd considered calling Niki earlier for any recollections she might have of the teenage Tabitha but had concluded it would only make her query why he was asking and lead her to make assumptions. She'd already sent him a cheeky message:

Tabitha would make a great sister-in-law. Just saying!

Just saying? If he hadn't avoided responding to the message he would have teased her about her English slang usage.

He did not want to feed any speculation about their relationship until Tabitha consented to marry him.

He kept his eyes fixed on the road. 'Why did she do that?'

'Because she hates me,' she answered flatly before he felt the weight of her gaze fall on him. 'She's like your wife. She married my father for his money. The only saving grace I have is that he died not knowing what she was really like.'

His grip on the steering wheel tightened so much his knuckles turned white.

'What happened with her?'

Her silence was broken with a jaded laugh. 'Nothing.'

'She kicked you out for no reason?'

'She kicked me out so she could keep the inheritance for herself and her daughters.'

'*Your* inheritance?'

From the corner of his eye he saw her wipe her hair from her face. 'My father put his fortune in a trust. I don't know how things work in Greece but trusts are very common in England for those who want to preserve their wealth through the generations. The trust he had written was for the benefit of myself and Emmaline.'

'Emmaline's your stepmother?'

'Correct. Emmaline was also named as one of the trustees. The trustees control how the money is spent. My father's wishes were just that—wishes. Legally, I had to be supported by his estate and my education paid for until I turned eighteen. I turned eighteen during the first half-term break of my final school year. She was no longer obliged to pay the fees, so she didn't, and I didn't complete my secondary education.'

'Didn't the other trustees object?'

'There was only one other trustee. My father's best friend. Emmaline was sleeping with him. She had her claws in him as greatly as she'd had them in my father.'

Thinking her father must have been an incredibly weak man, but not voicing this private opinion, Giannis said, 'None of this sounds legal. Whether it was held in a trust or not, your father's wishes should have been carried out. Didn't you fight?'

'I couldn't.'

'Why not?' he asked incredulously. 'I'm certain any lawyer worth anything—'

'I had *nothing*,' Tabitha interrupted. A deep, itchy feeling had formed beneath her skin just to remember how helpless she had felt. 'When she threw me out she'd already packed a case for me. All I had was seventy pounds. It didn't cross my mind that I could fight her.'

'Why ever not?'

Hating the incredulity in his voice, she tried to explain. 'Because overnight my life became a matter of survival. Don't you understand that? I had nowhere to go and no one I could turn to for help. Both my parents were only children, all my grandparents were dead.'

'What about friends?'

'They were schoolgirls the same as me. What could they do? My closest friends weren't even English so I could hardly knock on their door and beg for help, could I?'

There was a long pause before he asked, in a softer tone, 'What did you do?'

'Hitched into Oxford and slept in a hostel for a couple of nights. It was the owners there who helped me find a live-in job at a small hotel in Northamptonshire. The pay was awful but I had a bed to sleep in and they fed me too. Fighting back…?'

Hating the memories that were swarming out of her, Tabitha clasped the bag in her hands and twisted tightly. 'You have no idea what Emmaline is like. She puts on a façade that is so believable but beneath it she's rotten.'

'You are frightened of her?'

She had to swallow the dry lump in her throat before she could answer. These were things she had never spoken about. 'My father married her when I was ten. I was so excited and happy that I was going to have a new mummy and two sisters. I was desperate for siblings. They were older than me but really sweet to me. Emmaline was lovely to me too. It wasn't until after the marriage that their masks began to slip and I learned how rotten they were.'

'What did they do to you?'

'Lots of little cruel things. Fiona liked to hide pictures of clowns under my bedsheets. She knew I was scared of them. The first time she did it, I went running to my father and he scolded them. Fiona and Saffron both said sorry but then later that night they came into my room and woke me up. They stood either side of my bed and both pinched me hard on the underside of my arms. They said if I ever told on them again they would drown my cat. I believed them. I never told on them again.'

'They did more?'

'They couldn't touch me when I was at school—they went to a different one, thank goodness—but holidays were torture. They would bide their time and then when I was least expecting it do things like throw ink over my clothes or hide photos of horrible things like clowns and autopsies and stills from horror films in my drawers or bedsheets. Things that would either freak me out or get me into trouble.'

'And your father knew nothing of this?'

'I was too scared to tell him and I'd begun to be afraid of Emmaline. Her mask slipped too, but not as blatantly as her daughters'…nothing that anyone would notice. My father certainly didn't and there was nothing specific I could say to justify my feelings. It was more the way she looked at me when we were alone than anything. Like I was something unpleasant the cat had brought in. When he died there was no need for her to keep the façade up. The day after his funeral, she took down every photo of my mother and when I asked where they were she laughed.'

It still made her skin crawl to remember the coldness in that laughter. 'She still did her legal duty in feeding and clothing me but she acted like I was invisible. The times she did talk to me…' A shiver ran down her spine. 'She was like an ice sculpture that had come to life. She was cruel.'

'Why didn't you tell anyone?'

'And say what? And who could I have told? I was sixteen when my father died. I just kept telling myself all I had to do was work hard at school, get the grades I needed in my A Levels and then I could go to university and be free of her. I thought once I reached eighteen or went to university they would pay me enough of an allowance out of the trust that I wouldn't need to ever go back.'

'You wanted to leave your home to *her*?'

'I wanted to be *free* of her. I just assumed that one day she would die and I would be able to move back into my family home. I never thought for a minute she would go as far as to kick me out of it.' Hot, fat tears she'd been fighting back suddenly broke free and once they'd started she couldn't stop them.

Embarrassed at her weakness, she covered her face with her hands and pressed herself tightly against the window.

She'd never wanted to cry over her stepfamily's actions ever again but telling Giannis about it all had brought the pain back and made her realise how pathetic she had been.

Only when she felt a strong arm hook around her neck and haul her against his hard chest did she realise Giannis had pulled the car over. The unexpected comfort, and from Giannis of all people, only made her cry harder.

Giannis pressed his mouth into the cloud of hair beneath his chin and breathed deeply, trying hard to fight the rage swirling inside him that wanted to fly straight to England and destroy the woman who had destroyed Tabitha's life.

This Emmaline was as duplicitous as Anastasia had been but with added cruelty.

'She took everything,' Tabitha sobbed, her slender frame shaking in his arms, her tears soaking into his shirt. 'She took my home and my past and my future, and I let her.'

'You didn't.'

'I *did*. I never fought back because I was too scared. I never even went back to clear the rest of my bedroom. I told myself she would only have burned it all but the truth is I was too scared to face her, just like I was too scared to face you that morning. The truth is I'm a coward and I *hate* myself for that.'

Unwilling to listen to Tabitha castigate herself, he gently took her face in his hands and stared intently at her. 'Do not blame yourself for things that were out of your control, *koritzi mou*. What that woman did to you is despicable.'

And it would not go unavenged.

Her lips trembled, tears spilling over his fingers.

Hating to see her misery, he did what felt like the most natural thing in the world to give her comfort. He slipped his hands around to cradle the back of her neck and kissed her.

This kiss was nothing like the kisses they had devoured each other with before but a gentle, lingering brush of his lips to hers.

When he broke away her tears had stopped and she looked at him with an expression of bewilderment.

He pressed his forehead to hers and closed his eyes, inhaling the wonderful fragrance that made every cell in his body come alive.

After long moments had passed he heard her take a deep inhalation before pulling away.

'Thank you,' she whispered.

'Parakalo.'

They sat in silence, no longer touching, until she said, 'Giannis...if we marry...'

His heart gave a sudden leap.

There was no longer bewilderment in the bloodshot eyes now staring at him as intently as he'd been staring at her.

'What are you thinking?'

'That if you do one thing for me, I will marry you.'

'What is that one thing?' He drew the line at setting a hitman on her stepmother. That would be too kind.

'I want you to write a will or contract that explicitly states that, if you die, everything you have goes to our child. It has to be cast-iron. Nothing ambiguous or open to interpretation. A cast-iron guarantee that, if anything happens to you, our child will be protected.'

'What about you?'

She gave a fierce shake of her head. 'I don't want anything other than the right to be a mother to our child until he or she comes of age. If I die first then you will be the only parent. I know nothing is irreversible but—'

'I will get it done,' he interrupted, understanding why she was asking this of him. Her father had thought he'd protected his only child but it hadn't been enough to stop her stepmother taking everything. 'Our child will be named as my successor in my business and my sole heir.'

Her shoulders loosened and her head bowed. 'Thank you.'

Then their eyes met again and the spark that always flickered when he was with her flashed between them.

Knowing that now was the time to push aside the torrid emotions flowing through him, and harness the cool logic that had served him so well his whole adult life, Giannis turned the engine back on and pulled out of the spot where he'd carelessly parked.

'I will speak to my lawyer when we get home and get the wheels in motion,' he said conversationally. 'The documents will be drawn up and signed by the end of the week. We can marry next week. We will invite my family and leave it at that. Unless there is someone you would like to have there too?' He couldn't imagine who she would invite. She had no real family left.

There was a long pause before she sighed heavily and said, 'Actually...there is someone I would like to invite. My benefactor. Her name is Amelia Coulter and she's a live-in resident at your hotel.'

He had to concentrate hard to stop the car swerving off the road.

He'd forgotten all about Tabitha's mysterious benefactor, and it was the reason why he'd forgotten all about her existence that had him struggling to keep his concentration.

Without even realising it, he'd taken Tabitha at her word about her benefactor. He'd believed her without seeking proof as he always did.

Amelia Coulter was a name he'd become familiar with

in his search for Tabitha, it having been on the guest list for his masquerade ball.

Keeping his voice as steady as he could manage, he said, 'She gave you her invitation?'

'She bought it for me.'

'Why?'

'As a thank you for taking care of her when she was sick.'

'That's an extravagant way to thank the hired help.'

He saw a slim shoulder rise in a shrug. 'There's sixty years between us but we'd become friends. She's mostly estranged from her family. They live in England. Her husband's buried in Vienna and she loves the city too much to want to leave it.'

'And what did you get from the friendship?' Only a day ago he would have added, 'Apart from a rich benefactor?' to his question but such cynicism would be wrong now.

'She reminds me of my grandmother.' There was a wistfulness to her voice and he found he didn't need her to explain any further.

Tabitha's life must have been lonely.

Giannis had never known loneliness. He'd always had his family, always had good friends, always been surrounded by people he could rely on. The only person who had ever let him down was the woman he had fallen in lust with and foolishly married. His humiliation at Anastasia's hands had been an unspoken secret within his circle but not one of them had taken the gossip to the press.

And now he was going to marry Tabitha, a woman who elicited more desire in him than he'd known possible. A woman he felt the strangest compulsion to avenge. And protect.

He'd never wanted to protect anyone before. Not Anastasia, not even his sisters, who he'd always considered perfectly capable of protecting themselves.

These were all the feelings he'd sworn to avoid when he married again.

He'd had his head turned with lust before and had paid the price for it.

He had to get control of it all before it took control of him.

'I will arrange for an invitation to be given to her when we've set the date,' he said in a far more temperate voice than what lay beneath his skin. 'I will see the mayor tomorrow and get everything organised. He can marry us at my home.'

'Don't we have to marry in a church?'

He shuddered at the thought. 'No. We'll keep it a small affair. I've done the big, white wedding. I have no wish to go through that again.'

Her ensuing silence sat uncomfortably in his guts.

CHAPTER NINE

THE FOLLOWING WEEK sped by. Tabitha signed more documents and read through more paperwork in that time than she'd done in her entire life. She'd been taken aback at the speed with which Giannis had got things done but barely had time to blink let alone think. Which was probably just as well. She had a big enough headache as it was without adding thinking to the list.

And now their wedding was only one day away.

For the first time since Tabitha had agreed to marry him, Giannis had left the villa without her. He'd flown to Athens and would be spending the evening in his apartment there, the one traditional part of a wedding he intended to embrace.

Was that because he wanted a breather from her? Or because he genuinely feared it would bring bad luck to their marriage if they saw each other the night before the wedding?

Until that morning, she had spent all her waking time with him. He'd included her in everything: lawyers' meetings and the visit to his family to break the good news about their wedding. He'd flown her to England so they could get her birth certificate and had visited the embassy. He'd taken her to Athens for a day shopping for clothes, insisting on buying every single item that caught her eye, even those on which she had done nothing more than brush her fingers. As a result she had a wardrobe stuffed with beautiful, expensive clothes, which she had no chance of wearing all of before she became too big with child to fit in them, and a dressing table crammed with more cosmetics than a professional make-up artist possessed and more perfumes than a perfumer could sniff in a career.

When she had protested at this unnecessary extravagance, she'd been rebuffed with a, 'You are going to be a Basinas. When it is time for you to wear maternity clothes, we will go shopping again.'

She should be grateful for this time away from him, should be making the most of her last few hours of freedom, not moping around as if she missed him.

But she found she was missing him. The gregarious man she had fallen into a romantic dream with the night of the ball was slowly emerging from the austere shell into which the truth of her identity had put him.

She found she had to keep reminding herself that their marriage was not about them. It was all for their baby. She was not his wife of choice and now she feared he no longer even desired her.

He hadn't laid a finger on her since that small, comforting kiss in his car.

There had been more occasions than she could count when she had found herself trapped in the heat of his gaze but he'd made no move. What was stopping him from touching her?

And what was stopping her from touching him? She *ached* to touch him but something kept holding her back.

To keep the demons in her head from plaguing her too much, she decided to tidy her bedroom and clean her bathroom. Tomorrow they would no longer be hers. She would be in Giannis's bed, a thought that made her scrub the shower door that little bit harder.

'What are you doing?'

She whipped round to find Giannis at the bathroom doorway, a bemused expression on his face.

'What are you doing here?' she asked dumbly.

The ghost of a smile appeared on his lips then disappeared as a furrow cleaved his forehead. 'I'll answer that once you've answered my question. Why are you cleaning? I pay staff to clean.'

'I needed to do something.'

Now his brow rose quizzically. 'Did it have to involve cleaning bathrooms?'

'No, I cleaned my room too,' she answered tartly, desperate to cover the mortification soaking her. Who wanted to be caught scrubbing a shower dressed in a pair of designer denim shorts and a designer short-sleeved shirt she'd tied around her midriff, clothing he'd spent a small fortune on?

Taking a softer tone, she added, 'Cleaning's therapeutic and, let's be honest, something I'm good at.'

He nodded slowly, his expression softening too. 'We will have to think of something else for you to do when you're in need of something therapeutic to do, or Zoe will be worried for her job, but that is something for us to think about after the wedding. The reason I'm here is because I have a gift for you.'

From behind his back he produced a small box, the logo on it signalling that it contained a smart phone.

'I've already set it up for you,' he said while she examined it, hands shaking at his unexpected appearance.

He'd flown back just to give her a phone?

'It's the latest model,' he continued. 'I've programmed my number into it and downloaded an app that acts as a translator. It means you'll be able to converse with Zoe and anyone else without a language barrier.'

'How does it work?'

She put the phone into his open hand and sat next to him on the sofa. She didn't even remember walking from the bathroom to the bedroom with him.

Eyes alight with curiosity, she watched him press an icon. The screen lit up and he brought it to his mouth and said something in Greek. A moment later a disembodied voice rang out, 'Your hair needs a brush.'

She gave a shout of laughter and met clear blue eyes gleaming with an amusement she hadn't seen since the ball. It was a gleam that made her heart leap and suddenly she was aware that they were sat closer together than they had been in the past week. For all the time they'd spent together, this was the first time they'd been within touching distance of each other when alone.

The gleam in his eyes as they stared at each other slowly dimmed, the amusement on his lips fading. Tabitha's own lips began to tingle, the nerves on her skin firing, anticipation lacing through her as their faces tilted and closed in...

But then Giannis pulled back, cleared his throat and, without missing a beat, without any hint that he'd just been about to kiss her, murmured, 'Now you say something into it. It's programmed to translate both our languages.'

Blinking rapidly, trying to pretend that what had nearly happened just then hadn't, she took the phone back and brought it up to her chin. Striving for the same lightness he'd displayed when speaking into it, she said, 'You need a shave.'

Again, barely a moment passed before the same disembodied voice rang out, this time in Greek.

Tabitha put the phone onto her lap and stared at it, suddenly aware that hot tears were burning the back of her eyes and desperate not to let them fall.

This phone, although a drop in the ocean for a man of Giannis's wealth, was the most thoughtful gift he could have given her. It stopped her being isolated when she didn't have him there to translate.

'Thank you,' she whispered when she was reasonably confident she could speak without blubbing. Who cried over a *phone*? How ridiculous! The pregnancy hormones must be getting stronger.

Hormones or not, she had to start tempering the wild feelings Giannis evoked in her. Being with him heightened every normal emotion. He could turn her from joy to despondency and twist it all back again in the time it took to switch on a light. One look and her body's responses took a life of their own, her entire being practically salivating for him.

How could she contain it, she thought with despair, especially now that he'd stopped treating her like the Antichrist? Little acts of kindness had the capacity to melt her heart in the same way one little look from him melted her bones. Combine the two and she became a puddle of mush for him.

'It is my pleasure.' He took the phone from her lap without touching her skin and continued in the same nonchalant tone. 'It's retina-activated like my own phone. Once it's done, only you will be able to access it.'

Minutes later and it was all set up and Tabitha was trying hard to concentrate on some of the other features Giannis was showing her. He said something about a music app but his words had become distant, a direct effect of his body having inched closer to hers, her senses catching whiffs of the spicy scent she'd become greedy for.

He swiped the screen at the same moment his thigh pressed against hers.

Tabitha gritted her teeth and tried her hardest to ignore the fresh heat careering through her.

But then he put his hand on her thigh.

Holding her breath, she stared down at the long, tanned fingers resting on her bare flesh…

'What kind of music do you like to listen to?' Giannis repeated, wondering why Tabitha had suddenly become mute. 'You can put in bands and genres and it will select…'

And then he followed her gaze and realised his hand was on her thigh, his middle finger making little circles over the silky skin.

For a moment all he could do was stare at it dumbly before cursing himself.

Would his weakness for this woman ever be controlled?

Being with Tabitha meant being in a constant state of arousal, a condition he'd spent the past week controlling. It had been an internal battle he'd been determined to win, a battle to prove to himself that he could master his reactions around her, a battle he'd thought he was winning.

For the first time since she'd agreed to marry him, he'd unintentionally dropped his guard and now his hand was resting on her thigh as if it were the most natural gesture in the world.

He inhaled deeply to counteract the thuds of his suddenly heavy heartbeats and moved his hand away without comment.

He'd made a vow to himself not to touch Tabitha again until their wedding night, thinking he would have mastered his reactions to her enough by then that when they did make love, it would be an enjoyable experience but not in the world-shifting way it had been on their one full night together.

'We've had a package couriered over,' he said into the electrified silence, his voice sounding thick to his ears. 'Your Mrs Coulter sent it. A wedding gift.'

'That's sweet of her,' Tabitha whispered, her own voice containing the faintest hint of a tremor.

Mrs Coulter had regretfully declined the invitation to their wedding, not feeling physically strong enough to make the journey over. To make up for Tabitha's disappointment, Giannis had suggested she fly to Vienna with him for his next monthly trip to his hotel.

He opened his mouth to remind her of this but the words fell away from his tongue when he met cornflower eyes wide and stark on his.

The groan escaped from his throat before he could hold

it back, turning into a growl when his hands cupped the cheeks heightened with colour.

He could control this...

He brought his mouth down to capture the beautiful heart-shaped lips in one long, hot, wet, devouring kiss.

His loins sang their delight but he mastered his reactions with a ruthlessness that would have made a Tibetan monk proud. Breaking the kiss, he captured her chin, and this time allowed himself to stare deep into eyes pulsing their own desire back at him, the fingers of his other hand twisting the long, silky locks of her hair.

A sudden wave of possessiveness crashed through him along with an overwhelming urge to gather her into his arms, carry her to the bed and make her his in every way possible.

'Tomorrow night, *matia mou*, you will be my wife and in my bed. Until then...' He pressed one more, lighter kiss to her lips, breathing in her scent for good measure. It infused him, sinking deep into his veins...

He got abruptly to his feet.

He'd played with the flame of Tabitha's fire enough. A man had his limits and the burning ache in his loins proved he'd reached his.

'I will see you on the sun terrace tomorrow. Enjoy getting acquainted with your new toy.'

Tabitha watched him leave with her hand pressed tightly to her chest, her heart hammering against her palm.

Her blood pumped thick and strong inside her veins, as it did every time he kissed or touched her, her skin alive in a way that was becoming familiar to her but there had been none of the rightness she'd felt since their very first dance.

Giannis had flown back from Athens especially to give her the phone.

He was doing everything he could to make her transition into his life as easy as it could be.

Their wedding night promised so much…

So why did she feel so wretched?

The answer to Tabitha's wretchedness came to her three hours before they exchanged their vows.

She'd eaten a light, plain lunch alone on the pool terrace and then, limbs heavy, had gone to her bedroom to get ready for the wedding.

Two members of staff were in there, moving the last of her new wardrobe and accessories to the marital bedroom she would from that night share with Giannis.

It was the bedroom Anastasia must have shared with him.

Anastasia's ghost was the cause of her wretchedness, she realised with a strong churn of nausea.

Every step Tabitha took in this magnificent villa had been taken by the woman before her.

Giannis might desire her but he would never feel for Tabitha what he'd felt for his first wife.

It shredded her insides to know she was being denied a proper wedding because he'd already shared one with Anastasia.

She remembered that wedding picture of the two of them. It was one of dozens to be found on the Internet. Giannis and Anastasia's wedding had been a humungous affair with guests including the cream of Hollywood and European royalty. It had been a true celebration of their love.

For Tabitha's wedding, the only people he was inviting were his immediate family. No cousins or aunts and uncles. No friends. Their wedding was no celebration.

It shredded her insides even more to know she shouldn't care if they had what she considered to be a proper wedding or not. She shouldn't care that she would exchange her vows on Giannis's sun terrace and not in one of the beautiful, blue-topped white churches Santorini was famous for, and that she would be wearing a simple white summer dress instead of the big, flouncy traditional dress she'd dreamed of wearing when she'd been young and dreams had still existed within her.

She shouldn't care that Giannis didn't love her and would never love her.

It might have ended horrendously but he'd already had a marriage for love. With Anastasia.

She didn't want his love, she told herself with a stubborn desperation. She was marrying him to protect her unborn child's future, the exact same reason he was marrying her, and her irrational jealousy towards his first wife was…well, irrational. More than irrational. Heinous. Anastasia was dead, her life extinguished before she'd reached the age of thirty. What kind of monster was Tabitha to feel jealous of a ghost?

Emotions threatening to suffocate her, she opened one of the bedroom windows but was met with blazing heat.

She needed to get ready! She was hours away from marrying Giannis and all she could do was pace her bedroom, working herself into a lather.

If only she had someone with her, she thought despairingly, wishing her father could be there. She remembered him telling her as a child never to settle for second best, that she was worthy of only the greatest man to marry.

She wasn't settling for second best. Giannis was. He desired her. She thought he might even be coming to like her. But she was the woman with whom he'd had a one-night stand and he was marrying her from the consequence of that one night so he could claim their child as his own.

Her father would have loved Giannis, not for his mega-wealth and rumoured royal connections, but for his strong family bonds. Those were the kinds of bonds he'd been eager to create for Tabitha when he'd married Emmaline.

If her father had been alive she would have put her foot down and insisted on a big, white wedding but without him there, without any guests of her own, how could she complain? She wasn't contributing anything to their marriage financially or otherwise.

But how she wished Giannis thought enough of her that he would want to recite their vows in a sacred, sanctified building and give her the dream of her childhood.

Feeling herself on the verge of crying, she sucked the unshed tears back in at the loud rap on her door.

Thinking it must be the staff returning to collect more of her stuff, she opened it and found her heart lightening to see Niki there, arms laden with flowers, beaming widely. 'Hello, future sister-in-law. I've appointed myself your maid of honour, hairdresser and make-up artist. It's time to turn you into a beautiful bride.'

Giannis stood on his sun terrace, adorned with cascades of flowers and balloons, courtesy of his sisters, and closed his eyes at the warmth of the late-afternoon sun on his face.

Anyone looking at him would assume he was a man at complete ease with the vows he was about to exchange.

They would not see the tight knots coiling in his guts that were at odds with what felt suspiciously like butterflies in his stomach.

He could not remember the last time he'd felt so...nervous?

He pushed that irrational thought away. What was there to be nervous about? Whatever happened in this marriage, his fortune was protected. Tabitha would be provided for in the event of divorce or his death but he had taken her at her word and made his will, their pre-nuptial agreement and the contract he'd had drawn up for the business iron-tight. His child and any other children they might have would receive everything.

His phone buzzed in his pocket and he pulled it out to read the email from his private investigator. It was an update on the investigations Giannis had instructed be done on Emmaline Brigstock and Tabitha.

He experienced the now familiar twinge of guilt about having Tabitha investigated too, although the investigation of her was very much secondary to her stepmother. He was being prudent. He'd been bitten badly before and would not be fooled again. If there were skeletons in Tabitha's closet she had failed to tell him about, or discrepancies in her version of events of her past, he would learn them.

Tabitha had enchanted him from the first moment he'd set eyes on her. She had more power than she could ever know but he would not allow the spell she wove around him to entangle him any tighter than it had ensnared him before.

He sent a quick response, reiterating his desire for thoroughness over speed, and had just put his phone back in his pocket when the sound of loud chatter filled the air.

His family had arrived.

He greeted them warmly, sharing embraces and kisses with his parents, three of his four sisters, his three brothers-in-law and his handful of noisy small nieces and nephews.

As much as he would have preferred a wedding with only the two of them, his family would have been outraged to miss it. Tabitha was joining their family. She would become one of them. It was only right they be there to witness the union. And there was not a single member of his family who didn't love a good party.

There had been a complete lack of surprise when he'd introduced Tabitha to his family as his fiancée. Tabitha had been as white as a sheet but they'd welcomed her as if they'd known her for years. In Niki's case, she had. Her obvious bout of gossiping about his and Tabitha's relationship had eased the path to acceptance. Tabitha came from a good family, was well-educated, beautiful, shy but friendly and already had Niki's affection. That she was already carrying Giannis's child was simply the icing on the cake.

His youngest sister had been the only one annoyed that he wasn't having a traditional wedding. She'd pulled him aside to demand answers, which he had brushed off, using the same excuse he had with Tabitha—that he'd done the big, white wedding and saw no need for another.

'And is Tabitha happy to be denied her own white wedding?' she'd asked shrewdly.

'She is in agreement with me.'

His sister had snorted in reply but wisely let the matter go.

He'd been the one unable to let it go. Until Niki had asked him the question it had never occurred to him that Tabitha hadn't responded to his declaration that theirs would be a simple wedding.

As his family parted to take their seats and their chatter turned to hush, indicating that his bride was making her way up the pebbled steps to join them, Giannis reminded himself yet again that the only reason either of them was taking this step was for their child.

And then she appeared, Niki at her side beaming from ear to ear.

The ballooning of his heart pushed the air from his lungs.

Suddenly he was transported back to the night of the ball when he'd first glimpsed Tabitha on the stairs, when his pulses had raced and he'd been unable to tear his eyes from her.

Her beauty that night had dazzled him.

He'd wondered the next morning if she could be the one his family had urged him to find. He'd never had the chance to find out because she'd vanished. So much had happened since that early morning that he'd forgotten the question had played in his head.

Her eyes found his. A small, shy smile curved on her cheeks.

His heart stopped. It shuddered. It kick-started back to life.

The white cotton dress she wore was long and flowing and would look as at home on a beach as it did for this simple ceremony. On her feet were flat Roman-style sandals. Her long hair hung in loose curls around her shoulders and down her back. Her small hands, the once functionally short nails now elegant and polished, clutched a posy of flowers.

When she reached his side the mayor who was officiating the ceremony cleared his throat.

The vows they exchanged were as simple as the ceremony itself and, as Tabitha recited hers, cornflower-blue eyes never leaving his, Giannis's throat closed as the truth hit him.

Tabitha deserved better than this.

She wanted nothing for herself other than the right to be a mother to her own child. She could have demanded anything and everything but her only thought was for their child to have the love of both parents. It was for love of their unborn child that she was committing her life to his.

She deserved more than this simple exchange of vows on the roof of his home, even if the location and views were as stunning as anywhere else on his island.

When it was his turn to recite his own vows, he gazed deeply into her eyes and made a silent vow to himself to be the husband she deserved.

He would never love her but he would give his last breath to protect her.

Tabitha had magic in her veins. When he kissed her to seal the vows they'd exchanged, he felt its power seep through his lips and into his bloodstream.

CHAPTER TEN

TABITHA HADN'T HAD a drop of the champagne the rest of the Basinases had consumed in vast quantities but she felt as drunk as if she'd downed a whole magnum of it.

The vows they'd exchanged...

Somehow they'd contained far more meaning than she'd expected.

In truth, she'd expected the ceremony to feel like a farce but it hadn't. She'd meant every word she'd said and, from the look in Giannis's eyes when he'd spoken his vows, he'd meant it too.

Afterwards, they stayed on the terrace and shared a feast with his family.

Her family.

They didn't say it in words but they didn't need to. The Basinas family accepted her as one of their own. Their acceptance filled her heart to the brim.

For hours they talked, laughed, ate and drank. Toasts were made, blessings given for their marriage and the safe delivery of their child and childhood escapades revealed, all the while Giannis's small nieces and nephews ran around chasing each other and playing pranks on any family member they could.

This was the family life Tabitha had dreamed of when she'd been a child, the family life her father had wanted for her. When the full moon rose high in the night sky she looked up at it and wondered if he was up there too, looking down at her. If he was, she knew he would have a smile the size of that moon on his face.

But it wasn't just his family. It was Giannis too. She hadn't seen him so at ease since the night of the ball, not just with his family but with her too. Every time she looked at him his eyes would pulse and a knowing smile tug at his lips.

Anticipation laced her veins but there was dread mingled with it too.

For all the unexpected joy she'd found in their ceremony and small celebration, she just could not shift the image of Anastasia from her head.

How could she share Giannis's bed knowing he'd shared it with the love of his life before her?

Eventually it was time to call it a night. The small children were rounded up, all protesting wildly that they didn't want to go home, that they weren't tired, even while their little faces stretched with the yawns they couldn't fight.

And then the front door closed and they were alone.

After all that boisterous noise the silence was stark.

She gazed at her husband, the only sound her rapidly accelerating heartbeats.

He locked the door then slowly stepped towards her. 'You enjoyed yourself?'

'Very much.' She attempted a smile. 'I never knew you were such a troublemaker as a child.' His sisters had recounted many of his escapades with glee.

He stood before her and caught a lock of her hair in his hands. 'Did I ever tell you why I hosted the ball?'

'Wasn't it to find a wife?'

He brought the lock to his face and inhaled. Shivers cascaded up her spine. 'That was part of it. The ball itself came about because of a debt owed from my school days. When I was fifteen I broke into the headmaster's office and superglued all his furniture to the floor and all his stationery and books to his desk and shelves.'

'Why?' she whispered in fascination.

'One of the other boys dared me to. In those days I could never resist a challenge. The headmaster knew it was me but couldn't prove it. I was on my final warning. If Alessio hadn't given me an alibi, I would have been expelled.'

'You hosted a ball as repayment for an alibi twenty years ago?'

'A man must always pay his debts, *matia mou*. Without that alibi, my life might have taken a very different path.'

Giannis had always been a risk-taker. Being the only boy of five children probably had something to do with it. His sisters had always been good. Apart from Niki but, seeing as she'd looked up to him as her role model, that probably explained her own mischievous behaviour.

He'd delighted in driving his sisters to distraction, especially Katarina, the only one older than him and thus the bossiest, by climbing the tallest trees and buildings, stealing the gardener's ride-on mower for illicit joyrides, and then progressing to their father's car and stealing cigarettes, defiantly smoking them one after the other until he'd made himself sick. Anything they said he shouldn't do, he'd made it his business to do.

That had included marrying Anastasia, he now realised.

His sisters had all hated her on sight. They had never said it in words but the Basinases were a close-knit bunch and he'd been able to read his sisters' feelings all too well.

Their disapproval had only added to Anastasia's allure.

Skimming his fingers down the swan of Tabitha's elegant neck, revelling in the way her lips parted and her breathing shallowed, he ruefully considered what his reaction would have been if they'd disapproved of her.

Tabitha had an unidentifiable *something* that was far greater than mere allure, something that sang to all his senses, a conductor tuning them into harmony. The desire ringing from the cornflower eyes was more intoxicating than the strongest of spirits.

She could have no greater appeal. Not to him.

It was not humanly possible for him to desire her more than he did.

The past week spent attempting to master that desire had been torturous but, he felt sure, successful.

The spell she wove on him was nothing but an illusion and now he would prove it.

He would make love to her and when it was over the earth would still be on its axis.

Trailing his fingers down her arm, he took her hand in his and tugged it gently. 'Time for us to go to bed, Kyría Basinas.'

Fingers entwined, they climbed the stairs in silence to the room that now belonged to them both, sexual chemistry thick in the air surrounding them.

But, when they reached the door, she hesitated at the threshold.

He brought her hand to his lips and stared into the eyes brimming with uncertainty. 'Is something the matter, *matia mou*?'

She stilled, teeth sinking into her bottom lip, her stare now filled with something he didn't recognise. 'Did you share this room with Anastasia?'

Taken aback at both the question and her first ever mention of his dead wife, it took a few seconds for him to realise why she was asking it.

'Anastasia hated Santorini. She loved the city life. She didn't spend one night here. No woman has shared this bed with me.'

While it sank in that Tabitha had insecurities about his first wife, and what the implications of that could mean, something happened that distracted his thoughts entirely.

Right before his eyes, Tabitha grew in stature and a light came into her eyes that didn't just shine from them but infused the whole of her in a warm glow.

Before he could register the change, she put a hand to his chest then stepped forward and rested her cheek on it and breathed deeply.

She was inhaling his scent…

Then she tipped her head back and gave him a smile of such knowing radiance, every cell in his body tightened.

Gently she pushed him across the threshold and kicked the door shut behind them with her heel. And then she slid her arms around his neck and pulled his head down so she could kiss him.

Heat licked through his veins, his physical awareness—always there, always a part of him around her—flickering at the first brush of her lips to his. When her tongue darted into his mouth and she pressed herself tightly against him, the flickering turned to full arousal.

Hunger exploded in him and he wrapped his arms tightly around her. His hands delved into the silky tresses, fingers coiling in it as he devoured her…and she devoured him.

Tabitha was the one to steer them to the bed, to push him onto it, the one to break the kiss, to run her lips over his cheeks and down his neck as he had done to her, scorching his flesh with every mark from her mouth and tongue. It was her fingers that worked their way down the buttons of his shirt and then pushed it apart, pulled it down his arms and threw it onto the floor. It was her hands pushing at his chest until he was laid flat on his back, breathing deeply, wondering where this vixen had suddenly appeared from.

She put her mouth to his ear and bit the lobe gently. 'Don't move,' she whispered before reaching out an arm to turn on his bedside light.

He had no intention of moving anywhere.

Giannis had anticipated this night in detail, over and over, imagining her breasts in his mouth, his fingers caressing her, inside her, his mouth tasting her, exploring every inch of her so thoroughly that every part of her was as familiar as his own reflection was to him.

But never had he anticipated that she would be the one making the moves. Taking control.

Every inch of his body throbbed with anticipation, heat thick through his loins and veins.

She jumped off the bed with all the grace of a dancer, bounded to the main light switch by the door and hit it. Immediately the light in the room went from full illumination to dusky, casting them both in shadow.

Tabitha stared at the man she'd committed her life to, drinking in his devilish beauty, then bent over to remove her sandals. When they were off, she pinched the skirt of her dress in her fingers and brought it up and over her head.

The suck of air he took only added to the heady thrills zipping through her veins.

Their wedding might not have been the one of her dreams but she felt as if she'd slipped into another Giannis-filled dream. The relief at being told no other woman had shared this room with him had been dizzying, unleashing an enormous wave of emotion she could never find the words to explain. That wave had filled her entirely and suddenly she had found herself emboldened to act on her desires, and emboldened to express in a language they both understood everything she felt for him in that moment.

She wanted him, this beautiful Greek man who could sear her skin with nothing more than a look. She wanted him so much that there were times she could hardly breathe for her longing.

Hooking her arms behind her to undo her lacy bra, she pulled the straps down her arms and threw it onto her discarded dress.

The seductive appreciation in his hooded eyes sent arrows of bittersweet longing shooting from her breasts to her pelvis and gave her the courage needed to remove the last item of clothing and stand before him naked.

Giannis swallowed. His greedy eyes devoured every detail.

The incredible womanly body he'd relived every inch of every night since they'd conceived their child was there before him. The differences the pregnancy was making were there too, subtle but to his eyes obvious.

They only made her more beautiful.

The full breasts were larger, the hips a little wider…the stomach a little rounder.

He wanted to tell her how beautiful she was but his throat had closed.

He couldn't speak.

He didn't need to.

She must have read his thoughts for she smiled then walked slowly back to the bed, climbed onto it and straddled him.

Impossibly, his arousal grew, the ache in it a pain he was unable to relieve.

Gazing down at him, she placed her hands on his chest and let her fingers drift over it.

He reached out an arm to touch her silky skin but she stopped him and shook her head. 'Not yet,' she whispered.

And then she leaned forward and kissed him deeply. Her breasts brushed lightly against his chest, a tease of sensation he craved so much more of. When he tried to wrap his arms around her she shrugged him off and nipped his bottom lip. 'Not *yet*,' she repeated sternly.

She bestowed him with one more kiss on his mouth and then her lips trailed down his neck again. But this time she didn't stop.

This time she continued her oral exploration, tongue and mouth kissing and licking every inch of his chest, his nipples, down to his abdomen, her fingers working on his trousers, which she pulled down with his underwear and threw unceremoniously onto the floor.

This time she was the one to feast her eyes on him, lashes sweeping, a look of wonder on her face as she gazed at his jutting erection.

She put a hand to it.

He gritted his teeth as it throbbed at her touch.

And then she leant down to cover it with her mouth.

A loud, unbidden groan escaped his throat and he had to fist the sheets and grit his teeth even tighter to fight back the orgasm already threatening release.

'Tabitha...'

He could speak no more.

All he was capable of doing was raising his head to gaze dazedly down at the honey-blonde hair over his lap and submit to the pleasure she was giving him.

It was possibly the clumsiest but most incredible experience of his life.

He'd never known sensation like it.

She was doing this because she wanted to give *him* pleasure.

From the soft sounds she was making, she was enjoying it too.

The tension he fought against releasing was building inside him, every part of him thick with it, enveloping the whole of his body, the conductor of his senses harmonising them to a perfect pitch.

Suddenly he could take no more.

He wanted to come. Badly. More than he'd ever needed to come before. But he wanted to be inside her and watch as she came too.

He gathered her hair in his hands and gently raised her head. 'Come here,' he commanded thickly.

Eyes dark with desire met his and then her hands were patting over his chest as she moved gracefully back up to straddle him again. But this time she positioned herself exactly where he ached for her to be.

Her lips found his mouth at the same moment she sank fully onto him, taking him whole inside her hot, wet heat.

His groan came from deep within him.

Theos...

Giannis screwed his eyes closed and fought back the release his tortured body burned for.

She'd stilled. Her pubis was ground against him, his erection fully sheathed inside her, but she made no effort to move.

He took a deep breath and opened his eyes.

The expression on her face almost made him come there and then.

Cupping her cheeks with his hands, he gazed at the flushed face in wonderment. 'Do whatever you want, *matia mou*.'

Her eyes closed briefly and then she carefully raised herself back so her hands rested on his chest and she was gazing down at him with that heady, glazed look.

'That's it,' he urged. 'You set the pace.'

She rode him slowly to start with, her fingers digging into his chest, lips parted, eyes fixed on his face, adjusting her position until she found the one that had her moaning and her movements increasing.

It was the most erotic experience he had ever known.

Holding her hip with one hand to steady her, he reached his other up and cupped one of the breasts swaying so gently.

Her breathing deepened.

He brushed a thumb over the tip and watched her eyes widen and dilate in response, taking as much enjoyment and pleasure from watching Tabitha's expressive face as he did from the incredible sensations raging through him.

How he held on, he didn't know. It was an elemental torture he'd never known existed, pleasure and pain entwined together, and when she threw her head back with a cry and ground down on him one final time, the tight thickening pulled him as deep inside her as it was possible to go and pushed him over the edge.

His orgasm burst through him with a force that had him shouting out her name, pulsations of indescribable pleasure crashing through every part of him.

Tabitha, her face burrowed in Giannis's neck, his arms wrapped tightly around her, slowly came floating back down to earth.

She could feel the beat of his heart on her breasts crushed against his chest. She could hear the deep raggedness of his breaths.

He was still inside her.

She didn't want to move.

She didn't want to break the spell.

His arms loosened as his fingers wound through her hair.

'Where the hell did that come from?' he asked with a choked laugh.

She nuzzled into his neck and gave a short giggle. 'I have no idea.'

But of course she knew. It had been a release from her fears of the ghost of Anastasia, something for just Tabitha and Giannis, an embrace of the start of the rest of their lives together.

She wanted to hold on to this closeness she felt at that exact moment and bottle it for ever.

She felt so much. Too much, she feared, although it was a thought to be dealt with another time, when she wasn't still feeling the thrills of their love-making vibrate through her skin.

Moving her face from the heaven that was the crook of

Giannis's neck, she rested her chin on his chest. 'We can have a good marriage, can't we?' she asked in a small voice.

He was silent for a moment before he shifted from beneath her and rolled her over so he was the one lying on top of her.

His face hovered over hers, his hands smoothing her hair from her forehead.

He kissed the tip of her nose.

'I meant my vows,' he said seriously.

'So did I,' she whispered.

'I know you did. There has been much distrust between us and many misconceptions but we can make this marriage work. If we use our vows and the rings we wear on our fingers as lines in the sand, we can put the doubts and distrust behind us.'

Warmth filled her heart. With a soft sigh she put her hand on the nape of his neck and gazed into the eyes staring at her with such sincerity. 'I want to make it work.'

His lips brushed against hers. 'You already are.'

CHAPTER ELEVEN

THE SUN POURING into the bedroom woke Tabitha from the deep slumber she'd finally fallen into.

Giannis's side empty, she stretched and climbed out, looking for something to wear. She settled on the shirt she'd practically ripped from his body, still discarded on the floor where she'd thrown it.

A powerful sense of *déjà vu* hit her but she was too full of bliss from a night spent making exquisite love to fear the irony that the last time she'd spent the night with him she'd also woken to an empty bed and helped herself to his shirt.

They were married now. She carried his child in her belly.

For the first time since she'd been ten years old, Tabitha woke without a single fear in her mind.

It was liberating.

As she fastened the buttons of the shirt that fell to her knees, she gazed around at Giannis's bedroom. *Their* bedroom.

It was like a whitewashed cave with curved ceilings, thick arches and an abundance of alcoves, some covered with doors, others with seats carved into them or modern artwork placed in them.

She found a bathroom that thrilled her feminine heart, a dressing room filled with Giannis's clothes, another dressing room filled with *her* clothes… She quickly shut that door so she didn't have to change out of his shirt.

Padding to the other side of the room to one of the huge arched windows, she was astounded to find a private balcony with an infinity pool and immediately set about locating the door to it.

She found it behind the silk drapes hanging at the far end of the room and stepped out onto it. The sun's rays were already strong that morning, the cloudless sky a deep royal-blue.

'I was afraid for a moment that you'd done another early-morning vanishing act.' Giannis's deep, rich voice rumbled deliciously through her ears and she turned with a smile to face him.

He wore only a pair of shorts and carried a tray with coffee, orange juice and a variety of pastries and fruits.

He grinned, placing the tray on the glass table by the thick-walled balustrade. 'But I see you have stolen another of my shirts.'

As her heart had lodged into her throat at the first sight of him, it took a few moments before speech came. 'You wasted all that money on clothes for me when you could have just given me your discarded shirts.'

'If you wore only my shirts neither of us would ever leave my room.' And then he pulled her to him and kissed her so thoroughly, her knees weakened. 'Good morning, *matia mou.*'

Staring into the gleaming eyes, she smiled again. She couldn't stop smiling. 'Good morning.'

Anticipating another kiss, she was disappointed when he let her go and pulled a chair out for her. 'Sit. Eat.'

She raised a brow at his authoritative tone.

He winked and took his seat. 'I find I have a great appetite this morning.'

Laughing, she sat and helped herself to a glass of orange juice.

She could hardly credit that only twenty-four hours ago she'd been filled with dread. Now she felt as light as air, as if she could fly.

Giannis gazed in wonder at the radiance shining from his new wife, his relief at finding her still there now tamed.

While he'd waited for the coffee to brew he'd had an unexpected feeling of *déjà vu* flash through him.

The last time he'd made her coffee after a night of making love, he'd returned to an empty room.

This time the room had been empty but she had still been there.

The smile she had greeted him with could have melted an iceberg.

The night they had shared...

Theos, his loins still thrummed from the effects.

Biting into an apple, he chewed and swallowed the bite before saying, 'We have the next three days to ourselves. Is there anything you would like to do?'

She pulled a face as she considered the question. 'Can we stay in bed?'

'You read my mind.'

Their eyes met. His heart thumped hard against his ribs.

That was to be expected. After the night they'd shared, all of him felt out of kilter. Three days of making love to his beautiful bride would be enough for everything to right itself.

She broke into a bread roll and spooned honey on it. 'What happens after the three days are up? Are you going back to work?'

'I have to,' he answered regretfully. 'And I might have to answer the occasional urgent email while we're here. I have many business interests and, while I employ the best people to run them for me, any issues are ultimately my responsibility.'

She bit into the roll and shrugged, clearly conveying that she understood.

'What did you want to do?' he asked curiously.

She looked at him with a frown, her mouth still full of food.

'Before Emmaline kicked you out of your home and cut your education off. What did you hope to do? Would you have gone to university?'

She swallowed her mouthful and took another drink of orange juice. 'I wanted to do a business degree.'

He raised a brow in admiration. 'What would you have done with it?'

'The plan was for me to take over my father's business.'

'What business was he in?'

'He owned a brewery.'

Recognition flashed through him. 'Brigstock Brewery? That's your family's business?'

He remembered it well. His first illicit pint of beer at boarding school had been in one of its pubs.

'It's been in the family for over two hundred years,' she said with a touch of pride. 'We own over two thousand pubs and restaurants and brew many of our own beers.'

'Who runs it now?'

She gave a shrug but he caught the sadness in her eyes. 'It's not been family-run since my mother died. My father gave up day-to-day control of it so he could look after me. It's run by a board of directors but he was still the majority shareholder. He'd started easing back into the business a couple of years before he died. The plan was always for me to one day take my place on the board too.'

It was an answer that led to so many further questions, he hardly knew where to start. 'How old were you when your mother died?'

'Four. She died of cervical cancer. My father died when I was sixteen, of a heart attack. Probably the stress of being married to Emmaline,' she added with a bitter murmur.

'If he was the majority shareholder then presumably he was entitled to a majority share of the profits?'

Her eyes met his. There was a stoniness in them he'd seen only once before. 'Those profits go into the trust.'

He felt his own blood turn stony. 'Meaning they go to Emmaline?'

She nodded.

He drummed his fingers on the table, thinking hard, biting back irrational heated thoughts of hitmen and torture. 'You need to fight this.'

'I wouldn't know where to begin.'

'You begin at the start. With Emmaline. She has taken—'

'I know what she's taken and done,' she interrupted with a hint of anger. 'I've lived with the consequences for almost five years.'

'You don't have to live with them any more. Let me help you. We can take back what was yours.'

'No!' Tabitha's shout of disagreement surprised her as much as it clearly surprised him. Lowering her voice, she said evenly, 'The thought of seeing Emmaline again terrifies me.'

'You won't have to see her alone. I'll be by your side.'

'The effect would still be the same. All I have to do is think about that woman and my hands go clammy.' This conversation alone had her heart racing in the sick, frightened way it had done all those years ago when she'd walked for hours along the side of the road with her thumb out, praying that whoever stopped for her wouldn't be an axe murderer, no clue where she was going to go or what she was going to do when she got there. She'd been lost and terrified, feelings she remembered all too vividly to ever feel safe from them.

'Emmaline and her evil daughters put me through hell and I will not put myself or our baby through the stress that seeing them again would cause.'

'So you let her win?' he challenged.

Tabitha threw her hands in the air. 'She's already won!'

I'm not going to put myself through a huge court battle while I'm pregnant.'

His eyes narrowed. 'Once the baby's born? Will you fight her then?'

'Maybe.'

'I don't like the word "maybe". It's weak.'

His comment landed like a wound to her heart. 'Is that what you think of me?'

'No, *matia mou*, it's what you think of yourself. You don't see how strong you are.'

'I'm not strong.'

'The fact you are still here proves you are strong. How many people in your position could have done what you did?'

'I didn't do anything. I've been a chambermaid for years.'

'That takes strength in itself. Think of the girls you were at school with. How many of them would have found the strength to lower their hands into doing the menial work of their household staff? It would be beneath their dignity. Most of them would have ended up on the streets or selling their stories to the tabloid rags for money. You didn't.' He reached across the table to take her hand in his, bringing it up to his face to stare intently at it before turning his gaze back to her. 'You worked your fingers into callouses to support yourself. One day you will find you *do* have the strength to face your stepmother and fight her for what is yours. The power is yours. You just need to believe it.'

Tabitha's heart thumped so hard, there was danger it could burst out of her.

To hear Giannis say those things…

She stared into his eyes and found she could cry to see only sincerity staring back at her.

She'd spent so long thinking herself weak that it was

incredible to hear that Giannis, a man who epitomised strength and power, thought her strong.

Her head was still dazed when he brushed a kiss on her knuckles, the gleam returning to his eyes. 'Finish your roll, *koritzi mou*. And then I would suggest you eat another.'

She blinked a couple of times before finding her voice. 'Why would you suggest that?'

'Because I'm taking you back to bed. You will need all your strength for that.' And then he winked and took a huge bite of his apple.

Two weeks after the wedding Giannis was sat in his office reading his investigator's report on Emmaline.

The report on Tabitha had been emailed too but, when he'd hovered over the icon to open it, he'd found himself plagued by a violent bout of nausea and deleted it unread.

His wife deserved better than to have her husband poking into every last detail of her history. It was a violation she had done nothing to warrant and he was sickened with himself for authorising it.

He had no such qualms about reading the report on Emmaline.

By the time he'd finished, reading it a second time for good measure...

He had never felt such fury, not even when he'd received confirmation he was not the father of Anastasia's child.

Emmaline Brigstock was a greater piece of work than even Anastasia had been. The woman was vile. Clever, manipulative and cruel.

Her first husband had died in a motorboat accident when their daughters, Fiona and Saffron, had been small. He'd recognised their names from the guest-list of his ball. Tabitha's tormentors had been there the night they'd conceived their child. Had Tabitha seen them?

He thought of the shattered glass in her hand and knew the answer was yes.

Emmaline's first husband's family described Emmaline as an arch manipulator. Her own family described her as cold. Her sister, estranged for many years, described her thus: 'the kind of woman children would lovingly follow into her home believing they were going to be shown a litter of puppies, only to watch the puppies be drowned'.

Transcripts of interviews with ex-members of staff who'd borne witness to her treatment of Tabitha—all undertaken on condition of confidentiality—proved that Tabitha's treatment at her stepmother's hand had been far more wretched than she'd confided to Giannis, especially after her father had died. The day after his death, the cook had witnessed Emmaline slap Tabitha around the face. She'd no longer been permitted to eat in the dining room, forced to eat alone in the kitchen. She'd been excluded from all family occasions. Christmas had been spent with the staff. She'd received no presents. Her birthdays had gone unremarked and certainly not celebrated.

Pages and pages of testimony of the cold cruelty Tabitha had endured.

Not a single member of staff had a bad word to say about Tabitha herself. On the contrary, they'd all adored her and had been heartbroken when she'd run away on her eighteenth birthday, all having believed Emmaline's explanation for Tabitha's sudden disappearance from Brigstock Manor.

'She'd been such a happy child but those years after her father died...well...she become a shell of herself,' the housekeeper had explained. 'It was no surprise that she left the moment she legally could. Their treatment of her was barbaric.'

Calling out to his PA to cancel his next meeting, Giannis opened his oak cabinet door and pulled out the bottle of

Scotch he kept there for the occasions he worked late and wanted to wind down before returning to his apartment. He filled the glass to the brim, drank half of it then reached for his phone.

First he forwarded the report to his English lawyer with instructions to check for any illegalities in Emmaline's activities. Instinct told him that she must have broken a swathe of English laws.

Then he called his sister.

Niki answered on the first ring.

Cutting out the usual pleasantries, he said, 'It's Tabitha's birthday next week. How do you feel about organising a party for her? I thought we could book that restaurant we took our parents to for their fortieth wedding anniversary.' The restaurant was one of the best in Athens, excellent food, location and atmosphere combined with attentive but relaxed staff, making it a memorable venue for all the right reasons.

Her response was exactly what he had known it would be—enthusiastic—and she promised to get straight on to it.

Knowing he'd put the wheels in motion to bring a smile to his wife's face eased the fury pumping through his blood a little.

What hell she must have lived through.

He imagined a miniature Tabitha, with chubby cheeks and honey-blonde hair, and his heart twisted to think of that little girl losing her mother at such a tender age. Her father had found a new mother for her, and sisters too, not knowing he was bringing a black widow and her venomous offspring into his home.

It would be easy to sneer at her father for falling for Emmaline's lies but Giannis had been the victim of his own gold-digging witch.

Tabitha could not be more different if she tried.

What was she doing right then? Was she reading one

of the books he'd had shipped over by an English retailer, after she'd said in passing that she had always loved to read but that she'd only read one book since having been kicked out of her home? It hadn't been time or finances that had stopped her reading. For almost five years she had worked long, physical hours. She'd been too exhausted to read a book. She'd been too exhausted to do anything.

He swiped his phone and found her number before his brain registered what his fingers were doing and he turned it off before he could put the call through.

He downed the rest of his Scotch. The ease he'd just found disappeared. His skin felt suddenly uncomfortable, as if it had tightened around his bones and was constricting his lungs.

Since when did he call a woman just to hear her voice? Never.

And since when did he cut meetings short and cancel appointments just so he could read non-work-related reports? Since when did he focus on anything at work other than the work itself?

Since Tabitha.

It had been the same even before they'd married, he thought, remembering the weeks spent in his fruitless search for her.

In the course of a normal working week he stayed in his apartment in Athens or his other apartments or hotels if he was travelling. He returned to Santorini only at weekends. He worked long hours. Adding an hour's flight at the end of it was a hassle he could do without.

Since their wedding he'd flown back to Santorini six times. He'd had to physically restrain himself from flying back the other times.

He'd meant what he'd said about making their marriage work but there had to be a balance. He'd told himself he had a duty to spend time with his new wife during the week, and not just weekends, but the uncomfortable truth was that he ached to be with her.

She was never far from his mind.

Even with an hour's flight between them the spell she'd woven on him proved strong.

Sooner or later the spell would break.

Tabitha was his wife. He had a duty to provide for her, to protect her and to make life as good and as easy as it could be. He would give her everything she desired. He would treat her like a princess. He would worship her body when he was with her and be faithful when he wasn't.

But his heart he would—must—keep for himself.

Only a fool would allow it to be placed in another's hands after having had it smashed the first time he'd handed it to someone.

CHAPTER TWELVE

THE LATE-SUMMER Santorini heat showed no sign of abating so, while Tabitha's days were spent in glorious sunshine, it was nice to return to the more familiar heat of Vienna.

Tabitha didn't know if she was more excited at seeing her elderly friend or at the fact that she was finally accompanying Giannis somewhere away from Santorini.

In the weeks since their wedding she'd had plenty to keep her occupied but also the luxury of doing nothing if that was what she wanted. After years of toil, proper down time was a true luxury.

It had given her the time she needed to think. About her life, her future and the eternal question of whether Giannis was right that she should fight Emmaline for her inheritance.

He thought she was strong.

She still didn't feel it. She still couldn't picture her stepmother's face without needles of fear pricking on her skin.

Giannis's family all lived close by. If during the working week he stayed away from home for the night she was inundated by them with offers to feed her in their own magnificent homes. Electra, the second-youngest sister and currently on maternity leave, had dropped in a couple of times with her toddler in tow and Niki had taken her out for lunch and kept pressing for another one.

For the first time that she could remember, she wasn't lonely.

But still there lived in her the feeling that something was missing. She just wished she knew what it was.

She missed Giannis when he wasn't there. That could be it. A simple case of missing her husband.

Who wouldn't miss him? He was smart, attentive, sharp-witted, amusing, devilishly handsome and as sexy as sin. She simply couldn't get enough of his love-making. If she had her way they would never leave the bedroom.

But they did have to leave the bedroom, she accepted wistfully.

She just wished she could be with him on the nights he couldn't make it back to Santorini. When she'd suggested she accompany him to Athens, which was his main base during the working week, or wherever else he happened to be business-wise, he'd dismissed it with a, 'You'd be bored'.

She wished, too, that on the nights they spent apart she had any evidence that he missed her. Would it hurt him to pick up the phone and call her? The one time she'd called him, just for a chat, just to hear his voice, he'd been polite but distant.

It felt as if she was deliberately being kept in the shadows of his life. When they were together he couldn't keep his hands off her but when they were apart he didn't spare her a thought.

On the plus side, she had their forthcoming date on Saturday night to look forward to. Giannis was taking her to an exclusive event at the Palvetti production facility in Lake Como. Palvetti was an iconic jewellery and perfumery company, its boss, Alessio, Giannis's oldest and closest friend, the man whose debt Giannis had repaid by throwing the masquerade ball. Tabitha was very much looking forward to going. It would be the first time Giannis had taken her anywhere resembling an actual date since they'd married.

She kept that thought strong inside her when they entered the Basinas Palace Hotel and she found herself wanting to cry when not a single member of staff congratulated them on their marriage.

They didn't know. Unless they looked at the ring on her finger, they would have no reason to think Tabitha was Giannis's wife. Even if they did realise they were married, the hotel staff would look at her and think only that Giannis's new wife looked a lot like one of their old chambermaids.

There had been no announcement of their marriage but she'd thought word must have got out by now that one of Europe's richest men had married, especially after the tragic demise of his first wife. Outside of Giannis's family and his household staff, she doubted anyone knew.

She shoved her darkening thoughts away as she approached Mrs Coulter's door.

Her elderly friend was expecting her.

Tabitha was alarmed at how frail she looked compared to the last time she'd seen her. However, she was in excellent spirits, and after they'd shared a round of sandwiches and a pot of loose-leaf tea she got the playing cards out and insisted on hearing everything that Tabitha had been up to since their last lunch together. She wanted details on everything. How she and Giannis had met, details of the wedding, the whole works.

Tabitha obliged, sparing nothing apart from the bits that could make her blush.

In truth, it felt wonderful to confide it all.

'You're in love!' the elderly woman said, clapping her hands with glee. 'I cannot tell you how happy this makes me.'

'We're not in love,' Tabitha refuted, although her heart had started to thump. 'We married so our baby could have two parents under the same roof.'

'Poppycock. That was an old-fashioned notion even back in my day. That man's rich enough to build you adjoining houses if he'd wanted only for his child to have a mother and father on hand at all times. And you're very naughty for not telling me you spent the night with him at the ball,' she continued. 'You promised me full details, young lady.'

Even though perspiration had broken out on her back, Tabitha found a smile. 'It was too personal for me to share.'

'First love always is personal, my dear,' Mrs Coulter mused before a dreamy expression drifted over her wizened face. 'I remember my first love. He was a bad boy. My father thought he was scum. He was right—Billy was only interested in one thing—but I didn't care. I thought he was marvellous. The first time we made love was in the shed at the bottom of my garden. My father nearly caught us. He thought foxes had broken in. We only escaped when he went back in the house to get his gun.'

'What happened to him?' Tabitha asked, fascinated at this generations-old tale of young love.

'Who? My father or Billy?'

'Billy.'

Her eyes crinkled with mischief. 'I married him, my dear. Billy was my sweet William. And we had fifty happy years together.'

Could she love Giannis? Was Mrs Coulter right? It was a question still playing in her head four days later when she awoke to find Giannis in bed with her.

'Shouldn't you be at work?' she mumbled with a sleepy smile. He'd surprised her by flying back from Athens the night before when she'd assumed he'd be staying in his apartment.

He shook his head. There was something smug about the look on his face...

'What?'

His brow creased slightly. 'Don't you know what day it is?'

'Friday?'

'Tabitha, it's your birthday.'

'Oh.'

It had been so long since she'd celebrated that she'd stopped caring about it. It had become nothing but another date on the calendar.

He put his hand under his pillow and pulled out a slim gift-wrapped box. 'Happy birthday, *matia mou.*'

Dumbstruck, Tabitha took it from him with a hand that shook.

She hadn't received a birthday present in seven years.

Giannis, noticing her hesitancy, caught her downcast chin and raised it so he could look at her.

Those beautiful eyes were swimming with tears. 'What's the matter?'

She swallowed and shook her head.

Speaking gently, his guts twisting at what he suspected was the reason for her tears, he said, 'You're not supposed to cry until you've opened it and decided that you hate it—and then you're supposed to cry in private so my ego isn't bruised.'

She managed a smile. 'Is that the law?'

'*Nai.*'

'I'm sorry for breaking the law.' Then she palmed her hand to his cheek and kissed him. 'Thank you.'

'You haven't opened it yet.'

'Then I will thank you again when I have.'

She took her time opening it, treating the wrapping paper with a respect he'd never seen before. When Giannis had a gift, he ripped into it.

It had been a long time since Tabitha had received a gift of any kind, he suspected.

After taking much longer than the average person would take opening a present, the wrapping was off and she prised the lid open.

Her hand flew to her mouth. When she looked at him

again fresh tears were brimming in her eyes. 'Oh, Giannis, it's beautiful. Thank you.'

'It's a bespoke Palvetti creation especially for you.' He cleared his suddenly tight throat. 'You can wear it tonight.'

'Wear it where?'

'To the restaurant I'm taking you to in Athens.' Taking the box with the gift in it from her hands, he put it on the bedside table and rolled on top of her. He kissed her mouth. 'First, I'm going to make love to you.' He kissed her cheek. 'And then we will eat breakfast.' He kissed her neck. 'And then I will make love to you again. And then we will take my plane to Athens.'

He didn't get any further with his itinerary for the day. Tabitha had hooked her legs tightly around him.

Instead of heading straight to his apartment, Giannis took Tabitha to the Acropolis, where they walked around the great ruins hand in hand, her husband acting as her tour guide as he filled her in on the history of the ancient monument and all the ancient buildings that were a part of it.

Afterwards, they had a late lunch before finally getting to his apartment.

Tabitha had been in it only the once, when they had dropped in after a meeting with his lawyer when they'd been sorting out their pre-nuptial agreement. It was a beautiful, spacious apartment in, naturally, the most affluent area of the city and the contrast to his villa in Santorini was stark.

This time she took no notice of the differences. Her eyes were too busy popping out at the enormous display of roses that covered every available surface.

'I'll have them flown back to Santorini in the morning,' he murmured into her ear as he wrapped his arms around her.

After they'd whiled away the afternoon making love and

sharing a bath in his massive sunken tub, they got ready for their meal out.

When she was dressed she asked Giannis to do the clasp on the beautiful choker he'd had made for her.

Gold and covered with gems of all colours in a glimmering pattern, it was the most beautiful item of jewellery she had ever seen.

The next surprise came when they walked into the restaurant and were greeted by his family, all bearing gifts of their own for her.

They were the only guests there. The restaurant had been opened specially for them and decorated with balloons and streamers.

They ate, they drank, music played…there was even a birthday cake for her.

Yet the happiness that had fizzed through her veins that day slowly dissolved as the feeling of being kept in the shadows crept back on her.

Giannis had gone to all this effort for her but had again kept her away from prying eyes. Obviously he wasn't keeping her existence a secret but neither was he flaunting it.

That would change tomorrow, she reminded herself on the drive back to the apartment, when they flew to Lake Como for the Palvetti party.

Everything he'd done for her…

It was incredible.

When they'd ridden the elevator to the top floor, which Giannis owned entirely, and stepped inside his apartment he pulled her into his arms and kissed her. 'I have one more surprise for you,' he murmured.

'A kinky surprise?'

His lips quirked. 'Not quite but I can give you one of those too if you want.'

She admired the tightness of his buttocks as he strode to the bureau and pulled a thick envelope out of a drawer.

'What is it?' she asked when he handed it to her.

'The means for you to fight back. Evidence of your stepmother's fraudulent behaviour.'

Stunned, she clutched the envelope to her chest. 'How did you get this?'

'I had Emmaline investigated.' A muscular arm slid around her waist and pulled her to him. His breath was warm against her hair. 'When you are ready to fight and reclaim what is yours, I will be there to help you. You don't have to do this alone.'

'So you don't think I'm strong.'

'Being strong does not mean having to do things alone. This is the ammunition you need for when you are ready to confront her. You have much strength, *matia mou*. You just have to believe it.'

Tabitha pressed her cheek to his chest and listened to the steady beat of his heart echo in her ears and vibrate through her skin.

At that moment her own heart had bloomed enough to burst.

Tabitha did not think she had ever been so happy in her entire life. Possibly when she'd been a small child before her mother had died, but as she could hardly remember that far back she couldn't really count it.

Certainly not since, though.

That morning they flew from Athens to Milan but, instead of touring the city, they spent the day in bed in Giannis's magnificent Milanese apartment, only surfacing when it was time to get ready for the Palvetti party.

The envelope he'd given her sat in her oversized handbag. She had yet to open it but every time she caught a glimpse or brushed it with her fingers her heart filled with such love for him it choked her.

Because, of course, Mrs Coulter was right. Tabitha loved

her husband. She'd loved him from the moment he'd taken her into his arms and waltzed her around that wonderful dance floor and she wasn't going to deny it to herself a moment longer.

Lying in the foamy water of his huge roll-topped bath, her back pressed against his sopping chest, his fingers making lazy circles around her nipples, the need to declare her feelings was strong.

She'd never told anyone who wasn't her parent that she loved them.

How would he react when she did declare herself? Surely, *surely*, Mrs Coulter was right and he had strong feelings for her too? All the effort he'd gone to for her birthday, his anger at Emmaline's treatment of her, the fact he'd hired an investigator to prove her stepmother's fraud, his inability to keep his hands off her...surely that all meant something?

His hand moved lower to stroke her softly swelling belly. She turned her head to place a kiss on his biceps.

And then she twisted round to kiss his mouth.

Tonight, she thought as she sank onto his length and gasped at the incredible feelings flooding through her, feelings she just could not get enough of.

She would tell him her feelings tonight.

Giannis sucked in a breath when Tabitha finally emerged from their bedroom. After their steamy bath, he'd shaved and donned his suit, then worked his way through his email inbox while she'd got herself ready.

Tonight, wearing a sparkly deep blue dress that accentuated her growing curves in all the right places, the choker he'd had custom-made for her birthday snug around her neck, that glow that must be innate in her shone brighter than ever.

She never failed to take his breath away.

'You look beautiful, *glikia mou.*'

Colour stained her rounded cheeks and she bestowed him with a smile of such brilliance it dazzled him.

Something sharp pierced through his chest and then, without any warning, his heart began to thud. But these erratic beats were different, heavier than the thundering beats he'd become accustomed to with Tabitha.

These beats vibrated to the tips of his toes and filled him with such an ache that alarm bells clanged loudly in his head and he stopped mid-step towards her.

After an age passed he loosened his shoulders and pulled out his phone to instruct his driver to collect them.

Despite the motion sickness Tabitha's first helicopter ride induced, she found herself enchanted by her first glimpse of the Palvetti production facility. Nestled between two mountains in Lake Como, it appeared through the darkness of the night sky in shimmering white lights looking more like a castle than anything else, including the monastery it had started its life as.

The moment they touched down, a limousine appeared.

They were driven past masses of security to a huge courtyard and then they passed through scanners and she found herself in the midst of a select number of people whose faces she recognised as some of the wealthiest in the world. They were all clearly buzzing to be there: the first ever visitors at the facility behind one of the world's most iconic brands.

A touch intimidated, she reached for the security of Giannis's hand. He gave it a quick squeeze then dropped it to stride forward and embrace his old friend Alessio Palvetti. Disappointment lashed her when he introduced them and made not so much as a passing reference to her being his wife.

She told herself it was because there was no time, and

that he would introduce her properly later, for Alessio called for everyone's attention and announced the start of the tour.

Moments later, she found herself dumbstruck. It felt as though she'd stepped into a futuristic sci-fi film. She had never seen so much white: floors, ceilings, walls, not a mark to be seen. Contained within the whiteness were laboratories, indoor greenhouses, testing rooms…

As they toured the vast, deliciously scented rooms, their guide, a Palvetti whose name she'd already forgotten, touched on the history of the company in almost mythical terms. Tabitha's only disappointment was that they weren't invited into the workshop part of the facility where their wonderful jewellery was created. She lightly fingered the beautiful choker that Giannis had bought her for her birthday, which glittered with diamonds, emeralds and rubies, awed that it was the incredibly talented brains within this compound who'd made it for her.

When the tour was over, they were led into a vast yet surprisingly intimate room so different from the corridors and laboratories they had just walked that for a moment it felt as if she'd stepped back in time to Italy's mediaeval past.

Thick velvet gold drapes hung on the exposed ancient stone walls, crystal chandeliers hung on the frescoed ceiling and gold life-sized statues stood in each corner while a string quartet played jaunty yet sophisticated background music. Stunning models dressed in silver and adorned with Palvetti jewellery carried trays of canapés, champagne and, mercifully, alcohol-free drinks.

Ravenous though she was, Tabitha found herself feeling too tight inside to eat.

Giannis had kept by her side throughout the tour but the easy affection he displayed when alone with her was nowhere to be found. She had the distinct impression he was avoiding her touch. He was certainly avoiding touching her.

There were only twenty guests and a handful of Palvettis yet somehow he managed not to mention their marital state to any of them. She caught a few curious eyes clock her left hand but these people were the cream of high society and it would have been the height of poor manners to ask a stranger, which she was to them, if the gold band she wore on her wedding finger was a wedding ring.

Her mood lowered further when Giannis discussed business with an Agon prince in his native language. She could hardly use her phone app to translate for her benefit in this situation, so she was forced to stand decoratively beside them pretending that she didn't feel like a wallflower.

Mercifully, Alessio's new wife Beth, a fellow English girl, took pity on her. Though her eyes were alight with curiosity, they had a lovely long chat about Tabitha's new necklace, which Beth recognised as a Palvetti, and about Beth's new role within the company. Discovering that Beth was the brains behind this event, Tabitha found herself envious that her fellow countryman had settled into this world so well and so quickly. Or had she? She noticed that Beth's eyes kept flickering to her husband, the tiniest crease on her face, as if she were concerned about something.

By the time the evening came to a close, Tabitha's mood was as low as it had been the morning of their wedding. Not even the goody bag she'd been handed—which contained a beautiful gold and emerald bracelet and a perfume set with her name on the packaging, with a note in beautiful calligraphy stating all the contents had been made especially for her—could lift it.

They'd spent their first evening together in the company of Giannis's peers, some of whom he considered good friends, and he had not made a single allusion to their marriage.

CHAPTER THIRTEEN

'WHAT'S THE MATTER?' Giannis asked when they were back inside his Milanese apartment. Tabitha had hardly said two words to him since they'd left Lake Como. When he'd asked if she'd enjoyed herself, she'd raised one slim shoulder in a half-hearted shrug.

Troubled cornflower eyes connected with his before she turned her back to him, kicked her shoes off and headed to the kitchen.

'Tabitha?'

She opened a cupboard and removed a cup. 'What?'

'Something is bothering you. Talk to me.'

Instead of answering, she filled the cup with water, drank it, refilled it and drank again. Only when she'd put the empty cup on the draining board did she face him.

Folding her arms across her waist, she stared at him silently.

Now he was the one to ask, 'What?'

Her eyes narrowed before she bluntly asked, 'Are you ashamed of me?'

Taken aback at the ludicrous question, he laughed and pulled her into his arms. 'Of course not.'

She made no attempt to return his embrace, her frame as stiff as a mannequin's.

'You didn't touch me all night,' she said, her voice as stiff as her frame.

Tabitha was pregnant, he reminded himself. When his sister Helena had been pregnant, her hormones had made her irrational enough times that Giannis had felt sorry for her husband. He'd been lucky that, up to this point, Tabitha had been nothing but rational and considered. Outside of the bedroom, that was. In the bedroom, she was a vixen, as much a slave to their desire as he was.

'It was business,' he explained with a murmur, nuzzling into her delectable neck, fingers sliding up her back to find the zip. He was already rock-hard for her.

Theos, when *wasn't* he hard for her? Sharing the same air as her but not being able to touch her had been a masochistic form of torture but a necessary one after the violent emotions that had pulsed through him before they'd left the apartment. To master his control he needed space from her. Being surrounded by company that evening had given him the distance he'd needed to regain control of himself and, now they were alone again, he could hardly wait to…

She put a hand to his shoulder and pushed him back an inch. 'No it wasn't.'

'Most of the guests there were business associates of mine. It was not the place for displays of affection.' This wasn't a lie, he assured himself. Not the whole truth but certainly not a lie.

'So you feel affection for me, do you?'

Groping her bottom, he pressed her to him so she could feel his excitement. 'There, *matia mou*,' he whispered into her ear, her scent dancing straight into his bloodstream. 'Solid evidence of my affection for you.'

'Sex, you mean. You can have that with anyone.' Then she ducked out from his hold and walked out of the kitchen.

Perplexed, loins throbbing, he followed her into the living room. 'Do you want me to order food?' he asked carefully. 'You didn't eat much this evening. You must be hungry.' Which was probably what was making her irritable.

She sat on the sill of the bay window and crossed her legs. 'You noticed?'

Propping himself against the wall, he flashed the smile that normally made her grin. 'You must know by now that I notice everything.'

Her stony expression didn't alter. 'I notice things too. Like that you didn't once refer to me as your wife tonight.'

'Tonight wasn't about us.'

'That shouldn't stop you telling people—your friends—that you've married and that you're going to be a father.'

'I didn't think you would want people outside of the family to know about the baby until the first trimester was clear.'

'You could have discussed that with me first but, regardless, it shouldn't stop you telling people that you've married again. We've been married for three weeks. Tonight is the first time I've met any of your friends. Alessio is your best friend and you seemed pretty pally with that prince you were talking to too. Did you tell either of them we're married?'

'As I just said, tonight wasn't about us.' He found himself speaking through gritted teeth. 'Tonight was a big deal for Alessio and it wouldn't have been right to take the attention away from him.'

Again, this might not be the whole truth but it certainly wasn't a lie. Announcing that he and Tabitha had married would have caused a stir amongst his peers but he'd planned to mention it casually. Before the words could form, however, he'd remembered the fanfare of his marriage to Anastasia which they had all been privy to and a cold chill had run down his spine at how it had all ended.

'So when are you planning to tell people?'

'People know. I've not hidden that we're married to anyone—all anyone has to do is look at my wedding ring to see that I'm married.'

'Your family know but if you weren't so close I doubt you'd even have invited them to our wedding. You didn't want to include anyone else.'

'You didn't want to invite anyone apart from Mrs Coulter,' he reminded her.

His visions of returning to the apartment and ripping Tabitha's clothes off, fantasies that had burned through him the entire night, had been doused in ice. Tabitha had ambushed him with a conversation he'd been completely unprepared for and it was clear it was heading in a direction in which he did not want to go.

'That's because I have no one left who really matters to me. You do. You have a whole network of friends and far more family than even those you invited. How many of them know about my existence?'

'The ones who matter—my immediate family—but I have no objection to people knowing we're married.' He strode to the bar in the corner of the room. 'Eventually anyone who needs to know will know because we took our vows for life.'

He grabbed a bottle of Scotch. The first drops of liquid hit the glass when Tabitha, quietly but with a large dose of steel in her husky voice, said, 'What do you feel for me?'

Perspiration broke out on his back. 'You know what I feel for you. Don't I show it in every possible way?'

'You're talking about sex again.'

'Sex is important.'

'Only if it comes with emotions. When we're not together, when you're alone in your Athens apartment…do you even think about me?'

He tipped the Scotch down his throat and fought to hear his own voice above the suddenly ferocious beats of his heart. 'Of course I do.'

'Then why do you never call?'

The echoes from his heart now drummed in his head. 'I didn't know you wanted me to.'

'I want you to *want* to call me.' Tabitha's exasperation was fleeting, her stomach too knotted for anything to hold inside her. This was a conversation she wished desperately that she hadn't started but one she knew it was essential to have. 'How can we sustain a life together if all there is between us is good sex?'

'It's a damn sight more than a lot of other couples have, but that's not all we have. We'll have a child too.'

'What about love?' she challenged, an icy chill creeping down her spine. 'Where does that come into it?'

He froze right before her eyes but not before a look of abject horror flashed across his face, freezing his features with the rest of him.

It was a look that spoke a thousand words.

Then the horror vanished as quickly as it had appeared and he nonchalantly poured himself another drink. 'I told you from the start that I don't want love. I've been there…'

'I know. It tastes bitter,' she finished for him. The room began to spin and she had to grind her toes into the carpet to keep herself upright. Hoarsely, she added, 'Yes, I remember you saying that, but so much has happened between us since you said it that I foolishly hoped your feelings towards me had changed.'

'Of course they've changed. Things have been great between us but I've never made false promises to you. I've never lied to you. We married for our child.'

Her entire body now cold but her brain *burning*, she stared at him for the longest time as everything became clear to her.

She'd fallen in love with this man the night they'd conceived their child. Her feelings for him since had been like a runaway train on an incline and she found herself hurtling towards a sheer drop at the end of the track. If she didn't pull the brake now she would plunge over the edge head-first onto the jagged rocks below.

He gazed back at her, gripping his glass, knuckles white.

She swallowed the sharp lump lodged in her throat. 'My feelings for you are simple,' she said slowly. 'I want your heart and I want you to be as proud and happy to call me your wife as I am to call you my husband. I want everything, Giannis, but I can see that it's not possible for me to have it. I think for both our sakes, and our child's sake, we should call it quits.'

'What the hell are you talking about?' He was staring at her as if she'd suddenly sprouted a second head.

'That I think we should cut our losses and end things now while we can keep things amicable.'

Anger darkened his features and he slammed his glass on the bar. 'No! You do not get to call it quits because I don't call you. If you're not happy with something, you talk about it and we deal with it.'

'I *am* talking to you but your answers are only confirming my worst fears. We are never going to have the marriage I want.'

Like a panther stalking its prey, he prowled towards her. 'I've given you everything you've asked of me. I've arranged for our child to have everything on my death, I only have eyes for you and intend to remain faithful for the rest of our lives—what more can you possibly want?'

Somehow she managed to get her watery legs to stand and face him. 'I want to feel that, even if there was no baby in my belly, you and I would still be here.'

'We're only here *because* of the baby. That is a fact, *matia mou*.' Before she knew what was happening, he had her pressed against the wall. His breath was hot against her ear, hot enough to seep through her skin and melt her love-sick bones. 'The night we created our child was the best of my life, surpassed only by the other nights we've shared since we married. I want you more than I have ever wanted anyone. The nights I'm apart from you I fantasise about making love to you. My blood burns for you…and I know your blood burns for me.' And then, as if proving his point, he crushed her mouth and kissed her, filling her senses with his dark taste.

For a few glorious moments she sank into the heat of his mouth, a small fix like a shot of caffeine to temper all the torrid emotions swirling inside her.

Heat pulsed through her, hard, strong, undeniable. Her aching body taking control, she hooked her arms around his neck, her lips parted…

And then sanity crashed through her harder than the caffeine shot and she wrenched her mouth away and pushed her hands to his chest. *'No!'*

With a muttered curse he stepped back, brow creased in confusion, breathing heavily.

'I know you want me *here*,' she cried, placing her hand on his groin, feeling for the very last time the strength of his desire for her before moving her hand and placing it on his chest. The thuds of his heart were heavy beneath her palm and she could have screamed with the anguish of what she must do.

'But I want you to want me *here* too, in your heart. I want you to call me when we're not together because you need to hear my voice. I want you to miss me when we're not together as much as I miss you. I want you to take me with you when you travel because you can't bear to be parted from me but, the truth is, if I'm not with you then I don't exist for you. Your feelings for me are all wrapped up in your desire for me and when that fades what are we going to be left with?'

He dragged his fingers violently through his hair, a tumult of emotions flickering over his face. 'No one knows what the future holds.'

'And you're not denying anything I've just said! We could have something really special here but you're not even prepared to try.' And, as she said the words, fury laced her veins and she shoved hard at his chest with all the pain ravaging her heart. 'You won't try because you're a coward. Love turned bitter for you with Anastasia so you're punishing me for it by refusing to embrace what we have.'

'That is the most ridiculous thing I have ever heard you say,' he snarled. 'I'm not punishing you for anything. You've been insecure about Anastasia from the start. How many times do I have to tell you—whatever feelings I had for that woman died the day I learned another man had fathered her child!'

'But at least you *had* feelings for her before it all turned to hate. You've punished me for her sins since the day I told you I was pregnant! It's infected every part of our relationship because you refuse to let go of your hate for her and embrace a future with me.'

His face whitened, the pulse on his jaw throbbing madly.

'I want happiness, Giannis, and I can't have that if I'm spending my life waiting for your interest in me to fade while holding on to the futile hope that one day you'll let me into your heart. I've spent enough of my life living in the shadows and having my very existence denied and I'm not prepared to go through it any more. I can't hold on to a dream that doesn't exist. If you can't even try to let go of the past and embrace a true future with me then I leave now.'

He grabbed hold of her arm and pulled her back to him. 'I'm not letting you go. You're my *wife*.'

'Then start treating me like your wife.' She yanked her arm from his hold. 'You think I want to go? This is breaking my heart, Giannis, but if I stay as things stand it's going to destroy me.'

The darkness shadowed his face again, his features contorting with a mixture of menace and anguish. 'I'm not letting you take my child from me.'

'I'm not taking it from you.' She kneaded her temples and blinked back the hot tears, terrified to unleash them. 'You're still its father, but right now it's being nurtured in my belly, and until it's born I will care for it.'

'What about the stable life we married to provide it with? If you leave then everything we've done will have been for nothing.'

'No, Giannis, it won't have been for nothing.' Hating to see the pain on his face, even though she knew his pain wasn't for her but their child, she flung her arms around his neck for the last time and pressed the lightest of kisses to his mouth. Then she stared into the clear blue eyes brimming with all the emotion she wished could be for her. 'It's for our baby's sake as much as mine that I must do this. I don't want it to live with a mother who's miserable all the time. Better he or she has two happy parents even if they are apart. You're the one who's taught me to be strong and the strength you've given me will make me a far better mother than I would have been.'

The strength he'd given her had also given her the spine she needed to put her future in her own hands.

She pulled away from him, no longer able to look at him, and walked out of the living room.

He followed her to the front door as she was hooking her handbag over her shoulder. Luckily her passport was already in it.

'Where will you go?' he asked stiffly.

'Back to England.' She blinked back the tears still fighting for release and swallowed. 'I'm going to do what you keep telling me to do and fight for what is mine. I'm going to get my inheritance back for me and our baby.'

He shut the door before she'd made it to the elevator.

* * *

She could do this. She was strong as Giannis had told her.

Leaving him had proved it as nothing else could.

She would not be second best any more. And she would not allow her inheritance and her child's inheritance to be stolen from her a minute longer.

She wouldn't even bang on the door.

This was her home. She had no intention of waiting politely for entry to be granted.

She took one deep breath and turned the handle.

The moment she crossed the threshold, Tabitha's bravado almost deserted her. Her palms went clammy and her heart began that awful sick thud of dread.

She closed her eyes and took another deep breath. Clearing her throat, she parted her lips, but before she could call out her stepmother appeared.

For a moment neither of them said anything, then the frigid mask that was Emmaline's Botoxed face spoke. 'What are you doing here?'

Tabitha wiped her hands on her trousers and fought for air.

'What are you doing here?' Emmaline repeated icily.

In desperation Tabitha brought Giannis's face to mind and his stern assurance that she was strong enough to confront her stepmother and reclaim what was hers.

This was something she *had* to do.

Ignoring the tremors in her hand, she pulled out the document from her bag and held it out.

'What is that?' Emmaline sneered.

Tabitha cleared her throat and looked her square in the eye. 'Copies of the documentary proof I've obtained that you used fraudulent methods to evict me from my home and steal my inheritance.'

Giannis's investigative team had been more thorough than she could have imagined.

She'd read through it in the hotel suite she'd checked into in England six days ago, the day after she'd left him. She was still using the hotel as her base and had no intention of leaving until her home was her own again and she could move back to the place she belonged.

She had to keep ignoring the voice that kept whispering Santorini was where she belonged.

Emmaline's mouth dropped open. Now she was the one struggling to speak.

Tabitha straightened and lifted her chin. 'I'm here to give you notice. You have one week to leave this house and transfer all my father's assets into my name or I call the police and have you prosecuted for theft and fraud.'

'You can't do that.'

'Every time you argue with me, I decrease it by a day. This house is not yours. It was never yours. You had no right to it and you always knew that—this house belonged to my mother. My father transferred it into her name when I was a baby as a gift to her and she bequeathed it to me when she became ill.'

Her parents *had* protected her inheritance. When it had been clear her mother couldn't survive, they'd drawn up a separate trust for the house which allowed her father to live in it for the rest of his life, but the ownership of it would become Tabitha's. He'd intended to surprise her with this when she turned twenty-one.

She knew why Emmaline had thought she could get away with stealing it. She'd thought Tabitha weak and she'd been right.

Not any more. Tabitha would never allow anyone to walk over her again. She would never again accept that things were the way they were and that all you could do was endure and survive.

She wanted to live.

'You stole my home from me and I have documentary

proof that you stole much more too. All you're entitled to is half of the income from the brewery. Considering you have had all that income for your greedy self these past five years, you can have no objection to signing the document that's also enclosed transferring your share into my name.'

She didn't have to threaten her again. The rouge on Emmaline's cheeks was stark against the whiteness of her cheeks.

'One week,' Tabitha said sweetly as she turned back to the door to leave. 'You know what you have to do. Oh, and before I go, send my love to your daughters.'

Walking back down the long gravelled driveway, fallen autumn leaves crunching beneath her feet, she climbed into the waiting taxi without looking back.

Only when the driver pulled onto the narrow backroad did her posture dissolve and the adrenaline that had carried her through the ordeal slump.

Before all her courage deserted her, she snatched her phone out of her bag and, after deliberating how best to phrase it, fired off a message to Giannis.

I've seen Emmaline. She'll be gone from the house in a week. Thank you for your help.

However things had ended between them, he'd done this for her. He'd gathered the evidence she needed to reclaim her inheritance and helped her find the strength she needed to confront Emmaline.

She would call him soon and speak to him but she wasn't ready for that yet. Her strength could only take her so far and, until she knew she could be in a room with him without falling to her knees and begging him to take her back, it was best she kept her distance.

But, God, she missed him. All that had kept her going this past week had been gearing herself up for that confrontation with her stepmother. It had given her a focus that had dulled the ache she carried in every cell of her body.

She would not go back to him. She couldn't. She could not live her life by his side knowing her love would never be reciprocated. Eventually it would destroy her. And what kind of example would it set for her child? She wanted her child to find love and fulfilment. One day she hoped to find it for herself too.

CHAPTER FOURTEEN

'WHAT ARE YOU doing here?'

Niki barged her way past Giannis uninvited. 'I'm going on a date and thought I'd see if Tabitha was in—I want to borrow that gorgeous choker you got her for her birthday. Is she here?'

'She's gone,' he answered baldly, his stomach clenching.

'Gone where?'

He shrugged again. It was easier than talking. In the week since Tabitha had walked out on him in Milan, he'd found his vocal cords too tight to make more than monotonous grunts. After a merciful week doing business in Toronto away from his inquisitive family, five hours back in Santorini and his peace was shattered.

'When will she be back?'

Another shrug.

'Have you turned into a mute?' Not waiting for an answer, she strolled through to his bar and began rummaging through the rows of liqueurs, spirits and wines. 'You're running low on white wine,' she observed cheerfully as she pulled a bottle of white out of the fridge. 'How did the party go?'

'What party?' he asked tiredly.

'Alessio's party.'

'It wasn't a party. It was a function.' And it felt like a lifetime ago.

She poked her tongue at him and poured them both a large glass. 'How did the "function" go?'

'Fine.'

'What did Alessio say when you told him you'd got married again? Was he cross that he wasn't invited?'

He took the glass she thrust in his hand and took a large drink of it. 'The subject didn't come up.'

'Why not? And if you give another shrug as an answer I'm going to punch you.' But before he could answer Niki's eyes narrowed as she looked properly at him. 'When was the last time you had a shave?'

'What?'

She put her face to his neck then pulled away with her nose wrinkling. 'You need a shower too.' Then she stilled and bit her lip. 'Giannis…where's Tabitha?'

The clenching in his stomach became a vice as he finally admitted, 'I don't know.'

'What do you mean, you don't know?'

His heart twisted so tightly he had to force the words out. 'She's left me.'

And she hadn't come back. All her clothes, her jewellery, her cosmetics, every single item he'd bought her, were still in her dressing room. She had money he'd given her in her bank account and, from the message he'd received a few hours ago—the first message she'd sent since leaving—had her house back.

She had no reason to come home to him.

The horror on his sister's face landed like a punch in his guts and he struggled to drag air into his lungs.

'What happened?' she eventually whispered.

'A difference of opinion.'

He could feel Niki's troubled eyes on him as he paced the vast living area—a space that had grown disproportionately since Tabitha had gone, enhancing her absence—to stand outside on the terrace overlooking the sea.

Far in the distance he spotted a yacht. He kept his gaze fixed on it when his sister joined him.

Something hot and rancid had been building up in him,

right from the pit of his stomach, for days. He'd smothered it and doused it but now he could feel it rising sharply inside him.

Niki sighed and placed her hand on his.

But her attempt at comfort felt like needles on his skin and he snatched his hand away.

'Is it fixable?' she asked quietly.

He shrugged.

She punched him on the arm.

'What was that for?' he growled.

'I did warn you I would punch you if you shrugged another answer. Tell me what happened.'

'I don't want to talk about it.' He downed the rest of his wine.

There was a long period of silence before she said, 'What are you going to do to get her back?'

'Nothing. She doesn't want to be with me any more.'

'Don't be stupid. She's crazy about you.'

His breath grew ragged and he gritted his teeth. 'We married to legitimise our child. It is disappointing that things haven't worked out but we are both agreed that we will continue to put our child's best interests first.'

'And you're happy with this? Because from where I'm standing you look as miserable as sin. Did you sleep in those clothes?'

The build-up of rage in his stomach suddenly exploded. Turning on his favourite sister, Giannis shouted, 'For once in your life can you keep your nose out of my affairs? My marriage is none of your business. Tabitha is none of your business. *I'm* none of your business, so do us both a favour and get out of my face and go meet your date.'

Niki was nothing if not his sister, and uttered words at him that would have once earned her a slap from their mother. 'What is wrong with you, Giannis? Where's the fearless brother I've always adored? You love Tabitha…'

'Love has *nothing* to do with our marriage.'

'Oh, get over yourself, you blind fool. Anyone can see you're crazy about each other, but instead of getting out there and doing everything in your power to bring her home you're moping like a love-sick teenager. Tabitha is the best thing that ever happened to you and if you're too stupid to see that and apologise for whatever you've done to make her leave then you really don't deserve her.'

'You automatically put the blame on me?' he roared.

'She left *you* which, yes, does imply that you're to blame. Tabitha loves you. There is no way she would have left if she didn't think she had no alternative…'

He couldn't listen to another word. With a roar that seemed to come from the depths of his soul, Giannis hurled the glass over the wall and onto the jagged rocks below where it shattered into a thousand shards.

It was the perfect mimicry of his own shattered heart.

A week later and Brigstock Manor was Tabitha's again.

Emmaline and her daughters were gone, as was most of the garish furniture they'd replaced her parents' furniture with.

Tabitha kept wandering through the mostly empty rooms as if she were in a dream. It didn't feel real.

This was her home. This was the place where all the ghosts of her past lived. The echo of her mother's laugh, the one thing she remembered about her with any clarity, was contained in these walls. Everything else about her parents had been erased. A part of her wanted to confront Emmaline and demand she replace everything she'd thrown away but her thickening waistline was all she needed to dissuade herself.

She had her home back. She would receive a regular income from the business and, after her child was born, she would do that business degree she'd always wanted to do and eventually take her rightful place on the Brigstock Brewery board.

Everything was going in the right direction. Now it was time to live her life again.

She just wished she didn't feel so lonely.

She wished she didn't still miss Giannis so much.

She still hadn't found the courage to call him. They'd exchanged a few polite messages about her health and the baby but nothing more than that.

She feared hearing his voice. But she heard it in her dreams, every single night. She would reach out for him in her sleep, the tears spilling before she could stop them.

She never cried when she was awake.

Three days after taking possession of the manor and hiring a cleaning firm to come in and blitz the place—she might be a master cleaner but this was a job much too big for her—she decided to get out of the cleaning crew's way and take a look in the attic. Maybe Emmaline had forgotten about the Brigstock stuff that had been stored up there for generations and had left it unharmed.

Checking her watch first—a specialist decorating firm was coming over later to give her a quote on redecorating the manor back to its original glory—she climbed the creaky narrow stairs that led to it and opened the hatch.

The attic covered the entire ceiling space. Tabitha remembered poking her head in it as a child and being frightened of the shadows.

What a scared little girl she had been to be frightened of shadows. No wonder her stepsisters had found her such an easy target to terrorise.

Judging from the dust that swirled in the air as she walked through it, no one had been in the attic in years, but she was cheered to find old furniture in there: a chesterfield sofa and armchair, a dressing table and wardrobe that would have been fashionable in the nineteenth century, a variety of ottomans amongst other smaller items and dozens and dozens of boxes.

A short while later, she opened the lid of another ottoman and found a nest of white lace. Her mother's wedding dress and Tabitha's christening outfit.

Hands shaking, she hugged the wedding dress to her chest and carried it to the full-length mirror carelessly left against one of the walls.

This was the dress her mother had worn the day she'd married her father, the day her father had once whispered had been the second-happiest of his life. The happiest had followed three years later when Tabitha had been born.

Suddenly she found her legs could hold her up no more and she sank onto the floor, tears flowing down her cheeks as if a dam had burst.

She would trade everything to have them back for just one day. One hour. One minute.

If they'd been there she would have had their comforting arms around her easing the pain of her broken heart.

Oh, she *missed* him. That so-called great healer called Time hadn't healed anything. She missed Giannis's smile, his laughter, his sardonic wit, his love-making, his tenderness. Everything. She missed everything. Her arms ached to hold him and touch him. She longed to see him—had to resist searching his name on her phone just as she had to resist speaking to him. She had never known pain like it and it tore at her then, in a way she'd fought letting it tear at her before, shredding her already broken heart.

Only when there was a loud bang on the attic hatch did she drag herself off the floor.

'Miss Brigstock?' came the voice of one of the cleaners. 'You have a visitor.'

'Tell him I'll be down in a minute,' she called back, hurriedly wiping her face. It must be the decorator.

She winced to see her reflection. Her face was puffy, her eyes red from crying.

So much for crying being cathartic. The first time she'd cried in over a fortnight and she felt worse than ever.

Neatly folding the dress back into the ottoman, she retied her loose ponytail, wiped the dust from her clothes and headed back down the narrow stairs.

Moving through to the drawing room where he would be waiting for her, she almost had a heart attack when she walked in and found Giannis sitting there stiffly on the window ledge.

Struck mute, she could only stare at him, heart thumping into immediate overdrive.

Their eyes connected and in that moment a wave of emotion so strong pulsed through her that she pressed her back to the wall to keep herself upright.

'Hello, Tabitha.'

Just to hear her name fall from his lips was enough to make her veins dance and she crossed her arms tightly across her chest, grinding her feet to the floor, doing everything in her power to stop her treacherous body from flying over to fling herself at him.

She cleared her tight throat and forced herself to speak. 'This is an unexpected surprise.'

But not a welcome one, Giannis suspected ruefully.

He stared at the beautiful face that had haunted his every waking moment for what felt like for ever and felt his heart rip.

She looked like she'd been crying.

'What brings you here?' She spoke politely but he heard the rawness in her voice.

'I wanted to see you...see the home you grew up in. Is something the matter, *matia mou*?'

Her shoulders rose and, though she pulled a rueful face,

she blinked numerous times, as if trying to hold back more tears. 'I just found my mother's wedding dress in the attic.'

She'd been in the attic? That explained the dust clinging to the slender frame that had thickened a touch in the seventeen days since he'd last seen her.

Chin wobbling, she pulled at her ponytail. 'Can I get you a drink? I don't have any alcohol but I've got tea and coffee.'

'No, thank you.'

'A tour of the house?' She didn't wait for a response, springing away from the door and heading straight out of the room.

Without ceremony she guided him quickly through the many rooms of the sprawling manor house. He didn't need to close his eyes to imagine Tabitha as a small child running happily through the spacious rooms, her happiness coming to a crashing end when her father had married the stepmother from hell.

He didn't make any comment until she opened a door on the first floor and muttered, 'This was Fiona's room.' Then she muttered something under her breath and stepped inside it to snatch something from under the bed.

She held the photograph up with a frown. 'I can add this to the bonfire.'

He looked at the three faces staring into the camera's lens and shuddered. All three were pretty—beautiful, even— and immaculately made up but their eyes were empty.

'Your stepfamily make the witches of Macbeth look like angels,' he quipped, trying to break the tension radiating from her. He hadn't come here to distress her.

She gave a bark of laughter and wiped a stray tear from her cheek as she walked out of the room. 'The witches of Macbeth would have been easier to live with,' she said over her shoulder but before she could walk away he put his hand on her shoulder.

It was an instinctive action that came from a hand that

had yearned to touch her from the moment she had stepped into the drawing room.

'I'm proud of you,' he said in a low voice, dropping his hand to hang uselessly by his side. 'You defeated the witches. I hope you can be happy now.'

Her rigid torso didn't move. 'I couldn't have done it without your help.'

'You would have. Everything my investigators discovered, you would have found out for yourself in your own time.'

He could hear her breathing.

Long moments passed before she rolled her shoulders and turned to face him.

'You should go,' she said quietly. 'I've got decorators coming over to give me a quote and a hundred other things I need to be getting on with.'

She gave him no time to answer, walking away from him to the end of the corridor and disappearing from his view down the ancient cantilevered stairs.

Throat closed, he followed her until he stood at the top of the stairs and she was taking the final step at the bottom.

'I fell in love with you when I saw you walking the stairs of my palace hotel,' he called to her.

Her foot hovered mid-air, hand tightening on the banister.

'You enchanted me from that first glance. When I found you gone the next morning... I spent weeks trying to find you.'

Slowly she turned to look up at him, her expression disbelieving.

Putting one foot before the other, Giannis reached into his pocket and pulled out the one reminder she'd left of their night together until she'd walked back into his life.

When he reached her at the bottom of the stairs he held it out to her in his open hand without speaking.

Slowly she plucked the earring from him and stared at it. Then shining cornflower eyes stared at him.

'I have carried that with me every day since that night,' he told her. 'I could not forget you. I tried. God knows I tried, but you were with me all the time, in my head, in my heart... I could not forget you. It's been the same since you left me but so much worse. You're in my head, *matia mou*, under my skin and in my heart. I have missed you more than I thought it was possible to miss another.'

To Tabitha's utter bewilderment, he sank down onto his knees before her and took her hand in his.

'Since you left me I can't breathe properly and I am here to ask you—to beg you—to please give me another chance.'

His words were like nectar to a starving, exhausted bee but Tabitha had been through too much, had wrung her heart out too much over him, to believe that the dream she had for them could come true.

She pulled her hand from his hold and stepped back. 'I'm sorry, Giannis, I want to believe you...'

He closed his eyes. His throat moved a number of times. 'You were right that I kept you at a distance. When I'm with you my feelings overwhelm me. I needed to keep control. I never lost control of my feelings with Anastasia but her infidelity still shattered me. What I felt for her... I won't insult you by downplaying it but my feelings for her were nothing compared with what I feel for you. I'm not going to lie—they terrified me. I never called you when we were apart, not because I didn't want to, but because I was trying to prove to myself that I didn't need you. The truth is, every minute spent apart from you was spent missing you and needing you.'

Tabitha covered her mouth. She wanted to cover her ears too but the nectar coming from his mouth was too sweet to resist.

Her aching, broken heart yearned to believe him.

He rose back to his feet and closed the space she had created between them.

'I spent our marriage trying to free myself from the spell you'd put me under, but I was a fool, because I couldn't see that it wasn't a spell of your creation but a spell binding us both.' Giannis took both her rigid hands in his and pulled them to his chest so she could feel the aching thuds of his heart. 'You felt it too, didn't you?'

The shining eyes finally spilled into tears and she gave an almost imperceptible nod that gave him the strength to continue.

'This heart beats only for you. You have my heart, my body and my soul. Without you I am nothing. I love you, *matia mou*, and if it takes me the rest of my life to make you believe that then that is how I will spend it. I am sorry for the pain I have caused you. I understand why you left me, and I swear on our child's life that if you give me another chance I will be the husband you deserve, and the husband I should have been from the start if I'd only had the courage to believe what my heart was telling me.'

It felt as if the earth made a full rotation before her beautiful mouth parted.

'I fell in love with you that night too,' she whispered, a dreamy smile playing on her heart-shaped lips. 'When I danced in your arms…it felt as if I'd been dropped into heaven. There were so many times when we were together when I felt that heaven again and being without you…' She sighed and pressed herself closer to him. 'I never wanted to leave you, Giannis. Being without you has been like living with a part of myself missing. You're my life.'

Unable to hold himself back a moment longer, he wrapped his arms around her and pulled her trembling frame tightly to him. 'I love you, Tabitha, with all that I am. Please come back to me.'

Her lips brushed against his throat then inched their way to his mouth. The kiss she bestowed on him was filled with such sweet tenderness that it spoke her answer for her.

Lifting her into his arms, Giannis carried his wife up the stairs to her bedroom where the passion that had always consumed them came alive once more. But this time it was for ever.

EPILOGUE

THERE WASN'T A cloud in the cobalt Santorini sky. The late-afternoon sun beamed down, its rays matching the rays bursting out of Tabitha's heart.

Giannis's sisters fussed with her hair and her dress. Helena, the fashion designer sister who'd made the alterations needed for the wedding dress to fit Tabitha's post-baby frame, anxiously checked it every five seconds. Katarina, dressed in an identical bridesmaid's dress to her sisters, rocked a fractious baby Elise in her arms, refusing to hand Elise back to Tabitha in case the three-month-old baby was sick on her dress. It was with much relief that Giannis's mother, who was the designated babysitter for the day, returned from greeting the entire extended Basinas family, all squashed like sardines within the confines of the blue-topped church, snatched her newest grandchild into her arms and bustled back inside with her.

The only one of their small party stood on the steps of the church not nervous was Tabitha. She couldn't wait to get in there.

A sharp elbow landed in her ribs. 'Look,' shouted Niki, laughing.

Tabitha followed her gaze and saw a small plane flying over them with her and Giannis's names trailing behind it on a long banner.

She saw something else too that filled her heart with equal joy at this public declaration of her husband's love. The moon had risen on this long summer's day too, as if it had come out early to celebrate with them. She imagined her parents sat on it, watching her. She thought they would approve that this time, the time when the vows she was going to exchange meant everything, she was wearing the wedding dress that had belonged to Elise, her mother. And she thought they would approve of how she had given Brigstock Manor to the local authority to be turned into a children's home.

She blew the moon a kiss, then stepped inside the church to renew her wedding vows to the man who had made her the happiest woman on earth.

* * * * *

WED FOR THE SPANIARD'S REDEMPTION

CHANTELLE SHAW

For Adrian.
Being a writer's husband is no easy job!
Love you.

CHAPTER ONE

Spanish Stud's Sex Romp with
Cabinet Minister's Wife!

RAFAEL MENDOZA-CASILLAS SCOWLED as he sifted through
the pile of newspapers on his desk. All the tabloids bore
similar headlines, and even the broadsheets had deemed
that it was in the public interest to report his affair with
Michelle Urquhart.

The story wasn't only in the UK. All across Europe people were eating their breakfast while studying
a front-page photograph of the heir to Spain's biggest
retail company entering a top London hotel late at night
accompanied by the voluptuous Mrs Urquhart. A second photo showed him and Michelle leaving the hotel
by a back door the next morning.

One can only speculate on how Europe's most
prolific playboy and the Minister's wife spent the
intervening hours!

That was one journalist, writing in a particularly
tacky tabloid.

'It is one scandal too many, Rafael.'

Hector Casillas's strident voice shook with anger and Rafael held his phone away from his ear.

'On the very day that the company's top-selling Rozita fashion line launches a new bridal collection *your* affair with a married woman is headline news. You have made the Casillas Group a laughing stock.'

'I was not aware that Michelle is married,' Rafael said laconically when his grandfather paused to draw a breath.

Not that her marital status interested him particularly. He was not responsible for other people's morals—especially as his own morality was questionable. But if he'd known that Michelle's husband was a public figure he would not have slept with her. Even though she had made it clear that she was available within minutes of him meeting her in a nightclub. Rafael never had a problem finding women to occupy his bed and, frankly, Michelle had not been worth this fallout.

He leaned back in his chair and watched the rain lash the windows of his office at the Casillas Group's UK headquarters in London's Canary Wharf. The Casillas Group was one of the world's largest clothing retailers, and as well as Rozita the company owned several other top fashion brands.

Rafael visualised his grandfather sitting behind his desk in the study of the opulent Casillas family mansion in Valencia. There had been many occasions in the past when he had been summoned to that study so that Hector could lecture him on his failings and remind him—as if Rafael needed to be reminded—that he was part *gitano*. The English word for *gitano* was gypsy, and in other areas of Europe the term was *Roma*. But the meaning was the same—Rafael was an outsider.

'Yet again you have brought shame on the family

and, even worse, on the company,' Hector said coldly. 'Your mother warned me that you had inherited many of your father's faults. When I rescued you from the slums and brought you into the family I intended that you would succeed me as head of the Casillas Group. You are my grandson, after all. But sadly there is too much of your father's blood in you, and tacking Casillas on to your name does not change who you are.'

Rafael's jaw clenched and he told himself he should have expected this dig. His grandfather never missed an opportunity to remind him that he did not have the blue blood of Spanish nobility running through his veins. His father had been a low-life drug dealer, and his mother's relationship with him, a rebellion against the Casillas family's centuries-old aristocratic heritage, had ended when she'd fled from Ivan Mendoza, leaving behind Rafael and his baby sister in a notorious slum on the outskirts of Madrid.

'The situation cannot continue. I have decided that you must marry—and quickly.'

For a moment Rafael assumed that he had misheard Hector. 'Abuelo…' he said in a placating tone.

'The board want me to name Francisco as my successor.'

A lead weight dropped into the pit of Rafael's stomach. 'You would put a *boy* in charge? The Casillas Group is a global company with a multi-billion-dollar annual turnover. Frankie would be out of his depth.'

'Your half-brother is twenty and in a year he will finish studying at university. More importantly he keeps his pants on.'

Bile burned a bitter path down Rafael's throat. 'Has my mother put you up to this? She has never made it a secret that she thinks her second son is a true Casillas and should be the heir to the company.'

'No one has put me up to anything. I make my own decisions,' Hector snapped. 'But I share the concerns of the board members and the shareholders that your notoriety and frequent appearances in the gutter press do not reflect well on the company. Our CEO should be a man of high principles and an advocate of family values. I am prepared to give you one more chance, Rafael. Bring your wife to my eightieth birthday celebrations at the beginning of May and I will retire from my position as Chairman and CEO and appoint you as my successor.'

'I have no desire to marry,' Rafael gritted, barely able to control his anger.

'In that case I will appoint your half-brother as my heir on my eightieth birthday.'

'*Dios!* Your birthday is six weeks from now. It will be impossible for me to find a bride and marry her in such a short time.'

'Nothing is impossible,' Hector said smoothly. 'Over the last eighteen months you have been introduced to several high-born Spanish women and any one of them would be a suitable wife for you. If you want to be my heir badly enough you will present your bride to me and we will have a double celebration to mark my landmark birthday and your marriage.'

Hector ended the call and Rafael swore as he threw his phone down on the desk. The old man was crazy. It was tempting to think his grandfather had lost his marbles, but Rafael knew that Hector Casillas was a shrewd businessman. The CEO-ship had been passed down to the next generation's firstborn male since Rafael's great-great-great-grandfather had established the company, one hundred and fifty years ago.

Hector Casillas's only offspring had been a daughter so Rafael, the oldest grandson, was next in line. But he knew that many on the board of directors and many of his relatives were not in favour of an outsider—which was how they regarded him—being handed the reins of power.

Hector's words taunted him. *'If you want to be my heir badly enough...'* Rafael bared his teeth in a mirthless smile. Becoming CEO of the company was the *only* thing he wanted. Being named as his grandfather's successor had been his dream, his obsession, since he was a skinny twelve-year-old kid who had been taken from poverty into the unimaginably wealthy lifestyle of his aristocratic family.

He was determined to prove that he was worthy of the role to his detractors, of whom there were many—including his mother and her second husband. Alberto Casillas was his mother Delfina's second cousin, which meant that their son Francisco was a Casillas to his core. Like that of many aristocratic families, the Casillas gene pool was very exclusive, and the majority of Rafael's relatives wanted it to stay that way.

But the retail industry was going through big changes, with increasing focus on internet sales, and Rafael understood better than most of the board members that the Casillas Group must use innovation and new technology so that it could continue to be a market leader. His grandfather had been a great CEO but now new blood was needed.

But not a gitano's blood, taunted a voice inside him. Once he had begged for food like a stray dog on the filthy streets of a slum. And, like a dog, he had learned to run fast to avoid his father's fists.

Rafael shut off the dark memories of his childhood and turned his thoughts to the potential brides his grandfather had mentioned. He'd guessed there must be an ulterior motive when his mother had invited the daughters of various elite Spanish families to dinner parties and insisted that Rafael should attend. But he hadn't taken the bait which had been dangled in front of him and he had no intention of doing so—despite Hector's ultimatum.

He would have to marry, but he would choose his own bride. And it would *not* be a love match, he thought cynically.

A psychologist would probably suggest that Rafael's trust issues and avoidance of commitment stemmed from his being abandoned by his mother when he was seven. The truth was that he could forgive her for deserting *him*, but not for leaving his sister, who had been a baby of not even two years old. Sofia's distress had been harder for him to bear than his father's indifference, or the sting of Ivan Mendoza's belt across the back of Rafael's legs.

His determination to gain acceptance by the Casillas family was as much for his sister as for himself. He *would* be CEO and he was prepared to offer a financial incentive to any woman who would agree to be his temporary wife.

Once he had achieved his goal there would be no reason to continue with his unwanted marriage, Rafael brooded as he grabbed his briefcase and car keys and strode out of his office.

His PA looked up when he stopped by her desk. 'I'm going to my ten o'clock meeting and I should be back around lunchtime,' he told her. 'If my grandfather calls again tell him that I am unavailable for the rest of the day.' He paused on his way out of the door. 'Oh, and, Philippa—get rid of those damned newspapers from my office.'

The day couldn't get any worse, surely?

Juliet chucked her phone onto the passenger seat of the van and slid the key into the ignition. She wouldn't cry, she told herself. After she had lost her parents in the car accident which had also ended her dancing career she'd decided that nothing could ever be so terrible that it would warrant her tears.

But today had started disastrously, when she'd read a letter from an Australian law firm informing her that Bryan intended to seek custody of Poppy. A knot of fear tightened in her stomach. She couldn't lose her daughter. Poppy was her reason for living, and even though her life as a single mum was a struggle she would fight with the last breath in her body to keep her little girl rather than hand her over to her father, who had never shown any interest in her until now.

A phone conversation with her business partner Mel a few minutes ago had been the final straw on this day from hell. *Her life was falling apart!*

Juliet watched the rain streaming down the windscreen and blinked back her tears. There was no point sitting here in the car park behind the Casillas Group's plush offices in Canary Wharf. She still had sandwich deliveries to make to other offices in the area. Her business, Lunch To Go, might be facing ruin, but her customers had paid for their sandwiches and wraps and they were expecting her to turn up.

She sniffed as she started the engine and pulled her

seat belt across her lap before putting the van into gear and pressing her foot down on the accelerator pedal. But instead of moving forward the van lurched backwards, and there was a loud bang followed by the tinkling sound of broken glass.

For a split second Juliet couldn't think what had happened. But when she looked in her rear-view mirror it was obvious that she had reversed into the car which had swung into the parking bay behind her.

And not just any car, she realised with mounting horror. The sleek gunmetal-grey Lamborghini was one of the most expensive cars in production—so Danny, the parking attendant who allowed her to park her van in this car park, which was reserved exclusively for Casillas Group executives, had told her.

The day had just got a whole lot worse.

She watched the owner of the Lamborghini climb out of his car and stoop down to inspect the front bumper. Rafael Mendoza-Casillas: managing director of the Casillas Group UK, international playboy and sex god—if the stories about his love-life which regularly appeared in a certain type of newspaper were to be believed.

Juliet's heart collided with her ribs when he straightened up and strode towards her van. The thunderous expression on his handsome face galvanised her into action and she released her seat belt and opened the driver's door. God, she hoped the damage to his car wasn't too bad or too expensive to repair. A claim on her vehicle insurance would bump up her premium next year.

'*Idiota!* Why did you try to reverse out of your parking space? If you'd had the sense to use your mirror you would have seen that I had parked behind you.'

His gravelly voice with its distinct Mediterranean

accent was clipped with anger. But it was the sexiest voice Juliet had ever heard and her skin prickled with awareness of the man who towered over her.

She was five feet four—the minimum height for dancers in the *corps de ballet*—and she had to tilt her head so that she could look at him. His eyes were an unusual olive-green, glinting furiously in his tanned face. And what a face. Juliet had caught sight of him occasionally at the Casillas Group offices, when she'd been delivering sandwiches, but he hadn't so much as glanced at her whenever she'd walked past him in a corridor. One time she'd entered the lift as he had stepped out of it and the sleeve of his jacket had brushed against her arm. The spicy scent of his aftershave had stayed with her for the rest of the day, and now her stomach muscles contracted when she inhaled his exotic fragrance.

'I'm not an idiot,' she muttered, stung by his superior tone and dismayed by her unbidden reaction to his potent masculinity.

The torrential rain was flattening his thick black hair to his skull, but nothing could detract from his film star looks. With chiselled features, razor-edged cheekbones and a square jaw shaded with dark stubble, he was utterly gorgeous. Beneath her apron, which was part of her uniform, Juliet felt her nipples tighten.

Heavy black brows winged upwards, as if he was surprised that she had answered him back. 'The evidence suggests otherwise,' he drawled. 'I hope your vehicle insurance will cover you for an accident on private land. This car park has a notice which clearly states that it is for the Casillas Group's senior staff's use only. You are trespassing, and if your insurance is not valid you can look forward to receiving a hefty repair bill for the damage you have caused to my car.'

Of course she would be covered by her insurance—wouldn't she? Doubt crept into Juliet's mind and her shoulders sagged. 'I'm sorry. It was an accident, as you said. I didn't mean to reverse into your car.' Panic swept through her. 'I don't have the money to pay for your repairs.'

The rain had soaked through her shirt and was dripping off her peaked cap. She remembered how excited she and Mel had been when they had ordered the red caps and aprons with their company logo on. They'd had such high hopes for their sandwich business when they'd started up a year ago, but the two bombshells Juliet had received today made it likely that now Lunch To Go would fold.

To make matters even worse, the most handsome man she'd ever set eyes on was now glaring at her as if she was something unpleasant that he'd scraped off the bottom of his shoe.

Misery welled up inside her and the tears that she'd managed to hold back until now ran down her cheeks, mingling with the rain. 'The truth is that I don't even have enough money to buy my daughter a new pair of shoes,' she said in a choked voice.

She'd felt so guilty when Poppy had said yesterday that her shoes made her toes hurt. And now there was a pain in Juliet's chest as if the oxygen was being squeezed out of her lungs. She couldn't breathe. She felt as if a dam inside her had burst, releasing the emotions she had held back for so long.

'I certainly can't afford to pay for work on your fancy car. What will happen if my insurance company refuses to pay for the damage? I can't take out a bank loan because I already have debts…'

Her logical thought processes had given way to near

hysteria. Ever since her parents had been killed in that horrific accident she had subconsciously been waiting for another disaster.

'Could I be sent to prison? Who would look after my daughter? If I'm deemed to be a bad mother Bryan will be allowed to take Poppy to Australia and I'll hardly ever see her.'

It was Juliet's worst fear and she covered her face with her hands and wept.

'Calm yourself,' Rafael Mendoza-Casillas commanded. 'Of course you won't go to prison,' he said impatiently as her shoulders shook with the force of her sobs. 'I am sure your insurance will cover the cost of the repairs to my car, and if it doesn't I will not demand money from you.'

Juliet's relief at his assurance was temporary. Her other problems still seemed insurmountable and she couldn't stop crying.

Rafael swore. 'We need to get out of this rain before we drown,' he muttered as he took hold of her arm and led her towards his car. He opened the passenger door. 'Get in and take a few minutes to bring yourself under control.' Moments later he slid into the driver's seat and raked a hand through his wet hair. He opened the glove box and thrust some tissues into her lap. 'Here. Dry your tears.'

'Thank you.' She mopped her eyes and took a deep breath. In the confines of the car she was conscious of his closeness. She smelled rain, and the cologne he wore. Another indefinable scent which was uniquely male teased her senses.

'I'm making your car wet,' she mumbled when she was able to speak. She was conscious that her rain-soaked clothes were dripping onto the car's cream leather upholstery. 'I really am sorry about damaging your car, Mr Mendoza-Casillas.'

'You can call me Rafael. My surname is a mouthful, don't you think?' There was an oddly bitter note in his voice. 'What is your name?'

'Juliet Lacey.' She supposed he needed to know her name and other details for the insurance claim.

Her eyes were drawn to his hard-boned profile and a sizzle of heat ran through her, counteracting the cold that was seeping into her skin from her wet clothes. He glanced at her and she quickly looked away from him. She could not bear to think what she must look like, wet and bedraggled, with her face blotchy and her eyes red-rimmed from crying.

'I apologise for losing my temper. I did not mean to frighten or upset you,' he said curtly. 'You said that you have a child?'

'Yes, a three-year-old daughter.'

'*Dios*, you can only be—what?—nineteen?—and you have a three-year-old?' He sounded faintly appalled. 'I assume that as you are not wearing a wedding ring you're not married.'

'I'm twenty-four,' she corrected him stiffly, 'and, no, I'm not married. Poppy's father didn't want anything to do with either of us when she was born.'

'Who is this Bryan you mentioned?'

'He's Poppy's father. He has now decided that he wants custody of her. Under Australian law both parents are responsible for their child, even if they have never married or been a couple. Bryan can afford the best lawyers and if he wins the court case he intends to take Poppy to live in Australia with him.'

More tears filled Juliet's eyes and she scrubbed them away with a tissue.

'It's so unfair,' she blurted out. 'Bryan saw Poppy once when she was a baby. He told me he might have been more interested if she'd been a boy. But it's my word against his that he rejected his daughter. His lawyers are twisting everything to make it seem as though I refused to allow him to see his child. But I only brought Poppy back to England because Bryan insisted he wanted nothing to do with her.'

Juliet had no idea why she was confiding in Rafael when she didn't know him, and she was sure he wouldn't be interested in her problems. But there was something strangely reassuring about his size and obvious strength, the air of power that surrounded him. Words had tumbled from her lips before she could stop them.

'I've heard through my cousin, who lives in Sydney, that Bryan is dating the daughter of a billionaire and he wants to marry her. Apparently his girlfriend can't have children of her own because of a medical condition, but she desperately wants a child. My guess is that Bryan hopes to persuade his heiress to marry him if he can present her with a cute little daughter.'

Juliet bit her lip. 'Eighteen months ago Poppy spent a few weeks in temporary foster care when I had to go into hospital. She was very happy staying with the lovely family who looked after her. But somehow Bryan has found out that Poppy was fostered and he's using it as proof that I can't give her a secure upbringing and she'll be better off living with him.'

'Couldn't someone in your family have looked after your daughter while you were in hospital?'

The anger had gone from Rafael's voice and the sexy huskiness of his accent sent a little tremor through Juliet.

'My parents are dead and my only other relatives live in Australia. My aunt and uncle were kind to me when I stayed with them after my parents died, but they have busy lives and I try to manage on my own.'

'Why are you short of money?' Rafael turned his head towards her and Juliet felt his gaze sweep over her cap and apron. 'I take it that you have a job? What do the initials LTG stand for?'

'Lunch To Go is my sandwich business, which I co-own with my business partner. We've only been running for a year and our profit margins have been low while we have been getting established.' She gave another sniff and crumpled the soggy tissue in her hand. 'Things are finally looking up. But today I was called in by your HR manager and told that the contract we have to supply sandwiches to the Casillas Group's staff will finish at the end of the week because a new staff canteen is to open.'

Rafael nodded. 'When I established the London headquarters of the company it was always my plan to open a restaurant and a gym in the basement of the building for staff to use in their lunch break. The construction work took longer than anticipated and I asked HR to make a temporary alternative arrangement for staff to be able to buy their lunch from an outside source but still be subsidised by the company.'

'I didn't know about the staff restaurant,' Juliet said dully.

She'd never been down to the basement level—although she had overheard a couple of secretaries talking about the new staff gym. Her contract with the Casillas Group only required her to be given a week's notice.

'Will losing the contract have an impact on your business?'

'It will halve our profits,' she admitted heavily. 'I thought we could advertise for new customers at other offices—although a number of other food delivery companies have started up in this area, and the competition is high. And then I spoke to my business partner after my meeting and Mel told me she's going to sell the bakery shop where we're based. Her decision is for personal reasons—she and her husband want to move out of London. Mel owns the shop, and I can't afford to buy it or rent a new premises.'

'If your business closes what will you do?'

She shrugged. 'I'll have to look for another job, but I don't have any qualifications, or training in a career, and it will be almost impossible to earn enough to cover childcare for Poppy.'

Juliet thought of the home study business degree she had started but had had to abandon because she hadn't been able to afford the fees for the second year. That degree would have enabled her to find a better-paid job, or at least given her knowledge of the business strategies which would have been useful to develop Lunch To Go. But without Mel she simply could not manage, either financially or practically, to run the sandwich business.

Rafael was drumming his fingers on the steering wheel and seemed to be deep in thought. He had beautiful hands. Juliet imagined his tanned hands sliding over her naked body, those long fingers curving around her breasts and caressing the sensitive peaks of her nipples. Heat swept through her and she was startled by her wayward thoughts.

Bryan had broken her heart when he'd dumped her the morning after she'd given her virginity to him. A month later, when she'd tearfully told him that she was pregnant with his baby, his cruel rejection of her and her unborn child had forced her to grow up fast. She had felt a fool for falling for his easy charm and had vowed never to be so trusting again.

Being a single mother had left her little time to meet men, and it was a shock to discover that she could still feel sexual awareness and desire. Perhaps she was attracted to Rafael because he was so far out of her league that there was no chance that anything would come of it—a bit like a teenager with a crush on a pop star they were never likely to meet in real life, Juliet thought ruefully.

'I may be able to help you,' Rafael said, jolting her out of her reverie.

Her heart leapt. If he agreed to allow her to continue selling sandwiches to his office staff her business might just survive.

'Help me how?'

'I have an idea that would resolve your financial worries and also be advantageous to me.'

Juliet stiffened. 'What do you mean by "advantageous"?'

Was he suggesting what she thought he was? She knew that some of the women on the housing estate where she lived worked as prostitutes. Most of them were single mothers like her, struggling to feed their children on minimum wages. She didn't judge them, but it wasn't something she could ever imagine doing herself.

She put her hand on the door handle, ready to jump out of the car. 'I won't have sex with you for money,' she said bluntly.

For a few seconds he looked stunned—and then he laughed. The rich sound filled the car and made Juliet think of golden sunshine. She felt as if it had been rain-

ing in her heart since her parents had died and she'd
been left alone. How wonderful it would be to have
someone to laugh with, be happy with.

With a jolt she realised that Rafael was speaking.

'I don't want to have sex with you.'

His slight emphasis on the word *you* made Juliet
squirm with embarrassment, which intensified when
he skimmed his gaze over her. His dismissive expression said quite clearly that he found her unattractive.

'I have never had to pay for sex with any woman,' he
drawled. 'What I am suggesting is a business proposition—albeit an unusual one.'

'I make sandwiches for a living,' she said flatly,
wishing the ground would open up and swallow her. 'I
can't think what kind of business we could do together.'

'I want you to be my wife. If you agree to marry me
I will pay you five million pounds.'

CHAPTER TWO

'VERY FUNNY,' JULIET muttered, disappointment thickening her voice. 'I'm not in the mood for jokes, Mr Mendoza-Casillas.'

'Rafael,' he corrected her. 'And it's not a joke. I need a wife. A temporary wife—in name only,' he added, evidently reading the crucial question that had leapt into her mind. He stared at her broodingly. 'You have admitted that being a single parent is a financial burden. What if, instead of struggling, you could live a comfortable life with your daughter without having to work?'

'Some hope,' she said ruefully. 'I'd have to win the lottery to be able to do that.'

'Consider me your winning ticket, *chiquita*.'

His sudden smile softened his chiselled features and stole Juliet's breath. When he smiled he went from handsome to impossibly gorgeous. He reminded her of the male models on those TV adverts for expensive aftershaves—only Rafael was much more rugged and masculine.

She tore her eyes from him, conscious that her heart was beating at twice its normal rate. 'You're crazy,' she told him flatly.

And so was she, to be still sitting in his car. Five million pounds! He couldn't be serious. Or if he was serious there must be a catch. She felt hot, remembering his amused reaction to her suggestion that he was offering to pay her for sex. God, what had made her say that? Many of today's newspapers had a photo on the front page of Rafael and a beautiful blonde woman with an eye-catching cleavage. Juliet glanced down at her shapeless figure. She looked like a stick insect compared to Rafael's latest love interest.

'If you need a wife why don't you marry your girl-friend, whose picture is all over the front pages of the papers?'

'For one thing, Michelle is already married—but even if she were free to marry me she would not be suitable. All of my lovers, past and current, would expect me to fall in love with them,' he said drily.

He was so arrogant! She wanted to come back with a clever comment but she was mesmerised by the perfect symmetry of his angular features, which were softened a little by his blatantly sensual mouth.

'But you're not worried that *I* might fall in love with you?' She'd intended to sound sarcastic, but instead her voice was annoyingly breathless.

'I don't recommend that you do,' he said in a hard voice. 'I do not believe in love,—or marriage, for that matter. I'm not crazy,' he insisted. 'I have a genuine reason for needing to be married.'

He swore when his phone rang, and then took his mobile out of his jacket pocket and cut the call.

'We can't talk now. I'll meet you this evening and we can discuss my proposition.'

She shook her head. 'I'm not interested.'

'Not interested in earning yourself five million pounds for being my wife for a couple of months?' He reached across her and put his hand over hers to prevent her from opening the car door. 'At least give me a chance to explain, and then you can make up your mind whether I'm crazy or not. Although, frankly, you would be foolish to miss out on the chance to earn a life-changing amount of money. Think what you could do with five million pounds. You would never have to worry about the cost of buying your little girl a pair of shoes ever again.'

'All right.' Juliet released a shaky breath. He was relentlessly persuasive. She couldn't think properly when his face was so close to hers that as he leaned across her body she was able to count his thick black eyelashes. 'I'll meet you to discuss your proposition, but I'm not saying that I'll agree to it.'

She pressed herself into the leather seat, hoping he would not notice the pulse at the base of her throat that she could feel thudding erratically. It would add to her humiliation if he guessed that she was attracted to him—especially as he quite obviously did not feel the same way about her.

'It will have to be after nine,' she told him. 'I work the evening shift as a cleaner at a shopping centre close to where I live.'

Juliet felt a mixture of relief and disappointment when Rafael straightened up and moved away from her.

He handed her a business card. 'Here is my phone number. Text me your address and I'll collect you from your home at nine-fifteen.' He frowned. 'What about your daughter? Does someone look after her while you are at work in the evenings?'

'Of course I have childcare for Poppy. I certainly wouldn't leave her on her own,' she said indignantly, stung by his implication that she might be an irresponsible mother.

It was the accusation that Bryan's lawyer had levelled against her, and remembering the custody battle she was facing over her daughter evoked a heavy sense of dread in the pit of her stomach.

Five million pounds would enable her to hire her own top lawyer to fight Bryan's claim on Poppy, Juliet thought as she climbed out of Rafael's car and ran through the rain back to her van. But she would be nuts even to consider the idea.

Rafael parked his Lamborghini outside a grim-looking tower block and his conviction that it had been a mistake to suggest to a woman he had never met before today that she should marry him grew stronger. He visualised Juliet Lacey, who had resembled a drowned rat when he'd shoved her into his car out of the rain. Her voluminous apron had covered her figure, but from what he'd been able to see she was skinny rather than curvaceous. Her face had been mostly hidden behind by the peak of a baseball cap that was surely the most unfeminine and unflattering headwear.

In Rafael's opinion women should be elegant, decorative and sexy, but the waif-like sandwich-seller failed on all counts. His fury that she had damaged his beloved Lamborghini had turned to impatience when she'd burst into tears. He was well aware of how easily women could turn on the waterworks when it suited them. But as he'd watched Juliet literally fall apart in front of him he'd felt a flicker of sympathy.

He had heard a woman sob brokenly only once before, in the slum where he had spent the first twelve years of his life. Maria Gonzales had been a neighbour, a kind woman who had often given food to him and his sister. But Maria's teenage son had been drawn into one of the many drug gangs who'd operated in the slum and Pedro had been stabbed in a fight. Rafael had never forgotten the sound of Maria's raw grief as she'd wept over the body of her boy.

When Juliet had told him of her financial problems and her fear that she might lose custody of her young daughter the idea had formed in his mind that she would make him an ideal wife. The money he was prepared to pay her would change her life, and more importantly she would have no expectations that their marriage would be anything other than a business deal.

Maybe he *was* crazy, Rafael thought as he climbed out of his car and glanced around the notoriously rough housing estate—a concrete jungle where the walls were covered in graffiti. A gang of surly-looking youths were staring at his car, and they watched him suspiciously when he walked past them on his way into the tower block. He guessed that the older male in the group, who was wearing a thick gold chain around his neck, was a drug dealer.

Rafael had grown up in a shanty town on the out-skirts of Madrid, where dire poverty was a breeding ground for crime and lawless gangs ruled the street. His father had been involved in the criminal under-world, and as a boy Rafael had seen things that no child should see.

His jaw tightened as he took the lift up to the eleventh floor and strode along a poorly lit walkway strewn with litter. The tower block was not a slum but a sense of poverty and deprivation pervaded the air, as well as a pungent smell of urine. It was not a good place to bring up a child.

Juliet and her young daughter were not his responsibility, he reminded himself. But it was hard to see

how she would turn down five million pounds and the
chance to move away from this dump.

He knocked on the door of her flat and it opened
almost immediately. Rafael guessed from the unbe-
coming nylon overall Juliet was wearing that she must
have returned from her cleaning job only minutes before he'd arrived. Without the baseball cap hiding her
face he saw that she had delicate features, and might
even have been reasonably pretty if she hadn't been so
pale and drawn. Her hair was a nondescript brownish
colour, scraped back from her face and tied in a long
braid. Only her light blue eyes, the colour of the sky
on an English spring day, were at all remarkable. But
the dark shadows beneath them emphasised her waif-
like appearance.

A suspicion slid into Rafael's mind, and when Juliet
took off her overall to reveal a baggy grey T-shirt that
looked fit for the rag bag he studied her arms. There
were none of the tell-tale track marks associated with
drug addiction.

He flicked his gaze over cheap, badly fitting jeans
tucked into scuffed black boots and thought of glam-
orous Camila Martinez, the daughter of the Duque de
Feria and his grandfather's favoured contender to be
Rafael's bride.

The difference between aristocratic Camila, who
could trace her family's noble lineage back centuries,
and Juliet, who looked as if she had stepped from the
pages of *Oliver Twist*, was painfully obvious. It would
show his grandfather that he was not a puppet willing
to dance to the old man's tune if he turned up at Hector's birthday party and announced that he had married this drab sparrow instead of a golden peacock,

Rafael mused, feeling a flicker of amusement as the scene played out in his imagination.

'I told you to call me when you arrived and I would meet you outside the flats,' Juliet greeted him. 'If you've left your car on the estate there's a good chance it will be vandalised. There's a big problem with gangs around here.'

Rafael shuddered inwardly at the thought of his Lamborghini being damaged. 'This area is not a safe place for you to be out alone at night,' he said gruffly, thinking that she must have to walk through the estate in the dark every evening when she'd finished her cleaning shift.

He looked along the narrow hallway as a door opened and a small child darted out.

'Mummy, where are you going?'

The little girl had the same slight build and pale complexion as her mother. She stared at Rafael warily and he was struck by how vulnerable she was—how vulnerable they *both* were.

Juliet lifted her daughter into her arms. 'Poppy, I've told you I'm going out for a little while with a…a friend and Agata is going to look after you.'

An elderly woman emerged from the small sitting room and gave Rafael a curious look. 'Come back to bed, *kotek*. I will read to you and it will help you to fall back to sleep.' She took the child from Juliet. 'The baby will be happy with me. Go and have the nice dinner with your friend.'

'Who is looking after your daughter?' Rafael asked when Juliet followed him out of the flat and shut the front door behind her. She had pulled on a black fake leather jacket that looked as cheaply made as the rest of her outfit.

For a moment he wondered what the hell he was doing. Could he *really* marry this insipid girl who looked much younger than mid-twenties?

But her air of innocence had to be an illusion, he reminded himself, thinking of her illegitimate child. And besides, he did not care what she looked like. All he was interested in was putting a wedding ring on her finger. Once he had fulfilled his grandfather's outrageous marriage ultimatum he would be CEO of the Casillas Group. He did not anticipate that he would spend much time with his wife and would seek to end the marriage as soon as possible.

'Agata is a neighbour,' Juliet said. 'She's Polish and very kind. I couldn't do my cleaning job if she hadn't agreed to babysit every evening. Poppy doesn't have any grandparents but she loves Agata.'

'What happened to your parents?'

'They were killed in a car accident six years ago.'

Her tone was matter-of-fact, but Rafael sensed that she kept a tight hold on her emotions and her breakdown earlier in the day had been unusual.

'I believe you said that you have no other family apart from some relatives in Australia?'

She nodded. 'Aunt Vivian is my mum's sister. I stayed with her and my uncle and three cousins, but they only have a small house and it was a squeeze—especially after I had Poppy.'

So Juliet did not have any family in England who might question her sudden marriage, Rafael mused as they stepped into the lift. Once again he imagined his ultra-conservative grandfather's reaction if he introduced an unmarried mother who sold sandwiches for a living as his bride. It would teach Hector not to try to interfere in his life, Rafael thought grimly.

The lift doors opened on the ground floor and he took hold of Juliet's arm as they passed the gang of youths, who were now loitering in the entrance hall and passing a joint between them.

'Why do you live in this hellhole?' he demanded as he hurried her outside to his car. 'It can't be a good place to bring up a child.'

'I don't live here out of choice,' she said wryly. 'When Poppy was a baby we lived in a lovely little house with a garden. Kate was my mum's best friend, and the reason why I left Australia and came back to England was because she invited me and Poppy to move in with her. She was a widow, and I think she enjoyed the company. But Kate died after a short illness and her son sold the house. I only had a few weeks to find somewhere else to live. I had already started my sandwich business and needed to live in London, but I couldn't afford to rent privately. I was lucky that the local authority offered me social housing. Living on this estate isn't ideal, but it's better than being homeless.'

She ran her hand over the bonnet of the Lamborghini. 'You are a multi-millionaire—you can have no idea about the real world outside of your ivory tower.'

You think?

Inexplicably Rafael was tempted to tell her that he understood exactly what it was like to live in poverty—wondering where the next meal was coming from and struggling to survive in an often hostile environment. But there was no reason why he should explain to Juliet about his background. He dismissed the odd sense of connection he felt with her because they both knew what hardship felt like. His childhood had given him a single-minded determination to get what he wanted, and Juliet was merely a pawn in the game of wills with his grandfather.

He opened the car door and waited for her to climb inside before he walked round to the driver's side and slid behind the wheel.

'I know that five million pounds could transform your situation and allow you to provide your little girl with a safe home and a very comfortable lifestyle free from financial worries.' He gunned the Lamborghini away from the grim estate and glanced across at her. 'I'm offering you an incredible opportunity and for your daughter's sake you should give it serious consideration.'

It occurred to Juliet as she sank into the soft leather seat of the sports car that this might all be a dream and in a minute she would wake up. Things like this did not happen in real life. A stunningly handsome man offering her five million pounds to be his wife was the stuff of fantasy and fairy tales.

She darted a glance at Rafael's chiselled profile and felt a restless longing stir deep inside her. It was a long time since she had been kissed by a man, and she'd never felt such an intense awareness of one before.

Bryan had been her first and only sexual experience. She'd spent her teenage years at a boarding ballet school, and although she'd known boys, and danced with them, she had been entirely focused on her goal of becoming a prima ballerina and hadn't had time for boyfriends.

The scholarship she had been awarded had paid the school's fees, but there had been numerous other costs and her parents had scrimped and saved so that she could follow her dream. She'd always felt that she owed it to her mum and dad to succeed in her chosen career.

But the car accident which had taken her parents' lives had left Juliet with serious injuries—including a shattered thigh bone. The months she'd spent in hospital had intensified her sense of isolation and loneliness.

She had been painfully naïve when she'd met Bryan Westfield, soon after she'd moved out to Australia to stay with her aunt Vivian and uncle Carlos. She'd been looking for someone to fill the hole in her heart left by her parents' deaths, and blonde good-looking Bryan had seemed like 'the one'—until she'd realised he had only wanted sex.

'You're not the first young woman to have your heart broken and be left with a baby and you won't be the last,' Aunt Vivian had said briskly when Juliet had admitted that she was pregnant.

Her aunt had meant well but Juliet had felt stupid, as well as bitterly hurt by Bryan's rejection, and she'd vowed never to lay herself open to that level of pain again. It made her reaction to Rafael's undeniable sexual magnetism all the more confusing.

The look of distaste that had flickered over his face when she'd opened the door to him wearing her cleaning overalls had made her shrivel inside. She knew from photographs of him in gossip magazines—invariably with a blonde glamour model or actress hanging on to him—that she was as far from his ideal woman as the earth was from Mars. But his lack of interest in her made it easier to consider his proposition.

'You said I would be your wife in name only? Does that mean the marriage would not be…' she hesitated '…consummated?'

She was thankful that her scarlet cheeks were hidden

in the dark interior of the car. If he laughed she would die of mortification.

'Physical intimacy between us will not be necessary,' he said coolly.

He did not actually state that he wouldn't touch her with a barge pole but the message was clear. Juliet swallowed, feeling ashamed that the gorgeous man beside her found her repellent. They were both wearing jeans, but his were undoubtedly a designer brand, and she'd noted when he had walked around to his side of the car how the denim clung to his lean hips. His tan leather jacket looked as if it had cost the earth, while her clothes came from a discount store and her boots had seen three winters.

With a sigh, she turned her head and stared out of the window.

'We're here.'

Rafael's voice pulled Juliet from her thoughts and she discovered that he had turned the car onto the driveway in front of a large and very beautiful house.

'Where is "here"?' she asked when he switched off the engine.

'My home in England—Ferndown House. It's too dark to see now, but the house backs on to Hampstead Heath.'

Juliet looked down at the rip in her jeans. 'I suppose you don't want to be seen with me in public when I look like this,' she said flatly.

He turned his head towards her but she could not bring herself to look at him and see his disdainful expression.

After a moment he sighed. 'I brought you to my home because we will be assured of privacy while we talk, which we would not be in a bar or restaurant. There is no shame in being poor. It is obvious that you work hard to provide for your daughter, but I can help you. We can help each other. Now, come inside and meet my housekeeper. Alice has prepared dinner for us.'

If Juliet could have designed her dream home Ferndown House would have been perfect in every way. From the outside it was a gothic-style Victorian property, but inside it had been cleverly remodelled and refurbished into a sophisticated modern house which still managed to retain many original period features.

She caught her breath when Rafael showed her one huge room, with a stunning parquet floor and floor-to-ceiling mirrors on one wall.

'The previous owners enjoyed hosting parties in here, but I don't entertain very often and the room is not used much,' he told her.

The room would be an ideal dance studio, Juliet thought. It was her dream to one day own a ballet school, and she visualised ballet *barres* along the walls and a box of the powdered chalk called rosin on the floor, for dancers to rub onto their pointe shoes to help stop them slipping.

She followed Rafael along the hall and looked into another reception room, a study, and a library that overlooked the garden. Outside lighting revealed a large, pretty space with wide lawns, where Poppy would love to play. Juliet gave a faint sigh, thinking of the couple of rusty swings in the playground on the housing estate where she sometimes took her daughter.

Upstairs on the second floor they walked past what she guessed was the master bedroom, with a four-poster bed. Juliet carefully avoided Rafael's gaze as she wondered how many women had spent the night with him in that enormous bed.

'There is a nursery along here,' he said, leading the way along the corridor. He opened a door into a large room with painted murals of fairies on the walls and laughed at her startled expression. 'I'm not planning to fill the nursery with my own children, but my sister has four-year-old twin girls who sometimes come to stay here.'

They went back downstairs to the dining room, where a cheery fire burned in the hearth and velvet curtains were drawn across the windows.

'You have a beautiful home,' Juliet murmured when Rafael drew out a chair at the table and waited for her to sit down before he took his place opposite her.

He was silent while Alice served a first course of gooey baked brie with warm pears. Then the housekeeper left the main course on a heated trolley for them to serve themselves and Rafael poured wine.

'If you agree to my proposition Ferndown House will be yours and your daughter's home for the duration of our marriage. When, after a few months, the marriage is dissolved, five million pounds will be transferred into your bank account and you will be able to buy a property of your own. Have you any ideas about where you would like to live?'

'Somewhere on the coast,' she said instantly. 'When I was a child my parents took me on holiday to Cornwall a few times. We stayed in a caravan next to the beach.' Memories of a happy childhood full of love and laughter tugged on her heart. 'I've always thought how wonderful it would be for Poppy to grow up by the sea.'

'Agree to my deal and you can make your dreams reality,' Rafael said in a softly persuasive tone.

Excitement fizzed inside Juliet, overriding the voice of caution in her head. With the money that Rafael was offering she could buy a little cottage with a garden and a sea view. She didn't want a mansion—just a place that she and Poppy could call home. But what Rafael was asking was *wrong*, her conscience whispered. Marriage should be a life-long commitment. Her parents had enjoyed a happy marriage and, although Juliet had learned a harsh lesson with Bryan, she still hoped that one day she would fall in love with someone special who would love her in return.

She took a small sip of her wine, determined to keep her wits about her. 'I'm curious to know why you need a wife so badly that you're prepared to fork out five million pounds for one.'

'My grandfather has demanded that I marry before he steps down as head of the Casillas Group and appoints me as CEO of the company and Chairman of the board of directors,' Rafael said curtly. 'The dual roles have been passed down to the eldest son for generations. My mother does not have any siblings, which means that I am the next firstborn male and I should be Hector's successor. *Dios*, it is my *birthright*.'

He slapped his hand down on the table and Juliet flinched.

'Why does your grandfather want you to marry?'

'He disapproves of my lifestyle.'

She nodded. 'You do have a reputation as a playboy, and your affair with the wife of a prominent politician was reported in most of today's newspapers.'

'I spent one night with Michelle two months ago. The paparazzi must have seen us leave the nightclub together and go to a hotel, but those pictures did not appear in the papers the next day.' Rafael's jaw hardened. 'My guess is that someone paid the photographer to delay offering the pictures to the tabloids until the day the Casillas Group's biggest-selling retail line Rozita launched a new bridal collection.'

Juliet stared at him. 'Why would anyone do that?'

'It could have been a competitor, hoping to damage the company's reputation, or more likely someone who wanted to blacken my name and convince my grandfather that I would not be a responsible CEO.'

'Do you have any idea who?'

'In all probability it was someone on the Casillas Group's board who does not support my claim to be Hector's successor, or one of my relatives for the same reason.'

'How awful that someone in your own family might have betrayed you,' Juliet murmured. 'Families are supposed to support one another.'

Rafael stared at her broodingly. 'The pursuit of power is a ruthless game, with no place for weakness or emotions,' he said harshly.

While he served their main course of chicken cooked in a creamy sauce Juliet played his words over in her mind and felt a little shiver run through her. She had no doubt that Rafael was ruthless, and he must be utterly determined to become CEO if he was prepared to pay such an incredible amount of money for a wife.

Could she do it? His proposition had seemed crazy at first, but now she understood that his grandfather was forcing Rafael to marry. What he was suggesting was a business deal, she told herself.

The chicken was delicious, and a welcome change from the cheap, microwavable ready meals she tended to live on because fresh, good-quality produce was so expensive. She concentrated on eating her dinner, glad of the distraction.

Rafael got up to throw another log on the fire. The

flames crackled and an evocative scent of applewood filled the room. The wine, the food and the general ambience of the room was helping Juliet to relax, and she gave a soft sigh.

'Can you honestly tell me that you're not tempted?'

Rafael's seductive voice curled around her. She took another sip of her wine.

'Of course I'm tempted. To be honest I can't even *imagine* having five million pounds. It's an unbelievable sum of money and it would certainly transform my life. But I have to consider what is best for Poppy. I'm worried that she might become attached to you while we're married and be upset when we divorce and you're no longer around.'

Rafael frowned. 'I think that scenario is extremely unlikely. Immediately after our marriage you and Poppy will accompany me to Spain to attend my grandfather's eightieth birthday party. I will present you as my new wife to Hector and he will announce me as his successor. The transition of power will take a little while— maybe a month or two—and we will need to attend a few social engagements together to show the Casillas board members and shareholders that I have reformed my playboy lifestyle since my marriage,' he said sardonically. 'After a suitable period of time you and your daughter will be able to return here to Ferndown House—we'll make the excuse that you prefer her to attend a nursery school in England. It will be necessary for me to spend much of my time at the Casillas Group's headquarters in Valencia, and the truth is that I won't come to England very often.'

'How romantic.'

Juliet told herself it was stupid to feel disappointed

that Rafael had made it clear he would avoid her as much as possible.

'I am not offering you romance,' he said in a hard voice. 'I want you to be my wife for no other reason than to fulfil my grandfather's command that I must marry before he will make me CEO.'

He stood up and walked over to the sideboard, returning to lay some papers on the table.

'We are required to give twenty-eight days' notice of our intention to marry at the register office. My lawyers have prepared a contract stating that five million pounds will be transferred into your bank account when I succeed my grandfather as head of the Casillas Group. All you have to do is sign your name. I will take care of all the arrangements for our wedding, and for you and your daughter to move from your current home into Ferndown House.'

Juliet stared at the document in front of her and imagined Poppy running around the garden and playing with the dolls' house in the nursery.

She swallowed. 'It seems too easy.'

'It *is* easy. Everything will be as I have explained to you. There are no catches.'

Rafael's voice was like warm honey sliding over her. Tempting her. She wished her dad was around so that she could ask his advice—although she knew in her heart that he would advise her against marrying for money.

But five million pounds! Her heart was thudding so hard she was surprised it wasn't audible in the silent room. If she accepted Rafael's proposition her money worries would be over, but would she be selling her soul to the devil?

'I need time to think about it,' she whispered.

'I don't have the luxury of time. I have to be married by my grandfather's eightieth birthday, which is six weeks from now, or he will appoint my half-brother as his successor.' Rafael picked up a pen from the table and held it out to her. 'I am offering you a chance to give your daughter a better life. If you walk away now you will have thrown away that chance. I won't make the offer again and I will find another bride.'

The clock on the wall ticked loudly.

Do it. Do it.

Juliet snatched the pen from Rafael and signed her name where he showed her. It was for Poppy, she tried to reassure herself. A better future for her daughter.

'Bueno!' Rafael did not try to disguise the satisfaction in his voice. He picked up their wine glasses and handed Juliet hers. 'Let us drink a toast, *chiquita*, to the shortest marriage on record.'

CHAPTER THREE

A MONTH HAD never passed so quickly—or so it seemed to Juliet.

For the first couple of weeks after she had agreed to Rafael's marriage proposition she had been busy winding down her sandwich business. Mel had found a buyer for the bakery shop and it had been an emotional moment as they'd closed the door for the last time.

'I'm intrigued to know more about your new business opportunity in Spain,' Mel had said. 'Why are you being so secretive?'

'I'll tell you more if it happens.'

Juliet hadn't revealed to her friend the true reason why she would be going to Spain. She was sure Mel would think she was mad if she explained that she had agreed to marry a man she did not know for money.

As the date of the wedding had drawn closer her doubts had multiplied. But Rafael had promised that there was no catch to their business deal.

Deciding what to tell Agata had been more difficult. Juliet was fond of the Polish woman who had helped her and Poppy so much, and after some soul-searching she'd told Agata the white lie that she was marrying Rafael after a whirlwind courtship.

Today, packing her's and Poppy's belongings hadn't

taken long, and a member of Rafael's staff had come and taken the few cardboard boxes down to an SUV.

Juliet strapped Poppy into the child seat and as the car drove away from the estate on its way to Ferndown House she felt a mixture of relief, apprehension and excitement that refused to be quashed at the prospect of seeing Rafael again.

She had spoken to him once on the phone, when he'd called her to check some details he needed in order to complete the paperwork for their wedding. His gravelly voice with its sexy accent had made her feel hot all over, and she'd closed her eyes and pictured his devastatingly handsome face.

Remembering his disdainful expression when he'd seen her wearing her cleaning overalls, she had taken a bit of time over her appearance today. The pink jumper that Agata had given her at Christmas lent some colour to her washed-out complexion, and the old tube of mascara she'd found at the back of the bathroom cabinet had still had enough in it to darken her pale eyelashes.

But when they arrived at Ferndown House Alice the housekeeper greeted Juliet and explained that Rafael had left the previous day for a business trip to America.

'He is not sure when he will be back but he asked me to give you his PA's phone number. Miss Foxton will answer any queries you might have.' Alice smiled at Poppy. 'I've made some cookies. Would you like one?'

Juliet tried to shrug off her disappointment at Rafael's absence. There was no reason for them to spend any time together. Their marriage would be a formality which would allow Rafael to become CEO of his family's company and he was paying her an astounding amount of money to be his temporary wife, she reminded herself.

And sitting alone in the elegant dining room at Ferndown House, enjoying one of the delicious meals that the housekeeper had prepared, was a lot nicer than sitting in her flat with a microwaveable meal after Poppy had gone to bed—although she felt just as lonely.

Rafael finally phoned her the evening before they were due to marry the following day. 'My plane has just touched down in London and I'm going straight to the office,' he told her.

His gravelly voice had its usual effect of bringing Juliet's skin out in goosebumps.

'I don't know what time I'll get back to the house. Make sure you're ready to leave for the register office at ten-thirty tomorrow morning.'

On her way up to bed she wondered if he really was going to the office so late, or if he planned to spend the night with a mistress. Perhaps he wanted to enjoy his last night as a bachelor before he was forced into a marriage that he patently didn't want.

It was none of her business what he did, Juliet reminded herself.

There was no logical explanation for her dismal mood. In a few months' time she would have five million pounds in the bank—more than enough to buy a cottage by the sea and for her to establish her own dance school.

It was after midnight when she heard a car pull up outside the house, and when she hopped out of bed and ran across to the window her heart skipped a beat as she saw Rafael's tall frame unfold from his Lamborghini. The moonlight danced across his face, highlighting his chiselled jaw and sharp cheekbones.

Tomorrow he would be her husband.

Butterflies leapt in her stomach—nerves, she supposed. But around dawn she woke feeling horribly sick. Frequent trips to the bathroom followed, and the severe bouts of vomiting left her feeling drained.

She certainly did not look like a blushing bride, Juliet thought as she stared at her ashen face and lank hair in the mirror. It was ten o'clock and she needed to hurry up and get ready.

Choosing what to wear did not take her long. She lived in jeans or a denim skirt, and the only vaguely smart item of clothing she owned was a mustard-coloured dress she'd bought in a sale years ago when she had first moved to Australia and needed something to wear to job interviews. The colour hadn't looked so bad in the Australian sunshine, but on a grey spring day in England it made her pale skin look sallow.

She would have liked to buy something pretty to wear on her wedding day, but since her sandwich business had closed down and she'd given up her cleaning job she hadn't had an income. Living at Ferndown House meant that she hadn't had to pay for food, but she'd spent the last of her money on new shoes for Poppy.

Juliet had no time to worry about her appearance when another bout of sickness sent her rushing into the bathroom, and she emerged feeling shivery and hot at the same time. Then she spent ten minutes searching for Poppy's favourite teddy, knowing that her daughter would not sleep at night without Mr Bear. Finally they were ready.

Was she doing the right thing?

It was too late for second thoughts now, she told herself. She had already given up her flat and her job. If she did not marry Rafael she would be homeless.

As Juliet walked down the stairs a wave of dizziness

swept over her. She clung to the banister rail with one hand and held on to Poppy with the other.

Rafael strolled into the hall and an expression of horror flickered across his face as he studied her appearance, before he quickly schooled his features and gave her a cool smile. He looked utterly gorgeous in a grey three-piece suit that emphasised his broad shoulders and athletic build. His black hair was swept back from his brow and the designer stubble on his jaw gave him an edgy sex appeal that was irresistible.

'I couldn't afford to buy a new outfit for the wedding,' Juliet told him stiffly.

She wished the ground would open up beneath her feet when she caught sight of herself in the hall mirror. She hadn't had the energy to do anything fancy with her hair and it hung in a heavy braid down her back.

'You look fine,' Rafael assured her smoothly.

It was a blatant lie, she thought.

She wished she wasn't so agonisingly aware of him. Her breath snagged in her throat when he lifted his hand and lightly touched her face.

'Although I'm guessing from the dark circles beneath your eyes that you did not sleep well last night,' he murmured. 'You will do very well,' he added, in a satisfied tone that puzzled her.

But then he hurried her out to the car and she was too busy strapping Poppy into the child seat to think about Rafael's odd statement.

From then on everything about the day had an air of unreality. The wedding ceremony took place in an unremarkable room at the council offices, and the two witnesses were Rafael's PA and his chauffeur.

Juliet had asked Agata to come to the register office to look after Poppy during the ceremony, and Poppy's joy when she saw Agata brought tears to Juliet's eyes. Her parents would have loved their little granddaughter as much as Poppy would have loved to have grandparents.

Rafael had told her that he had a large extended family and that several of his relatives, including his mother, lived at the Casillas family mansion in Valencia. Perhaps his mother would enjoy having a child around and would make a fuss of Poppy? Juliet hoped so.

She must have made all the right responses to the registrar, and even managed to smile—although she felt numb and her voice sounded strangely disembodied. Rafael slid a gold band onto her finger and she tensed when he lowered his face towards hers. She realised with a jolt of shock that he was going to kiss her. She had secretly longed to feel his lips on hers, but not like this—not to seal their farce of a marriage.

His mouth was centimetres from hers, and she quickly turned her head so that he kissed her cheek. He frowned, and she guessed that no woman had ever rejected him before. But then the registrar was presenting them with the marriage certificate and Juliet felt as brittle as glass as she stepped into the corridor, hardly able to believe that she was now Mrs Mendoza-Casillas.

'I hope you know what you are doing,' Agata said when Juliet hugged her outside the register office. 'You told me that you fell in love with your husband at the first sight, but I do not see love between you.'

Somehow Juliet dredged up a smile. 'I'm very happy.' She tried to sound convincing. 'I'll bring Poppy to visit you soon.'

Rafael was uncommunicative in the limousine that took them to the airport, and once they had boarded his private jet he opened his laptop, saying that he needed to work.

Juliet devoted herself to keeping Poppy entertained during the flight, and by the time the plane had landed in Valencia and they were in a car on the way to his family home she had a thumping headache—although thankfully the sickness seemed to be over. Poppy was tired and fretful, and Juliet felt frazzled, and she was relieved when the car turned onto a long driveway.

'You didn't tell me you lived in a palace,' she said to Rafael in an awed voice as the Casillas mansion came into view.

Built over four storeys, the villa had white walls and tall windows gleaming in the bright afternoon sunshine. The car drove past manicured lawns and a huge ornamental pool and fountain before coming to a halt by the imposing front entrance which was framed by elegant colonnades.

Juliet knew, of course, that Rafael was wealthy, but travelling on his private jet and seeing his family's palatial home had made her realise that she'd entered a world of incredible luxury and opulence which was a million miles away from her tower block in one of London's most deprived boroughs, and from her life as a single mother.

They climbed out of the car and her tension escalated as she lifted Poppy out of the child seat and attempted to set her down on her feet. Tears ensued until she picked the little girl up again.

'Poppy is tired from travelling,' she told a grim-faced Rafael. 'I'd like to get her settled and give her something to eat.'

'You will be able to do that soon, but first I will introduce you to my family. My grandfather has arranged a reception to celebrate our marriage.'

Was it her imagination or did Rafael sound as tense as she felt?

She bit her lip as he strode up the steps leading to the front door of the villa, leaving her to trail behind him with Poppy balanced on her hip.

On the top step, he turned to her and frowned. 'Let me take the child. She is too heavy for you to carry.'

Juliet felt beads of sweat running down her face—which was strange, because she was shivering even though the sun was warm. Poppy clung to her like a limpet and shrank away from Rafael when he tried to take her into his arms.

A man whom she guessed was the butler opened the door and ushered them into the villa. Juliet's stunned gaze took in a vast entrance hall with pink marble walls and floor. Rafael placed his hand between her shoulder blades and propelled her forward as the butler flung open a set of double doors into another enormous room that seemed to be filled with people.

The hum of voices became quiet and silence pressed on Juliet's ears. An elderly man stepped out of the crowd and came to greet them—but the smile of welcome on his face faded and his eyes narrowed.

'Rafael, I understood that you would be bringing your new wife with you.' The man spoke in Spanish and his harsh tone sent a shiver through Juliet.

'Abuelo...' Rafael drawled. 'I would like you to meet my bride.'

There was a collective gasp from the people in the room and the old man swore. He flicked his sharp black eyes over Poppy before he spoke to Juliet in English. 'Were you a widow before you married my grandson?'

Confused by the question, she shook her head. 'No. I've never been married before.'

His implication suddenly became clear, and a terrible certainty slid into her mind when the man whom she realised was Hector Casillas glared at Rafael.

'*Tu esposa y su bastarda son de la cuneta!*' he hissed in a venomous voice.

He was white-lipped with anger, but his grandson laughed.

'What is the matter, Abuelo?' Rafael drawled. 'You demanded that I marry and I have done what you asked.'

'There is something you should know.'

Juliet's teeth were chattering so hard that she could barely get the words out. Anger burned like a white-hot flame inside her, but she was determined to control her temper in front of Poppy, who was running around in the little courtyard behind the kitchen. Her daughter had been subjected to enough ugly emotions from Rafael's grandfather.

Rafael. *Judas.*

'What should I know?' he said indifferently.

'I understand Spanish. I learned to speak the language when I lived with my aunt Vivian and her husband Carlos, who is Spanish by birth.'

His brows lifted. 'Ah…'

'Is that all you can say?' she choked.

She wanted to scream at him. Worse than her rage was her sense of hurt, which felt like an iron band wrapped around her chest that was squeezing the breath from her lungs.

'Your grandfather said that I am from the gutter and he called Poppy a bastard.' Juliet swallowed hard. 'Technically, I suppose it's true. Poppy's father did not offer to marry me when I fell pregnant, and he refused to have any involvement with his daughter when she was born. But I don't regret for one second having my little girl, and I will not allow your grandfather or anyone else to upset her.'

'My grandfather has very old-fashioned views.' Rafael gave a shrug. 'He is disappointed because he hoped I would marry the daughter of a duke. Hector sets great store on aristocratic titles,' he said drily.

'You threw me to the lions deliberately. Your grandfather said those awful things about me and you didn't defend me.'

It was not just raw emotion that was making it hard for Juliet to swallow. Her throat was sore and she recognised that the shivery feeling and her jelly-like legs were signs of a flu-like virus, the start of which must have been the sickness she'd experienced that morning.

'Mummy, can I give some yoghurt to the cat?'

She forced a smile for Poppy. 'I don't think cats eat yoghurt, darling. And I want you to sit down and finish your tea.'

Juliet lifted her daughter onto a chair at the wooden table in the shade of a pergola. Although Poppy could not have understood the things that had been said by Rafael's grandfather, she had sensed the tension in the room and burst into tears. Rafael had brought them to the kitchen and asked the cook to find some food for the little girl.

Luckily Poppy had been distracted when she'd seen a tabby cat in a pretty courtyard where terracotta pots were filled with a profusion of herbs.

While Poppy tucked into a bowl of fresh fruit and yoghurt, Juliet said in a low tone to Rafael, 'I don't understand why you chose me to be your wife if you knew that your grandfather would not approve of me.'

She stared at him and saw a ruthlessness in his hard-boned face that sent a shiver through her.

'That was the point, wasn't it?' she whispered. 'You were angry that your grandfather had insisted on you being married before he would make you CEO, so to pay him back you married a woman you knew he would despise—a single mother from the gutter.'

She was mortified to think of the vision she must have presented to Rafael's family, looking like Little Orphan Annie in her horrible dress and scuffed boots, with a child on her hip.

'You are not from the gutter.' Rafael sounded impatient rather than penitent.

'I come from a run-down council estate where the police have given up trying to arrest the drug dealers because there are too many of them,' she said flatly.

Juliet wasn't ashamed of her background. Her parents had worked hard in low-paid jobs to give her the chance to pursue her dream of being a ballerina. And most of the families living in that tower block were good people who struggled to make ends meet.

None of them had judged her for being a single mother—like Rafael's grandfather had and perhaps Rafael himself did. One thing was certain—she did not belong in the Casillas mansion with Rafael's so-phisticated relatives.

'I can't stay here knowing that your family despise me,' she told him. 'More importantly, I don't want Poppy to meet your grandfather again. I'll book us onto the next available flight to England.'

She kept a credit card for extreme emergencies and her current situation definitely qualified as an emergency. Poppy had been terrified when Rafael's grand-father had shouted at them. But Juliet had no idea how she would pay the credit card bill, or where she would go when she reached London. Perhaps Agata would allow her and Poppy to stay at her flat for a few days.

'My grandfather will calm down,' Rafael told her. 'Even if he doesn't, you are my wife and there is nothing Hector can do about it.'

'You can't use me and especially not my three-year-old child as pawns in your row with your grandfather. I don't understand why such bitterness exists between the two of you. There is poison here in paradise and I want no part in an ugly war of wills between two men who have more money than people like me—people from the *gutter*,' she flung at him, 'can only dream of.'

She could tell from the way his dark brows slashed together like a scar across his brow that he hadn't expected her to stand up to him.

It was about time she grew a backbone, Juliet told herself grimly. But even though she had discovered the unedifying reason why Rafael had married her she still could not control the heat that coiled low in her pelvis when he pushed himself away from the wall that he had been lounging against and crossed the small courtyard to stand in front of her.

Too close, she thought, lifting her hand up to her throat to try and hide the betraying leap of her pulse.

'You became part of this when you signed our marriage agreement and it is too bad if you don't like it,' he said curtly. 'Let us not forget that your motives were hardly altruistic, *chiquita*. You sold yourself to me for five million pounds.'

'I see now that I sold my soul to the devil.' She put her hand on his arm and felt the iron strength of sinew and muscle beneath his olive-gold skin. 'It's not too late to end this madness. We can have our marriage annulled.'

'And give up what should be mine?' Rafael gave a harsh laugh. 'I am afraid not. I will be CEO, whatever it takes. We are in this together.'

A violent shiver shook Juliet and she gripped the edge of the table as the ground beneath her feet lurched.

'What's the matter?' Rafael demanded. 'You're even paler than you were at the register office.'

'I've been feeling unwell all day,' she admitted.

She turned away from him and started to walk across the courtyard, but the ground tilted and she felt herself falling. From a long way off she heard Rafael call her name.

She mustn't faint because Poppy would be frightened, she thought before blackness blotted out everything.

When he was growing up Rafael had learned to run fast—to escape his father's temper, or shopkeepers who chased him for stealing food, or to avoid the dealers who forced the slum kids to deliver drugs.

As an adult he still ran to escape his demons. His favourite route took him through the Albufera Natural Park, where a huge freshwater lagoon was separated from the sea by a narrow strip of coastline. There he could run along the beach before heading into the sand dunes and the pine forest beyond.

The Casillas mansion overlooked the beach, and right now Rafael, gazing out of an upper-floor window, would have liked nothing better than to be pounding along the shoreline, with the sea breeze ruffling his hair and the sun on his back. Running gave him the head space to find solutions to his problems—but there was no easy solution to the situation he found himself in, with a marriage that he had been forced into against his will.

There had even been a chance of a reprieve. It might not have been necessary to go ahead with the wedding at all. He would have paid Juliet off and thought it a small price to pay for his freedom.

An opportunity had arisen to buy out a popular American fashion brand, and Rafael had spent the past month in California, determined to secure the deal which would give the Casillas Group a major stake in the US clothing retail market. The acquisition would, he hoped, prove to the board members and shareholders that he *should* be CEO.

But even his success had not been enough to persuade his grandfather to withdraw his marriage ultimatum.

'A wife will be good for you. Now that you are thirty-five it is time for you to settle down and think about the future,' Hector had said when Rafael had phoned to tell him that the Casillas Group now owned the US fashion brand Up Town Girl. 'I am an old man, and when I die I want to be certain that the next generation of my family will lead the company into the future.'

If Hector believed that having great-grandchildren would be ensured by forcing his eldest grandson to marry he was going to be disappointed, Rafael brooded. He had no burning desire to have children. His parents had hardly been ideal role models, and although he was fond of his nieces he was too driven by his ambition to believe that he could be a devoted parent like his sister, or like Juliet.

His wife.

Dios. He pictured the sickly waif who had occupied his bed for the past two nights while he slept on the sofa in his dressing room. He hadn't thought about what he would do with Juliet once he'd married her, and he resented his nagging conscience which insisted that he was now responsible for her and her child.

Damn his grandfather for issuing his ridiculous marriage ultimatum. Rafael's jaw clenched. Once his temper would have made him lash out and punch something—or someone. At fifteen he had been expelled from an exclusive private school for fighting with another pupil who had taunted him for his rough manners.

'You grew up in the gutter, Mendoza. You call yourself Casillas but everyone knows your father was a *gitano*.'

Rafael had wiped the grin off the other boy's face with his fists, but when he'd cooled off he'd felt ashamed of his behaviour. As a child he had often been on the receiving end of his father's violent outbursts, but he wanted to be a better man than Ivan Mendoza and prove to his grandfather that he deserved the name Casillas.

From then on he'd learned to control his emotions. *Don't get mad, get even* had become his mantra.

At a new school Rafael had ignored the boys who'd reminded him about his background. Instead of losing his temper he had focused his energy on his studies, determined to catch up on the education he'd missed while he'd lived in the slum.

That single-mindedness had seen him gain a master's degree from Harvard Business School before he had joined the Casillas Group in a junior role and worked his way up the company ladder.

He pulled his mind back to the present when a small hand slipped into his, and glanced down at Juliet's daughter. Poppy was an enchanting child, with a knack of disarming Rafael's defences which he would have sworn were impenetrable.

'Will you read me a story, Raf?'

He hunkered down in front of her. 'Go and find a book from the shelf. I'll read you a story and then we will go and see if your *mamà* is feeling better.'

Across the room Rafael caught his sister's amused expression.

'*Raf?*' Sofia murmured.

'My name is unfamiliar for the child, and hard to say, so she shortens it to Raf. I seem to have made a hit with her,' he said ruefully.

'"The child" has a name,' his sister reproved him. 'Poppy is younger than the twins and you are the only person she knows in a house full of strangers. It's hardly surprising that she wants to be with you while her mother—*your wife*—is too unwell to look after her.' Sofia sighed. 'What made you do it, Rafael?'

He did not pretend to misunderstand, or to try to convince his sister that his marriage was anything other than a calculated ploy which would give him what he wanted.

'Abuelo blackmailed me into choosing a wife by threatening to name Francisco as his successor if I did not marry. The CEO-ship should be *mine*—and not only by birthright. I don't feel a sense of entitlement,' he insisted. 'When I joined the company I started at the bottom—sweeping the floor in a warehouse. Hector did not want me to receive special favours just because I am his eldest grandson. I quickly rose through the managerial ranks because I worked harder than anyone else. I have *proved* my worth.'

Rafael's gaze met his sister's eyes, which were the same shade of olive-green as his own. Their unusual eye colour was a physical sign of the difference that set them apart from the rest of the Casillas family.

'You and I are still seen as outsiders. Especially me,' he muttered. 'You smile and say the right things, and you are not viewed as a threat to Madre's ambition to see her beloved Francisco—the true Casillas heir, in her opinion—made CEO.'

Sofia moved to break up a squabble between her two daughters. 'Ana, give the doll to Inez if she was playing with it first. Your uncle says he will read a story. Why don't you help Poppy choose a book?'

She turned her attention back to Rafael.

'I'm sorry I wasn't here two days ago, when you introduced your wife to the rest of the family. Madre says the girl you have married is so thin and pale perhaps she is a drug addict.'

'Dios!' Rafael growled, biting back a curse when he caught his sister's warning look to remind him that children were present. 'Juliet fell ill with a gastric virus shortly after we arrived.'

He was angered by his mother's unjust accusation. But his conscience pricked. When he had first met Juliet her hollow cheeks and extreme pallor had made *him* suspicious that she was a drug user. And her drab appearance was one reason he had picked her for his bride, he acknowledged, feeling a faint flicker of shame as he pictured her in the ghastly creased dress she'd been wearing when he had introduced her to his grandfather.

He hadn't realised that she was ill when they had arrived at the Casillas mansion. With another stab of discomfort Rafael admitted to himself that he'd been busy taking a vicious pleasure in Hector's fury when he'd announced that the waif clutching her illegitimate child in her arms was his wife.

Juliet was as far removed from any of the high-society daughters of Spanish aristocratic families whom

Hector had expected him to marry as chalk was from cheese. But her lack of sophistication did not warrant his family's scorn.

'Juliet is a devoted mother—which is more than can be said for *our* mother,' he said harshly. 'Delfina is embarrassed by us because we remind her that she was once married to a low-life drug dealer. Sometimes I think she would have preferred it if Hector *hadn't* found us and brought us into the family.'

Sofia looked at him closely. 'I hope you have not led your wife to believe that you are in love with her?'

'Juliet understands that we have a business deal and she will be well recompensed after she has served her purpose.'

'Oh, Rafael,' his sister murmured. 'I worry about where your ruthless ambition will lead you. When can I meet your bride?'

He shrugged. 'Perhaps later today. The doctor I called in to examine her has said that the virus hit her hard. But the nurse reported that Juliet's temperature was nearly back to normal this morning and she should be well enough to attend Hector's eightieth birthday party on Saturday evening.'

When *he* would be named as his grandfather's successor, Rafael thought with satisfaction. He had met the old man's stipulation for him to marry and now it was time for Hector to publicly recognise his firstborn grandson as the true Casillas heir.

There was a knock on the door and the butler entered the nursery. 'Yes, Alfredo, what is it?'

'Señor Casillas wishes to speak to you,' the butler told Rafael. 'He is waiting for you in his study.'

CHAPTER FOUR

RAFAEL LOOKED DOWN at Poppy, who was holding a book out to him, before he responded to the butler. 'Tell my grandfather that I am with my stepdaughter and I will be along in ten minutes.'

'Why do you have to antagonise Hector?' Sofia demanded when Alfredo had left.

'He needs to realise that I am not one of the yes-men he surrounds himself with,' Rafael muttered. 'I am sick of his attempts to manipulate me. Besides, I promised to read to Poppy.'

He had felt oddly protective of Juliet's daughter since the ugly scene with his grandfather when they had arrived at the house had upset the little girl.

'You and Abuelo are both too proud,' Sofia said impatiently. 'It's like a clash of bulls.'

She broke off as the nursery door was flung open.

Rafael glanced across the room and saw Juliet standing in the doorway. She was wearing a pair of baggy pyjamas that had faded to an indeterminate colour and her hair was scraped back from her white face.

'Where is my daughter?'

She gave a low cry when she saw Poppy, and flew across the room to scoop the little girl into her arms.

'Oh, munchkin, there you are. I was scared I'd lost

you.' Juliet's relief was palpable and tears spilled down her cheeks as she looked at Rafael. 'I thought you had taken Poppy away. I woke up and I didn't know where she was. I thought…' She shook her head and hugged her daughter to her. 'I hope that no one has upset her. Your grandfather…?'

'Hector has not met Poppy again since we arrived two days ago,' Rafael assured her gruffly.

He was not completely heartless, and Juliet looked pathetic in her rag-bag clothes that hung off her angular body, with her face blotchy and wet with tears.

'As you can see, Poppy is quite safe. I have been taking care of her.'

'*You?*'

The mistrust in her voice exasperated him, but he felt uncomfortable as he remembered how she had accused him—rightly—of failing to defend her and Poppy in front of his grandfather.

'I am not an ogre,' he said curtly. But the wounded expression in Juliet's eyes made him feel like the evil villain in a Victorian melodrama.

'I can't believe that we have been here for two days,' she said unsteadily. 'What happened to me?'

'You have been ill with a virulent virus which gave you a high fever. The doctor I called in gave you medication to bring your temperature down and it knocked you out.'

Rafael did not add that the doctor had voiced his concern that Juliet was underweight and most likely undernourished, which had lowered her immune system, allowing the virus to take a hold.

'I don't remember putting my pyjamas on.' She looked at him with something akin to horror in her eyes. 'Did you undress me?'

'The nurse I hired put you to bed.'

Dios, Rafael thought irritably. Juliet had sounded appalled at the idea of him taking her clothes off. It was not a response he'd ever had from a woman before.

He recalled that at their wedding, when the registrar had invited him to kiss his bride and for the sake of convention he had tried to brush his lips over Juliet's, she had turned her head away to prevent him from kissing her mouth. Her behaviour had been puzzling because he knew she was attracted to him. Rafael always knew.

Before he was twenty he had discovered that he could have any woman he wanted with minimum effort on his part. No doubt his wealth and the name Casillas were partly responsible for his popularity, but he indulged his high sex drive with countless affairs with women who understood that commitment was not a word in his vocabulary.

He wasn't interested in his poor, plain bride. Although those attributes were the reason he had married her, he acknowledged, feeling guilt snaking through him as he remembered the crushed look on her face when his grandfather had insulted her. How was he to have known that Juliet understood Spanish? Rafael asked himself irritably.

'Rafael, are you going to introduce me to your wife?' Sofia walked up to Juliet and held out her hand. 'I apologise for my brother's lapse in manners. You must be Juliet. I'm Sofia, and my daughters are Ana and Inez. The twins have had a wonderful time playing with Poppy. She really has been quite happy with Rafael and me and the nanny, Elvira.'

'I panicked when I woke up in a strange place and couldn't find her.' Juliet set Poppy on her feet and the fierce look of love on her face as she watched her daughter tugged on emotions buried deep inside Rafael.

He had long ago got over the fact that his mother did not love him and that his relatives—with the exception of his sister—resented his existence. He'd never felt that he belonged anywhere or with anyone, and he had assured himself that he did not care. No one had ever looked at him as though they would give their life for him…as if they loved him more than anything in the world.

'Rafael—quick!'

Sofia's urgent tone jolted him from his thoughts and he sprang forward and caught Juliet as her legs crumpled beneath her. She weighed next to nothing, he thought as he carried her over to the door.

'You are not fully recovered,' he said, ignoring her attempts to slide out of his arms. 'You should be in bed. I'll ask the nurse to check your temperature and bring you something to eat.'

'Poppy will be fine with me,' Sofia assured Juliet. 'I'll read the girls a story.'

'As soon as I'm better—which I'm sure I will be by tomorrow—I want to take Poppy home,' Juliet told Rafael when he'd carried her into the bedroom and sat her on the edge of the bed.

She was a slip of a thing, perched on the huge bed like a little sparrow, he mused. But as he straightened up he noticed that her eyes were really a quite remarkable bright blue. His gaze dropped to her mouth, which was pulled down at the corners in a sulky expression.

'Where is home, exactly?' he asked sardonically. 'I made it clear when you signed the marriage contract that you cannot return to Ferndown House until after we have attended my grandfather's eightieth birthday party and he has appointed me as CEO.'

'I wish I'd never signed the contract. You said there were no catches, but you didn't tell me that you had chosen me as your bride to punish your grandfather,' she said in choked voice. 'You certainly didn't think about my feelings when your family looked at me as though I had crawled out of the gutter.'

Rafael ignored the prick of his conscience. 'I'm paying you five million pounds,' he reminded her harshly. 'It is regrettable that my grandfather spoke to you the way he did, but I'm sure you'll get over it when the money is in your bank account and you can buy yourself nice clothes and jewellery—whatever you want.'

'All I want is security for Poppy,' she whispered. 'I'm not interested in jewellery and clothes.'

'That much I can believe,' he muttered, flicking his gaze over her revolting pyjamas before he stalked out of the room, away from the accusing expression in Juliet's eyes that made him feel ashamed of himself.

Dios, she should be grateful that she and her daughter would no longer have to live in poverty, Rafael brooded as he strode down the grand staircase.

His foul mood was not improved when he entered his grandfather's study and saw the company's senior lawyer, Lionel Silva, seated behind the desk next to Hector. Rafael strolled across the room and lowered himself into a chair facing the two men, resting his ankle across his opposite thigh. His appearance was relaxed but his instincts sensed trouble.

'Lionel, I am glad to see you,' he drawled. 'I presume my grandfather asked you here today to set in motion the transfer of the CEO-ship to me, now that I am married. It is what we agreed, did we not, Abuelo?'

His grandfather gave a snort. 'Once again you have disappointed me, Rafael. I cannot say that I am surprised, when you have so often proved to be a disappointment. But this time you have excelled yourself.'

Rafael felt a flare of irritation mixed with something raw that he assured himself wasn't hurt. He'd spent the past twenty-odd years trying to earn Hector's approval—hoping to win his grandfather's love—although he refused to admit as much even to himself. Now all he cared about was his right to be recognised as the Casillas heir.

'I trust you were not *disappointed* when I secured a deal to buy out the biggest clothing retail company on America's west coast?' he said drily. 'The acquisition puts Casillas Group among the top five largest apparel retailers in the world.'

'I do not dispute that your business acumen is impressive,' Hector barked. 'But, as I have said before, our CEO is the figurehead of the company—all the more so because the role is combined with that of Chairman. It is a position of great power and responsibility that requires a sense of humility—which you lack, Rafael.'

'I have met the condition you imposed on me and brought my wife to Spain in time for your eightieth birthday celebrations. How does that show a lack of humility?' Rafael said grittily.

'Do not insult my intelligence. You know that I expected you to make a good marriage, befitting the Casillas family's noble heritage, but you have deliberately sought to undermine me by marrying an unprepossessing girl. Your wife looks no more than a teenager and yet she already has one illegitimate child and no doubt lives off hand-outs from the state.'

'Juliet is in her mid-twenties and she has always worked to support her daughter.'

Fury simmered inside Rafael at his grandfather's

unfair description of Juliet. But his conscience prodded him that his reason for marrying her *had* been to infuriate Hector by introducing an untitled and unsophisticated bride.

The lawyer cleared his throat as he picked up a printed document. 'This is the agreement between you, Rafael, and your grandfather, stating Hector's intention to name you as his successor following your marriage.'

Rafael nodded. 'I have given you a copy of my marriage certificate.'

'Yes, it seems to be legitimate,' Lionel murmured, studying the other document in front of him. 'Nevertheless your grandfather has expressed his concern that your marriage to Miss Juliet Lacey is in fact a marriage of convenience which you have entered into for the purpose of gaining benefit or advantage arising from that status. In other words, your marriage to Miss Lacey is a sham, meant to deceive Hector and persuade him to name you as his heir and the next CEO of Casillas Group.'

'The marriage is perfectly legal.'

Rafael's grip on his temper broke and he jerked to his feet, slamming his hands down on the desk. He noted that the lawyer flinched but Hector remained absolutely still. A clash of bulls, his sister had once said, describing his battle of wills with his grandfather.

'I have kept to my side of our agreement and I expect you to honour your word, Abuelo.'

'What do *you* know of honour?' Hector snapped. 'It is my belief that you do not intend your marriage to be a permanent arrangement and that once you are CEO you will seek a divorce. But the wedding took place in England, and under UK law you cannot apply for a divorce until you have been married for one year.'

Rafael stiffened. 'So? Where is this leading?'

His grandfather gave a smug smile.

'On my eightieth birthday this Saturday I will announce that you are my successor, as we agreed, but I will not step down until the date of the first anniversary of your marriage—and only then if I am convinced that your marriage is genuine rather than an attempt to trick me.'

Hector gave Rafael a sly look.

'I am certain that there will be no need for me to try to prove or disprove the validity of your marriage A year will, I suspect, seem like a lifetime to a playboy such as you are, to maintain the pretence of a committed relationship with your unappealing bride.'

'You can't do that,' Rafael gritted. 'You agreed—'

'I can do whatever I think best protects the interests of the Casillas Group,' Hector interrupted. 'If I handed the company over to you and you divorced after only a few months of marriage it would suggest that you lack commitment. Instead I will appoint you CEO-in-waiting, and it will make sense that you should be based in Valencia in order for us to be in daily contact and ensure a smooth hand-over of leadership. I will expect you and your wife to spend the first year of your marriage living here at the Casillas mansion. If you return to your home in England it might lead to rumours of a rift between us, which would worry the board and our shareholders, who already have reservations about your suitability to head the company.'

The old man was as wily as a fox, Rafael thought furiously. 'I am certain that Juliet will not want to stay here after the vile way you spoke to her. Her daughter is settled at my home in London and it would not be good for the child to be brought to live in a different country.'

'Children are adaptable,' Hector said coolly. His black eyes bored into Rafael. 'Either you remain married for a year, or Lionel and his legal team will convince a court of law that your marriage is a fraudulent exercise intended to dupe me into appointing you as CEO.'

Rafael swore savagely. 'You cannot dictate where I choose to live or how I conduct my marriage.'

But he would not give his grandfather the satisfaction of seeing him lose his temper, and he swung round and strode out of the study. The truth was that the old man could do whatever he liked. Hector had won this round in their battle of wills, but he would not win the war. Whatever it took, he *would* claim his birthright, Rafael vowed.

An hour on the treadmill relieved some of his tension, but he was still in a black rage when he left the gym and returned to his private suite of rooms. He headed straight to the bar and took a beer from the fridge. He could do with something stronger, but spending the afternoon getting drunk on Orujo—a fiercely strong spirit sometimes referred to as Spanish firewater—would not be a good idea. Especially as he was expected to attend a family lunch later with his wife.

His wife.

Rafael swore under his breath as he stepped outside onto the balcony which ran along the entire length of his apartment at the back of the mansion and overlooked the extensive gardens. In the distance the swimming pool glinted in the sunshine, but he wasn't interested in the view. His attention was fixed on Juliet.

She was standing a little way along the balcony, leaning against the stone balustrade. He knew it must be her, but his brain could not believe what his eyes were seeing. Gone were the saggy grey pyjamas and instead she was wearing an ivory-coloured silk chemise that skimmed her slender body. Her hair was even more of a surprise. Freed from the tight braid she usually wore, it reached almost to her waist and was not a dull brown, as Rafael had thought, but red-gold, gleaming like silk in the sunshine.

She was unaware of him and he stood and stared at her, not daring to move in case she was an illusion that might disappear if he alerted her to his presence. He was stunned to realise that the unflattering clothes he had always seen her wearing had hidden a slender but definitely feminine figure, with graceful lines and delicate curves.

As Rafael watched Juliet tilted her face up to the sun and lifted her arms above her head, stretching like a sleepy kitten. The gentle breeze flattened the silk chemise against her body, drawing his gaze to her small, high breasts. He could see the faint outline of her nipples, and heat rushed to his groin as he imagined sliding the straps of the chemise down her arms and peeling the silky material away from her breasts.

He cursed silently when he felt his arousal press against the thin material of his running shorts. *What the hell was happening to him?* Discovering that his mousy little wife might be more appealing than his initial opinion of her had suggested was not something he had ever anticipated.

Nor had he anticipated that his grandfather would react the way he had, Rafael thought grimly. He'd guessed Hector would be annoyed that he had not chosen a bride from the Spanish aristocracy, but he'd never imagined that the old man would break their agreement and refuse to appoint him CEO.

Rafael did not know if Juliet had heard him sigh or if she'd sensed that she was no longer alone. She was still half turned away from him, but when she spun round he felt another jolt of shock when he saw how her features were softened by the hair now framing her face. Her high cheekbones and almond-shaped eyes gave her a fey prettiness.

Now that he was really looking at her—rather than flicking an uninterested gaze over her—he noticed that her mouth was a little too wide for her heart-shaped face and the sweet curve of her lips was unexpectedly sensual.

He walked across the balcony, and as he came nearer to her he saw the rosy flush on her face spread down her throat and across her décolletage. Her eyes widened, the pupils dilating. These subtle signals her body was sending out betrayed her awareness of him—which might work in his favour in light of the news he was about to break to her, he brooded.

Juliet watched Rafael saunter towards her and the wariness she felt for this stranger who was her husband was muddled with other confusing emotions that evoked a dragging sensation low in her pelvis.

It wasn't fair that he was so gorgeous, she thought ruefully. It had been difficult enough to keep her eyes off him when he'd been wearing a suit, or jeans and the navy polo shirt that he'd worn earlier when she had found him in the nursery with Poppy.

Now he must have come from the gym, and his black shorts and matching vest top revealed his powerfully muscular physique. His legs and arms were tanned a deep bronze, and she wondered if the sprinkling of black hair visible above his gym vest covered the whole of his chest.

She hated her reaction to his smouldering sensuality, very aware that he did not find her remotely attractive. But it was odd that he was staring at her intently, almost as if he had never seen her before. When she glanced down at the silk chemise she understood the reason for his scrutiny.

'Your sister lent me a nightdress because my pyjamas have been sent to the laundry,' she explained. 'I should have them back later today.'

'I do hope not,' Rafael said drily.

She grimaced, thinking of her pyjamas, which were as old and cheaply made as everything else she owned. After paying the bills and the monthly repayments on the money she'd borrowed from a loan company which charged a high interest rate, she used any spare cash to buy clothes for Poppy.

'It hardly matters to you that I have horrible pyjamas,' she said defensively. 'You won't see me wearing them. It's not as if we will have to spend any time together, or so you assured me.'

'I only meant that the temperature here in Valencia is much warmer than in England and you won't need to wear thick pyjamas to sleep in.'

'No, you didn't. You think I look terrible and so do your family—apart from your sister, who is very kind.'

Juliet was grateful to Sofia for taking Poppy to play in a summerhouse in the garden with her twin daughters. Sofia had explained that she was married to an Englishman—Marcus Davenport. Her husband worked for a bank in Valencia and the family lived at the Casillas mansion. The twins had been brought up to be bilingual and happily chatted away to Poppy in English.

'I don't care what you or your relatives think of me. I have never pretended to be anything other than a working class single mother—which is precisely why you chose me for your bride,' Juliet reminded Rafael sharply, desperate to hide the hurt she felt.

She was quite aware that he had married her because he needed a wife, but it was humiliating to realise that he'd picked the most disgusting woman he could find so that he could antagonise his grandfather.

He exhaled heavily. 'I'm sorry that I subjected you to my grandfather's temper. Hector is angry with me, not you, but I should have considered your feelings when I involved you in my conflict with him.'

She bit her lip. Rafael's apology had sounded genuine but it did not change the situation. 'I don't want to stay here when it is patently obvious that Poppy and I are not welcome. It don't suppose your grandfather will want me to attend his birthday party. You said that he would make you CEO if you were married by the time of his birthday, and presumably that will still happen. There is no reason for me to stick around and I'm sure you will be relieved when I go.'

'I'm afraid you won't be going anywhere for a while,' Rafael said smoothly. 'For a year, in fact.'

'What do you mean?'

A frisson of unease ran the length of Juliet's spine as she stared at his hard face. He was so beautiful that just looking at him made her insides melt. But she had already experienced his ruthlessness and she did not trust him.

'Hector is refusing to make me CEO because he believes that our marriage is not genuine.'

'Well, that's that, then. Your plan has backfired.'

'Not entirely. On Saturday my grandfather will name me as his successor, and in a year's time he will stand down as head of the company as long as I am still married.' While Juliet was digesting this information, he continued. 'All we have to do is prove that our marriage is the real thing for a year.'

'No way.' She shook her head. 'Our agreement was that we would separate after a couple of months and divorce as soon as legally possible.'

'The contract you signed states that you will receive your money when I become CEO,' he reminded her.

'Then I'll forfeit the money.' She should have known it was too good to be true. 'I should never have agreed to a fake marriage. I just want to take Poppy back to England and forget that I ever met you.'

Rafael's eyes narrowed. 'Five million pounds for a year of your life doesn't sound unreasonable. The deal will be the same, except that you will live here at the Casillas mansion rather than at Ferndown House.'

'With one major difference. You said you wouldn't visit your home in Hampstead very often, but you're asking me to share your family's home in Spain with you. Even though the mansion is huge, we won't be able to avoid each other completely.'

'That's the point,' he said, in that sardonic way of his which made Juliet feel small and insignificant in the grand scheme of his determination to be CEO of his family's business. 'We'll have to live together to show my grandfather that our marriage is real.'

'But it isn't…' she whispered.

An image flashed into her mind of her parents, who had celebrated their wedding anniversary a few weeks before they were killed. Her mum had baked a cake in the shape of a heart, and her dad had gone to his allotment before dawn and come back with a huge bunch of colourful, fragrant sweetpeas which he'd left on the kitchen table next to a card addressed to his darling wife.

Her parents hadn't needed money to make them happy. Their love for each other and for her had been more precious than gold, Juliet thought, blinking away her tears before Rafael saw them.

'It doesn't make sense that your grandfather is insisting on you staying married to me when he doesn't approve of me and knows that I am not the kind of woman you're attracted to,' she muttered.

Rafael's expression was inscrutable, but Juliet was mortified as the truth dawned on her.

'Hector thinks that you won't be able to bear being married to me for a whole year, doesn't he?'

'He is mistaken. I will do whatever I have to,' he said grimly.

'*You* might be willing to lie back and think…not of England, in this case, but of the CEO-ship that you'll gain from being married to the Bride of Frankenstein,' Juliet snapped, 'but I won't do it. You can't force me to stay.'

'You're being melodramatic.' Rafael sounded amused. 'I can't force you to remain in our marriage, it's true. But I suggest you think about what you stand to lose if you walk away now. You told me that your daughter's father wants custody of her and will try to prove that you are unfit to have Poppy living with you. It's hard to see how a judge would back your claim over your ex's if you were homeless or placed in a hostel by social services.'

Juliet swallowed hard, knowing that Rafael was right. 'However,' he continued, 'you are my wife, and Poppy is my stepdaughter, and I will ensure that you have the support of my best legal team. I think it is likely that a family court will look favourably on the fact that Poppy is living in a comfortable home in a secure family unit and she will be allowed to remain with her mother.'

She couldn't argue with Rafael's logical assessment of the situation, Juliet acknowledged despairingly. He had said he would do whatever it took to get what he wanted and she understood that, because she would walk over hot coals to keep Poppy.

'If your grandfather suspects that you've tried to trick him how can we convince him that our marriage is not fake? No one will believe that you fell for someone like me.' When his brows lifted, she said crossly, 'You've dated some of the most beautiful women in the world and you are frequently photographed by the paparazzi with a supermodel or a famous actress draped around you. I'm under no illusions about the way I look. I've always been thin, and I was clearly in the wrong queue when breasts were given out...'

He laughed, and it was so unexpected that Juliet stared at him, mesmerised by the way his lips curved upwards at the corners.

'You're funny,' he said, and there was faint surprise in his voice, as if he had discovered something unexpected about her. He stretched out his hand and touched her hair. 'I see now where your daughter gets her strawberry blonde hair from.'

Suddenly it was hard to speak because her mouth had gone dry. 'Poppy's hair is much fairer than mine,' she muttered.

'Your hair is the colour of amber. It suits you when you leave it loose.'

'After a shower I came to sit outside, so that my hair would dry in the sunshine. Usually I keep it tied up, because it gets in the way when I'm playing with Poppy...'

Juliet knew she was waffling, to distract herself from

suddenly finding that Rafael was much closer. How had he moved without her noticing?

He was so much taller than her and she found herself staring at the ridges of his impressive pectoral muscles visible through his tight-fitting sports vest. The scent of him—spicy cologne, sweat, *male*—assailed her senses. She tilted her head so that she could see his face and her heart missed a beat when she discovered that he was looking at her intently. The gleam in his olive-green eyes startled her, and she told herself she must be imagining the very male interest in gaze.

Rafael wasn't interested in her as a woman. To him she was merely a tool to help him get what he wanted, she reminded herself.

She backed away from him but found herself trapped between his partially clothed muscle-packed body and the wall of the balcony. He placed his hands flat on the top of the balustrade on either side of her and frowned when she shrank from him.

'We are going to have trouble convincing my grandfather that our marriage was made in heaven if you flinch every time I come near you,' he said impatiently. 'You did the same thing during our wedding.'

'You didn't warn me before the ceremony that you would kiss me, and I wasn't expecting it.'

He gave her a sardonic look, but slowly the expression in his eyes changed to something else—something hot that caused Juliet's heart-rate to quicken. 'In that case I'm giving you fair warning that it will be necessary for us to kiss whenever any of my relatives are around and we are on show, so to speak.'

Her tongue darted out to moisten her dry lips. 'You don't want to kiss me…' She would never forget his appalled expression when he had seen her in the mustard-coloured dress she had worn for their wedding.

'I'm coming round to the idea,' he drawled. 'And by the way, I don't think you look like the Bride of Frankenstein.'

'I'm flattered.' She tried to sound sarcastic but her voice was a thread of sound.

Her breath hitched in her throat when Rafael bent his head towards her so that he blotted out the sun. He was so gorgeous, and it would be so easy to fall under his magnetic spell, but it would be dangerous.

She turned her face away and felt his warm breath graze her cheek. 'I don't want you to kiss me.'

He captured her chin between his long fingers and exerted gentle pressure so that she was forced to look at him. 'How do you know until you've tried it? You might enjoy it.'

That was what she was afraid of.

She could not hide the tremor that ran through her when he dragged his thumb pad over her bottom lip.

'You are not my prisoner, and I am not doing anything to prevent you from going back inside the house,' Rafael murmured. 'But if you don't move in the next ten seconds I *am* going to kiss you.'

It was true that she could easily step past him. But her feet seemed to be cemented to the floor. Her instinct for self-protection urged her to run, but a stronger instinct that was deeply rooted in her womanhood held her there against the balustrade as Rafael's mouth came nearer.

Her heart was beating at three times its normal rate and he placed his finger over the pulse that was going crazy at the base of her throat. And then he brushed his lips across hers and the world tilted on its axis.

She had expected him to kiss her with the bold arrogance that was integral to him, but his mouth was gentle on hers, warm and seductive, disarming her defences so that her lips parted without her volition. Even then he kept it light, undemanding, tasting her with little sips that teased and tantalised so that she pressed her body closer to his and placed her hands flat on his chest.

Juliet felt the powerful thud of his heart beneath her fingertips and with a little sigh of capitulation kissed him back. Her eyelashes swept down and her senses became attuned to the taste of him on her lips, the warmth of his breath filling her mouth and the evocative masculine scent that wrapped around her as she melted, soft and pliant, against his whipcord body.

CHAPTER FIVE

'THAT WASN'T SO difficult, was it?'

Rafael's voice broke through the sensual haze that had wrapped around Juliet and she blinked at him, half blinded by the bright sunshine in her eyes as he lifted his head and she was no longer in his shadow. She wondered why he had stopped kissing her, but then reality hit and she remembered he had been demonstrating how they would have to act in public to convince his grandfather that their marriage was genuine.

And she had just demonstrated to Rafael that she couldn't resist him!

Following his gaze, she glanced down and a fresh wave of embarrassment swept over her when she saw the outline of her pebble-hard nipples beneath the silk chemise. She looked back at him, expecting to see mockery in his eyes, but he seemed unusually tense, and it was obvious that he couldn't wait to get away from her when he swung round and strode across the balcony.

He paused as he reached the bi-fold glass doors. 'The nurse said that your temperature has returned to normal and you are feeling much better?' When Juliet nodded, he continued, 'We are expected to attend a family lunch later, so that you can meet more of my relatives.'

She thought of the sea of faces that had stared at

her as if she had been beamed down from Mars when Rafael had brought her to the Casillas mansion. 'You mean there are *more*?'

'My grandfather is the oldest of seven siblings, and there are numerous uncles, aunts and cousins, many of whom work within the company and have an opinion on who they think should succeed Hector. Some of them support me—rather more of them don't,' he said sardonically.

It sounded like a family at war. Juliet bit her lip. 'I'd rather not be subjected to further humiliation and I don't want to risk Poppy being upset again. Can't you say that I am still unwell?'

'My grandfather will expect us to be at the lunch and it will be an opportunity to show him that we are a couple who are in love.'

Juliet wondered why his words evoked an ache in her heart. She had never been in love. Her crush on Bryan had ended abruptly when he'd brutally told her she had been a one-night stand. And Rafael had warned her not to fall in love with him. But now he was asking her to pretend that he was the man of her dreams.

'I'm not that good an actress,' she muttered.

'I thought your performance a few moments ago was very convincing—unless it wasn't an act and you actually *enjoyed* kissing me?' he said silkily.

While Juliet was searching her mind for a clever retort, he spoke again.

'Sofia's twins will have their lunch in the nursery with the nanny—Poppy might be happier staying with them.'

He had kissed Juliet to show her how they would have to act like happy newlyweds in front of his grandfather.

That was the *only* reason, Rafael assured himself. Although perhaps there had been an element of curiosity too, he conceded.

The realisation that he had been too hasty when he'd dismissed his wife as being plain and unattractive had stirred his interest. But he had been unprepared for his reaction to the feel of her soft lips beneath his. Quite simply he had been blown away by the sweet sensuality of Juliet's response, and his gut had clenched when she had kissed him with an intriguing mix of innocence and desire.

Dios, there had been a moment when his cool logic had almost been superseded by fiery passion, and he'd been on the verge of deepening the kiss and drawing her slender figure up close against his hard body. Fortunately he had remembered in time that it would be a mistake to become involved with her. Juliet was more vulnerable than he had thought when he'd suggested their marriage deal.

Face it, Rafael told himself grimly, you didn't think about *her* at all.

She was simply a means by which he could achieve his goal of becoming CEO, and nothing in that respect had changed—except that out there on the balcony it had fleetingly crossed his mind that he would like to have sex with her. But that would further complicate an already complicated situation, he brooded as he slid his arms into his suit jacket.

Rafael's private apartment in the mansion consisted of an open-plan lounge-cum-dining room, a kitchen and his study. There was also a large master bedroom, with his-and-hers dressing rooms and en suite bathrooms. He had asked the staff to put a single bed in Juliet's dressing room, so that Poppy could sleep near to her mother, and he had been sleeping on the sofa in his dressing room, leaving the bed for Juliet while she was ill.

There would have to be a change to the sleeping arrangements, he decided. He was six foot three, and he couldn't spend every night for the next year with his feet hanging off the end of a sofa.

Pushing open the bedroom door, he stifled a sigh when he saw Juliet. It had suited him that she looked like a drab waif when he'd wanted to annoy his grandfather with his unsuitable bride. Now there had been a change of plan, but unfortunately Juliet's dress sense had not improved.

Her outfit of a denim skirt with a frayed hem and a flamingo-pink jumper that clashed with her reddish hair was only marginally less unflattering than the abomination of a dress she had been wearing when he had introduced her to his family two days ago.

'I should have mentioned that lunch will be a formal affair,' he said.

At least she had made a bit of effort with her hair, and it was piled on top of her head in a neat bun. The style showed off the elegant line of her throat, but inexplicably Rafael wished she had left her hair loose so that he could run his fingers through it.

Her face was no longer unhealthily pale. Spending some time outside in the sunshine had put a pink flush on her cheeks. He would have to make sure that she wore sunscreen, he thought. Her English rose complexion would burn easily.

She shrugged. 'I don't own any designer clothes. There wasn't any need for them at my cleaning job,' she told him drily.

He strode into her dressing room and opened the wardrobe door, grimacing when it was immediately obvious that she had spoken the truth. 'You *must* own other footwear besides those things,' he muttered, looking at her scuffed winter boots.

Instead of replying she took a pair of tatty trainers out of the wardrobe and waved them in front of him. 'You married me precisely because my clothes look like they came from a jumble sale. Frankly, your plan to try and convince your grandfather that you've married your fantasy woman is just not going to work.'

'We both have a vested interest in *making* it work,' he reminded her. 'And we will have a better chance if you are a little less lippy.'

Against his will his gaze was drawn to her mouth, and he remembered how her lips had parted beneath his, so soft and moist and willing. He'd sensed her disappointment when he'd ended the kiss. Beneath her belligerent attitude she was attracted to him. But it would not be fair to lead her on or let her believe that he could fulfil any romantic notions she might have about him.

'I will arrange an appointment for you with a personal stylist who can advise you on what clothes will suit your figure instead of swamping you,' he said abruptly. He glanced at his watch. 'We had better go downstairs. Lunch is in ten minutes.'

He escorted Juliet out of his private suite, and as they descended the grand staircase and walked through the house he had to wait several times while she stopped to admire the artwork on the walls.

'Don't tell me that's an original Van Gogh?' she said, sounding amazed. 'And a Cezanne and a Renoir? It's an impressive art collection. Do the paintings belong to your grandfather?'

'Some of them are mine. I bought the Jackson Pollock at auction a year ago.'

He was curious about where a girl from a council estate who sold sandwiches and cleaned for a living had gained such an in-depth knowledge of art. Juliet intrigued him... Rafael frowned as he admitted to himself that she was the only woman ever to have done so.

She stood in front of the Pollock and studied the painting. 'It looks like the artist just threw paint at the canvas. I don't like it. Do you?'

He shrugged. 'I've never thought about whether I like it or not. I paid one hundred and twenty million dollars for the painting, which I bought as an investment.'

She tilted her head to one side and studied him thoughtfully, the same way she had looked at the painting. 'Fancy paying all that money for something that doesn't fill your heart with joy.'

'I will be paying a lot of money for *you*, but I am not feeling joy right now, *chiquita*. I'm feeling exasperated,' he growled. He glanced at her, clumping along next to him in her scuffed boots, and sighed. 'I had forgotten that you haven't had a chance to look around the house because your illness has confined you to bed. I'll give you a tour after lunch.'

He was about to open the dining room door but Juliet put her hand on his arm. 'Is it going to be as awful as last time?' she said in a low tone.

Why hadn't he thought that she would be nervous about meeting his family again—especially his grandfather? And who could blame her? Guilt snaked through Rafael at knowing he had put Juliet in this situation.

Her eyes were huge in her face and her small hand was cold when he wrapped his fingers around hers. 'I have explained that Hector is not angry with *you*.'

'He's disappointed with me because I'm not good enough to be your wife.'

He grimaced. 'No, *cariño*. My grandfather has always been disappointed with *me*. You have done nothing wrong and I won't allow him to insult you again.'

Despite Rafael's reassurance, Juliet felt sick with nerves when he ushered her into the dining room and led her over to the group of people who were gathered by the open French doors where pre-lunch drinks were being served.

He introduced her to his numerous relatives and she was conscious of the curious glances they gave her.

Worse were the unflattering comments she overheard his mother make about her clothes. Perhaps Rafael had not informed his family that she understood Spanish.

The tangible antagonism between him and his mother, the icily elegant Delfina Casillas, was another puzzle. She remembered that Rafael had mentioned he had a stepbrother, but he didn't seem to be at the lunch.

When they sat down for the meal she was relieved that Hector was seated at the far end of the table. He did not pay her any attention, but she was too on edge to enjoy the five courses, and she opted for water rather than wine so that she kept a clear head. She was toying with her dessert—a chocolate confection that at any other time she would have adored—when Hector spoke to her in English.

'Rafael tells me that you ran your own business in London. What type of business?'

Conversation around the table suddenly stopped and Juliet sensed that everyone was looking at her. She lifted her chin. 'I sold sandwiches and delivered them to office staff at lunchtimes.'

'You worked in catering?'

Hector's tone was as scathing as if she'd announced that she had worked as a stripper. Her temper simmered. She hated snobbery, and having been subjected to it at ballet school by some of the other pupils she had learned to stand up for herself.

'Yes. I also had a cleaning job in the evenings— pushing an industrial floor-polishing machine around a shopping centre.'

'Santa Madre! Ella es un domestico!' the old man muttered to Rafael's mother, who was sitting next to him.

Delfina's expression became even haughtier as she glanced along the table at Juliet.

'Abuelo, there is no need for you to be rude about my wife,' Rafael said curtly.

Juliet's heart lifted at his defence of her—until she remembered that he was determined to convince his grandfather he was in love with her.

She looked over at Hector. 'Presumably you are un-aware that I speak Spanish and that I can understand the horrible things you have said about me? I am not from the gutter. My parents weren't wealthy but they were hard-working, and they taught me good manners— which you seem to lack.'

A gasp went around the table, and beside her she felt Rafael stiffen, but she was too angry to care.

'And there is no shame in doing domestic work. Without the staff who run this house you would have to clean your own floors.'

As quickly as her temper had flared it cooled again, and she wished she was anywhere but sitting at this table, with Hector Casillas looking at her disdainfully as if she were a piece of rubbish. What if he decided not to appoint Rafael CEO because she had allowed her pride to get the better of her? She did not dare glance at Rafael, certain that he must be furious with her, and she was startled when he gave a shout of laughter.

'Well said, *querida*.' He looked over at his grandfather. 'As you have just discovered, Abuelo, my wife is petite in stature but she is as fierce as a lioness.'

Juliet turned her head towards her husband and her heart lurched when he smiled at her, showing his even white teeth. She must have imagined that note of admiration in his voice, she told herself.

Following her outburst the atmosphere in the dining room among his relatives was strained and she could not wait for the meal to be over. It was Sofia who broke the awkward silence.

'Where did you learn to speak Spanish, Juliet?'

'My aunt is married to a Spaniard and Uncle Carlos insisted on speaking Spanish at home with Aunt Vivian and my cousins. I lived with them for a couple of years, and quickly picked up on how to speak the language, but I'm not confident at reading and writing in Spanish.'

It was for that reason she had been unable to find a better paid job as a translator, Juliet thought ruefully.

'Did you live in Spain with your aunt and uncle?' Sofia asked.

'No—Australia. They settled in Sydney twenty years ago, but my uncle wanted to feel a connection to his birth country.'

'What about your parents? Do they also live in Australia?'

She shook her head. 'Mum and Dad died before Poppy was born.'

'I'm so sorry,' Sofia said gently. 'I assume your parents were not very old. Did they lose their lives in an accident?'

'Their car broke down on a motorway and they were waiting for the rescue truck. It was a foggy night and a lorry ploughed into them. They were both killed instantly.'

'What a terrible tragedy. You must have been devastated.'

'Yes.'

Memories flooded Juliet's mind of the night that her life had been blown apart. She missed her parents so much and she felt very alone—an outsider in Rafael's family home, made to feel unwelcome by his relatives. Tears blurred her eyes and she stared down at the table while she struggled to bring her emotions under control. To her horror she felt a tear slide down her cheek and drip onto the tablecloth. The bead of moisture darkened the pristine white cloth as it soaked into the material.

Rafael made a low sound in his throat, almost like a groan, and placed his hand over hers, where she was resting it on the table. That human connection—the warmth of his skin as he threaded his fingers through hers—tugged on her heart.

For a few moments she allowed herself to daydream that he actually cared about her as he lifted her hand to his mouth and pressed his lips against her knuckles. Her eyes flew to his and he held her gaze, his expression softer than she had ever seen it. Time seemed to be suspended, and it was as if there were only the two of them floating in a private universe.

Juliet released a shaky breath—but when she glanced around the table she saw that Hector was watching them and understanding dawned. Rafael was acting in front of his grandfather and she was a fool for wishing that his concern was genuine.

When the lunch was over, and they stood up and

walked out of the dining room, she tried to snatch her hand out of his. 'Hector can't see us now, so you can stop pretending to be sympathetic,' she muttered.

'I wasn't pretending.' He stopped walking and stared down at her, tightening his fingers around her hand so that she could not pull free. 'I am not without compassion. You have been through a hell of a lot.'

She shook her head, refusing to allow herself to fall for the huskiness in his voice. 'Like you *care*, Rafael,' she said sarcastically. 'I realise that for the next year I will have to act like your loving wife in public, but I don't want your pseudo-sympathy or your fake kisses.'

Something indecipherable flared in his eyes. 'There was nothing fake about the chemistry we both felt this morning or the way you responded when I kissed you. Perhaps I should remind you?'

Without being aware of how she'd got there, Juliet found herself standing in a small alcove off the marble-lined entrance hall. Rafael ignored her renewed attempts to free her hand by the simple method of re-positioning it behind her back.

He swore when she kicked his shin. 'Calm down, you little wildcat.'

She glared at him, her heart thudding unevenly as he lowered his head. 'I don't want you to kiss me.'

'We've been through that once.'

He sounded bored, but his eyes glittered with something that Juliet was stunned to realise was desire. For *her*. He lifted his other hand and pulled the pins out of her bun, so that her hair unravelled and spilled over her shoulders.

'No one is around to see us so why are you doing this?' she asked desperately.

'You need to practise kissing,' he told her.

His voice was deadpan, but there was a wicked gleam in his eyes that made her stomach swoop.

'It's my guess that you haven't had much experience.'

'I'm sorry if you were disappointed by my efforts earlier,' she choked. 'Do you take pleasure in humiliating me?'

'I find this much more pleasurable,' he murmured against her lips, his breath mingling with hers as he brought his mouth down and kissed her with a possessiveness that decimated her defences.

And Juliet surrendered. She suspected that she would hate herself later, but right now she was powerless to fight the restless longing that stirred low in her belly as Rafael deepened the kiss and explored the shape of her lips with his tongue before he dipped it into her mouth, demanding a response that she could not deny him.

She had never felt like this before—wild and hungry and aching with a passion that stung her nipples and tugged sharp and needy between her thighs. Rafael had been right to think that she hadn't had much experience of kissing or anything else.

She'd only been on a few dates with Bryan before he had suggested they spend the night together. Naively she'd believed that he was in love with her, as she had been with him, and so she had agreed.

Her first and only sexual experience had been uncomfortable and unsatisfactory—which he had assured her was *her* fault. Bryan had not wanted her for more than one night—and Rafael did not want her at all. Not really.

He had married her because she was unattractive and now he was stuck with her for a year. He couldn't resume his playboy lifestyle while he had to convince his grandfather that his marriage was genuine. Faced with a choice of celibacy or sex with his wife, perhaps he had decided that she was the better of the two options.

Shame doused the fire inside her and she jerked her mouth away from his. 'No.'

'*No?*' He sounded as dazed as she felt and he was breathing hard. 'I could very easily persuade you to retract that statement, *chiquita*...' he rasped.

'Why would you want to? We both know that I am the last woman you would desire. I am too thin and plain.' She bit her lip. 'I've seen pictures of the supermodels you take to bed.'

His eyes narrowed. 'You are not plain. You just need the right clothes for your shape.'

'My mother used to say that you can't make a silk purse out of a sow's ear. I know what I am, and more to the point I know my lack of looks and sophistication are the reasons you married me.'

It hurt more than it should, and she pushed past him, hating the idea that he might pity her.

She ran up the grand staircase and then hesitated on the landing when she realised that she had no idea where Rafael's suite of rooms were or, more importantly, the location of the nursery. Her arms ached to hold her daughter and feel the unconditional love that Poppy gave her and she returned a thousandfold.

'Are you lost?' Rafael's sister walked along the corridor towards her and laughed when Juliet nodded. 'The house is huge, isn't it? When Rafael and I first came to live here we couldn't get over how grand it is.'

'I assumed you were both born here. Where did you live before you moved into the mansion?'

Sofia gave her a thoughtful look. 'You should ask my brother. Here's the nursery.' She seemed relieved to change the subject. 'I promised to take the twins swimming this afternoon. Will you and Poppy join us?'

'Neither of us have swimwear. I've never taken Poppy swimming. The local pool where we lived in London was closed down by the council. There was a pool at a private gym but I couldn't afford the membership fees.' Juliet flushed and looked away from Rafael's elegant sister.

'I'm sure you have always done your best for your daughter,' Sofia said gently. 'But Poppy can use one of the swimsuits that the girls have grown out of, and I'll lend you a swimming costume.'

Juliet's conscience would not allow Poppy to miss out on her first experience of swimming, and the little girl's excitement when they arrived at the pool later that afternoon helped her to overcome her reluctance to slip off the towelling robe and reveal the sky-blue swimsuit that Sofia had lent her.

The twins were already in the water and Juliet noted that they were proficient swimmers. She felt guilty that her circumstances meant that Poppy had missed out on so many things—especially a father, she thought as she watched Sofia's husband playing with his daughters. He waded up the steps carrying Ana and Inez in each arm, and Sofia introduced him to Juliet.

'I was meant to arrive back in time for lunch but my flight was delayed,' Marcus Davenport explained. His pleasant face broke into a grin. 'I hear that you stood up to Hector? I wish I had been there to witness it.'

Sofia and Marcus were so friendly that Juliet started to relax as she played in the pool with Poppy, who was wearing armbands and bobbing about happily in the water.

'There's an indoor pool too, and Poppy will soon

learn to swim without water aids if you bring her every day,' Sofia said.

For the first time since Rafael had dropped the bombshell that they would have to remain married for a year and live at the Casillas mansion Juliet realised that there would be some benefits—especially for her daughter. Poppy was already picking up a few Spanish words from the twins, and she would have so much freedom to play in the gardens or at the beach, which had been visible when Juliet had stood on the balcony that morning.

Her stomach hollowed as she remembered what had happened when Rafael had found her on the balcony. He had kissed her, and it had been so much better than she'd imagined.

And she had imagined it often.

Her secret fantasies, in which he swept her into his arms and claimed her mouth with his, had not been disappointed by the sensual expertise of his kiss. Just thinking about it made her breasts tingle, and when she glanced down she was dismayed to see the hard points of her nipples outlined beneath her swimsuit.

The sound of a familiar gravelly voice with a sexy accent caused her to spin round, and she quickly ducked her shoulders under the water when she saw Rafael standing at the edge of the pool. A pair of navy blue swim shorts sat low on his hips, and Juliet's gaze skittered over his hair-roughened thighs before moving up to his flat abdomen and broad, tanned chest covered in silky black hair.

Oh, my! She edged into deeper water to hide her body's reaction to his rampant masculinity.

Poppy gave a squeal of delight when she saw Rafael. 'Raf—are you coming swimming?'

'Would you like me to, *conejita*?'

He swung himself down into the pool and dived below the surface before reappearing and raking his wet hair off his brow with his hands.

'Let me see you swim, little rabbit,' he said to Poppy, and she immediately kicked her feet the way Juliet had tried to persuade her to do for the past twenty minutes.

They stayed in the water for a while longer, until Poppy started to shiver, and then Rafael lifted her onto the poolside where Elvira was waiting with a towel. He turned back to Juliet and frowned when he saw her tense expression. 'What's the matter? We are meant to be playing happy families but you haven't stopped glaring at me.'

'That's just it. This is a game to you,' she said tautly. 'But while you are *"playing happy families"* to impress your grandfather, there is a danger that Poppy will become fond of you. When I agreed to our marriage deal it was only going to be for a couple of months, but now we have to stay together for a year and it will be harder on Poppy when I take her back to England.'

'Are you saying that I should *ignore* your daughter?' Rafael's frown deepened. 'I realise the situation has changed and I won't suddenly drop out of Poppy's life in a year's time.' He swore beneath his breath when Juliet gave him a disbelieving look. 'It is not my intention to upset Poppy. She is a delightful child and a credit to you,' he said gruffly.

'She likes you,' Juliet muttered. 'You are good with her and your nieces.'

The truth was that she'd felt a tug of jealousy when Poppy had wanted to play with Rafael rather than with her. She had been surprised that he was so patient with her daughter and his sister's little girls.

'You'll make a good father when you have children of your own.'

'That's never going to happen.' His tone dropped several degrees. 'I've no desire to have children.'

'What if your wife wants a family? I don't mean me,' she added hastily. 'But in the future you might meet the right woman and fall in love with her.'

'I told you when you agreed to be my wife that I do not believe in love.' He walked up the steps out of the pool and grabbed a towel from a nearby sunbed. 'Lust is an emotion I understand, but that doesn't last for ever. Unfortunately too many people only discover that after they have made a legal commitment to spend the rest of their lives together, and the only winners are the divorce lawyers.'

'Why are you so cynical? My parents were as much in love with each other when they died as they were on the day they married. They were happy together for more than twenty years.' She swallowed. 'It might sound odd, but I'm glad they were together when they were killed. I don't know how one would have survived without the other.'

Juliet followed Rafael out of the pool and stopped dead when she saw him staring at her leg. She had been so engrossed in their conversation that she'd forgotten about the scar that ran from the top of her thigh to just above her knee. The scar had faded over the years, but she was chilly after being in the pool and it was now a vivid purple welt on her pale skin.

Avoiding his gaze, she hurried over to where she had left her robe and wrapped it around her, thankful that it covered her leg. She had come to terms with the scar, or so she'd thought, but she wished Rafael hadn't seen it. No doubt now he thought she was ugly as well as plain.

'What happened to you?' he asked quietly.

'I was in my parents' car when the lorry crashed into the back of it.'

'Dios.' He dropped his towel and strode over to her, settling his hand on her shoulder. 'I didn't realise that you were with your parents when they died.'

'I don't remember much about the accident.' Juliet automatically turned her head to check on Poppy, and saw her playing in a sandpit with the twins. 'The car developed a problem while we were driving along the motorway and my dad pulled over onto the hard shoulder. It was winter and very foggy. I was sitting in the front passenger seat and Dad told me to stay there while he went to get my coat out of the boot. Mum got out with him, and that's when the lorry smashed into us.'

She was conscious of Rafael curling his fingers tighter around her shoulder. She had never really spoken about what had happened to anyone before, but now the words came tumbling out.

'All I remember is a loud noise like an explosion. I was in a coma for two weeks, and when I came round I was told that my femur had been shattered by the impact of the crash. At first the surgeon thought that my leg would have to be amputated, but he did everything he could and saved it. My thigh bone is held together with several metal pins.' She swallowed. 'My aunt had flown over from Australia and she broke the news about my parents when I came out of Intensive Care.'

'Dios!' Rafael repeated roughly. 'Has your leg healed fully?'

'It's fine now, but eighteen months ago I had to have some more surgery and I was in hospital for a few weeks. Aunt Viv couldn't come over from Australia then, because she was ill herself. There was no one to look after Poppy so she stayed with foster parents.'

Juliet felt a pang, remembering how desperately she had missed her daughter while they had been apart. She watched the sunlight glinting on the surface of the pool. It was so bright that it made her eyes sting. That was the reason for the tears that blurred her vision, she assured herself.

'Poppy is all I have,' she whispered. 'Bryan has never been interested in her but now he's threatening to take my baby away from me.' She spun away from Rafael and his hand fell from her shoulder. 'I won't let that happen,' she said fiercely. 'That's why I agreed to your marriage deal and why I am determined to see it through.'

She stared at his beautiful face, at the mouth that had wreaked such havoc on hers.

'I'm using you as much as you are using me. Let's hope that we both end up with what we want in a year's time.'

CHAPTER SIX

RAFAEL STROLLED THROUGH the marble and gold entrance hall in the Casillas mansion, clearly designed to impress, with a champagne flute in one hand and a smile on his lips that anyone who knew him well—which only his sister did—would realise was entirely fake. He stopped to speak to his uncle, but although he was fond of Tio Alvaro, who was one of his supporters, Rafael's attention was on the grand staircase where he expected to see Juliet appear.

Where the hell *was* his wife?

When he had knocked on the door of her dressing room before he'd come down to greet the guests who were arriving for his grandfather's birthday party Sofia had called out that Juliet would be ready in ten minutes. That had been a quarter of an hour ago, and Rafael was growing concerned that she did not want to leave her room because she was afraid of being subjected to another frosty reception from certain members of his family.

He had barely seen her for the past two days, while he had been at work at the Casillas Group's head office in Valencia. He'd arranged for her to go shopping with a personal stylist who would advise her on a new wardrobe, and Sofia had offered to look after Poppy.

However, Rafael had yet to see if the stylist had been successful in finding some clothes which suited Juliet's figure.

She had been fast asleep in his bed by the time he'd returned to the mansion late in the evenings, after long days of business meetings. And, aware that she had only recently recovered from the virus that had made her so unwell, he had been reluctant to disturb her and had slept on the sofa in his dressing room again.

But she had been on his mind a lot. Too much. Instead of concentrating on what was being said at the meetings he had found himself thinking of Juliet when they had been at the pool. He'd pictured her in that light blue swimsuit which matched the startling blue of her eyes. The clingy material had revealed her slender figure and small, round breasts. She was as fragile as a bird, and when he'd seen that scar on her leg, before she had quickly wrapped her robe around her to hide it from him, he'd been struck once again by her mix of vulnerability and incredible courage.

The realisation that Juliet might have died along with her parents in the car accident, and that he might never have met her, disturbed Rafael more than it should. After all, it was not as if she meant anything to him. He kept his affairs short and sweet, aware of the damage that the unstable mix of emotions and relationships could produce. His mother had followed her heart when she'd eloped with his father, and Rafael was the damaged product of his parents' messed-up lives.

'It is a big night for you tonight, eh?' said Tio Alvaro.

Rafael nodded his head, not entirely sure what his uncle meant.

'I have heard rumours that Hector is going to announce you as his successor. It is what you have wanted for a long time?'

'Ah, yes.'

Rafael did not explain that his grandfather's announcement would contain a caveat and that the handover of power would not happen immediately. To his astonishment he realised that he had not given Hector's announcement a thought. He had waited for years and fought hard to claim his birthright, but tonight his mind was on Juliet rather than the CEO-ship.

He raked a hand through his hair and asked himself why he was allowing a slip of a girl with an understated sensuality and eyes that he could drown in to affect him. Something caught his attention, and when he looked up towards the top of the staircase he felt the new experience of his heart colliding painfully with his ribs.

'Ah, querida...' he murmured beneath his breath.

He had already been surprised by Juliet—by her unexpected fiery nature and the sensual heat of her kiss that had made him ache for hours afterwards. But as he watched her begin to descend the grand marble staircase, one hand holding lightly onto the banister rail, he was quite simply awestruck.

She shimmered. There was no other way to describe her. The effect was created by the hundreds of gold sequins that covered her ball gown, but there was something else that made Juliet sparkle. It was self-confidence and pride, Rafael thought as he strode across the hall to the base of the staircase. It was also, he mused as he stood there, unable to take his eyes off her, her own realisation that she was beautiful. So very beautiful.

And she was certainly making an entrance. The eyes of every person in the hall were focused on his stunning, sexy wife as she walked down the stairs towards him.

How had he not seen before how utterly lovely she was? Well-fitting clothes helped, of course. The gown had been designed to mould her slender frame and emphasise the narrowness of her waist. The bodice was strapless and her small breasts were displayed like perfect round peaches above the low-cut neckline. The shimmering gold material followed the gentle contours of her hips before finally flaring out trumpet style to the floor.

She seemed to glide down the stairs, and Rafael caught a glimpse of gold stiletto heels beneath the hem of her dress. He lifted his gaze up to her hair, which had had three or four inches cut off its length and now fell to mid-way down her back, gleaming like polished amber beneath the bright lights of the chandeliers. A stylist had added some wispy layers to the front sections of her hair, which framed her face and drew attention to her high cheekbones and forget-me-not-blue eyes.

When she halted two steps above where he was waiting for her Rafael saw that her fair eyebrows and lashes had been darkened with make-up and her mouth was coated in a rose-coloured gloss. The finishing touch to her transformation was her perfume—floral notes mixed with an edgier, more sensual fragrance that assailed his senses and evoked a kick of heat in his groin.

As he studied her he saw a wariness in her expression that he instantly wanted to banish. *'Bella,'* he murmured, capturing her hand in his and lifting it to his mouth. 'I'm speechless, *chiquita.* I would never have believed…'

'That a sow's ear could be turned into something passably attractive?' she suggested.

'I never want to hear you use that terrible expression again. You are not and never have been a sow's ear.'

But he had been blind, Rafael acknowledged. Worse, he had been arrogant enough to believe that he could use Juliet to further his raging ambition. He had chosen her because of her downtrodden appearance. *Dios*, he had treated her as scornfully as his grandfather had. But Juliet's ethereal beauty hid an incredible strength of will. She was a survivor—as he was—and he knew how lonely that felt.

Shame ran through Rafael. Distaste for his presumption that Juliet's lack of money made her less worthy of his respect. He had spent the past twenty years fighting prejudice from his family because of his lowly background—part-*gitano*, born in the gutter to a drug-dealer father. But he had ruthlessly exploited Juliet's financial problems to persuade her to marry him without considering how humiliated she would feel to be despised by his rich relatives.

'You look exquisite,' he assured her. 'I take it that your shopping trip was a success?'

She caught her lower lip between her teeth, making him want to soothe the place with his tongue. 'The personal stylist insisted that I needed dozens of outfits to reflect my position as your wife. She spent a *fortune* on clothes. But I'll pay you back when—' She broke off and glanced around to check that they could not be overheard by anyone. 'When our marriage deal ends.'

Rafael laid his finger lightly across her lips, refusing to question why he did not want to think of the motive behind their marriage. 'I believe in living for the moment,' he said softly. 'And at this moment, *querida*, I will be honoured to escort my beautiful wife into the ballroom.'

Juliet smiled and her elfin beauty made his gut clench. He drew her arm through his and walked her into the ballroom, where most of the three hundred guests were now assembled and waiters were serving champagne and canapés. Many of Spain's elite—a mix of old money aristocrats and nouveau riche millionaires—were on the guest list.

He took a glass of champagne offered by a waiter and gave it to Juliet before he took a glass for himself. *'Salud.'*

She sipped her drink. 'Is it real champagne? I've only ever had sparkling wine.'

'Of course it's real champagne. My grandfather would not allow fizzy wine to be served at his eightieth birthday party,' he said drily.

'It's lovely.' She took another sip and giggled. 'It feels like the bubbles are exploding on my tongue.'

Rafael stared at her. He could not stop himself. Juliet was like a breath of fresh air, and he realised how stultifying and predictable his life had become until she had burst into it.

He did not know what to make of the feelings she stirred in him. The hot rush of desire that went straight to his groin was something he understood, but he felt possessive, protective, and a host of other emotions that had never troubled him before.

Juliet bit her lip and he realised that she had mistaken his brooding silence for irritation. 'I'm not sophisticated,' she mumbled, rosy colour running under her skin.

'Thank God,' he reassured her.

The band had started playing and he led her over to the dance floor, handing their empty glasses to a waiter before he drew her into his arms. Even in high heels she was so much smaller than him that he could rest his chin on the top of her head.

She danced with a natural grace that captivated him, and he swore silently when he felt the predictable reaction of a certain part of his anatomy to the sensation of Juliet's lithe body pressed up against his hard thighs. He was in trouble, Rafael acknowledged, seizing the excuse that the tune had finished to step away from her.

'Come and meet some people.'

He took her hand and felt her tense as he led her across the ballroom.

'Relax,' he murmured, bending his head so that his mouth was against her ear and his breath stirred the tendrils of her hair. 'Tio Alvaro and his wife Lucia are nice. Just be yourself.'

Rafael introduced Juliet to his aunt and uncle and fielded their curiosity about where and when he had met his bride. He was conscious of the simmering look Juliet darted at him when he explained that it had been love at first sight when they had met in London.

Lucia glanced at Juliet's hand. 'I see you are not wearing an engagement ring. Shame on you, Rafael.'

'We married quickly—there wasn't time to choose a ring,' he said smoothly.

'Alvaro and I will be visiting London next month,' Lucia said to Juliet. 'I want to visit Buckingham Palace. Did you live near it?'

'Not very near,' she replied without a flicker.

Rafael pictured the tower block in the rough part of London where Juliet had lived, and was fiercely glad that she and her little daughter would never have to go back there.

'Where else do you recommend we visit while we're staying in the capital?' Lucia asked.

'Well, if you like music, or ballet, I recommend booking tickets for the Royal Albert Hall. It's a won-

derful venue to enjoy a concert. Or there's the Royal
Festival Hall and the Royal Opera House. All are spec-
tacular.'

'I suppose you worked as a cleaner in the Opera
House?' a voice said sarcastically.

Rafael looked round and saw Hector was standing
close by. His grandfather had obviously been listening
to the conversation. Furious with the old man, he tightened his arm around Juliet's waist, hoping she was not
upset. *Dios*, his grandfather was a snob.

'Abuelo…' he began tensely.

'Actually, I danced at all three venues,' Juliet said
calmly. 'I was a ballerina, and in my very brief career
I performed on stage at several of London's best concert halls.'

Shock ran through Rafael. He heard Hector give a
disbelieving snort but Tia Lucia clapped her hands together and said excitedly, 'I *love* the ballet—especially
Swan Lake.'

'That's one of my favourites too,' Juliet said with
a smile. 'I once performed the Dance of the Cygnets.'

'Do you still dance?' Lucia asked.

Juliet shook her head. 'Not professionally. I was
badly injured in an accident and couldn't continue with
my ballet career.'

Hector walked away and Rafael made an excuse,
leaving Juliet to chat to his aunt and uncle, while he
strode after his grandfather.

'Abuelo.' He caught up with the old man and scowled
at him. It occurred to Rafael that he had spent all his
adult life trying to win Hector's approval—without success. He *was* the best person to take over running the
Casillas Group—he knew it and so did his grandfather.
But he could never escape his gypsy heritage and the

prejudice and mistrust it evoked—not just in his family but in people generally.

'Do not *ever* treat my wife with disrespect again,' he told Hector savagely. 'You have no right to make judgements upon her. You know nothing about Juliet.'

Hector's bushy brows rose. 'Do *you*?' he challenged.

He stared at Rafael, and the curiosity in his expression slowly changed into something which might have been begrudging respect. But maybe he'd imagined it, Rafael thought. And then he realised that he did not care about his grandfather's opinion of him. His only concern was that Hector would treat Juliet with the consideration and courtesy she deserved.

As he threaded his way back across the crowded ballroom he was waylaid by his half-brother. 'How are you, Francisco?' he greeted the young man.

'I'm in shock,' his brother said with a grin. 'Mamà has told me that you have a wife, but she seems to think it is suspicious that you married so quickly.'

Rafael knew it was not his half-brother's fault that their mother favoured him, her youngest son, and would do anything to see him succeed Hector. He did not like deceiving Frankie, but he could not risk Delfina discovering that his marriage was fake.

'No one was more surprised than me when I fell in love with Juliet,' he murmured. It was odd how easily the lie fell from his lips.

'I can't wait to meet the woman who finally persuaded you up the aisle. She must be amazing.'

'She certainly amazes *me*,' said Rafael, thinking of Juliet's latest startling revelation. 'I'll introduce you to her when I find her.'

He frowned as he scanned the ballroom but failed to see a sparkly gold dress.

* * *

Juliet stepped through the glass doors leading from the ballroom onto a wide balcony. Immediately the buzz of chattering voices and the music from the band became muted. It was a clear night, and she tipped her head back and studied the stars glittering like diamonds against the inky backdrop of the sky.

The party wasn't as daunting as she had expected, and apart from an awkward moment when Rafael's grandfather had made an unpleasant comment to her she was enjoying herself.

She had never dreamed when she'd been cleaning floors in the shopping centre that she would ever wear a beautiful ball gown, drink champagne and dance cheek to cheek—well, cheek to chest, she amended—with her impossibly handsome husband.

She leaned her elbows on the top of the stone balustrade and stared out over the dark garden. The mingled scents of jasmine and bougainvillea filled the air and she breathed deep, trying to slow the frantic thud of her pulse as she remembered the expression on Rafael's face when she had walked down the stairs in her glittering gold ball gown.

He had looked stunned—as if he couldn't believe it was her. And she understood the feeling because when she'd seen her reflection in the mirror after Sofia had applied the finishing touches to her make-up she had hardly recognised herself.

'My brother is in for a shock,' Sofia had said in a satisfied voice. 'You look amazing.'

Juliet *felt* amazing. Rafael had told her she looked beautiful and her heart had leapt when she'd seen the unmistakable gleam of desire in his green eyes. It had restored her pride after he'd looked at her with such disdain on the day of their wedding, when she had walked down the stairs at Ferndown House wearing that hideous dress.

But none of this was real, she reminded herself. Oh, the ball gown which shimmered every time she moved was real, as were the dozens of new outfits—some formal, some more casual, but all of them exorbitantly expensive—that filled her wardrobe. She had new shoes too: numerous pairs of elegant high heels made of softest Italian leather in a variety of colours, with matching handbags, and accessories including silk scarves and some pieces of modern, chunky costume jewellery made from semi-precious stones. She had thrown away all her old clothes, apart from a couple of leotards and her pointe shoes that she'd kept as reminders of her life as a ballerina.

Juliet knew it would easy to be swept away by the magic that had transformed her from looking and feeling unattractive to a realisation that she looked quite nice in clothes that fitted properly. But she must not forget the reason why Rafael had married her, and she must not allow herself to be seduced by a self-confessed playboy who had made clear his scathing opinion of love.

Not that she would be foolish enough to fall in love with him, she assured herself.

'Why are you out here alone?'

Rafael's gravelly voice sent a prickle of awareness across Juliet's skin and she spun round and found him standing close beside her. Much too close. Heat exploded inside her when his thigh brushed against hers.

He looked incredible, in a superbly tailored black tuxedo, white silk shirt and a black bow tie. A lock of his hair fell forward across his brow, and the shadow of black stubble covering his jaw gave him a rakish look that was spine-tinglingly sexy. Memories assailed her of the way he had held her tightly against his strong body while they had danced together. She had felt the warmth of his skin through his shirt and seen the shadow of his black chest hair beneath the fine silk. She'd wanted so badly to tear open the buttons and run her hands over his naked torso…

'I came outside for some air.' She gave him a rueful smile. 'I am no more alone out here than in the ball-room, where I don't know anyone.'

'You know me.'

'Not really. We are strangers, thrown together in this crazy marriage.'

He frowned. 'We need to spend some time getting to know each other or we won't manage to convince my grandfather that our relationship is genuine. For a start, why didn't you mention before that you trained as a ballerina?'

'I didn't think you would be interested. You picked me to be your wife because you believed I was uncul-tured and came from a poor background.'

His jaw tightened. 'I have already apologised for the way I treated you.'

'You don't have to apologise when you're going to pay me five million pounds.'

If she kept reminding herself of the deal they had made she might find it easier to ignore the burning in-tensity in his gaze that made her wish their marriage was real in every sense.

Rafael exhaled heavily. 'The car accident that took your parents' lives also ended your dancing career, didn't it?'

'I had just danced the role of Giselle in London— one of the youngest ballerinas to have been chosen for the part.' Juliet hugged her arms around her. 'Mum and Dad died because of *me*,' she whispered. 'They were driving me to Birmingham, because the ballet was due to open next at the Symphony Hall there. I could have gone on the coach with the other dancers but my parents always came to my first night performances.'

'The accident was not your fault—you have to believe that,' Rafael said roughly. He pulled her into his arms and held her close to his chest. 'Thick fog and a speeding lorry—you had no control over those things.' He stroked his hand over her hair. 'It sounds as though your parents loved you very much.'

There was an odd note in his voice that Juliet could not define.

'They sacrificed so much so that I could follow my dream of being a ballerina,' she said. 'I won a scholarship to a boarding ballet school when I was eleven. The fees were paid but there were many other expenses, and my parents worked extra hours to buy my ballet shoes and cover all the costs.'

She sighed.

'I was the only scholarship student in my year and most of the other pupils were from wealthy families. I was made to feel that I didn't belong there by some of my peers because of my background. In the same way your grandfather made me feel that I was an outsider when you introduced me as your wife.'

Rafael's chest rose and fell. 'Why did you stay at the school if the other pupils upset you?'

'I was determined to be a ballerina and I didn't care about anything else. The other kids stopped teasing me when I consistently came top of the class in my dance exams. And I did make some friends. My best friend Chloe is the daughter of the famous art collector Derek

Mullholland. I used to stay with her in the school holidays and her father would show us around his private
art gallery and talk about the paintings.'

Beneath her ear Juliet heard the steady thud of Rafael's heart.

'Chloe is a soloist ballerina. We keep in touch, but I
am envious of her career,' she admitted.

He said nothing, but he tightened his arms around
her as if he understood, as if he cared—*which of course
he doesn't*, whispered her common sense.

'I plan to use some of your money to set up a dance
school for children and young adults. My leg isn't strong
enough for me to dance on the stage, but I can teach ballet and give other little girls the dream that I fulfilled
for a short time.'

Juliet's heart missed a beat when she felt Rafael
brush his lips over her hairline. Time seemed to be suspended and she did not know how long they stood there,
with his arms wrapped around her and her cheek resting on his shirt front. But gradually she became aware
of the hardness of his thighs pressing against her, and
the heat of his body through his shirt.

The spicy scent of his cologne filled her senses,
and when she looked up at him she discovered that he
was staring at her with an intent expression that made
her stomach swoop. She felt dizzy, as though she had
drunk too much champagne, although she'd only had
one glass.

He slid his hand beneath her chin and his eyes narrowed, gleaming with a sensual promise that set her
pulse racing. Once again she had the feeling that none
of this was real. It was a beautiful dream and she never
wanted to wake up. Her eyelashes drifted closed and
she felt Rafael's warm breath graze her lips.

'Open your eyes,' he commanded in a husky growl that sent a delicious shiver down her spine.

She obeyed, and as her gaze meshed with his she instinctively arched towards him as he angled his mouth over hers and kissed her. At first he kept it light, teasing her lips apart while he moved his hand from her jaw to cradle her cheek in his palm. He tasted divine and she pressed herself closer to him, wanting more, wanting...

'Oh!' Her soft gasp was muffled against his lips as he deepened the kiss, crushing her mouth beneath his so that her head was tilted back and she was powerless to resist his passionate onslaught.

Heat swept through her veins and a wildness bubbled up inside her as Rafael coaxed her lips apart in a kiss that transported her to a place where there was only sensation. He made a rough sound in his throat and moved his hand from her waist to the base of her spine, forcing her pelvis into contact with his so that she felt the powerful proof of his arousal.

Astounded that she could have such an effect on him, Juliet melted against him, lifting her arms to wind them around his neck while he pushed his tongue into her mouth and the kiss became ever more erotic.

Sparks shot through her. She hadn't known that a kiss could be like this: a conflagration that swept away her inhibitions and her uncertainty and compelled her to burn in Rafael's fire.

It took a few seconds for her to realise that the brilliant white lights she could see were not shooting stars but actual lights, which had been switched on to illuminate the balcony. Even more puzzling was the sound of applause.

Rafael lifted his mouth from hers and she turned her

head to discover that they were in full view of the party guests in the ballroom—including his grandfather.

Understanding brought with it a wave of humiliation at the realisation that Rafael had kissed her so publicly in a bid to prove to Hector that their marriage was real. He must have known that the balcony lights were about to be turned on—or maybe he had instructed the staff to switch them on. Either way, that kiss had been under the spotlight…but only one of them had been acting.

Juliet wished a hole would appear beneath her feet and swallow her. But Rafael tightened his hold on her waist, as if he guessed that she wanted to tear herself out of his arms and slap his face. He strode across the balcony, giving her no choice but to walk with him back into the ballroom.

'I want to go and check on Poppy,' she muttered, making the excuse so that she could leave the party.

She was such an idiot. Rafael was a playboy, highly experienced in the art of seduction. And she had betrayed her fascination with him when she had responded to his heart-stopping kisses with an eagerness that made her cheeks burn when she remembered how she had come apart in his arms.

'You can't leave now. My grandfather is about to give his speech,' he told her. 'The nanny will see to Poppy if she wakes up.'

Hector stepped onto a dais at one end of the room and looked around at the guests. 'As you all know, today I celebrate my eightieth birthday. The time has come for me to think about the future of the Casillas Group and consider who will be the best person to succeed me as Chairman and CEO. I believe that person is my eldest grandson Rafael.'

Juliet glanced around the room and was shocked by

the look of fury on Delfina Casillas's haughty face. She wondered why Rafael's mother favoured her youngest son, and why there was no sign of affection between her and Rafael.

'However,' Hector continued, 'I have decided to remain as head of the company for the coming year, while I work closely with Rafael to ensure a smooth transition to his leadership. Rafael knows there are certain areas where he will need to prove his suitability before I step down. In my opinion, whoever ultimately succeeds me should be prepared to show commitment in all areas of his life—which is something that, frankly, Rafael has not done in the past. But his recent marriage suggests a change of heart.'

Hector paused, and from across the room Juliet felt the old man's sharp black eyes flick from Rafael to her. She felt Rafael tighten his grip on her waist, pinning her to him.

'Perhaps,' Hector said thoughtfully, 'Rafael will be able to convince me to retire before the year is up.'

CHAPTER SEVEN

'JULIET—WAIT.'

The sound of Rafael's voice behind her spurred Juliet on to increase her pace as she tore across the lawn, heading away from the twinkling lights of the mansion. But she wasn't used to walking, let alone running in high heels, with a long skirt swirling around her ankles, and he caught up with her in front of the chalet-style summerhouse.

His hand curled around her shoulder. 'Where are you going?'

'Anywhere as long as I'm far away from *you*.'

He swore and caught hold of her other shoulder, spinning her round to face him. 'What's the matter?'

The impatience in Rafael's voice fanned Juliet's temper. 'You are an expert at this game, but I'm just a novice and I don't know the rules,' she muttered.

Moonlight slid over his face, highlighting his razor-edged cheekbones and hard jaw. The mouth that had lived up to its promise of heaven was set in a grim line and his brows were two black slashes on either side of his nose.

'What game? Why did you disappear from the ballroom while the guests were making a toast to my grandfather? People will think we have had a row.'

'I doubt it, after you made sure that everyone, including Hector, witnessed that X-rated snog on the balcony.' Juliet bit her lip. She felt such a fool. 'I opened up to you in a way that I have never done with anyone else,' she told him rawly. 'I thought you'd kissed me because— Oh, not because you *cared*, but I thought you liked me a little. I should have realised it was an ideal opportunity for you to act the role of a loving husband in front of your grandfather when you found me on the balcony. The stage was set and all you needed were lights and action.'

To her horror, her voice wobbled, and she cringed because she could not disguise her hurt feelings. Just because she was wearing a beautiful dress it did not change who she was. She was still a single mother from a council estate, and no amount of clever tailoring could give the illusion that she had the kind of curvaceous figure that Rafael preferred—if the newspaper pictures of his last busty blonde mistress were anything to go by.

She shrugged her shoulders, trying to throw off his hands, but he held her tighter. A muscle flickered in his cheek when she dashed a hand across her wet eyes.

'That was not why I kissed you,' he said harshly. 'It had nothing to do with my grandfather. I didn't know that those damn lights would come on.'

'You can't deny it was convenient that we were lit up like a Christmas tree. And Hector hinted in his speech that he might make you CEO in less than a year, so I can't complain. The sooner he hands you the company the sooner we can end our farce of a marriage.'

'I did not know that we would be seen by everyone in the ballroom.'

Rafael's voice was as dangerous as the rigid set of his

jaw. He trapped her gaze, and her breath hitched in her throat when she saw heat and hunger flash in his eyes.

'I kissed you because I couldn't resist you,' he said tensely. 'Because I'd wanted to kiss you since I watched you float down the stairs looking like a princess in that golden dress with your hair like amber silk. Looking like every red-blooded male's fantasy woman.'

She shook her head, not allowing herself to believe him. 'What man would fantasise about *me*?' she whispered.

'This man, *chiquita*,' he growled.

He jerked her towards him, taking her by surprise, so that she slammed hard into his chest and the air was forced out of her lungs. Before she could draw a breath he'd lowered his head and claimed her mouth in a kiss of blatant possession and savage passion.

Her brain told her to resist him. Insisted she would be a fool to believe him. But there had been something so stark in his voice. And she *wanted* this, Juliet admitted to herself. She wanted his mouth on hers, kissing her with an urgency that was too fierce to be fake.

The world spun on its axis as he swept her into his arms and carried her along the path to the summerhouse, shouldered open the door and kicked it shut behind him while his lips remained fused to hers.

Moonlight shone through the windows and filled the summerhouse with a pearly gleam. Rafael strode over to the sofa that took up one corner of the room and sat down, settling her on his lap. He traced his lips over her cheek, nuzzled the tender place behind her ear and then nipped her earlobe with his sharp teeth, sending starbursts of pleasure through her entire body.

And then his mouth was on hers once more and he was kissing her—unhurriedly at first, and then with increasing passion when she responded to him with a fervency that made him groan. His pressed his lips to the pulse beating erratically at the base of her throat before he kissed his way along her collarbone.

Juliet felt his hand on the bare skin of her back and only realised that he had tugged the zip of her dress down when the strapless bodice fell away from her breasts. The air felt cool on her heated skin and her nipples swelled and hardened beneath Rafael's avid gaze.

'No bra,' he said thickly.

'I'm too small to need one.' Her tiny breasts were a constant regret to her.

'You're perfect.'

Dark colour ran along his cheekbones when he cupped one breast in his hand. Reaction shivered through Juliet as he rubbed his thumb-pad across her nipple, teasing the sensitive peak so that she made a choked sound. The pleasure of his touch was so intense that she could not control the little quivers that ran through her. Rafael was a sorcerer and she was spellbound by his magic.

She held her breath when he lowered his head to her breast. Moonbeams danced across his dark hair and Juliet sank her fingers into the rich silk as he captured her nipple between his lips and flicked his tongue back and forth over the dusky tip.

Darts of pleasure shot down to the molten place between her legs. Her ability to think was lost in the wondrous sensations he was creating with his mouth and his hands on her body. She was startled to realise that the husky moans that bounced off the walls of the summerhouse were coming from her throat.

Rafael pulled the bodice of her dress down so that it bunched at her waist and then leaned his head against the back of the sofa, his eyes glittering as he subjected her to a slow appraisal.

'You are exquisite,' he said, in a rough tone that made Juliet ache everywhere.

He cradled the pale mounds of her breasts in his big hands and played with her reddened nipples. The ache deep in her pelvis became an insistent throb. When he shifted their position, so that she was lying on the sofa and he was stretched out on top of her, she gloried in his weight pressing her into the cushions. He nudged her legs apart with his thigh and she felt the hard length of his arousal press against her feminine core through the dress.

And all the while Rafael kissed her with a mastery that made her shake with an incandescent need that blazed and burned until she was only aware of the heat of his body and the sweep of his hands across her skin.

He lifted the hem of her dress and skimmed a path up to her thighs, tracing his fingers over her tiny lace panties. Lost in the sheer delight of his caresses, Juliet held her breath and willed him to move his fingers higher. She shuddered when he dipped into the waistband of her knickers and stroked his finger lightly over her moist opening.

It was a very long time since a man had touched her so intimately. There had only been one other man before Rafael and she didn't want to think about Bryan and her solitary, uninspiring experience of sex with him. But the word floated in her mind. Was that where this was leading? Did Rafael want to have sex with her?

He was as hard as a spike beneath his trousers, and she imagined him pulling his zip down and pushing the panel of her panties aside so that he could drive his erection into her.

She was eager for him to make love to her. But like this? A frantic coupling in the dark in a glorified shed before they returned to his grandfather's birthday party?

More importantly, she wasn't prepared for sex—and while she had forgiven herself for one accidental pregnancy, two would be utterly irresponsible.

Even so, the temptation she felt to allow Rafael to continue caressing her with his clever fingers was strong, and her body throbbed with unfulfilled longing when she tore her mouth from his.

'I'm not on the pill.'

Rafael froze as Juliet's words kick-started his brain, which until that moment had been clouded in a red haze of desire. His first reaction was frustration that he wasn't carrying condoms in his jacket, as he invariably did on evenings out in London. He saw nothing wrong with one-night stands if both parties understood the rules.

But Juliet was not a woman he had picked up in a nightclub—she was his wife. In name only. That was what he had assured her when he'd suggested their marriage deal, and in all honesty he hadn't expected that he would *want* to take his unappealing bride who had behaved like a sullen teenager at the register office to bed.

He had been blind to her beauty and unaware of her vulnerability, which was evident now in her wary expression as he lifted himself off her and offered her his hand to pull her up from the sofa. The shadowy interior of the summerhouse could not disguise the flush that spread over her cheeks as she dragged the top of her dress up to cover her breasts.

'Will you zip me up?'

She presented her back to him and his stomach

clenched as he pushed her silky fall of hair over one fragile shoulder so that he could fasten her dress.

'I can't face going back to the ballroom,' she said in low voice.

Rafael studied her kiss-stung lips and the betraying hard points of her nipples, visible through her dress, and it occurred to him that his grandfather would have no doubt that his marriage was real if he saw evidence that he and Juliet had slipped away from the party to indulge their passion for each other.

But he couldn't bring himself to humiliate her in front of his family, who had already judged her so harshly because of their misplaced belief that money and an aristocratic lineage made them better than a cash-strapped single mother.

He looked away from her, struggling to bring his rampant libido under control. 'You can go into the house via the kitchens and use the back staircase to go up to the apartment so that no one sees you. I'll say that you were feeling unwell and have gone to bed.'

'Thank you.'

Instead of walking out of the summerhouse when he opened the door she stood on her tiptoes and pressed her lips to his cheek. His pulse kicked when he breathed in her feminine fragrance—perfume mixed with something muskier that clung to his fingers—and he recognised the scent of her womanhood.

'Rafael...'

He did not want a post mortem on what had happened between them. What definitely should not have happened and what must not happen again.

'I should get back to the party before my absence is noticed,' he said.

The flash of hurt in her eyes at his abrupt tone convinced him that he should have listened to the warning voice in his head when she'd fled from the party and he had chased after her.

Rafael stayed in the ballroom until after midnight, when the last of the guests departed. His grandfather had retired to bed some time ago and it had given him an excuse to remain downstairs and act as host.

When he entered his private suite he headed straight for his study and spent another half an hour there, nursing a large cognac. Juliet would surely be asleep by now, he thought as he entered his dressing room and threw a pile of bedding onto the sofa.

His cufflinks hit the dressing table, followed by his tie. He shrugged out of his shirt and undid his trousers, wincing when the zip brushed against his manhood, which was still semi-aroused several hours after he'd nearly lost his sanity in the summerhouse.

'I only discovered today that this is where you have been sleeping.'

Juliet's soft voice came from the doorway between the master bedroom and the dressing room.

'I assumed there were two bedrooms in the apartment and you were using the second one.'

He glanced at her and felt his blood rush south, his erection instantly and embarrassingly hard. Juliet had shimmered in the sequined ball gown, but in a black satin chemise with semi-transparent lace bra cups that exposed a tantalising amount of her small but perfectly formed breasts she simmered with sensual promise.

Once again he wondered how he could have dismissed her as drab. The uncomfortable truth was that he had seen what he'd wanted to see, Rafael acknowledged. The irony of finding himself fiercely attracted to his little sexpot wife wasn't lost on him.

'There is only a master bedroom in my private suite. Obviously the house has other bedrooms—twenty-five, I believe, although I have never counted them. But we need Hector to think we are sleeping together.'

'I can't imagine that sofa is comfortable for someone of your height…' Juliet hesitated and a rosy stain ran under her skin. 'We could share the bed. I mean—it's huge. Big enough for us to keep to our own sides of the mattress…unless you want…'

Her voice trailed off and the shy look she gave him very nearly made him forget that she was off limits.

'No,' he said curtly. 'That would be a bad idea.'

The pink flush on her cheeks spilled down her throat and across the upper slopes of her breasts, tempting him to rip the confection of satin and lace from her body, sweep her into his arms and carry her through to the bedroom so that they could both enjoy that big, soft bed—but not to sleep in.

He knew it was what Juliet wanted him to do. Her pupils were dilated so that her eyes were dark discs rimmed with brilliant blue. But he suspected that she wanted her sexual gratification wrapped up in a romantic ideal that he was incapable of giving her.

'I didn't get the impression earlier tonight that you thought our sharing a bed was a bad idea.' Her tongue darted out across her bottom lip. 'In the summer-house—'

'What happened between us there was a mistake.'

'You wanted to make love…and so did I.'

Dios, why not take what she was offering and satisfy his libido? Rafael asked himself. If Juliet expected hearts and flowers that was *her* problem.

But the nagging voice of his conscience insisted that he was responsible for her. She had no idea what he was. He had been born in the gutter and had grown up in a slum where every day had been a fight to survive. He knew how to keep himself together, but that was all he knew. There was nothing inside him but darkness and ruthless ambition.

Juliet had lost her parents when she had still been a teenager and he sensed her loneliness. She was looking for love, affection, caring—but he could not give her those things. How could he when he had never experienced them?

'I wanted sex,' he told her bluntly. 'To scratch an itch. And you happened to be there.'

The colour drained from her face as quickly as it had appeared. 'So you're saying that any woman would have done?'

Her eyelashes swept down, but not before he'd seen a wounded expression that gutted him.

Juliet was silent for a moment before her chin came up. Rafael though of all the other times she had picked herself up after life had delivered another knockout blow. Admiration curled through him when she met his gaze steadily. Only the faint tremor of her bottom lip betrayed her hurt, but she quickly firmed her mouth.

'Then there is nothing more to be said. But it's ridiculous for you to sleep on the sofa when I am so much smaller than you and will fit on it much better. You can have the bed and I'll sleep here.'

She turned towards the sofa and started to make up a bed. When she bent over to smooth out the sheet her satin chemise pulled tight across her pert derrière. Rafael swore beneath his breath. She would tempt a saint, let alone the sinner he knew himself to be.

He snatched a pillow out of her hands. 'Leave it,' he said savagely. 'Go—now—before I do something that we will both regret.'

Juliet's eyes widened. But she must have realised that his self-control was at breaking point and without another word she sped back into the bedroom and slammed the door behind her.

Juliet put off taking Poppy down to breakfast for as long as possible. She knew that Rafael was in the habit of drinking several cups of black coffee in the morning, while he sat on the balcony and glanced at the day's newspapers before he left for work at the Casillas Group's offices in Valencia. But she couldn't face seeing him.

She was mortified at the memory of how she had thrown herself at him and he had rejected her, so she read Poppy two more stories until the little girl hopped off the bed and ran over to the door.

'I'm hungry, Mummy.'

It was past nine o'clock—he must have left by now. 'Okay, munchkin. I'm coming.'

She followed her daughter into the kitchen and her heart leapt into her mouth when she saw that the bi-fold doors were open and Rafael was outside, sitting at the table with a newspaper propped against the coffee jug.

Poppy greeted him excitedly and climbed onto the chair beside him. 'Raf, will you read me *The Three Bears*?'

'Rafael has to go to work,' Juliet said quickly. She avoided his gaze and fussed over Poppy's breakfast. 'Would you like a peach with your yoghurt?'

'I'm not going to work today,' he told Poppy. 'And I'll

read the book if you eat all your breakfast.' He picked up the cafetière and looked at Juliet. 'Coffee?'

'Thank you,' she said stiffly, feeling her colour rise.

Her unsubtle suggestion that they should share the bed came back to mock her. She wished she didn't blush so easily. She wished Rafael wasn't wearing sunglasses which hid his expression. She wished she could prevent her eyes from straying to his broad chest and the denim shirt that was open at the neck, revealing a sprinkling of black chest hair.

Thankful that her body's reaction to his sexual magnetism was hidden beneath her robe, she hugged her coffee cup like a security blanket while Poppy chatted away to Rafael. His patience with the little girl surprised Juliet again, and made her wonder why he had been so vehement when he'd said he did not want children of his own.

She looked up when the nanny stepped onto the balcony. 'Would Poppy like to come and play with the twins in the garden?'

'Keep your sun hat on,' Juliet instructed as Poppy trotted off with Elvira.

She really did not want to be alone with Rafael, but just as she was about to rise from the table he pushed a plate of *churros*—little sticks of dough which had been deep-fried and sprinkled with sugar and cinnamon—towards her.

'You should have some breakfast.'

'I'm not hungry,' she muttered, her chair scraping on the stone floor as she stood up.

'Sit down and eat.'

Rafael's exasperated tone made Juliet feel like a naughty child. After a moment's hesitation she sank back down onto her chair.

'Sulking is not an attractive trait,' he drawled.

'I am *not* sulking.' Releasing her breath slowly helped to control her temper. 'I'm tired of the games you play. You blow hot and cold. I don't know where I am with you, or what you want from me, and frankly I don't care.'

She forced herself to look directly at him and ignored the leap of her pulse. Okay, he was so gorgeous that her heart did a flip every time she looked at him. *Get over it*, she told herself. He was also unbelievably arrogant and had an ego the size of a planet.

To her surprise, Rafael looked away first. 'We are having lunch with my mother and her husband Alberto. My dear *mamà* is desperate for my grandfather to choose my half-brother as his successor and she will do anything to discredit me.' His voice was emotionless. 'Delfina must not suspect that our marriage is fake.'

'I'll do my best to pretend that I think you're God's gift to womankind,' Juliet told him flippantly.

His heavy brows lowered. 'Do not test my patience, *chiquita*.'

'Or you'll do what?'

He pulled off his sunglasses and scowled at her. But the hard gleam in his eyes was not temper but desire, and the heat of it scorched Juliet even as it confused her.

Last night he had told her that he'd wanted sex with any woman who was conveniently to hand and it had happened to be her. But he was staring at her now as if she really was his fantasy woman—as if she was the only woman he wanted.

The air was so still that she could hear the rasp of his breath and the unevenness of hers. Awareness prickled across her skin. Sexual tension sizzled between them and suddenly she was afraid—not of Rafael, but of the way he made her feel. The way she made *him* feel if the hunger in his gaze was real…

She broke eye contact and took a deep breath. 'You said we should get to know each other so that we can convince Hector and other members of your family that we are genuinely a couple. I've told you a lot about me, but I know virtually nothing about you.'

He put his shades on again and leaned back in his chair, watching her. She had no idea what he was thinking.

'What do you want to know?'

'Why is there such animosity between you and your mother?'

He shrugged. 'A clash of personalities.'

'I assume your parents are divorced as your mother is remarried and you have a half-brother? Do you keep in contact with your father?'

'No.'

The word shot from him like a bullet.

Juliet said nothing, and he must have realised that she was waiting for him to continue because after a moment he muttered, 'My father died years ago.'

'I'm sorry.'

'Don't be,' he said harshly. 'I'm not.'

She could not hide her shock. 'That's a terrible thing to say about your own father.'

'He was a terrible man.'

Rafael shoved a hand through his hair, and although Juliet could not see the expression in his eyes she sensed that he was agitated—something she would not have believed possible for a man whose self-control was formidable.

'I suppose you will find out about my background at some point, so it might as well be now,' he muttered.

Juliet suddenly remembered that his sister had said something about how she and Rafael had felt overawed when they had come to live at the Casillas mansion.

'My mother eloped with my father because my grandfather disapproved of her relationship with him. Ivan Mendoza had a gardening job on the Casillas estate and apparently Delfina fell madly in love with him.' Rafael grimaced. 'I remember he could be charming to people when it suited him, but he was never anything other than violent and aggressive to me.'

She froze. 'Did your father hit you?'

'Frequently—until I learned to dodge his fists and run away when he undid his belt.'

'How old were you when he started hitting you?'

He shrugged. 'I don't remember a time when I wasn't afraid of him.'

Juliet felt sick, imagining Rafael as a little boy, perhaps no older than Poppy, being physically abused by his father. 'What about your mother? Didn't she try to protect you?'

'I don't know if my mother was aware when she married Ivan that he was involved in the drug scene. He was a petty crook, who worked when he could find a job, and had a sideline in drug dealing.' Rafael exhaled heavily. 'I think it's likely that my mother was a drug user then—probably encouraged into that lifestyle by Ivan. I have very few memories of her before she left. She was distant, uninterested—especially in me. I don't remember her ever showing me affection.'

'What do you mean when you say that your mother left?'

'She disappeared out of my life when I was about seven. Sofia would have been around two years old. I didn't find out my actual birth date until years later, when I saw my birth certificate,' he explained. 'My father never said where my mother had gone.' A nerve flickered in his cheek. 'I think my sister missed our mother at first and she clung to me.'

Juliet thought of her happy childhood, with parents who had adored her, and her heart ached for Rafael and his sister. 'Who took care of you and Sofia?'

He gave another shrug. 'My father was a *gitano*—a gypsy. The Roma community is tightknit, and *gitanos* have a strong sense of family. Sometimes the other mothers took care of Sofia and gave us food. But my father was always moving around and we didn't settle anywhere for long—which is why it was years before my grandfather found us.'

He caught Juliet's questioning look.

'My mother had returned to the Casillas mansion. Presumably she missed the wealth and status of belonging to one of Spain's foremost families,' he said drily. 'I don't know why she did not take us or at least my sister with her when she left. We ended up living with my father in a slum outside Madrid, where drugs were dealt openly on the streets and criminal gangs were in charge. We were there for a few years before Ivan was shot dead in a gang war and Sofia and I were placed in an orphanage. Once there was an official record of our whereabouts Hector managed to track us down, and he brought us to live at the Casillas mansion when I was twelve.'

Juliet was so shocked by Rafael's description of his childhood that she did not know what to say. It explained the toughness she sensed in him, and his obsessive determination to get what he wanted.

'Your mother must have been happy to be reunited with you and your sister...' she murmured.

He gave a short laugh. 'I was a surly teenager, with a chip on my shoulder and a hot temper. *None* of my relatives—including my mother—were pleased to have me around, although I'm glad to say that Sofia was made more welcome.' He gave a faint smile. 'My sister learned young how to smile and say the right things to people. I was far less amenable. But my grandfather saw something in me and pushed me to catch up on my education. Meanwhile my mother had married a distant cousin, and my half-brother Francisco is a *true* Casillas, in Delfina's opinion, and should be Hector's successor.'

Rafael picked up his coffee cup and swallowed its contents.

'You said you were made to feel that you did not belong at your ballet school by some of the richer pupils. I understand what it's like to feel like an outsider, because that's how I felt when I came to live here with my aristocratic family. Many of my relatives still think that a *gitano* is not good enough to be a Casillas.'

Juliet stared at him. 'Yet even knowing that your family would despise me, you brought me here and presented me as your wife. You didn't consider my feelings. Perhaps,' she said huskily, 'you thought I was too unintelligent to *have* feelings.'

His jaw clenched. 'I have never thought you unintelligent. I admit that when I first met you it crossed my mind that it would infuriate Hector if my bride was a single mother from a council estate...'

Juliet blanched and he swore.

'You have shown me that I was wrong to make assumptions about you based on the circumstances I found you in. But I won't lie to you. I needed to marry quickly, and your financial problems gave me the leverage to persuade you to be my wife.'

Rafael's voice was indecipherable, and his eyes were still hidden behind his sunglasses so that Juliet had no clue to his thoughts.

'Was my decision cold and calculating? Yes.' He answered his own question before she could speak. 'I told you once that my pursuit of power is a ruthless game, with no place for weakness or emotions—and nothing has changed.'

CHAPTER EIGHT

Something *HAD* CHANGED. Rafael suspected it was something inside him, but he refused to examine that unsettling thought and assured himself that the change was entirely in Juliet.

It was not only her appearance, he brooded, studying her where she sat opposite him at the dining table in his mother's over-fussy suite. The truth was that he hadn't been able to take his eyes off his wife throughout this tedious lunch with Delfina and her tedious husband.

Juliet looked deliciously cool and elegant in a pale blue silk sheath dress that skimmed her slender figure. The neckline was decorous, but cut just low enough to reveal the upper slopes of her breasts. Those perfect small handfuls that made Rafael's mouth water when he pictured the dusky pink nipples he had tasted once. He had come to the conclusion that he would *have* to lick and suckle them again—if his overheated body did not spontaneously combust first.

He forced his mind away from the erotic images and shifted in his seat in a bid to ease the uncomfortable tightness of his trousers stretched across his arousal. *Dios*, no other woman had ever made his heart pound the way Juliet did, nor made him feel like a hormone-fuelled youth instead of a self-confessed cynic who had become jaded with easy sex.

He was used to having whichever woman he wanted with minimum effort from him, but he had discovered that there was such a thing as too much choice, Rafael acknowledged sardonically.

Juliet's daughter was sitting beside her. Despite Poppy's young age she had behaved impeccably during lunch. She was a cute kid, he conceded. But like her mother Poppy had a way of looking directly into his eyes that disconcerted him. As if she saw something inside him that Rafael was quite certain did not exist.

'I did not expect that you would bring the child with you,' Delfina had said when he'd carried the little girl into the private apartment. Beside him, Juliet had stiffened as his mother had added coldly, 'Couldn't you have left her with the nanny?'

'Elvira offered to look after Poppy, but I like to spend as much time as possible with my daughter,' Juliet had replied calmly, but Rafael had caught the gleam of battle in her blue eyes.

Now Alberto was chatting to Juliet about three of Pablo Picasso's paintings, which he owned. Rafael knew his mother did not share her husband's interest in the famous Spanish painter, and she'd looked irritated when Juliet had revealed an impressive knowledge of the artist's work.

'Did your parents have professions?' Delfina asked during a lull in conversation.

'They both worked at a hospital.'

'Oh! Were they doctors?'

'Dad was a porter and Mum was a domestic assistant,' Juliet said cheerfully.

Delfina's brows arched in a supercilious expression. 'Domestic work seems to be a favourite in your family.'

'Madre...' Rafael said warningly. His mother could be a bitch and he would *not* allow her to upset Juliet.

'My parents worked hard so that I could follow my dream of becoming a ballerina. They were not rich, or particularly well educated, but they loved me and supported me.' Juliet looked directly at Delfina. 'They would never have abandoned me in a crime-ridden slum as you did Rafael and his sister when they were young children—Sofia just a baby and Rafael only seven years old.'

Delfina drew a sharp breath, but Juliet was continuing in a fierce voice.

'How *could* you have left your children with a father who was cruel and violent? You must have known that Ivan beat Rafael with his belt—'

Her voice cracked and a chink opened up in Rafael's heart.

His mother had paled and her highly glossed lips were a scarlet slash across her face. 'How dare you...?' Delfina breathed.

'I dare because I am Rafael's wife. And it is a wife's duty to stand by her husband. I was appalled when Rafael told me about how he suffered as a child, living in a slum.'

Juliet brushed her hand across her eyes and Rafael felt a jolt of something he could not explain when he saw that her lashes were wet.

'Hector brought him to the Casillas mansion to be reunited with you and his other relatives but he was made to feel unwelcome and unwanted. *You* did not defend him, but I will. Rafael is Hector's eldest grandson and *he* should succeed his grandfather as head of the Casillas Group.'

In the stunned silence that followed Rafael told himself that the pain he felt beneath his breastbone was indigestion…too much rich food. The ache could not be because Juliet had stood up for him, *fought* for him in a way that no one had ever done in his entire life. As if he mattered. To *her*.

His mother picked up her wine glass and drained it before she looked at Rafael. 'I was ashamed,' she said tightly.

'I know, Madre. You have always made it clear that you are ashamed of having a son who is part-*gitano*. I will never be the perfect son, like Francisco, but the CEO-ship *is* my birthright and I *will* claim my place within the family and the company.'

Delfina did not speak again, although as Rafael bade her goodbye and kissed the air close to her cheek he had an odd sense that she wanted to say something to him.

'Are you angry with me?' Juliet muttered as they walked through the house back to his apartment.

He glanced at her over Poppy's head. The little girl was walking between them and had insisted on holding his hand as well as Juliet's.

'Why would I be angry? You acted the role of supportive wife very convincingly.'

He opened the door of his apartment and as Juliet preceded him inside her long hair brushed against his arm and he breathed in the lemony scent of the shampoo she used.

Poppy spied her favourite teddy bear and ran across the room.

Juliet turned to him. 'I wasn't acting. What happened to you when you were a child was terrible. Your mother shouldn't have deserted you, and her failure to protect you has had a fundamental effect on you. I think it could be the reason why you have never allowed yourself to fall in love. You're afraid of being let down and abandoned, like Delfina abandoned you before.'

Her words opened that chink in his heart a little wider, and Rafael didn't know what to make of that—or her.

'I think you should stop trying to psychoanalyse me,' he said drily. 'And you should certainly stop looking for my redeeming features, because I don't have any.'

She shook her head. 'You took care of your sister—acted as a parent to her when you were just a child yourself. When I met you I thought you had only ever known wealth and privilege. The fact that you spent the first twelve years of your life in a slum doesn't make you less of a man, it makes you *more* of one—a better person than any of your pampered relatives who have no right to look down on you.'

'A better man would not have sat through lunch imagining stripping you naked and having wild sex with you on my mother's dining table,' he rasped.

Rosy colour winged along her high cheekbones, but she held his gaze. 'That itch still bothering you, is it?'

'You have no idea, *chiquita*...' He could not explain the restlessness inside him that seemed to get a whole lot worse when she smiled. 'I need to disabuse you of the idea that there is anything good in me.'

Juliet tilted her head to one side and looked at him thoughtfully. 'I wonder why you are so determined to do that,' she said softly.

Before he could reply—and the truth was that he did not *how* to respond—she walked away from him in the direction of her dressing room.

'Sofia has asked me to give Ana and Inez some ballet lessons. We're going to have our first dancing class this afternoon—unless there's anything else you want me to do?'

A number of highly erotic scenarios flooded his mind, which had an immediate and predictable effect on his body.

'I promised to play golf with Tio Alvaro,' he growled, his feet already taking him towards the door of the apartment and safety—away from the temptation of his wife who was not his wife. Not in any way that mattered. And Rafael was beginning to think that it mattered a lot.

Three hours spent on the Casillas estate's private golf course would ordinarily have given him time to clear his head.

'You seem to be distracted,' his uncle commented as they walked off the green. Alvaro was jubilant because he had won the game convincingly. 'I suppose you are thinking about business?'

Rafael hadn't spared a single thought for any of the business projects which until recently he had been obsessed with. The realisation that his new obsession with Juliet was interfering not just with his game of golf but with his focus on the company was disturbing. Work had always been his number one priority—the only mistress to command his fidelity.

The situation could not continue, he brooded. Juliet had got under his skin and there was only one way to deal with his unexpected fascination with her.

There was no one around when he entered the mansion. Most of his relatives and the household staff took a siesta in the afternoons, but as he walked across the entrance hall he heard music coming from the ballroom. Puzzled, he opened the door—and stopped dead when he saw Juliet dancing.

Rafael knew nothing about ballet, but he could tell instinctively that she was a talented ballerina. Dressed in a black leotard that revealed her ultra-slender figure, she seemed to glide across the floor on the points of her ballet shoes. Ethereal and graceful, strong and yet fragile. She did not simply dance to the music she lived it, breathed it, painting pictures in the air with each twirl and leap as if she had wings and could fly.

He stepped into the room and quietly closed the door, leaning against it while he watched her. He was utterly captivated…mesmerised. As a boy growing up in the slums he'd had no idea that such beauty existed. He could not take his eyes off her supple body, and his breath became trapped in his lungs as desire swept molten and hot through his veins, setting him ablaze everywhere.

Juliet danced with such passion, such fire, and he wanted all of it.

But her performance ended abruptly when she leapt into the air and seemed to land awkwardly. She gave a cry as she crumpled to the floor, trembling like a bird with a broken wing…a bird that could no longer soar into the sky.

Rafael's heart gave a jolt when he heard the sound of her weeping.

'*Dios, querida,* are you badly hurt?'

He was across the ballroom in seconds and kneeling on the floor beside her. 'Juliet, *cariño,*' he said huskily as she lifted her face and he saw tears streaming down her cheeks.

'My stupid leg.'

The words hung there, hurting him as much as she was hurting. Her voice ached with a depth of emotion he could barely comprehend. Loss—of her parents, and her ballet career, and more than that. The loss of the unique gift that Rafael had glimpsed when he'd watched her dance.

He had no idea what to say to her. 'You must miss dancing.'

'Ballet was my life,' she said, in a low voice that scraped his insides. 'It was like breathing—a necessary part of me. But now it's gone.'

'But you can still dance. You are incredible, *querida*.'

She scrubbed a hand over her eyes. 'I can manage for a few minutes, but I'll never be able to dance professionally. My leg isn't strong enough to cope with the relentless routine of rehearsals and performances, the pursuit of perfection. There's a reason why the life of a ballet dancer is called a beautiful agony.'

Her wry smile floored Rafael. The lack of self-pity in her voice humbled him, and that chink in his heart opened wider still.

'Come,' he said softly, lifting her into his arms.

'I can walk,' she protested as he carried her across the ballroom. 'I'll have a bath. It helps to relax the muscles in my thigh.'

'Put your arms around my neck,' he commanded, liking the feel of her small breasts pressed against his chest when she complied.

He strode up the stairs, and when he entered his apartment headed straight into the en suite bathroom and placed her on a chair. He ran a bath, tipping a liberal amount of scented bath crystals into the water.

He turned to find her watching him, and the lost look in her blue eyes, the shimmer of tears, evoked a reaction inside him that was too complicated for him to deal with right then.

Instead he knelt in front of her and curled his fingers

around the edge of her leotard. 'Let's get you undressed and into the bath.'

'I can manage. Please…' she whispered when he didn't move. 'I want to be alone. I don't need your help.'

Her rejection was no more than he deserved, Rafael acknowledged. But it hurt more than it should—more than he would have believed possible when he had prided himself for nigh on thirty years in not allowing anyone the power to hurt him.

He stood up and stared at her downbent head. Her hair was arranged in a classical bun that showed off the delicate line of her jaw and her slender neck.

'Don't lock the door,' he said tautly. 'I don't want to have to break it down if you have a problem.'

Juliet lay back in the roll-top bath and felt the ache in her thigh start to ease in the warm water. She had been an idiot to dance on points, she thought ruefully. But giving a dancing lesson to Rafael's nieces had reminded her of how she had fallen in love with ballet when she had learned those first simple steps as a child.

After the class Sofia had taken the twins and Poppy to play in the garden, and Juliet had found the temptation to dance in the huge ballroom too strong to resist.

She closed her eyes and allowed her mind to run over the other events of the day. Rafael's shocking revelations about his childhood, when his mother had abandoned him to his fate with his violent father. It had made her want to cry when he'd told her his story, and she hadn't been able to control her anger when they'd had lunch with his mother.

She did not care about Delfina's haughty disdain of her, but Rafael deserved better than to be treated like an outsider by the Casillas family.

The water was cooling and she rested her arms on the edge of the bath while she levered herself upright. Her thigh muscle spasmed and she couldn't hold back a yelp of pain.

Immediately the bathroom door flew open and Rafael appeared, glowering at her. 'What happened? Your leg…?'

'It's fine. It just twinged a bit.'

She caught her bottom lip between her teeth when it belatedly occurred to her that she was naked, standing there in the bath with water streaming down her body. Rafael was staring at her with an intensity that caused her stomach to swoop, and now his gaze dropped down from her breasts to the neatly trimmed triangle of pale red curls between her legs.

Her skin, already pink from being immersed in hot water, flushed even pinker, and there was nothing she could do to prevent her nipples from hardening so that they jutted provocatively, as if begging for his attention.

'Go away…' she muttered.

'You've got to be kidding.'

His rough voice rasped over her, setting each nerve-ending alight. The fierce glitter in his eyes caused her heart to kick in her chest as he walked purposefully across the bathroom.

She licked her dry lips and saw his eyes narrow on the movement of her tongue. 'Will you pass me a towel?'

He took a towel from the shelf and held it out to her. But when she unfolded it, she discovered that it wasn't a big bath sheet but a hand towel that was too small to cover her nakedness. *Seriously?*

His mouth curved into a wicked grin that destroyed her flimsy defences like skittles tumbling after a strike.

Modesty dictated that she should at least hold her hands in front of the pertinent areas of her body, to hide them from his hot gaze. But instead she burned in the fire that danced golden and bright in his green eyes.

'Rafael…' she whispered, with so much longing in her breathy voice that he gave a chuckle as he settled his hands on either side of her waist and lifted her out of the bath. 'I'll make you wet.'

She caught her breath when he settled her against him, so that one of his arms was around her back and the other beneath her knees, and carried her through to the bedroom.

'Not as wet as I am about to make you, *chiquita*.'

The promise in his voice echoed the desire in his eyes. His skin was stretched taut over the blades of his cheekbones, giving him a feral look that sent a quiver through Juliet. She felt boneless, and when he bent his head and angled his mouth over hers she parted her lips and gave herself up to the sweet seduction of his kiss.

The room tilted as he lowered her onto the bed and leaned over her, running his hands over her body from her hips up to her breasts, scalding her skin wherever he touched. She wanted him to surrender to the passion that she sensed he was controlling with his formidable willpower. What would it be like to see that control shatter? Would she survive the tsunami?

'You said that any woman would do,' she reminded him.

'I lied.'

His husky admission dispatched her doubts. He stopped nuzzling her neck and claimed her mouth once more, gentle seduction replaced by hungry demands that she was powerless to deny. He had fascinated her from the start, and she shuddered with delight when he moved down her body and flicked his tongue across one pebble-hard nipple and then the other, again and again, until the pleasure was too intense and she gave a keening cry.

Eyes closed, she felt the scrape of his beard over her belly—her thighs. Her eyelashes flew open. 'What are you doing?'

He lifted his head, amusement and something else that made her stomach muscles contract glinting in his narrowed gaze. 'What do you *think* I am about to do, *chiquita*?'

'I have no idea.'

His low laugh rolled through her and she tried to twitch her thighs together, to hide the betraying dampness of her arousal that scented the air.

'You cannot really be so innocent,' Rafael said half beneath his breath as he pulled her hips towards him, so that her bottom was on the edge of the bed, and dropped to the floor on his knees.

A suspicion finally slid into her mind. 'You can't...' she whispered, appalled yet fascinated, and excited when he pushed her legs apart and lowered his head to her feminine core.

'Want to bet on it?'

His accent was thicker than usual, and his breath fanned the sensitive skin on her inner thigh. One strong hand curled around her ankle. He lifted her leg and draped it over his shoulder. And then he simply put his mouth against her centre and ran his tongue over her opening, making the ache she felt there so much worse, so much *more*.

Juliet glanced down at his dark head between her thighs and knew there was a part of her that was hor-rified for allowing him to pleasure her in such a way. But she could not deny that he was giving her the most exquisite pleasure as he teased and tormented her with his tongue. She sank back against the mattress, twisting her head from side to side as the heat and the fire and the terrible need inside her built to a crescendo.

Nothing had prepared her for sheer delight of Rafael's intimate caresses, or his soft murmurs of approval when she arched her hips and offered herself to him. She was aware of a coiling sensation low in her pelvis that wound tighter and tighter, until she was trembling and desperate for something that hovered frustratingly out of reach.

And then it happened.

He flicked his tongue across the tight nub of her clitoris and the coil inside her snapped, sending starbursts of pleasure shooting out from her core in a series of exquisite spasms that made her internal muscles clench and release, clench and release, flooding her with the sticky sweetness of her earth-shattering climax.

Her first.

She would remember it long after their marriage was over.

Her heart contracted painfully as the thought slid like a serpent in paradise into her mind.

In the aftermath, as her breathing slowed, she realised that the most amazing sexual experience of her life could not have been satisfactory for Rafael. When he leaned over her and kissed her lingeringly on her mouth she tasted her own feminine sweetness on his lips and wondered if he expected her to afford him the same pleasure he had given her. But how to suggest it?

She felt frustrated by her inexperience. 'I—' She broke off, at a loss to know what to say. He had taken her apart utterly and she didn't know how to put herself back together again, or if she even could.

She watched him uncertainly when he stepped away from the bed. 'I can hear Poppy,' he murmured.

Her daughter! How could she have forgotten?

She scrambled off the bed when she heard voices from somewhere in the apartment and guessed that Sofia had returned Poppy after she'd spent the afternoon with the twins.

'I'll go and see her while you get dressed,' Rafael said, kissing the tip of her nose before he strolled out of the room.

It took Juliet seconds to slip into the blue silk dress she had worn at lunch. Silently cursing the tell-tale flush on her cheeks, she hurried through the apartment.

As she entered the sitting room Poppy ran towards her. 'Mummy, can I have my pyjamas?'

'It's not bedtime.'

Sofia laughed. 'The twins would like Poppy to come to us for a sleepover.' She glanced at her brother. 'Rafael has explained that you have a dinner engagement in Valencia this evening, so it's perfect timing.'

It was the first Juliet had heard of a dinner engagement, but Rafael seemed determined to avoid her gaze.

For the next ten minutes she was busy packing a bag with Poppy's pyjamas, toothbrush and an assortment of cuddly toys. She gave her daughter a big hug and felt a pang when Poppy trotted off happily with Sofia. Her baby was growing up so fast.

When they had gone she turned to Rafael. 'Who are we meeting? Some more of your relatives? Or is it a business dinner?' She did not relish the thought of either. 'What should I wear?' She frowned when he didn't answer. 'Is it a formal function?'

'It's a date.'

'A *date*?' Her confusion grew as dull colour ran along his cheekbones. 'I don't understand.'

'It's quite simple, *chiquita*,' he said, strolling towards her. 'I'm taking you to dinner, away from the Casillas mansion, so that we can spend some time alone.'

'I thought the point was for us to stay here in the house under your grandfather's nose so that we can convince him our marriage is real?'

Instead of replying, Rafael tucked a tendril of hair that had escaped from her chignon behind her ear. The unexpectedly tender gesture tugged on Juliet's heart.

'I would like to explore the attraction between us and I think you would like to do that too,' he said quietly.

She did not deny it and a heavy sigh escaped him.

'We have done everything in the wrong order—married before we had even spent a day together. I was arrogant enough to believe that it didn't matter. But I would like us to start again. So, *bella Julieta*, will you have dinner with me?'

She nodded, feeling suddenly shy, but excited too—and apprehensive, and a host of other emotions she was afraid to define. Rafael had made it clear that he desired her, and although it felt as if she was about to jump from the top of a precipice she was ready to leap into the unknown.

'I'd love to.'

'Good.' He dropped a swift, hard kiss on her mouth that left her lips tingling. 'I have some work to do in my study and we'll leave in an hour.' He paused on his way out of the room. 'By the way, you'll need to bring an overnight bag as we'll be spending the night at my penthouse in the city. Oh, and wear something sexy, *amante*.'

Juliet's heart missed a beat. *Amante* meant lover.

CHAPTER NINE

'WE COULD SKIP dinner and go straight to the penthouse.'

Rafael's voice was oddly hoarse and it sent a shiver across Juliet's skin. She tore her gaze from the unholy gleam in his eyes and glanced around the restaurant, which he'd told her was one of the best places to eat in Valencia. Situated in a charming little square in the old part of the city, it had plenty of atmosphere, and a band was playing traditional Spanish music.

He had promised her a date. 'I'm hungry,' she told him, unfolding her napkin.

'Same here,' he growled. 'You look incredible in that dress. Good enough to eat.' His accent thickened. 'I am looking forward to tasting you again later.'

Heat scorched her cheeks at the memory of how he had pleasured her with his tongue, and she buried her face in her menu. A black velvet dress clung to her slender figure and the low-cut neckline pushed her breasts up to give her a cleavage. Sheer black stockings and high-heeled strappy sandals completed the outfit, and she had left her hair loose, with just the front sections drawn back from her face with diamante clips.

She'd worn a lightweight wool coat when they had left the Casillas mansion, so Rafael had only seen her dress when they'd arrived at the restaurant. The sizzling look he'd given her had made her feel like a sex goddess and boosted her confidence.

When the waiter had taken their order Juliet sipped her champagne cocktail and gave a small sigh. None of this was real. She still expected to wake up in her flat in the tower block and find it had all been a dream. Especially Rafael.

Her eyes were drawn across the table to him. In tailored black trousers and a black silk shirt, casually open at the throat to reveal a vee of bronzed skin, he was darkly gorgeous, and the black stubble on his jaw gave him a dangerous sexiness that sent her heart clattering against her ribs.

'Were you in love with Poppy's father?'

Startled by his question, she gave him a wry look. 'I thought I was. I met him at a party given by some friends of my cousin. Bryan was good-looking, and he knew it, and I was naïve and grieving for my parents. I was flattered that he'd noticed me. But after we'd slept together he told me he'd only wanted sex.'

She sighed.

'I had been taking the contraceptive pill to regulate my periods, and I stupidly agreed to have sex with him without a condom. I'd been taking a herbal remedy to help with my feelings of depression following my parents' deaths and I had no idea that it could decrease the effectiveness of the pill. When I discovered I was pregnant Bryan wasn't interested, and he refused to support his child, although he did agree to have his name on Poppy's birth certificate.'

'He sounds like a jerk. It's Bryan's responsibility to make a financial contribution towards his daughter's upbringing.'

Juliet stared at Rafael. 'Would you support *your*

child? You're a renowned playboy, but if one of your mistresses became pregnant what would *you* do?'

'It won't happen because I always use protection,' he told her smoothly. Seeing her frown, he added, 'But in the extremely unlikely event that it did, I would make a settlement to ensure the child had financial security for life.'

She grimaced. 'Money isn't everything. A child needs to be loved and nurtured. My parents had little money but I had a wonderfully happy childhood, with the security of knowing they loved me.'

'I had a miserable childhood, living in poverty—and, believe me, money would have made a huge difference to my life and my sister's.' A nerve flickered in Rafael's cheek. 'The best thing—no, the *only* thing I could give a child of mine is access to my wealth.'

His harsh tone warned Juliet to drop a subject that was clearly contentious, but she couldn't. 'Are you saying you wouldn't want to be involved in your child's life? You wouldn't *love* your child?'

'The question is irrelevant,' he said coldly.

His expression was as haughty as his mother's, Juliet thought. Centuries of his family's aristocratic heritage were stamped on his hard features and revealed that he was every bit a Casillas. No doubt some of his noble ancestors had been as ruthless as Rafael was.

It was a relief when the waiter arrived at their table to serve the first course. When they were alone again Juliet stayed silent while she ate her grilled scallops with chorizo. The food was delicious, but tears pricked the back of her eyes at the thought that she had spoiled the evening.

Rafael sipped his wine. 'I thought you might like to visit the Museum of Fine Arts tomorrow. The building is very beautiful, and worth visiting simply to see the baroque architecture. It houses the second most important art collection in Spain.'

'I'd love to go.'

His mention of 'tomorrow' reminded her that they would be staying at his apartment in the city tonight.

'But what about Poppy? I'll need to get back for her.'

'My sister is planning to take all three girls to the beach, and she will have the nanny to help out. Valencia is a beautiful city and I think you would enjoy the City of Arts and Sciences and the aquarium—although both are a day's visit. But we don't have to do everything in one day. There will be plenty of time in the year ahead for you to enjoy all that Valencia has to offer.'

Rafael's words were a timely reminder of why she was there with him. Their marriage was a temporary arrangement and she would be a fool to hope for more than he was offering.

Why not use this opportunity to explore her sensuality and enjoy great sex, free from the expectations that came with a normal relationship? Juliet asked herself while the waiter cleared away her plate and served her main course. Life had taught her to seize the moment, and she would regret it for ever if she did not make love with Rafael. As long as she remembered that *love* wasn't involved.

She looked up, and her heart leapt when she found him watching her. His mouth crooked in a sexy smile that made her pulse race and her spirits soar as the awkwardness between them disappeared. For the rest of the meal they chatted with an ease that surprised her. Rafael had travelled widely and she was fascinated to hear of the places he had visited.

'I've only been to Australia—and now Spain,' she admitted.

'I have to go to New York for a few days next month. I'll take you with me.'

Going to New York was another dream of hers that she had never imagined she would fulfil when she had lived in the tower block.

Juliet licked the last morsel of the chocolate mousse she had chosen for dessert from her spoon. The light-as-air mousse felt sensual on her tongue and she closed her eyes while she enjoyed the sensory experience.

'*Dios...*' Rafael growled. 'Do you do that on purpose?'

Her eyes flew open. 'Do what?' she asked innocently.

Instead of replying, he dipped his spoon into his own dish of mousse and leaned across the table to hold the loaded spoon against her lips. 'You would tempt a saint, *bella*, and piety is not my strong point. Open your mouth,' he ordered softly.

Juliet could not resist the rich mousse, or Rafael, and she obediently parted her lips and licked the dessert from his spoon. He made a thick sound in his throat that provoked a flood of molten warmth between her legs.

She watched him dip the spoon back into his bowl and then lift it to his own mouth. She could not tear her gaze from his tongue as he licked his spoon clean. It was incredibly erotic, and heat coiled through her as she imagined him using that wicked tongue on her body.

She swallowed, searching her mind for something—anything—to say that would break the sexual tension that crackled between them.

'I've heard this music before,' she murmured, recognising the tune that the band were playing. 'My uncle

Carlos is a brilliant acoustic guitarist and he used to play this.'

Rafael pushed back his chair and stood up. 'Dance with me,' he said, holding out his hand to her. 'This music is flamenco. It originated in the gypsy communities in southern Spain and is as fiery and passionate as the people who created it.'

Dazedly Juliet put her hand in his and allowed him to lead her to the small dance floor in the centre of the restaurant, where a few other couples were already dancing. Rafael drew her into his arms and placed one hand in the small of her back, holding her so that her pelvis was pressed up against his. A tremor ran through her when she felt the bulge of his arousal through his trousers.

He danced with a natural grace and Juliet matched his rhythm, swaying her hips in time with his as the dance became a seduction of her senses. Nothing existed but the music and this man whose green eyes gleamed with a naked hunger as he lowered his head towards her, compelling her to slide her hand around his neck and pull his mouth down to hers.

She was drowning in the whirlpool of sensations that he was creating with his mouth as he plundered her lips in a kiss that left her trembling. He threaded his fingers through her hair while he trailed hot kisses along her jaw. Need clawed inside her, obliterating every sane thought and leaving a kind of madness, a wild restlessness that only Rafael could assuage.

And all the while they danced together to the music of the flamenco as the tempo quickened and became more intense.

'We need to leave,' he growled close to her ear.

Minutes later he'd settled the bill and escorted her out

of the restaurant to where his car was parked. Neither of them spoke on the short journey to his city apartment. The sexual tension in the car and then in the lift on the way up to the penthouse was tangible, and Juliet's heart pounded as Rafael leaned against the wall of the lift and studied her with a brooding intensity.

The penthouse was ultra-modern and stylish. A bachelor pad, Juliet thought as she took in the pale wood floors, white leather sofas and colourful modern art on the walls of the open-plan living space. She bit her lip as she wondered how many of his mistresses he had brought here.

'Would you like to take a look around the apartment?' Rafael offered, standing behind her to take her coat when she slipped it off her shoulders.

She felt his hand smooth her hair. 'Not really,' she said huskily.

'Can I get you a drink?'

'No, thank you.'

He placed her coat over the back of a chair and came to stand in front of her, his glittering gaze making her stomach swoop. 'What *would* you like, *chiquita*?'

'You.'

The word burst from her. She couldn't help it. He had driven her crazy with longing all evening with every smile he'd sent her as they had lingered over conversation and champagne—flirting with her, she realised.

He laughed, and the sound filled her with golden light and a fire that burned hotter still when he opened his arms wide.

'Have me, then, *bella Julieta.*'

His laughter stole around her as she literally threw herself into his waiting arms and he lifted her off her feet.

'Wrap your legs around me,' he told her, and when

she obeyed he gave a groan as her pelvis pressed hard against his arousal.

He carried her into the bedroom and set her down next to the bed. She was vaguely conscious of muted lighting and décor of black and gold, a printed throw on the bed. But then he bent his head to claim her mouth and she was only conscious of Rafael: the slide of his lips over hers, the heady scent of his cologne mixed with the indefinable musk of male pheromones, the heat of his body beneath her palms as she ran her hands over his chest and tugged open his shirt buttons.

He undressed her, taking his time to slide her zip down her spine and peel her dress away from her breasts, baring her to his hot gaze. But he didn't touch her breasts yet, focusing instead on tugging her tight-fitting dress over her hips so that it fell to the floor and she stepped out of it.

'Dios,' he said roughly as he stared at her sheer black stockings. 'If I'd known you were wearing these…' he traced his fingers over the wide bands of lace around the tops of her thighs '…we wouldn't have made it past the starter.'

He knelt to remove her shoes and then slowly drew one stocking down her leg, then the other, pressing his lips along her white scar, his gentle kisses healing the deeper scars inside her.

'You are so beautiful,' he murmured, and there was nothing but truth and hunger in his eyes when he stood and drew her into his arms.

He made her feel beautiful. And, oh, he made her want him when he kissed her as if he could not have enough of her, when he cupped her breasts in his palms and stroked his thumbs over her nipples so that they peaked and she shuddered beneath the pleasure of his touch.

His hands skimmed down to her panties and he hooked his fingers in the waistband to draw them down her legs.

'So beautiful,' he said again, his low tone aching with need, making the ache between her legs even more acute.

He stripped with an efficiency that caused her a tiny flicker of doubt. Rafael had done this a thousand times or more—perhaps he would be disappointed by her inexperience. But then he took off his boxer shorts, and the sight of his erection jutting so big and bold turned her insides to liquid.

Did he see the flash of uncertainty in her eyes when she viewed the awesome size of him?

He slipped his hand beneath her chin and tilted her face to his. 'We'll take things slowly, *cariño*,' he promised, rubbing his thumb across her lower lip. And then he lay down on the bed and pulled her on top of him, arranging her so that she sat astride him and the hard ridge of his arousal was *there*, pressing against her opening.

But he didn't push any further forward, and it was his finger that stroked over her moist vagina, gently parting her and easing inside her, swirling and twisting, making her gasp and rock her hips against his hand. A second finger joined the first, testing her, stretching her, while his other hand cradled her breast and he tugged her down so that he could close his lips around her nipple and suck hard, so that she gave a moan and molten heat pooled between her legs.

Juliet pushed herself upright and ran her hands greedily over his torso, loving the feel of his satin skin and the faint abrasion of his chest hair beneath her palms.

'Kiss me,' he ordered, and all that arrogance of his

was there in his gravelly voice and in his eyes that gleamed fiercely beneath his half-closed eyelids.

She did not hesitate—simply placed her hands flat on the bed on either side of his head and lowered her mouth to his. He might be arrogant but he wanted her— badly—and she kissed him with all her passion and need, with all her heart and soul, because she was intrinsically honest and her lips could not lie as they clung to his.

'*Querida…*' he groaned, and set her away from him while he reached across to the bedside drawer and took out a condom.

She watched him roll it down his hard length and her heart hammered in her chest, anticipation and the faintest apprehension causing her to catch her breath.

His gaze sought hers and she was entranced by the darkness of desire that had turned his green eyes almost black. She read the unspoken question in his eyes and her breath escaped her on a soft sigh of assent.

He lifted her into position above him and then pulled her slowly down so that his erection nudged her opening. Holding her hips, he guided her, his eyes locked with hers as his swollen tip stretched her and pressed deeper, deeper, filling her inch by inch, and it was so impossibly intense that she thought she would die in the beauty of his possession.

The feel of Rafael inside her was perfect—beyond anything she could have imagined as he began to move, thrusting into her with steady strokes while he slipped his hands round to cup her bottom. His head was thrown back against the pillows, his black hair falling across his brow, his eyes blazing into hers.

'Dance for me,' he said thickly.

And she did. Catching his rhythm, she closed her

eyes and lost herself in the magic of an age-old dance, arching her supple body above him, throwing her head back as they moved together in total accord and flew ever upwards towards the pinnacle.

It couldn't last. Fire this bright had to burn out.

The power of him moving inside her stole her breath and the perfection of each devastating thrust broke her heart. This was not just sex. Not for her. Deep down, she'd known it would be more, that *making love* with Rafael was exactly what she was doing.

She leaned forward so that her nipples brushed across his chest, making him groan and increase his pace. She kissed his mouth and her heart flipped when he pushed his tongue between her lips. The storm was about to break and she arched her body backwards, shaking her hair over her shoulders as the pressure built deep in her pelvis.

'*Dios*, what you do to me...' he muttered—raw, harsh, as if the words were torn from him.

His jaw was clenched and she sensed he was fighting for control—a battle he lost spectacularly when he exploded inside her at the same moment that she shattered. Her sharp cry mingled with his deep groan as they rode out the storm together, and she felt the flooding sweetness of her orgasm and heard the uneven rasp of his laboured breaths.

In the aftermath she lay sprawled across his chest, too exhilarated, too empowered, too *everything* to be able to move. But the idea that he would think she was clingy and needy finally stirred her and she attempted to roll off him—only for him to tighten his arms around her.

'Stay.'

The word rumbled through his chest and tugged on

Juliet's heart. She heard in his low tone the boy who had been abandoned by his mother. She heard the teenager shunned by his rich relatives because they believed his background was shameful, when it was they who should have been ashamed.

Don't, she told her heart sternly when it leapt at the feel of his hand stroking her hair. She must not allow the idea that Rafael was in any way vulnerable to breach her defences.

But when he rolled them both over so that she was beneath him, and he sought her mouth in a kiss of beguiling sweetness and the renewed flowering of passion, she knew that the warning was too late.

Something had changed and now Rafael knew it was him. It had started when he had told Juliet about his boyhood, which he had never spoken of to anyone— not even to Tio Alvaro, to whom he was closest out of all his relatives.

But perhaps it had started before that—when he had watched Juliet descend the stairs at his grandfather's birthday party, a vision of ethereal loveliness in that golden dress.

His wife.

He wasn't comfortable with the possessive feeling that swept through him, nor did he understand it. Rafael knew what he was—knew better than to think he could be a better man. The kind of man a woman might love. It was hardly likely when his own mother hadn't loved him and his father had used any excuse to beat the life out of him. A few times he had very nearly succeeded.

Rafael hated the name Mendoza, but he'd kept it because it reminded him of what he was—what he feared he could be. Tacking Casillas on to his name did not make him a member of the family, his grandfather had told him more than once. Which meant that he was no one—nothing.

Why, suddenly, did it matter? Why did he care? And, even worse, why did he wish that he could overcome the legacy of his past?

The answer to those questions circling like vultures in his mind was curled up beside him, sleeping as only the innocent could sleep, with her hand tucked under her cheek and her lips slightly parted so that when he put his face close to hers her sweet breath whispered across his skin.

It astonished him that he had once thought her plain. He wondered if she'd felt victorious when he'd come so hard inside her, three times the previous night, that his groans had echoed around the bedroom. Now the pearly grey light of dawn filled the room, and the only way to resist the temptation to pull her beneath him again was to get out of bed.

Juliet needed to sleep after he'd kept her awake for much of the night with his demands—which she had enjoyed, he reminded himself as he pulled on a pair of sweatpants. They were mercifully loose around his erection, which had sprung to attention when he'd pushed back the sheet and unintentionally exposed one of Juliet's pale breasts, tipped with a nipple that was rosy red from the ministrations of his mouth.

Rafael walked through the penthouse and made a jug of coffee. Then he stood in front of the glass doors and watched the sun rise over Valencia. Nothing had changed, he decided. He felt in control of himself once more as the caffeine entered his bloodstream. In a year he would achieve his goal of becoming CEO, and by then his fascination with Juliet would have faded. Desire was always transient, but for now she was his.

He shoved a hand through his hair, remembering her hungry little cries when they'd shared a bath last night and he'd made her come as he'd eased his long fingers inside her. Never before had he taken such delight in giving a woman pleasure. Juliet's curious mix of innocence and heart-stopping sensuality intrigued him.

'Rafael?'

Her voice sounded from behind him and he turned, frowning when he saw her wary expression, the vulnerability that she successfully hid from most people but not from him.

'I woke up and you'd gone, and I thought...'

She'd thought he had used her for a night of sex, in the same way that the father of her child had done.

Rafael did not question why he felt a tugging sensation beneath his breastbone. He simply strode across the room and pulled her into his arms. 'I'm an early riser,' he said lightly, aware of another tug in his chest when relief flashed in her eyes.

That's very apparent,' she murmured drily, moving her hand over the tell-tale bulge beneath his sweatpants.

He laughed. He couldn't help it. And it felt so good, so carefree, that he laughed again as he scooped her into his arms and carried her back to the bedroom.

Her impish smile stole his breath. 'Are we going back to bed? Because I've had enough sleep...'

'Who said anything about sleeping, *chiquita*?'

CHAPTER TEN

'WHERE ARE YOU GOING?'

Rafael's gravelly voice halted Juliet's attempt to wriggle over to the edge of the bed. They were in the bedroom of his private suite at the Casillas mansion. It was a huge bed, and for the past few weeks she hadn't slept in it alone. His stretched out his arm and hauled her back across the mattress.

'I was trying not to wake you,' she mumbled, pressing her face against his warm chest and listening to the steady thud of his heart.

'I've been awake for a while.' He chuckled. 'Did you really think I would remain asleep while you were taking liberties with my body, *querida*?'

'Oh.'

She burrowed closer to him to hide her hot face. She'd had no idea that Rafael had been aware when she'd pulled back the sheet and made a detailed study of his naked body with her eyes and hands. He was a work of art: lean and yet powerfully muscular, his bronzed skin overlaid with black hair that arrowed over his flat stomach and down to his impressive manhood.

'I'd like to know what you intend to do about *this* as you're responsible for it,' he drawled, flipping her over onto her back and settling himself between her thighs so that his rock-hard erection jabbed her belly.

'I was going to make coffee,' she said breathlessly. 'Don't you have to get up for work?'

'I'll go into the office late.'

'But you're coming back early for the twins' birthday party,' she reminded him, catching her breath when Rafael flicked his tongue across a turgid nipple.

'Mmm… There has definitely been a drop in my productivity since I married you.'

'I have no complaints about your performance,' she said, and gasped as she wrapped her legs around his hips and he surged into her.

He grinned and her heart contracted. She loved it when he smiled, and lately he'd smiled a lot. *She loved him*, whispered a voice inside her, but Juliet didn't want to admit that dangerous truth to herself, let alone to Rafael.

Much later, after they had shared a shower and he'd given her another bone-melting orgasm while she'd been bent over the side of the bath, he finally went to work. It was lucky that Poppy now slept in the nursery with Sofia's twins, Juliet mused as she stepped onto the balcony and found her daughter eating breakfast with the nanny.

Poppy had formed a real bond with Elvira, as she had with Sofia and Ana and Inez. It would be a wrench when she took Poppy back to live in England.

The thought sent Juliet's heart hurtling down to her toes. She had never imagined when Rafael had brought her to the Casillas mansion that she could be this happy and feel so settled. Some of his relatives had been cool towards her at first, but others, like his aunt Lucia and uncle Alvaro, were friendly and made a fuss of Poppy.

Rafael's mother had kept her distance since that explosive lunch, but Juliet didn't regret the things she'd said to Delfina. Rafael had told her more about his terrible childhood in the slum, and Sofia had also spoken to her about their early life.

'I don't remember much about the slum or my father,' she'd told Juliet. 'My brother took care of me and I felt safe with him.'

But no one had taken care of Rafael and protected him from his violent father—least of all his mother, who had abandoned him and then spurned him, or his grandfather, who had found him but refused to acknowledge Rafael as his successor.

Juliet knew she must not forget the reason why Rafael had married her, but over the past weeks she had felt closer to him than she'd ever felt to another person. Even though she had adored her parents and known they loved her, their love for each other had come first. But it would be the worst folly to start believing that Rafael was hers, or that he too felt a connection between them that went beyond the passion they shared.

Pushing her complicated thoughts to the back of her mind, she sat down at the table with Poppy and Elvira and poured herself a cup of coffee. A feeling of nausea swept over her and she set her cup down without taking a sip. She was probably hungry, she decided. But the sick feeling grew worse after she'd eaten some yoghurt and she hoped she wasn't coming down with another gastric virus.

Luckily the sensation of nausea soon passed, and she spent the morning at the pool with Poppy before Elvira took the little girl back to the house for lunch.

Juliet was aware that Rafael's grandfather had come to sit beneath a parasol on the pool terrace. She had barely spoken to him since he had been so unpleasant to her when Rafael had introduced her as his wife, but she had left her book on the table where Hector was now sitting.

Steeling herself for more of his rudeness, she walked over to him, puzzled to see two copies of a psychological thriller by a popular author on the table.

'Are you enjoying the book?' she asked as she picked up her copy.

Hector shrugged. 'It is good, but I have not read very much of it. My eyesight is poor because I have cataracts in my eyes which impair my vision. A surgical procedure could resolve the problem, but I also suffer from a heart condition and my doctor has advised me against having an anaesthetic.'

'I'm sorry. You must find it frustrating not to be able to read. I know I would.' Juliet hesitated. 'I could read to you, if you like.'

After a moment he nodded, and said rather stiffly. 'Do you have time? Your little daughter keeps you busy.'

'Oh, Poppy will have a nap after lunch.' Juliet picked up Hector's copy of the thriller and opened it at the page he had bookmarked. 'It's lucky this is the English edition. I'm not very good at reading in Spanish.'

'But you speak the language fluently.' He sighed. 'I must apologise for the reception you received when my grandson brought you here.'

Juliet was not one to hold a grudge. 'That's all right. I wasn't what you were expecting. I'm not the kind of wife you hoped Rafael would marry.'

'No,' Hector admitted. 'But I have watched you with Rafael and I think you are a good wife to him. You love him, don't you?'

She flushed. Were her feelings for Rafael so obvious? If so, had he guessed how she felt about him?

She met his grandfather's knowing gaze. 'Yes,' she said huskily.

It occurred to her that she was supposed to be trying to convince Hector that their marriage was genuine, but she didn't have to pretend that she had feelings for Rafael.

She looked down at the book in her hand. 'Chapter Four...' she began.

The Valencian sun grew hotter as the summer progressed, and Juliet spent much of her time slathering sun cream on herself and Poppy, cursing their pale Anglo Saxon skin that burned so easily. Even so she had developed a light golden tan, and Poppy brimmed with energy and had learned to swim without water aids.

Life couldn't get much better than this, she thought one afternoon. A few days ago she had received a letter from the Australian law firm informing her that Bryan was no longer seeking custody of Poppy.

The reason he'd given for dropping his claim was that he felt reassured that Poppy was now growing up in a stable family environment since Juliet's marriage. But her cousin in Sydney had heard that Bryan's heiress girlfriend had dumped him. Juliet had emailed, offering Bryan phone contact with his daughter, and possibly visits when Poppy was older, but she'd had no response.

It was a huge relief to know she would not lose Poppy. She looked over at where the little girl was busy building a sandcastle. They had spent the day at the Casillas estate's private beach—her, Rafael and Poppy, and Sofia, her husband Marcus and the twins. They had swum in sea that was as warm as a bath, and now the men were tending to a barbecue while the children played and she and Sofia had a chance to relax.

They must look like a typical family group, Juliet thought, looking over at Rafael and finding him staring at her. Their eyes met, held, and he smiled, his teeth flashing white in his tanned face, causing her heart to skip a beat.

It was tempting to believe that it was all real: the lingering looks he gave her when she glanced up from her book, his smile which was the first thing she saw when she opened her eyes every morning, the way he held her close after sex. And the sex… She bit her lip, thankful that her sarong hid the hard nipples jutting beneath her bikini top as she remembered how he had made love to her on this very beach the previous evening, after they had walked hand in hand along the shoreline at sunset and he'd tumbled her down onto the sand.

Rafael had told her that he would not fall in love with her. He didn't believe in love, only lust. But was it foolish to think, to hope, that he might see her as more than his public wife and private mistress?

Juliet sighed as her mind turned to the niggling worry that had the potential to shatter the fairy tale. Her period was late. Only by a few days, but it was enough for her to feel concerned. It had got her thinking about her period last month, which had been unusually light. She'd put it down to the gastric virus she'd had when she'd arrived in Spain. The feeling of nausea when she smelled coffee was another red light, but it was probably all in her imagination.

To put her mind at rest she'd bought a pregnancy test, and if her period didn't start in another couple of days she would take it. She closed her eyes and an image popped into her mind of a chubby olive-skinned baby with a mop of black hair and green eyes like his father's.

Startled, she jerked upright and blinked at Rafael as he dropped down onto the sand beside her.

'You fell asleep in the sun,' he murmured, brushing his lips across hers in a lingering kiss. 'What's the matter, *querida*, did you have a bad dream?'

She swallowed. 'Something like that.'

'Well, Madre, what is this about?'

Rafael did not hide his impatience. He didn't want to be cooling his heels in his mother's cushion-stuffed sitting room when Juliet was waiting for him in his own apartment. Hopefully she would already be in bed, but if not he would soon take her there.

An early-morning meeting meant that he'd left for the office before Juliet had woken up. Usually they had sex first thing, and he'd missed it—missed *her*, if he cared to admit it. Which he did not.

'I want to talk to you.' Delfina was twisting her hands together and seemed hesitant. 'When you brought your wife to lunch…it must be three months ago now… I told you that I was ashamed, and you assumed that I meant I was ashamed of *you*.'

'An easy assumption to make as you have barely been able to look at me for the past twenty-three years,' he said sardonically.

'I was ashamed of myself. I *am* ashamed of what I did to you,' Delfina whispered. 'When Juliet accused me of abandoning you, leaving you with your violent father, I saw the condemnation in her eyes and knew I deserved it. I knew what Ivan was like…the monster he was.'

She sighed.

'I had led a sheltered life and he was dangerously attractive. Within months of running away with him he'd persuaded me to take drugs. It was his way of controlling me, and as my life with him spiralled ever downwards I took more drugs to block out the grim reality of life with him.'

Delfina dropped her face into her hands.

'I don't even remember giving birth to you or your sister. I felt half alive. But then one day I saw my father on the television and all I wanted was to go back to my *papà*, who had always protected me. I took some money out of Ivan's wallet and somehow I made it back to my family.'

'*I* was your family,' Rafael said harshly. 'Me and Sofia. Your *children*. And you left us with him.'

His mother was crying. He had never seen her cry before and he was angry that her tears hurt him. She hadn't cared about *him*.

'I was afraid of him.'

'Do you think *I* wasn't? You called him a monster and that's exactly what the man who fathered me was.' A monster whose blood ran through *his* veins, Rafael thought, and something bleak and hopeless lashed his heart.

'I'm sorry,' his mother sobbed. 'I know you must hate me. I never knew how to try and reach out to you. When Hector brought you here you were so angry. And as you grew older you were cold and hard, and I knew it was my fault that you never smiled with your eyes.' Delfina took a shaky breath. 'This girl you've married...'

'Juliet,' Rafael gritted. 'My wife's name is Juliet.'

'She is a brave young woman,' his mother said quietly. 'She is good for you. She makes you smile.'

Delfina put her hand on Rafael's arm. It was the first time they'd had any sort of physical contact since— He frowned, unable to remember a time when his mother had touched him, let alone hugged him, unlike Juliet, who constantly hugged and cuddled her daughter.

'Rafael, I am reaching out now,' Delfina said in a trembling voice. 'I cannot expect you to forgive me, but I wish that some day we can be…friends.'

He should tell his mother to get lost and walk away. A few months ago he probably would have done, Rafael acknowledged. But life was short, as Juliet often said. Juliet, his wife, who had more courage in her tiny body than the tallest giant. Right now he didn't know if he could forgive his mother, but he found that he didn't want to walk away, so he placed his hand over Delfina's and gently squeezed her fingers.

'It's all right, Madre.'

Juliet did much more than make him smile, Rafael thought, recalling his mother's words as he entered his apartment. Juliet intrigued him, fascinated him, drove him crazy with her stubbornness and evoked an ache inside him that defied explanation when he watched her with her little daughter. She was an amazing mother and an amazing lover, and if he was a different man he might have hoped for things that he'd long ago accepted he could never have.

But he could not escape his past. He could not be a different man. So he would settle for having her in his bed, and if the nine months that were left of their marriage seemed not enough—not nearly enough—he would bury that thought and live for the day, which was how he had survived his childhood.

He found her standing outside on the balcony. She was wearing a simple white dress made of a floaty material that skimmed over her slender figure like gossamer, and her hair was loose, falling down her back like a river of amber silk.

'There you are,' he said, and there was satisfaction in his voice as he thought of the evening ahead and an early dinner and an early night—not necessarily in that order.

He waited for her to turn around and give him one of her smiles that lit up her face and did something peculiar to his heart rate.

But she seemed to stiffen before she swung round, and she didn't smile. Her eyes were very blue—as blue as the summer sky.

'I have something to tell you.'

Out of nowhere Rafael felt sick with dread. It was the same feeling he'd had when he was a boy and he'd heard the swish of his father's belt. The hairs on the back of his neck prickled with foreboding.

'So tell me,' he said evenly, while his heart thudded.

Juliet lifted a hand and let it fall to her side again. 'I'm pregnant.'

Silence. So intense it pressed on him. And then a roaring in his ears.

Every muscle in his body clenched in rejection of something that he knew from her face was true. But he rejected it anyway. 'You can't be. We've always been careful. Even on the goddamned beach I made sure I had condoms in my pocket.'

'It was before then.'

She swallowed and he saw her slender throat convulse.

'The test shows that I'm nine weeks.'

He shook his head. 'That's more than two months. How didn't you know before?'

Not that it mattered, Rafael thought grimly, turning

away from her and gripping the balustrade before his legs gave out. Juliet was expecting his baby. *Dios.* How could *he* be a father? The son of a monster? He'd decided long ago that his bloodline—the Mendoza bloodline—had to end with him.

'I know it's not what you had planned,' she said in a low voice.

He closed his eyes as her words struck him another blow. *What he had planned.* A fake marriage so that he could claim the CEO-ship. His arrogance mocked him and he felt ashamed of the ambition that was all he had, all he was.

He knew what he had to do. For Juliet's sake and for the child she carried. Especially for the child's sake.

'No,' he said unemotionally. 'A baby was not in my plans nor what I wished for.'

'Here's a newsflash, Rafael. Your wishes no longer matter.'

The bite in her voice made him turn his head and he saw anger on her face—and something else…something fiercely protective. A lioness defending her cub, he realised, and admiration joined the swirling mix of emotions he was trying to control.

'Like it or not, I am going to have your baby.'

He nodded and turned away from her again, to stare unseeingly across the gardens to the sea beyond. When this was done he would go for a run along the beach, but he knew he wouldn't be able to outrun his demons. They would sit on his shoulders, terrible and ugly, reminding him of why he dared not deal with this situation differently. Why his child and Juliet would be safer without him.

'I will ask my lawyers to begin divorce proceedings,' he told her flatly. 'Spanish law allows couples to seek a no-blame divorce after three months of marriage, a fact of which my grandfather is unaware. And I'll make immediate arrangements for you and Poppy to return to England. Ferndown House will be made over to you and five million pounds transferred into your bank account as per our agreement. I will also make further provision for Poppy and the child you are carrying.'

'*Your* child,' Juliet said fiercely. 'I am carrying *your* child.'

Rafael felt the glare she sent him but he didn't look at her, and after a moment she gave a heavy sigh.

'You know we can't divorce until we have been married for a year—your grandfather insisted on that before he will make you CEO.'

'Then I won't be CEO.'

If he allowed her to live at the Casillas mansion until their first wedding anniversary he would see her body change as her pregnancy progressed and he'd be tempted to hope for a miracle. If she was already two months pregnant the child would be born seven months from now, but their marriage had nine months to run, which meant that some sort of involvement with his child would be unavoidable. He couldn't risk it.

Juliet's silence compelled Rafael to look at her. He watched the tears roll down her face and hardened his heart. She would never know how much it was costing him to send her away. He was only just starting to realise that despite his best efforts to avoid this kind of situation, this level of pain, he had been reckless when he'd allowed Juliet close. All he could do now was try to limit the damage.

'Do you hate the idea of having a child so much that you're willing to give up your claim to be your grandfather's successor and head of the Casillas Group?'

Juliet stared at him, and when she spoke again her voice was cold—as cold as the ice around his heart.

'In that case the baby will be better off without any father rather than growing up with a father who does not love him.'

Rafael's jaw clenched and despite himself he was curious. 'Him? You know it's a boy?'

'It's too early for a scan to show the baby's gender, but I am sure I'm having a boy.' She reached out her hand towards him and let it fall again. 'Rafael... It doesn't have to be like this. I understand if you don't want me. That you might feel trapped—' Her voice cracked. 'But your son needs his father.'

'And what if I am my father's son?' he said harshly. 'No child needs a father like mine.'

He saw shock on Juliet's face, confusion. The wounded expression in her eyes felt like an arrow through Rafael's heart. He did not trust himself to be near her and without another word he walked away.

CHAPTER ELEVEN

JULIET CURLED UP in a tight ball in the bed that was much too big for her alone and cried until her head hurt and her eyes burned. Some time around dawn she slept fitfully, and when she woke she cried again because Rafael's head wasn't on the pillow beside her, He wasn't there to greet her with a smile that promised it would be another beautiful day.

Maybe there would never be another beautiful day. Just grey, sad days, like the days and weeks and months after that lorry had wiped out everything she'd cared about when she was a teenager.

She stumbled into the bathroom and splashed water on her puffy face. All that crying had made her look like a frog. It was lucky there was no chance that Rafael would see her.

He hadn't come back to the apartment after he'd stormed out the previous night, but he'd sent her a text telling her that he had gone to his penthouse in Valencia and would arrange for the Casillas private jet to take her and Poppy back to London.

More tears came into her eyes but she blinked them away. She had managed as a single parent when Poppy was born and she would manage just fine having this baby without Rafael's involvement, she told herself firmly. Being financially secure would help.

She'd considered refusing the money he'd agreed to pay her, but although it might restore her pride, which had taken such a battering, she could not let her children grow up in poverty. Rafael had made it clear he did not want his baby, but he was prepared to provide financial support.

His rejection of his child had forced her to accept that the closeness she'd sensed between them had been an illusion. By rejecting their baby he had also rejected her, and it hurt even though she knew she should have expected it. At the start he had warned her not to fall in love with him, and it was her own fault that she'd given him her heart only for him to trample all over it.

Refusing to wallow in any more self-pity, she went to find Poppy in the nursery. Sofia was there, with Ana and Inez, and she looked shocked when she saw Juliet.

'Has something happened? You look terrible.'

So Rafael hadn't told his sister.

Juliet forced a bright smile. 'I must be coming down with a cold—or maybe hay fever has made my eyes red.'

Sofia looked unconvinced, especially when Juliet went on to explain that she was taking her daughter back to England.

'Poppy is due to start nursery in a month, and I think it will be better for her to begin her schooling in England.'

'Is Rafael going with you?'

'You'll have to ask him.' Juliet avoided her sister-in-law's gaze and started taking Poppy's clothes out of the drawers, ready to be packed.

'I don't know what's happened between you and my

brother,' Sofia muttered while the children played. 'But I do know that Rafael has never been as happy as he has for the past months. He needs you, Juliet.'

Juliet bit her lip, fighting back tears. 'He doesn't need anyone. Rafael is…'

'A flesh and blood man—even though he lets people think he has ice in his veins. I *know* him,' Sofia said intensely. 'He bleeds when he is wounded, the same as the rest of us.' She grimaced at Juliet. 'I thought you were different from the other women. I thought you would fight for him—but you're giving up on him.'

Now was not the time to tell Sofia about the baby, Juliet thought wearily as she stood in her dressing room and picked out a few clothes to take with her. Her flight to London was later that afternoon and Rafael had said in his text that he would have the bulk of her belongings sent to Ferndown House.

Not that she would be needing ball gowns or the sexy negligees that she'd bought to replace her horrible old pyjamas. She would only need maternity clothes in the months ahead.

Her hand strayed to her flat stomach. It was hard to believe that a new life was developing inside her. Despite everything, her heart clenched with love for this baby. Another little one who would need her to fulfil the roles of both parents.

The positive pregnancy test had made her sink to her knees on the bathroom floor, her shock mixed with trepidation about Rafael's reaction to the news. She'd guessed he might be angry for a while, but he had been so much worse, so grimly adamant that he didn't want this baby.

She frowned, thinking of that strange comment he'd made. *'What if I am my father's son?'* She did not understand what he'd meant, and she was too tired and defeated to try and work it out.

She looked at the clock and realised that Hector would be waiting for her in his study. She read to him every day, and they were on the final chapter of the latest book they had enjoyed. It would be the last time she would read to him and her eyes brimmed again.

Never would she have believed when Rafael had brought her to the Casillas mansion that she would become fond of the elderly man.

Hector was in his study, but he shook his head when she picked up the book from his desk. 'Rafael came to see me last evening.' His shoulders sagged and he suddenly looked old and frail. 'I was shocked by what he told me.'

Juliet waited for Hector to mention her pregnancy, but what he said next sent a judder of shock through her.

'He explained why he married you. That it was a fake marriage to meet my stipulation that he must be married before I would make him CEO. I suspected as much,' Hector said heavily. 'But I could not really believe that Rafael's ambition would drive him to such an action.'

'We did a terrible thing,' Juliet whispered, shame rolling through her. 'I agreed to the marriage deal because I needed the money. It wasn't only Rafael. I am as much to blame for pretending that our marriage was real.'

His grandfather looked at her closely. 'You defend him?'

'I am his wife. It is my duty to defend my husband.'

Hector nodded. 'And for you the marriage wasn't fake, was it?'

'No.' To her horror Juliet heard her voice crack and she couldn't hold back her tears. 'Thank you,' she choked when Hector handed her a box of tissues.

'I do not think it was fake marriage for my grandson either. Last night Rafael looked more troubled than I have ever known him to be.' Hector sighed. 'I was wrong to insist that he choose a bride. I do believe that Rafael is the right person to succeed me, but any position of power can be a lonely place. I was lucky enough to have the support of my dear wife, until her death three years ago. Rafael had no one. I hoped that by forcing him to marry I could make him realise that there is more to life than his ruthless ambition.'

Hector patted Juliet's hand.

'Clearly something has happened to cause a rift between you. Is there no way to resolve the issue?'

She shook her head, remembering Rafael's look of abject horror when she'd told him she was pregnant. 'He doesn't want me and he certainly doesn't love me.'

'How can you be so sure?'

'He's never said so.'

But she thought of the vase of roses he had placed by her bed yesterday morning. He must have picked them from the garden before he'd gone to work, while she had been asleep. And last week he had spent two hours helping her search for the gold locket containing photos of her parents that she'd lost. When he had eventually found it on the pool terrace he had painstakingly fixed the broken clasp on the chain. But did those kind gestures and dozens more like them mean that he cared about her?

'Have you told Rafael how you feel about him?' Hector asked gently.

Even if she did find the courage to admit her love to Rafael he wouldn't want her now that she was pregnant, Juliet thought as she left Hector's study. Perhaps he was so against having a child because he thought he would feel trapped. He had looked so furious, but as she thought back to when she had announced her pregnancy she remembered there had been another emotion in his eyes. There had been fear.

'What if I am my father's son?'

She frowned. His father had been a violent bully who had beaten Rafael when he was a little boy. Surely he couldn't think...?

Rafael ran his hand over the thick stubble on his jaw. He guessed he should shave, maybe change out of the clothes that he'd worn for the past twenty-four hours. He tipped the last of the cognac out of the bottle into his glass and contemplated the effort of getting out of his chair, where he had been sprawled ever since he had walked into the penthouse, and decided that the only way to escape his personal hell was to drink himself into oblivion.

Hell had got even blacker when he'd looked at his watch a couple of hours ago and realised that Juliet would be on the Casillas jet heading for London. Heading away from him, and a good job too. She and her cute little daughter would be fine living at Ferndown House without him. And as for the baby. *His baby.* It... he—Juliet was sure she was expecting a boy, and maybe she had an instinctive mother's knowledge—would be well provided for.

Rafael had his own money from the property portfolio he'd built up. His fortune didn't match his family's billions, but he didn't much care right now. Besides he wasn't a Casillas. And he sure as hell didn't want to be a Mendoza. The truth was that he was a mess.

He moved his hand up from his jaw to his cheek and swore when his skin felt wet. He'd get over this, he assured himself. He'd get over *her*. Although it would help if he wasn't being haunted by a vision of her standing by the window, silhouetted against the fading light.

The vision came closer to him and wrinkled her pretty nose. 'Are you drunk?'

'If I am, it's no business of yours,' he growled. 'You should be on a plane.'

'About that...'

She knelt in front of his chair and pushed her long hair over her shoulders. Her perfume stole around him and he gripped his glass so tightly in his fingers that he was surprised it didn't shatter.

'I've decided to stay.'

He glared at her, because it was that or kiss her, and kissing her led to all sorts of trouble—like making love in the shower the one and only time he'd forgotten to use protection.

'Stay where?'

'At the Casillas mansion—or here.' She shrugged. 'A tent on the beach? I don't know. It doesn't matter as long as I'm with you.'

Rafael felt his heart kick hard in his chest. *Fear*, he recognised. Fear that he wasn't strong enough to send her away even though he knew he must.

'The only problem with your plan, *chiquita*,' he drawled, 'is that I don't want you. Surely you've re-alised that by now?'

'I've realised a great many things,' she told him se-riously. 'For one thing I've realised that you are a liar.'

He swore, but it didn't stop her leaning forward until her face was inches from his and putting her hands flat on his chest.

'You are making a fool of yourself,' he said harshly.

'Are you really going to beg on your knees for me to take you back?'

'If I have to. But as I never left you can't really take me back.'

There was a hint of laughter in her voice. *Laughter*. He'd accepted that he would never laugh again, and he would have told her that grim truth if she hadn't pressed her lips to his mouth so that he couldn't speak, couldn't think. He couldn't do anything but keep his mouth tightly closed until she got the message.

But it got harder and harder to resist the sweet seduction of her lips. He dropped the glass and put his hands on her shoulders to push her away. How, then, did she end up sitting on his lap, her hand holding his jaw, his hands tangled in the silken fall of her hair?

Her mouth was his downfall and his delight, and with a savage groan he took charge of the kiss and drank from her as if he had been lost in a desert and she was life-giving water.

'I love you.'

Dios. He stared into her eyes and watched a tear slide down her cheek. 'I told you not to. Why didn't you pay attention, you little idiot? I'm no good for you, and I'm certainly no good for that baby of yours.'

He tried to set her away from him but he was trapped by her hair wrapped around his fingers and by something invisible that wrapped itself around his heart.

'The baby is yours too. *Ours*.'

He sat upright and cupped her chin in both his hands so that she couldn't look away from him. 'I've told you what my father was—what he did to me. Suppose I am like him? I have a temper like Ivan did. I've learned to control it, but what if I *lose* control? What if I lash out and hurt the baby? Or you?'

'You won't.'

'I won't take the risk.'

Juliet stood up and walked across the room.

Finally, Rafael thought bleakly. *Finally she sees the monster.*

'Do you think I would risk my children's safety and wellbeing?' she said fiercely. 'I have seen you with Poppy and your nieces—your patience and your caring. You are not the evil man your father was.'

'How do you *know*?' he said, struggling to speak past the lump in his throat. 'How can you have such faith in me?'

She smiled and he rocked back on his heels, blinded by her beauty, humbled by her courage.

'Because I *know* you. I know you are capable of love and I understand why you are afraid. You are a good man, Rafael. You don't need to prove yourself to anyone, least of all me. I love you with all my heart. I need you, and so does our baby.'

He stared at her while his thoughts rearranged themselves and hope slipped stealthily into his heart. When he walked towards her he saw a shadow of vulnerability in her eyes that killed him.

'Say something,' she whispered. 'Can you love me just a little?'

'Querida—' His voice broke and he reached for her, hauling her into his arms and holding her against his chest where his heart was doing its best to burst through his skin. *'Te amo, mi corazón.'*

He kissed her wet eyelashes, the tip of her nose, her lips that parted beneath his as she kissed him back with all that sweetness and light that was his wife, the love of his life.

'I don't know when it began,' he said, resting his

chin on the top of her head. 'You got to me in a way no other woman had ever done. You defended me, and no one had ever done that before.'

'It wasn't love at first sight, then?' she said ruefully.

'I was a blind fool—but you showed me that you are beautiful, inside and out.' He looked into her eyes and read her unspoken question. 'It ripped my heart out when I sent you away but I thought it was for the best.'

His heart gave another kick when she held his hand against her stomach, where the new life they had created together linked them inextricably.

'I will love our baby, and Poppy, but more than anything I will love *you, mi Julieta*, for the rest of our lives. For always and for ever.'

EPILOGUE

Rafael stood in the hallway of Ferndown House and watched a troop of small girls wearing pink leotards run out of the room which Juliet had turned into a dance studio. Their parents were waiting in the lobby and there was general chaos while coats were found and ballet shoes were swapped for trainers.

'Your last class for a while,' he said to his wife when the house was quiet again.

'Yes, it will be nice to have a few weeks off, and the babies should arrive any day now.' She patted her swollen belly. 'In a couple of years' time I'll have two more pupils.'

He shook his head. 'I can't believe there will be another set of twin girls in the family besides Sofia's girls. Can you imagine the mayhem when we all get together at Christmas?'

Rafael looked at his son, who had run in from the garden holding a football. Diego Casillas was three years old, and chasing him was his big sister Poppy, who had just turned seven.

'Your grandfather will enjoy having the whole family to stay. You know how he dotes on all the children. And your mother will spoil them,' Juliet said serenely.

She was tired now, at the end of her third pregnancy, but Rafael thought she had never looked more beautiful.

They had made the decision to live in England after Diego was born. When Rafael had become CEO of the Casillas Group after Hector had retired he had insisted on sharing the role with his half-brother. Francisco now worked from the company's offices in Valencia, and Rafael was based in London. He and Juliet wanted their own home, where they could bring up their growing family, and Ferndown House was filled with love and laughter.

Especially love, Rafael mused as he drew Juliet into his arms and she lifted her face for his kiss. He adored her, and told her so daily. The bright blue sapphire and diamond ring he had slipped onto her finger next to her wedding band was just one token of his deep and abiding love for this woman who had brought him out of the darkness into her golden light.

'It feels like there's a riot going on in there,' he murmured when a tiny foot kicked his hand where his fingers were splayed possessively on Juliet's bump.

'Yes, I think your new daughters are ready to meet their daddy.' She looped her arms around his neck. 'You know what's supposed to bring on labour...?'

'Señora Casillas—are you suggesting that we...?' He whispered the rest of the sentence in her ear and she giggled.

'Yes, please, Señor Casillas, my love.'

Love and laughter. He couldn't ask for more, Rafael thought.

And three days later, when he held two little bundles whom they'd named Lola and Clara in his arms, he knew he was the luckiest man in the world.

* * * * *

COMING SOON!

We really hope you enjoyed reading this book. If you're looking for more romance, be sure to head to the shops when new books are available on

Thursday 11th July

To see which titles are coming soon, please visit

millsandboon.co.uk/nextmonth

MILLS & BOON

Coming next month

AN HEIR FOR THE WORLD'S RICHEST MAN
Maya Blake

Dr Chang returned just before midday.

Saffie, having managed to keep down a piece of dry toast
and two cups of tea, stood in the middle of the living room.
Aware of Joao's imposing presence beside her, she linked her
fingers in front of her as Dr Chang entered. The two technicians
who followed, wheeling in a large ultrasound machine, couldn't
have spelled out her condition louder if it'd been written in
fifty-foot letters in the sky.

The room spun around her but Saffie wasn't aware she'd
moved until Joao's arm wrapped firmly around her waist.

'This is our new reality, Saffie,' he rasped softly, almost
soothingly, in her ear. His voice was gruff, but there was a
layer of intent as he watched her that drew goosebumps across
her flesh.

Dr Chang approached, leaving the butler and technicians
at a discreet distance as he gave a shallow bow. 'Miss
Everhart, I have the results of your blood test.' He cast a
quick look behind him. 'You can probably guess what it is.
Congratulations.'

Her nod was shaky, her heart hammering against her ribs
so hard she feared she would pass out. 'Thank you,' she
murmured.

'Would you still like me to perform the ultrasound?'

Beside her Joao stiffened, a coiled tension seizing his frame.

'Yes, thanks.'

Joao relaxed a touch, his arm temporarily drifting over her
hip before claiming her waist once more.

Within minutes, she was lying on her bed, Joao's overwhelming presence beside her as Dr Chang rolled the wand over the cold gel on her abdomen.

When the coloured 3D image appeared on the screen, Saffie's heart leapt into her throat. A moment later, a rapid heartbeat joined the picture. A breath of wonder shuddered out of her, her eyes prickling as she watched the wriggling bean on the screen.

Her baby. Her family. Every hope and aspiration within reach. But as she watched the dancing blob, Saffie's breath caught for another reason. For as long as she'd yearned for this dream, she'd pictured just herself and her baby. Two against the world.

In all the years of hoping and dreaming, all she'd wanted was a mother. Someone to hold her close, tell her she mattered. Perhaps because she knew it was her mother who'd left her behind, she'd been the parental figure Saffie had wanted the most. A father had been an even more impossible dream. One totally out of her reach.

But now she was faced with an even more impossible scenario.

The shadowy shape of the stranger who would one day father her child had taken the form of the most formidable man she'd ever met. The richest man in the world, with endless power and influence, who would remain way out of her league for ever. A man who intended to claim her baby, but not her.

Continue reading
AN HEIR FOR THE WORLD'S RICHEST MAN
Maya Blake

Available next month
www.millsandboon.co.uk